"I may never marry at all," Abby said, her voice sounding noncommittal.

Jakob jerked his head up, blinking at her in surprise. Not marry? Ever? The idea was alien to him.

"You should marry. It is what *Gott* would want."

"I know you really believe that. I'm not so sure anymore."

Hmm, he didn't like the sound of that. And yet, how could he fault Abby when he was shunning marriage for himself?

"Of course you will marry one day," he said.

She smiled and Jakob felt a new awareness sweep over him. Abby wasn't just a girl from his past. She was now a beautiful woman. He hurried to his feet and moved away. He couldn't face the disloyalty he felt toward his late wife. Never once had he been tempted by another woman.

Until now.

He was definitely attracted to her, but that wasn't enough. After everything Abby had been through, she deserved for someone to adore her.

But that someone couldn't be him.

Leigh Bale is a *Publishers Weekly* bestselling author. She is the winner of the prestigious Golden Heart® Award and is a finalist for the Gayle Wilson Award of Excellence and the Booksellers' Best Award. The daughter of a retired US forest ranger, she holds a BA in history. Married in 1981 to the love of her life, Leigh and her professor husband have two children and two grandkids. You can reach her at leighbale.com.

By sixth grade, **Meghan Carver** knew she wanted to write. After a degree in English from Millikin University, she detoured to law school, completing a Juris Doctor from Indiana University. She then worked in immigration law and taught college-level composition. Now she homeschools her six children with her husband. When she isn't writing, homeschooling or planning another travel adventure, she is active in her church, sews and reads.

LEIGH BALE

Runaway Amish Bride

&

MEGHAN CARVER

Amish Country Amnesia

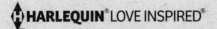

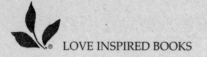

LOVE INSPIRED BOOKS

ISBN-13: 978-1-335-47015-7

Runaway Amish Bride and Amish Country Amnesia

Copyright © 2019 by Harlequin Books S.A.

The publisher acknowledges the copyright holders
of the individual works as follows:

Runaway Amish Bride
Copyright © 2018 by Lora Lee Bale

Amish Country Amnesia
Copyright © 2018 by Meghan Carver

www.Harlequin.com

Printed in U.S.A.

CONTENTS

RUNAWAY AMISH BRIDE

Leigh Bale

See that ye love one another
with a pure heart fervently.
—*1 Peter* 1:22

Chapter One

Abigail Miller sat primly on the edge of a tall-backed chair and stared at Jakob Fisher, his long fingers clenched around the letters Abby had given him.

He paced the length of the spacious living room in his home, his blue chambray shirt stretched taut across his overly broad shoulders and muscular arms. Even his black suspenders looked tight against his solid back. He had just arrived from working in the fields, and his plain trousers and black boots had dust on them. His dark hair was slightly damp and curled against the nape of his neck, confirming that the April weather was unseasonably warm. His straw hat sat on a table where he'd carelessly tossed it twenty minutes earlier. His high forehead furrowed as he scowled at his mother.

"I can't believe you told this woman I would marry her," he muttered.

Naomi Fisher met her son's gaze. She sat beside Bishop Yoder on the sofa, her hands in her lap. The friction in the room was palpable. Abby couldn't help wishing she had never come to Colorado. Even the abuse she had suffered back home in Ohio at the hands of her father and elder brother was preferable to this humiliating scene.

"I didn't make the offer, *mein sohn*. As you can see from his letters, your father did this, just before he died." Naomi spoke in a quiet, matter-of-fact voice, her expression calm but resolute.

Jakob handed the letters back to Abby. Several pages escaped her grasp and drifted to the floor. She bent over to gather them up, then placed them neatly inside her purse. They were like a shameful reminder that she'd done something wrong, but she hadn't. She'd merely agreed to what she thought was a marriage proposal.

"Did you know what *Daed* had done?" Jakob asked.

"*Ne*, I didn't know anything about it. Not until today. I just thought Abby was coming to Colorado to visit us," Naomi said.

The bishop cleared his voice. "Your *vadder* told me of his plans, although he led me to believe that you had agreed to the offer of marriage. I thought it was all arranged. I'm sorry that I didn't speak with you about it before now."

Jakob stopped dead and stared at the man. "*Ne*, I knew nothing. Why didn't *Daed* tell me about it? I never would have agreed to such a scheme."

Abby flinched at the irritation in his voice. She felt devious, as though she had plotted behind Jakob's back. She shifted her weight, wishing she could disappear. Wishing she were anywhere but here. She had arrived by bus only two hours earlier. Naomi, Bishop Yoder and his wife, Sarah, had been at the station to meet her. After traveling for twenty-six hours, Abby was hungry, exhausted and relieved to see a friendly face. She'd climbed into the back of the bishop's buggy and he had driven her here, to the Fishers' farm just nine miles outside town. She thought she was coming here to marry Jakob, the only man she'd ever trusted. Now, she realized she'd made a huge mistake.

"I'm already married. Susan is my wife," Jakob said, his voice sounding hoarse with emotion.

Abby jerked her head up at this information. Jakob had a wife? When had that happened? Obviously, Jakob hadn't known about his father's offer until this morning. Even among the Amish, an arranged marriage was considered old-fashioned. But Abby had suffered a lifetime of abuse at the hands of her father and elder brother, Simon. Desperate to escape, she had agreed to come to Colorado. Naomi had been childhood friends with her mother. Fourth cousins, to be exact. Abby had been a girl when they'd left Ohio, but she still remembered them.

Naomi lifted her head, her eyes shimmering with moisture. "Susan is gone, but your children still need a *mamm*. Perhaps that is why your *vadder* contacted Abby and told her to come here."

"My children have you to mother them. They don't need anyone else. And it wasn't *Daed's* place to find me a wife," Jakob said.

Naomi nodded. "You are right, of course. But Reuben is so angry all the time. He's becoming uncontrollable. Yesterday, his schoolteacher told me he put a frog in her desk drawer. It jumped out and nearly scared her to death. And he's constantly teasing Ruby and making her cry."

Abby listened intently. He had children, too! Reuben and Ruby. Those must be their names. And knowing that Reuben was picking on Ruby made Abby's defenses go up like a kite flying high. She couldn't help feeling instantly protective of the girl.

Jakob released a heavy sigh of frustration. "I will speak with him again."

"That's just it. He won't listen. He needs a *mamm*. So does Ruby. They need a complete *familye*," Naomi said.

Sitting next to the bishop wearing a black traveling bonnet, Sarah Yoder nodded her agreement.

A sick feeling settled in Abby's stomach. She hadn't known any of this information. That Jakob had been married before and had two children. That was more than she'd bargained for.

"I didn't know." She spoke in a quiet voice, needing to understand exactly what she was getting herself into. At his father's urging, she had agreed to marry Jakob, not become an instant mother.

Jakob turned, his eyes widening, as if he'd forgotten she was here. "What didn't you know?"

She swallowed, gathering her courage. "That you were married before and have *kinder*."

"*Ach*, it's true." He looked away, his gestures filled with impatience.

A dark, heavy silence followed.

"Jakob is a widower. Susan died in childbirth sixteen months ago," Naomi explained in a gentle tone.

Oh, dear. Jakob's father had neglected to mention that in his letters. Abby couldn't help wondering what the man had been playing at. Had he hoped to get her here and then convince her to become a stepmother to Jakob's children? Why hadn't he told her the truth before she traveled across the country? Since the man had died suddenly a few weeks earlier, she would never know.

It had taken her all that time to convince her brother to let her come here, and now it seemed a wasted effort.

"How old are your *kinder*?" she asked.

Jakob raked a hand through his short hair, showing his annoyance. "Reuben is seven and Ruby is five."

"I didn't know anything about them," she said.

Now what? She hadn't expected this. No, not at all.

The Western United States seemed strange and isolated to Abby, but it offered a chance at freedom. To begin a new life of peace and happiness. At the age of twenty-four, she should have already wed. But frankly, her father and brother had soured her toward all men.

Except one.

A rush of memory filled Abby's mind. She'd been twelve years old when Simon was beating her with a heavy stick...doing what he'd seen their father do so many times before. Up until then, Jakob had been friends with Simon. The two boys were both fifteen years old. Jakob had been working with his *daed* in a nearby field. When he'd seen what was happening, he'd marched through the tall wheat, jerked the stick out of Simon's hand and broken it over his bended knee. Simon had been furious that Jakob would interfere, but he hadn't dared challenge him. Jakob was bigger, stronger and fiercer. He'd shielded Abby, giving her time to flee.

When Jakob's *familye* had migrated to Colorado a year later, Abby never forgot his kindness. And every time her father or brother beat her, she thought about Jakob and his compassion. It was the only reason she had agreed to marry him. But now, she had a dilemma. If she returned to Ohio, she'd be forced to live in Simon's household, where she had no doubt the abuse would continue. And she couldn't stand that. No, not ever again. But maybe there was another option.

"I understand a marriage will not work between us." She spoke softly, her hands trembling.

Jakob tilted his head to the side. "What did you say?"

She forced herself to meet his dark, angry eyes and repeated herself. "There has obviously been a horrible misunderstanding. But now that I am here, is it possible that I might work for you? Surely you need help on the farm. I am eager not to return to Ohio. Please. Don't send me back there. Let me stay and work here."

She hated that she must resort to begging, but life was harsh for an Amish woman alone in the world. She didn't want to return to the misery waiting for her in Ohio, but neither did she want to abandon her faith for a life among the *Englisch*. She could work to make her way, if only Jakob would agree.

"I see no reason why you must leave, especially when you just got here," Bishop Yoder said. "Our district is anxious to bring new members into its fold, to increase our settlement. There are not enough women of our faith to marry our young men. You would be a great asset to our congregation."

Abby understood the implication of his words. If Jakob wouldn't marry her, then someone else would because they were in short supply of Amish women. But what they didn't know was that Abby would never agree to marry any of them. The fact that Jakob's father had misguided her only confirmed her belief that most men could not be trusted and they used women only to get what they wanted.

Naomi nodded eagerly. "Of course, you must stay. We can find room for you here. There's always work to be done, and we really could use more help. The bishop's wife runs a bakery in town, and we contribute baked goods on consignment. In fact, I have to make a delivery in town tomorrow morning."

Sarah nodded eagerly. "*Ja*, that is true."

"You could also assist me with keeping an eye on the *kinder*," Naomi continued.

Abby didn't mind looking after children, but she felt a little odd tending Jakob's kids. It was preferable to returning to Ohio. Everyone seemed eager for her to remain here. Everyone except Jakob.

"I would like that very much," Abby said.

In unison, they all turned to look at Jakob. Their eyes were filled with hope as they silently awaited his verdict. For the first time in Abby's life, it felt good to be wanted for a change, even if it was just Naomi, the bishop and Sarah who wanted her.

Jakob blinked, regarding them all as if he were a cornered rabbit facing a pride of mountain lions. Panicked and desperate. Abby held her breath, silently praying he agreed to let her stay.

Jakob took a deep breath, then released it slowly. He tried to calm his racing heart and troubled mind. Right now, he didn't know what to think. Confusion fogged his brain. Too much grief had struck his *familye* lately. First, his beloved wife, Susan, had died in childbirth. Then *Daed* had died of a heart attack a few weeks ago. But why had *Daed* written to Abby and said that Jakob had agreed to marry her? It didn't make sense.

Between the farm and his furniture-making business, Jakob already had more responsibilities than he could handle effectively without a wife. Though he tried, he had little time to comfort his grieving children. *Mamm* and his elderly grandfather had filled in the gaps. They'd been a great deal of help, but they were also still in mourning. He was responsible for each of them. To cope with his loss, he had buried himself in his work. It was easier to pretend that Susan was still alive, waiting for him at home at the end of each day. That his father was available anytime he needed advice or help with his labors. That they were a whole and happy *familye* again.

But they weren't.

He definitely could use assistance on the farm, but not a wife. Never that. He would not allow Bishop Yoder or *Mamm* to pressure him into marrying again. It hurt too much. But what should he do about Abigail Miller?

He reminded himself that he wasn't the only one who had been duped by his *daed*. After reading his father's letters to Abby, he realized she hadn't known that he was a widower with two young children to raise. Right now, they were with *Dawdi* Zeke, their great-grandfather, and not here to witness this difficult conversation. Reuben was still so angry that his *mudder* and grandfather had died. He and Ruby couldn't understand what had happened to their world.

Neither could Jakob. It seemed that *Gott* had abandoned them, and he didn't know why.

"I suppose we could make room for you here in the house, at least until you decide what you'd like to do. I can stay with *Dawdi* Zeke, so that there is no appearance of impropriety," he said.

There. That was good. His offer provided an immediate solution to Abby's needs without making any long-term commitments. And by staying with *Dawdi*, it would remove Jakob from the house so that no one could accuse him of indecency with a woman who wasn't his wife. Of course, he'd still be taking his meals here in the house, but with Naomi and *Dawdi's* presence, no member of his congregation could accuse him of being inappropriate.

"*Dawdi* Zeke?" Abby asked.

"My grandfather."

She nodded. "*Danke.* I am grateful to accept your offer."

She released a quiet sigh and looked away, her startling blue eyes filled with relief. He couldn't blame her. He remembered her *familye* well and could guess her reason for not wanting to return to them. *Mamm* had told him that her father had died a few years earlier, which left her to the questionable mercy of Simon. Jakob had no doubt the boy had grown up to be a cruel man just like his father, and he hated the thought of sending Abby back to him.

A clatter sounded outside the open window. Jakob stepped over to peer out and saw Reuben racing across the lawn toward the barn. A bucket was overturned in the flower bed, as though it had been used as a step stool. The boy's footprints were embedded in the damp soil, and he had tromped on Naomi's petunias.

Hmm. No doubt the little scamp had been listening in on their conversation. Jakob had no idea how much the boy had overheard, but he would have to deal with that later.

"*Wundervoll.* I am so glad we have come to an agreement. Abby will remain here, then." Bishop Yoder slapped his hands against his thighs and stood to signal his departure. Sarah rose also, smiling wide.

Naomi hopped up and escorted them out onto the front porch. "I appreciate your being here today."

"Any time. Let me know how things go…" The bishop's voice faded as the screen door clapped closed behind him.

Jakob turned and faced Abby. She'd been a young girl when he saw her last. Young, quiet and afraid. Now, she was an attractive, fully grown woman with magnetic blue eyes; smooth, pale skin; and golden-blond hair. Her light blue dress and matching cape looked perfectly starched, though her skirts were slightly wrinkled from her travels. She still looked quiet, still afraid. The complete opposite of his outspoken wife. Susan had been olive-skinned with dark hair, freckles, hazel eyes and an overly long nose. She wasn't what most people would call beautiful, but she'd been kind and energetic, and Jakob had loved her dearly.

Correction. He still loved her. He always would. And he had no room in his heart to love another woman. Not ever again.

Now, Abby sat with her battered suitcase resting beside her on the hardwood floor. Her shoulders sagged with weariness. Still wearing her black travel bonnet, she appeared tuckered out and in need of some time by herself. She reached up and slid an errant strand of flaxen hair back into her *kapp*, looking lost and all alone in the world.

A twinge of compassion pinched his heart.

"*Koom.* I will show you to your room." Without waiting for her, Jakob scooped up her bag and headed toward the back stairs. She followed. He could hear the delicate tapping of her sensible black shoes behind him.

Upstairs, he pushed the door wide to offer Abby

admittance. She stepped inside and looked around the tidy room. It included a simple double bed, a nightstand on each side with tall gas lamps, a chest of drawers, a wooden chair and an armoire. The oak furnishings were beautiful but plain. Jakob had crafted the wood himself as a wedding gift for his new bride. They complemented the lovely blue Dresden Plate quilt that covered the bed. The design included small gold hearts at the corner of each quilt block. A matching braided rag rug covered the bare wood floor. Susan had made the quilt, rug and plain curtains hanging across the window. She'd claimed that the hearts on the quilt were a whimsical reminder of their love. And though pride was not something Jakob should allow himself, he couldn't help feeling just a bit of *Hochmut* for her skill in making them.

Abby turned, her gaze riveted to the far corner of the room where a rocking cradle sat awaiting a little occupant. She made a small sound of sympathy in the back of her throat, her eyes filled with sadness. He'd made the cradle for his new child. As he looked at the empty mattress, a wave of lonely helplessness crashed over him. All his hopes and dreams seemed to have died with Susan and their unborn child. He should have removed it by now but hadn't been able to let go of the past. Packing the cradle off to the barn would seem like burying his wife and child all over again. So he'd left it here, a constant reminder of all he'd lost.

He looked away, trying to squelch the pain. Setting Abby's suitcase on the floor with a dull thud, he walked to the armoire and reached inside. It took only a moment to gather up his clothes. He didn't have much, just what he needed.

Abby watched him quietly, her delicate forehead

crinkled in a frown. Her gaze lifted to a hook on the wall where his black felt hat rested. He scooped it up, feeling out of place in his own home. Having this woman see the room he had shared with his wife seemed much too personal.

Abby looked at him, her eyes creased with compassion, and he felt as though she could see deep inside his tattered heart.

"This is your room," she said.

It was a statement, not a question.

"*Ja*, but it is yours to use now. I will join *Dawdi* in the *dawdy haus*. He turned ninety-three last month and is quite frail, but he still lives alone now that his wife is gone."

The *dawdy haus* was a tiny building next to the main house with a bedroom, bathroom, small living area and kitchenette. It included a front porch with two rocking chairs, although *Dawdi* Zeke didn't do much idle sitting even though he was so old. The cottage was the Amish version of an old folks' home, except that they cared for their elderly grandparents instead of turning them over to strangers. Jakob had no doubt the man would be happy to let him live with him for the time being.

"I'm sorry to chase you out of your room," Abby said.

He shrugged. "It's no problem, although *Dawdi* Zeke does snore a bit."

He showed a half smile, but she just stared at him, totally missing his attempt at humor.

"We will eat supper soon. Come down when you are ready." With one last glance around the room, he closed the door.

Alone for a moment, he stood on the landing, his

thoughts full of turmoil. He didn't want Abby here, but the situation wasn't her fault. She'd come to Colorado in good faith. No doubt she was hoping for a better life than what she'd had with her own *familye*. He knew how he would feel if Reuben were beating little Ruby with a stick, and he made a mental note to speak with his son right after supper. He'd feel like a failure if one of his children grew up to be cruel and abusive. He couldn't marry Abby, but neither could he turn his back on her in her time of need. If nothing else, he could shelter her. The Lord would expect no less.

Turning, he descended the creaking stairs and entered the wide kitchen. *Mamm* stood in front of the gas stove, stirring a pot of bubbling soup. Strands of gray hair had escaped her *kapp* and hung around her flushed cheeks. She looked tired, but he knew she'd never complain. It wasn't their way.

The fragrant aroma of freshly baked biscuits wafted through the air. *Mamm* paused, looking at his armful of clothes. Her gaze lifted to his face, as if assessing his mood.

"Jakob, I'm so sorry. Your *vadder* never should have interfered…"

He held up a hand. She hadn't been privy to his father's plans and it wasn't her fault, but he didn't want to discuss it any further. "Abby is welcome in our home until she wishes to leave, but I am not marrying her or any woman. Not ever. Now, I'm going to get *Dawdi* and the children so we can eat. I heard Abby's stomach rumbling and believe she is hungry. We should feed her before I complete the evening chores."

With that final word on the subject, he stepped out onto the back porch and walked past the yellow daffodils Susan had planted the first year they'd been married. He saw her presence everywhere on the farm. In the garden where she'd grown huge beefsteak tomatoes in spite of the short growing season, and in his children's eyes. They both looked so much like their mother that he could never forget. Nor did he want to.

No, he definitely would never marry again. It was that simple.

Chapter Two

"What's taking her so long?"

Abby heard the impatient words as she reached the bottom of the stairs. The voice sounded grouchy, like it came from a young boy. No doubt Reuben was hungry and she was keeping him waiting.

Smoothing one hand over her apron, she subconsciously patted her white *kapp* before entering the kitchen. A gas lamp hung from the high ceiling, filling the room with warm light. Through the window above the sink, Abby saw the dusky sky painted with fingers of pink and gold. The warmth from the woodstove embraced her chilled arms and hands along with the delicious aromas of food. She hadn't eaten since the day before and her stomach grumbled as she took another step.

"I'm sorry to keep you waiting." She stood in the doorway, gazing at the occupants of the room.

Two children, a boy and girl with identical chins and eyes, stared back at her. The boy sat on Jakob's left with the girl next to him. As Naomi turned from the woodstove with a plate of steaming biscuits, Jakob and an elderly man scooted back their chairs and rose from their places at the head of each end of the long table. Their respect was not lost on Abby, and she stared at them in surprise. No one had ever stood up for her in her father's home.

"Here she is." Naomi spoke in a lilting voice as she showed Abby a happy smile.

"*Willkomm* to our home." The elderly man hobbled over and took Abby's hands in his.

This must be *Dawdi* Zeke, Jakob's grandfather. His long beard was white as snow, his face lined with deep creases. A pair of wire-rimmed spectacles sat on the bridge of his nose, his gray eyes sparkling with humor and the experience of a long life. As Abby looked at him, she found nothing to fear.

"*Danke,*" she said, conscious Jakob was watching her.

"Sit here." Naomi pointed to a chair on Jakob's right.

As Abby rounded the table, the two children stared at her…the girl with open curiosity, the boy with open hostility.

"But that's *Mamm's* seat," the boy said.

Abby hesitated, her hand resting along the high back of the wooden chair.

Jakob's mouth tightened and he didn't say a word, but his dark eyes mirrored his son's disapproval.

"I can sit here." Abby sat across from Ruby instead, not wanting to stir up any more animosity.

In spite of her effort to please him, Reuben gave a gigantic huff and rested his elbows on the table, his chin cradled in the palms of his hands. He eyed her as though she were a stinky dog that shouldn't be allowed in the house.

"Sit up straight and mind your manners," Naomi told him with slightly raised eyebrows.

The boy did as asked, but his glare stayed firmly in place. Abby tried not to squirm beneath his unfriendly gaze and decided that ill-mannered children should be ignored. She instead focused on Ruby and was rewarded for her effort. The girl grinned, showing a bottom tooth missing in front.

"You're pretty," Ruby said.

"*Danke*. So are you," Abby said, feeling the heat of a blush suffuse her face. She wasn't used to such praise, even from a child.

"You're not our *mamm*. You never will be." Reuben blurted the words angrily, then scooted back his chair and raced out of the room. The chair toppled to the floor with a loud clatter.

Abby flinched.

"Reuben!" Jakob called, but the boy kept going.

Abby blinked, not knowing what to say.

"I'll go speak with him." Jakob stood and walked around the table to set the fallen chair back up, then left the room.

Abby stared at her hands. It was obvious that Reuben didn't like her. That he felt threatened by her. And if she were going to stay here, she must figure out a way to show him that she meant no harm.

"Where did Reuben and *Daed* go?" Ruby asked, her little chin quivering.

"Reuben isn't feeling well. Your *vadder* will look after him, but he will be fine," *Dawdi* said.

The girl accepted this without further complaint.

"It'll be all right," Naomi whispered and patted Abby's shoulder, then set the biscuits in the middle of the table and took her seat.

Dawdi smiled at each person in turn, as though trying to bring a better mood back to the room.

"Let us pray and give thanks to the Lord for the bounty we enjoy each day." He waited patiently for them to bow their heads.

His words warmed Abby's heart. She couldn't help comparing Zeke's actions with those of her father and brother. Back home, if she didn't hurry, she could find herself receiving a solid smack with the back of her brother's hand. There was never any tolerance waiting for children or women in his home.

In unison, they closed their eyes. Silently in her mind, Abby recited the Lord's Prayer from the New Testament. Then, she quickly thanked *Gott* for bringing her safely to Colorado and asked that He might comfort Reuben and help her make a successful life here. Everyone at the table released a quick exhale, and Ruby reached for the biscuits. Naomi hopped out of her chair and hurried to pour glasses of milk for them. The woman bustled around, seeing to everyone else's needs. Abby stood up to help, but Naomi pushed her back into her seat.

"You've had a long enough day. Just sit and eat your meal."

Feeling frazzled and exhausted, Abby sat down.

"How was your ride into town on the bus?" *Dawdi* asked as Naomi ladled thick soup into his bowl.

"It was long and tiring, but I saw some amazing scenery on my journey. Your mountains are so tall. I'm glad to be here," Abby said truthfully.

"I'd like to ride on a bus someday, but we only travel by horse and buggy," little Ruby said.

"Unless we need to travel a great distance, as Abby has done. Then we would take the bus," *Dawdi* said.

"Then I want to go on a long trip one day. Then I can ride the bus," she said.

Dawdi smiled. "I'm sure you will, one day."

Jakob returned a short time later with Reuben in tow. The boy sniffled, his face and eyes red from crying. He paused beside Abby's chair and stared at the toes of his bare feet.

"Go on. Do as you were told," Jakob urged the boy.

Reuben heaved a tremulous sigh. "I'm sorry for what I said earlier."

Overcome by compassion for the motherless boy, Abby couldn't resist reaching out and squeezing his arm. The moment she did so, she felt him tense beneath her fingertips, and she removed her hand. He might have apologized, but she could tell he wasn't really sorry.

"It's all right. No one could ever replace your good *mudder*," she said.

He glanced at her face, as though surprised by her words. Then a glint of suspicion flashed in his eyes. He didn't say anything as his lips pursed and he took his seat at the table. Keeping his gaze downcast, he ate his meal in silence. And then a thought occurred to Abby. Surely Jakob wouldn't have beaten the boy into submission. She knew many Amish parents adhered to the *spare the rod, spoil the child* mantra. But not Jakob. Not the man she'd known and trusted all these years. He wouldn't do such a thing. Would he? She hadn't seen him in years and didn't really know him anymore. Maybe he'd changed. And the thought that she might be the cause of Reuben suffering a spanking, or worse, made her feel sick inside. If so, he now had a viable reason to hate her. And if Jakob had struck the boy, she wouldn't be able to like him either. Maybe it was a blessing they would not be marrying.

She nibbled a biscuit but had suddenly lost her appetite.

Jakob lifted a spoonful of soup to his mouth. He chewed for a moment, then swallowed. "I'll start plowing the fields tomorrow, but I don't want to plant the feed corn too soon. We could still get a killing frost."

"I think we're safe now." *Dawdi* spoke between bites. "We can plant anytime. But tomorrow morning, you should go with the women to the bakery. They've got a lot of heavy items to carry and they'll need your strength. I can stay here and finish staining that oak hutch for Jason Crawley."

"But the day after tomorrow is the Sabbath. I won't be able to plant then," Jakob said.

Dawdi shrugged. "We can plant on Monday. That is soon enough. It'll give us a couple of extra days since you're worried about frost. It shouldn't keep us from having a bountiful harvest."

Jakob nodded, accepting his grandfather's advice without protest. *Dawdi* Zeke might be old, but he knew what he was talking about.

Jakob glanced briefly at Abby, and her senses went on high alert. She felt as though he could see deep inside her, but she couldn't understand why he made her so jittery. Perhaps it was because she doubted him now, just as she doubted all men. Was it possible the compassionate boy she had known had grown up to be abusive like her brother?

"*Ja*, you are right. I should drive *Mamm* into town," Jakob said. "She is low on flour, and I don't want her to lift the heavy bags. We will drop off her breads and pies at the bakery, then go to the store and purchase the other supplies she needs."

"*Ach*, I can lift those bags just fine," Naomi said.

"I can help. I'm strong and can do the lifting, too," Abby offered, wanting to earn her keep.

"Absolutely not. Naomi will be glad to have your help with the baking, but let Jakob lift the bags of flour," Zeke said.

Abby nodded, returning the man's warm smile. Back home, her brother expected her to do heavy work. In spite of the aches and pains in her muscles and joints, she'd learned not to ask him for help. Even with Reuben's outburst, it felt so good to be sitting here, having a *familye* meal and a normal discussion. It was her first day in Riverton and she was beyond grateful to be here.

She tasted her savory chicken noodle soup, and her hunger took over. Even though she was nervous, she ate her fill, enjoying strawberry preserves spread across her warm biscuits. They consumed one of Naomi's schnitz apple pies for dessert. And when the meal ended, the men scooted back their chairs.

"I will be out in the barn," Jakob announced.

Abby realized his evening chores must have been interrupted because of her arrival, and she felt the heat of embarrassment stain her cheeks. Normally, the majority of farm chores were completed before sitting down to the evening meal.

"I'll help you," Abby said, wanting to do her part.

"No need. Tomorrow, you can work. Tonight, you should rest," Jakob said.

Dawdi walked around the table and leaned down to kiss Naomi on the forehead. "Another delicious meal, my dear."

Likewise, Jakob kissed his mother's cheek. *"Danke, Mamm."*

"Gern geschehen." Naomi smiled with satisfaction. She squeezed *Dawdi's* hand but looked at her son. "Don't let him overdo or lift anything heavy out there."

Jakob nodded obediently. "I won't."

Dawdi pursed his lips. "You can both stop mothering me. I've worked all my life and raised a *familye*. I'll lift anything I want. I'm not a *boppli*."

No, he definitely wasn't a baby. He continued murmuring as he hobbled toward the door. Although his words sounded terse, his tone was light and pleasant. Abby knew they were just worried about the elderly man, but she wasn't used to this kind of loving banter and couldn't be sure.

"I would never question your skills, *Dawdi*. You know more about farming than anyone in the state," Jakob said, resting his arm across his grandfather's feeble shoulders.

"I'm glad I'm still good for something," Zeke replied with a laugh.

Abby stared in shock. Growing up, she'd never seen this kind of affection nor gratitude shown in her home. Was this normal in most Amish households, or just this one? It seemed so alien to Abby, and yet she wished she had been raised this way.

"I'll gather the eggs." Reuben stuffed half a biscuit into his mouth before pushing away from the table.

"I want to help, too." Ruby hopped out of her chair, and both children quickly carried their dishes to the sink before kissing their grandmother. Then they raced outside with the men.

Naomi released a huge sigh and finally sat at the table. She cupped her face with her hands, breathing hard.

"Are you all right?" Abby asked.

The woman nodded and sat back, seeming to relax now that her *familye* had been cared for. "I'm fine. There's just a lot to do."

She reached for a bowl and filled it with soup for herself. She began eating, and Abby thought she was overdoing.

"Now that I'm here, I can help take some of the load off you," Abby said.

Naomi smiled. "*Ja*, I'm so glad to have you here, my dear."

Again, the woman's words warmed Abby's heart. "The *kinder* are so eager to assist with the work."

She was thinking of home again. She'd never been opposed to hard work, but she hated being anywhere near her father or brother. Surely Reuben wouldn't be eager to help in the barn if his dad was inclined to beating him and Ruby.

Naomi nodded. "They are good children. I hope you know Reuben didn't mean any harm by what he said earlier."

"*Ja*, I understand that he has suffered a great loss. You all have."

Naomi showed a sad smile. "I am sorry for how this has turned out with Jakob. You must be very disappointed not to be marrying him."

Abby shrugged. "Not really. I am content not to be married. And I'm so grateful to be able to stay here with you. I promise not to be a burden. I'll earn my keep."

"Don't worry about that. I like having a house full of *familye*. But you should marry one day. It's a lot of work but also brings boundless joy. Losing my husband has been difficult, but we had many wonderful years together and I have my grandchildren to enjoy now. But I am very worried about Reuben and Jakob."

"How many children do you have?" Abby asked, standing so she could clear the table.

"Five, including Jakob, who is the eldest. They are all grown and married now. Three of them live in the Westcliffe area and come to visit us now and then. Colorado isn't like Ohio, where all of our *familye* lives close by. Here, we are spread far apart, but we are glad to have affordable land. There is plenty of room to grow. We can have a better future here. My daughter Ruth and her husband live here in Riverton. You'll meet them at church on Sunday. She is expecting her first child in August. Then I will have eight grandchildren to love. I hope to have many more."

Abby smiled at the thought, wishing she could have children someday. A husband and a large *familye* that loved each other had always been her dream. But children of her own would require marriage, which didn't appear to be in her future. Although it wasn't quite the same, she would just have to care for other people's children. Starting with Reuben and Ruby.

"How nice that your *familye* is growing so much. You must be very pleased," she said.

Naomi set her spoon in her empty bowl and pushed back from the table with a sigh. "I am. It is good to have a large *familye* in my old age, but I would feel better to see *mein sohn* happily married again. I can understand why my husband wrote to tell you that Jakob would marry you. The Amish settlements in Colorado are just beginning to grow. Bishop Yoder fears without enough women, our young men might start marrying outside our faith. I'm sure that is one reason he was eager for you to remain here with us."

Abby didn't respond to that. She thought it was better to let the topic die. And yet, she'd had such great expectations. Now, she wasn't so sure.

"Is *Dawdi* Zeke your father?" she asked.

Naomi nodded. "He is kind, yet firm in his convictions. He's lived a long, happy life. Jakob is just like him, although you wouldn't know it lately. He's still hurting over losing his wife. But one day, he will realize that *Gott* wants him to keep going and to be happy. That he cannot live in the past."

Abby agreed, yet she realized how difficult it must be for Jakob. He'd lost two vital people he loved very much, and she envied that love. How she wished someone in the world loved her the way Jakob loved Susan. Abby was so traumatized by her life in Ohio that she was desperate to leave it behind, yet Jakob wanted to cling to the past. She realized neither mind-set was healthy, but she had no idea how to overcome the problem.

"Now, tell me about Ohio and our old home. Who has married recently and who has had new babies? Tell me all the news." Naomi stood and walked to the kitchen sink.

Abby willingly complied, drying the dishes while Naomi washed. They laughed and chatted as they worked, soon having the room cleaned up and plans made for tomorrow's meals. That didn't diminish the worries in Abby's mind. She was a stranger in a new home. She'd come here to get married, but surely things had worked out for the best. The Lord knew of her needs and would care for her. She must have faith. Jakob had let her stay, and she didn't dare ask for more. So why did she feel an unexplainable sense of disappointment deep inside her heart?

The air smelled of a combination of cattle and clean straw. The horses were inside their stalls, blissfully munching on hay. The sun had all but faded in the western sky, highlighting the fields with shadows of dark purple and gray. Jakob lit a kerosene lamp and set it on the railing. He loved this late time of day, when he'd almost finished his work and could go inside and read or talk with his *familye* before the fireplace. But lately, he found no peace of mind.

Sitting on a three-legged stool, he set a clean bucket beneath one of their three cows.

"Abby is a sweet young woman, don't you agree?" *Dawdi* Zeke asked.

Jakob paused in his milking and glanced over at his grandfather. It was a good thing that Reuben and Ruby were outside feeding the pigs. It might have been a mistake, but he'd told *Dawdi* about his father's letters to Abby and that he had refused to marry her.

"She is a nice enough person I suppose," he said.

Dawdi leaned against the side of the cow he was milking. He sat at a hunched angle, indicating his arthritis was bothering him again. His bucket was almost filled with frothy white milk or Jakob might have tried to get him to go inside. He gave his fragile grandfather as few chores to do as possible. The *familye* couldn't stand to lose anyone else right now.

"Susan was a sweet woman, too," *Dawdi* said. "It was a shame to lose her. But it's been over a year and it's time for you to live again. If you open your heart to love, you will find more joy than you ever thought possible."

Open his heart to love? Jakob didn't know how anymore. Even if he could do it, he didn't want to try. When he'd married Susan, he'd locked his heart to all others. What if he loved another woman and lost her, too? He couldn't stand to go through that pain a second time, nor did he want to put his children through it again.

"I'll never love anyone the way I loved Susan," he said.

"True. Susan was unique and you loved her for who she was. But Abby is unique, too. She'll bring some man a lot of happiness. If you decide not to love again, then that's the way it'll be. But it doesn't have to be like that. It's your choice."

"It wasn't my choice when Susan died. I can't tell my heart what to feel or who to love," Jakob said.

How could he tell his heart to stop loving Susan and start loving another woman? He couldn't shut it off and on. It wasn't possible.

"*Ja*, you can. All you have to do is stop being angry at *Gott* and start living in the present instead of the past. Look for ways to feel joy and you'll find it." With a final nod, *Dawdi* stood slowly and carried his bucket out of the milking room. He set the container on top of the rough-hewn counter. When he turned, he staggered but caught himself against a beam of timber.

"*Dawdi!* Are you all right?" Jakob stood so fast that

he almost kicked his bucket over. A dollop of frothy
white milk sloshed over the pail.

"I'm all right." *Dawdi* Zeke held up a hand to reassure him.

Jakob was still worried. With his father passing away
so recently, they were shorthanded. To take up the slack,
Dawdi Zeke had been overdoing, but he would never
complain. Jakob would make a point of doing the milking earlier for a few days, to give his grandfather a rest.

He glanced at the buckets, mentally calculating how
many gallons of milk they would have tonight. He knew
Mamm would separate the cream later, to make butter
and other tasty fillings for the pastries she sold at the
bakery in town. During the past few years of drought,
the extra income she brought in had been a blessing.
With Abby's help, they should be able to increase their
production.

Jakob lowered his head and continued with his task.
Yes, Abby was a sweet person from what he could tell,
but that didn't mean he wanted to marry and spend the
rest of his life with her.

It would do no good to tell *Dawdi* that he wasn't
angry with *Gott*, because he was. Very angry. Yes, he
loved the Lord with all his heart, but why had He taken
Susan and *Daed* away when the *familye* still needed
them so badly?

Dawdi leaned against the doorway. "Your *vadder*
was wrong to bring Abby here without your approval,
but I believe he had your best interests in mind. No
doubt he intended to speak with you about it, but he
never got the chance. I hope you won't feel too harshly
toward him."

Jakob didn't respond, wishing they could talk about

something else. He had loved and respected his father, but he had no idea what the man's intentions had been. Jakob was no longer a young lad. He was a grown man with *kinder* of his own, and he had earned the right to choose whom he did and did not marry. His father had been out of line to make promises of marriage to Abby without asking him about it first.

"What are you going to do about Abby?" *Dawdi* pressed.

Jakob resisted the urge to look up from his milking. "Nothing. We will let her work and live here as long as she wants. I'm not inclined to send her back to her *familye* if she doesn't want to go."

He told his grandfather about his altercation with Simon all those years ago when they had been teenage boys. He didn't want to send her back to a life of abuse.

Dawdi grunted. "Her *daed* was no better. I knew him well when we still lived in Ohio. A cruel man, for sure. Everyone in the district knew he beat his horses, wife and kids. Some even believe he was responsible for his wife's death. His abuse was a constant point of contention in his home. The bishop and deacon spoke to him about it many times, but he never changed. The Lord taught us that loving persuasion is the way for us to lead our households. Otherwise, your *familye* learns to hate and fear you. And that's not the way for any man to be."

"I agree with you," Jakob said.

Many Amish spanked their *kinder*, but not Jakob. No matter how disobedient, he could never bring himself to beat his wife or children if they chose not to do as he asked. They were too precious to him, and he didn't want to become their enemy. But Reuben was getting out of control. Maybe a spanking was what he needed right now.

Dawdi made a *tsking* sound. "*Ach*, it's just as well that it didn't work out between you and Abby. But no matter. One of the other young men in our district will surely want to marry her. She's beautiful, young and filled with faith. I doubt she'll be living with us for very long."

With those words, *Dawdi* picked up his bucket and carried it outside, leaving Jakob alone with his thoughts. Jakob stared after the man, stunned by what his grandfather had said. The thought of another man paying attention to Abby bothered him for some odd reason. They wouldn't know about the abuse she'd suffered. Even Jakob sensed that he didn't know all the facts. She needed a man who was patient, kind and compassionate. Someone who would adore her and never raise a hand to her or their children.

He tried to tell himself it wasn't his business. Abby could marry whomever she liked. It wasn't his place to interfere. And yet, he felt responsible for her now, especially since she had come here with plans to wed him and was now living in his household. And for the first time since she'd arrived, he actually felt bad that he couldn't give her what she desired.

Abby was just preparing to go upstairs when Jakob brought the children inside for bed. They kissed their grandmother, then trolleyed off to brush their teeth with their father's supervision. Hiding a yawn, Abby soon followed. Standing on the landing, she peered into the room the children shared. Two twin beds sat apart from each other, budged up against opposite walls. Curious about the kids' relationship with their father, Abby listened for a moment.

"Will you read us a story, *Daed*?" Reuben asked, holding up a children's book.

"Of course." Jakob took the book and sprawled across the boy's bed, his long legs hanging over the edge.

He plumped the pillows as Ruby joined them, wearing a simple flannel nightgown. She cuddled against her father and laid her head back. Abby plastered herself against the outside wall so they wouldn't see her, but she couldn't bring herself to leave. Not once in her life could she remember her father reading her a bedtime story, and she was captivated by the event.

Jakob read a tale about an Amish girl named Lily and her adventures around the farm. He brought the story to life, using a different voice for each character. When his tone lowered to a deep bass as he read the grandfather's lines, Abby had to stifle a laugh. Soon, the story ended and Jakob urged the kids to sleep.

Abby peeked around the corner. With the children lying in their separate beds, Jakob snuggled the blankets around each of their chins, then kissed them both on the forehead. She had no doubt he loved his children with all his might. In fact, his show of affection told her that he hadn't spanked Reuben earlier. If he had, the boy would still be angry and pull away. Wouldn't he?

"I miss *Mammi*," Reuben said.

"Me, too," Ruby responded.

"I know. But she's with *Gott* now. She's also still here with us, in our hearts. She'll never leave us," Jakob said.

"How can she be with *Gott* and be in our hearts, too?" Ruby asked, her forehead furrowing.

"Because we remember her. If we think of her often and know what she would want us to say and do, she can be with us always. By that way, she lives in our hearts," Jakob said.

"Truly?" Ruby whispered.

"Truly," Jakob returned. "But you must be kind to Abby. It's not her fault that *Mamm* died. And Abby has her own sadness to deal with, too."

"Like what?" Reuben asked in a challenging voice.

"Both of her parents are gone and she's all alone in the world. Life has not been easy for her."

"Really? She doesn't even have a *familye*?" Ruby's voice sounded so sad.

"Not anymore," Jakob said. "Just a *bruder* who never treated her well. She came here looking for a *familye* of her own."

"*Ach*, she can't have mine. She should go back to Ohio." Reuben's tone was heavy with resentment.

"She's not trying to take any of us away from you, Reuben. She just needs a place to stay. We talked about this, and you will treat Abby with respect. You will treat your *schweschder* better, too. Understood?"

Abby was glad that Jakob told the boy to treat his sister well. But the boy made no verbal reply, and Abby wondered if he had nodded or merely refused to comply.

"*Gutte' nacht,*" Jakob said.

"*Ich liebe dich, Daedi,*" Ruby called.

"I love you, too, *boppli*," Jakob said.

He turned to leave and Abby darted into her room and carefully shut the door. She didn't want to be caught eavesdropping, and yet she was fascinated by Jakob Fisher and his *kinder*.

I love you.

The simple words of an innocent child to her father. How Abby longed to hear those words directed at her, but she knew now that it would never be. Other than her mother, no one had ever loved her, except *Gott*. And as long as she had the Lord on her side, she had faith that all would be well for her. She couldn't blame Reuben for feeling threatened and wanting to protect his mother's memory. He was just a young child who missed his mom. And once again, she envied Jakob and his loving, wonderful *familye*.

Chapter Three

Starlight gleamed through the windows in the *dawdy haus*. The cloying scent of the spearmint ointment *Dawdi* used on his arthritic joints lingered in the air. Jakob blinked his eyes, gritty with fatigue, and wished he could sleep. After a restless night, he'd finally dozed off and then awoken two hours early. He couldn't stop thinking about his father and how he'd arranged to bring Abby Miller to their farm under false pretenses. Nor could he stop worrying about Reuben, or the farm, or his mother, or a million other concerns. He needed to trust the Lord more, but lately his faith had wavered.

Staring into the darkness, Jakob lay on the small twin-size bed inside his grandfather's room. It had been his grandmother's bed before she'd died five years earlier. He listened to *Dawdi's* low, even snores and remembered a time when he'd been content enough to sleep through the night. Now, he was too troubled to rest more than an hour or two. His racing mind wouldn't settle down. After several years of drought, they had finally enjoyed a wet winter. They'd made it through the lean times, but they were short on funds and he was eager to get the fields planted so they could sell their crops. Once they delivered the hutch he'd recently finished, the payment would also help.

Sitting up, he tossed the quilt aside and padded across the wood floor in bare feet. In the tiny bathroom, he closed the door before lighting a kerosene lamp. He quickly washed and shaved his upper lip so that no moustache would accompany his tidy beard. Turning the lamp down low, he emerged from the bathroom and dressed in the dark, his grandfather's snores undisturbed by his movements. Walking outside, he closed the front door quietly behind him and stood on the porch for a moment.

Joe, their black-and-white dog, greeted him. His pink tongue lolled out of his mouth.

"*Hallo*, boy." Jakob patted the animal's head.

The chill morning air embraced him, and he took several deep breaths. Moonlight sprayed across the graveled driveway. His gaze swept over the open fields where their cattle grazed peacefully. A small stream ran past their place, swollen with spring runoff. He should speak with Reuben and Ruby about staying away from the swirling water where it deepened near the irrigation ditch…it could be dangerous to a young child. Thankfully, they should have enough water for their crops this year. Since his father brought his *familye* to Colorado ten years earlier, they had worked hard to build their farm into a prosperous place to live. Although they earned only half their living off the farm and the rest from the bakery and furniture he sold, Jakob loved it here and hoped to one day pass this land on to his children. Hope for a better future was the main reason his father had brought them here in the first place.

He held the lamp high as he walked to the barn. Joe trotted happily beside him, his stumpy tail wagging. Opening the heavy door, Jakob caught the warm earthy smell of dust, animals and straw.

"Abby!"

She stood in front of the grain bin, fully dressed and holding a silver pail and scoop of chicken feed. Another lamp had been lit and hung on a hook beside her head. The warm glow illuminated her lavender dress, white apron and *kapp*, making her look small and fragile among the shadows. Her eyes widened with momentary surprise, then she smiled and brushed a hand across her long skirts in a gesture that told him she was suddenly nervous.

"*Guder mariye*, Jakob."

"Good morning," he returned.

He closed the barn door to shut out the chilly air, then walked to her. "Why are you up so early?"

She took two steps back, not quite meeting his eyes. "I couldn't sleep, so I thought I'd make myself useful. I suspect I'm used to getting up two hours earlier in Ohio." She glanced at him. "Why are you up so early?"

He shrugged. "The same reason. I couldn't sleep either, although Ohio has nothing to do with it."

She laughed, her blue eyes twinkling and her face lighting up. In the lamp glow, she was absolutely stunning and he couldn't take his eyes off her. He realized she had as many worries on her mind as he did. And for some reason, he wished he could ease her fears and bring her a bit of comfort.

"It appears we both suffer from insomnia," she said.

"I guess so." He couldn't help returning her smile. Stepping closer, he reached up to remove a piece of straw from her *kapp*. She jerked back and lifted both hands, as if to protect herself. In the process, she dropped the pail and scoop. Chicken feed spattered across the barn floor. Her breathing quickened, her eyes wide and wary, as if she expected him to strike her.

Jakob drew back in surprise. He held perfectly still, waiting for her to relax. Then he plucked the piece of straw and held it out to her.

"I meant you no harm." He spoke gently, trying to soften the tense mood. But in his heart, he couldn't help wondering at her actions.

"Danke." She stooped over and swept up the spilled feed with her hands, funneling it into the pail.

He noticed that she never turned her back on him, but positioned herself so she could always see him. Something told him it was a protective instinct she'd learned from living with her father and brother, and he couldn't help wondering if they had a tendency to ambush her when she wasn't looking.

When he crouched down to help her, she drew away again, her entire body stiff. And then he knew. Simon and her father's abuse had been worse than he first thought. This gentle, soft-spoken woman was afraid of men.

She was afraid of him.

"I'll never hurt you, Abby. You are safe here. This I vow," he said.

She met his gaze, her lips slightly parted. Her eyes filled with doubt, and he wasn't sure she believed him.

She stood abruptly and gave a nervous laugh. "I had better get the chickens fed. Do you want me to turn them out into the yard, or leave them in the coop?"

"Ja, turn them out. The dog will not bother them,

and *Dawdi* will be here to watch over the place while we go into town."

"Unless you object, I'll feed the pigs also," she said.

He nodded and she hurried to the door, but paused there to look over her shoulder at him. "Are...are we taking the children with us into town?"

Her voice carried a bit of hesitancy, and he didn't need to ask why. No doubt she was still wary of Reuben and wished to avoid the boy.

"*Ja*, but we'll be dropping Reuben off at school. Ruby will spend the day with you and *Mamm*."

"*Gut*. I want to spend more time getting to know Reuben, so that he realizes I mean him no harm. I hope we can one day be friends."

Once again, she surprised him. She didn't want to avoid the boy. Instead, she sought the opportunity to be near him. Not what Jakob expected at all.

She stepped outside and closed the barn door. He felt the urge to go after her. To apologize once more for frightening her. To make her laugh again. But he knew that would be a mistake. It might make her think he had changed his mind and wanted to marry her after all. That there could be something between them. And there couldn't. Not ever.

"Reuben, get your coat. We're going to be late," Naomi called to the boy from the stairs. Her arms were laden with a shallow box of freshly wrapped blueberry muffins.

The boy's bare feet thudded against the stairs as he ran down them and hurried into the kitchen. He thrust his arms into his plain black sack coat. "Where's my lunch?"

"Here it is." Abby turned from the counter, holding a red personal-sized lunch cooler.

He came to a screeching halt. "Did…did you make my lunch?"

She nodded and smiled, handing the cooler to him. "*Ja*, and I put something extra special inside. I hope you like it."

He scowled at her but took the handle, careful to avoid touching her hand. As he studied the box, she could tell he wanted to stop right there and open the lid to view the contents, but Naomi called to him again.

"Reuben! *Koom* on."

The boy turned and ran outside. Picking up a box that contained six loaves of carefully wrapped home-made bread, Abby followed. On the porch, she set the box down on a table and closed the front door securely behind her.

"I'll see you all later," *Dawdi* Zeke called from near the workshop.

"Vaarwel." Abby waved as she picked up the box of bread and stepped down off the porch.

Jakob had already pulled the buggy wagon up in front of the house. The back of the wagon was filled with carefully packed breads, rolls, cupcakes, cookies and pies for the bakery. He hopped out of the buggy to help her put the box in the back. As he did so, his hand brushed against hers and she jerked back, the warm feel of his skin zinging up her arm.

Looking up, she noticed that Naomi had managed to climb in the back of the buggy with Reuben and Ruby. That meant Abby would have to ride in the front with Jakob.

He helped her into the buggy, then hurried around to

the driver's seat. Taking the leads in his strong hands, he released the brake and slapped the leather gently against the horse's back.

"Schritt."

The horse stepped forward in a steady walk. In the close quarters, Abby gazed out her open window, conscious of Jakob's knee brushing against her skirts from time to time.

When they reached the county road leading into Riverton, Jakob directed the horse over to the far right side of the road. Several cars and a truck whizzed past, and Abby was relieved when they took a turn onto another dirt road. Within fifteen minutes, they passed wide-open fields and an apple orchard.

"The Beilers live down there." Naomi pointed. "We buy our apples from them. You'll meet Lizzie at the bakery. She makes the best pies in the district."

"Not better than yours, *Grossmammi*," Reuben said.

"That's because I use her crust recipe. It's so tender and flaky. She's a very *gut* cook." Naomi smiled.

It wouldn't be appropriate for the woman to brag, but Abby could tell her grandson's words had pleased her.

Abby saw the schoolhouse long before they reached it. A white frame building with a small bell tower sat amid a fenced-off yard in the middle of a hay field. Two outhouses sat in one isolated corner. A teeter-totter and baseball diamond were the only play equipment in the yard.

The horse pulled the buggy wagon down the lane, and Jakob stopped them just out front of the schoolhouse. Several boys dressed in similar clothes waved at Reuben.

"Mach's gut." The boy bid farewell, then hopped out and ran toward them in bare feet.

"Wait! Your lunch," Abby called.

The boy stopped. Turned. With a huff, he walked back to the wagon. Abby picked up his forgotten cooler and handed it to him with a smile.

"Have a *gut* day," she said.

Under the heavy stare of his father, Reuben gave a slight nod, then turned and raced over to his friends.

Jakob made a clicking noise and the horse walked on. They passed another buggy coming into the schoolyard. They waved, but Jakob didn't stop to chat. Abby could see the woman craning her neck to look at her and was grateful he kept going. She would have plenty of people to meet and questions to answer at church on Sunday.

"Reuben said you put something special in his lunch box," Ruby said.

Abby turned in her seat, conscious of Jakob's interest in the conversation. *"Ja*, that's true."

"Is it a real nice surprise?" Ruby asked, obviously digging for more information.

"I think so. Would you like to know what it is?"

The girl nodded eagerly, a wisp of brown hair escaping her small *kapp.*

Reaching into her purse, Abby withdrew a carefully wrapped bag of chocolate chip cookies tied with a bit of yellow string. While Naomi made breakfast, she'd prepared them for the bakery.

"I was saving the cookies to give to you later on, but if it's okay with your *vadder*, you can have them now," she said.

Ruby leaned forward and pressed her cheek against

her father's shoulder. "May I have them now? Please, *Daedi*?"

Abby's heart melted. The girl asked so sweetly that it would be difficult for anyone to refuse her anything.

Jakob chuckled. "*Ja*, you may."

Abby handed the cookies over.

"*Danke.*" The girl undid the string and then made an exclamation of surprise. "*Ach*, what is this?" she asked, holding up a little slip of paper with writing on it.

"What does it say? Can you read it?" Abby asked, knowing very well what it said since she had written the note.

Ruby tried to sound out the words, but got only the first three correct.

"'You have an amazing smile.'" Naomi read it out loud for her.

"I do?" Ruby asked.

"You most certainly do," Jakob said from the front seat.

"*Ja*, you do." Abby faced forward and hid a satisfied smile. She'd written something similar on a piece of paper for Reuben, too. Simple words that would hopefully make him smile.

"That's nice," Naomi said.

The girl showed the paper to her father. "See what Abby gave me, *Daed*?"

Jakob nodded, looking at Abby with a thoughtful frown. "*Ja*, it was very nice of her."

"I hope it makes you feel *gut*," Abby said, thinking that Ruby and Reuben needed to hear something positive for a change. Maybe her notes would help them feel not quite so lonely for their mother.

"When I go to school, I'll learn to read better." Ruby

tucked the note into her hand, obviously planning to keep it.

"You'll learn many interesting things in school," Abby agreed, remembering her own education as some of the fondest times in her life. For those few hours each day, she had been free of her father and brother. Free to be herself. Free to be happy.

After eighth grade, she'd had to return to the house, where she'd been constantly at their mercy. When her father had died three years earlier, she'd had no choice but to live with her brother and his new wife.

"The Hostetlers live down that road. They raise nothing but hay and draft horses. They sell their Percherons to buyers all across the nation. They hire big trucks to come in and transport the hay for them," Naomi said.

She pointed out several other points of interest as they rode the rest of the way into town. Ruby munched on her cookies, even sharing one with her father. By the time they arrived in the alleyway behind the bakery on Main Street, they were in fairly good spirits.

"Guder mariye!" Sarah Yoder greeted them as Jakob pulled the buggy wagon to a stop and hopped out. Two other buggies were parked in the alleyway with men and women carrying baked goods into the store.

"How are you?" Naomi asked Sarah as she helped Ruby climb down from the buggy.

"Gut." Sarah smiled at Abby. "You look much more rested than when we first met yesterday."

"I am, *danke.*"

"Let me help you." The woman took the box of frosted cupcakes Abby had lifted out of the back of the wagon, leaving her free to retrieve something else.

"Danke." Abby smiled.

As they walked into the store, Sarah leaned closer and spoke low so that other people wouldn't overhear. "Have you decided to stay in Riverton after all?"

Abby nodded. "For the time being."

Sarah's gaze followed Jakob as he carried a heavy case of baked goods into the store. "Amos and I both hope you might soon find a reason to stay permanently."

Abby understood the woman's meaning perfectly, but didn't acknowledge it. She didn't want gossip to spread that she and Jakob were courting. Because they weren't.

Inside the shop, Abby helped fill the display cases with fragrant pastries, pies, breads and other baked goods. Ruby helped, too, picking up each wrapped loaf of bread carefully before handing it over to Abby.

"You're new to the district, aren't you?"

Abby looked up from her work. An attractive young woman with reddish-blond hair and wearing a sky-blue dress and white apron stood next to her, arranging a tray of frosted sugar cookies.

"*Ja*, I'm from Ohio."

"I'm Lizzie Beiler. My *familye* is from Lancaster County. We moved here eight years ago."

"I'm Abby. Abby Miller," she said.

Lizzie nodded, but her slight smile didn't quite reach her eyes and it quickly faded. "I'm glad to meet you, Abby. Are you going to be working here in the bakery now?"

Abby shook her head. "*Ne*, do you work here?"

"*Ne*, Sarah has two older daughters who help her run the place, but one of them will be marrying soon. Since you're new in town, I thought perhaps Sarah might have hired you."

"I'm just helping Naomi drop off her baked goods."

Lizzie slid the tray of cookies into the display case. "The store is only open two days a week, on Fridays and Saturdays. In a town this size, there isn't enough business to keep it open more often than that. Everyone knows the hours and they come in to buy their bread, pies and cookies for the week. A number of us make baked goods to sell. We use the same recipes for consistency. Sarah usually sells everything by close of business on Saturday evening."

"Ah, I see."

"Abby, we're ready to go," Naomi called to her from the doorway, wiping her hands on her long apron.

Ruby ran to her grandmother. Jakob stood just behind Naomi, speaking to Bishop Amos Yoder. He shifted his weight, seeming a bit nervous. He glanced at Abby, and she wondered what the two men were discussing. When Jakob nodded and turned away, she breathed in silent relief. No doubt he was eager to get their shopping done so he could return home to his work there.

"Goodbye," Abby said.

Lizzie waved farewell, but she still didn't smile.

Abby joined Naomi and stepped outside into the morning sunshine.

"I see you've met Lizzie," Naomi said.

"*Ja*, she was nice and friendly, but she seemed kind of sad." Her gaze drifted to the doorway where Lizzie had stepped outside with her empty basket. The young woman looked up, shading her eyes against the sun.

"That's because she's still missing Eli," Naomi said.

"Eli?"

"Eli Stoltzfus, her fiancé. He left a couple of years ago… I lose track of time. They were supposed to get married, but he wanted to go to college. The night before they were to be baptized together, he abandoned our faith and joined the *Englisch* in Denver. He didn't even have the common courtesy to say goodbye or write Lizzie a note. Nothing. He just left."

"Oh, how sad," Abby said, understanding how that must have hurt his *familye* and Lizzie.

"I understand from his *mudder* that he is doing very well in school," Naomi continued. "He hasn't even written to Lizzie. He broke her heart, and she hasn't been the same since. Now, she won't attend the singings or even think about getting married. I fear she's lost her trust in men."

Abby felt a powerful rush of sympathy. She didn't trust men either. Her heart had been broken, too, but for different reasons. Neither she nor Lizzie wanted to marry. Not after the painful betrayal they'd experienced at the hands of men they should have been able to trust.

Looking up, Abby saw Jakob leaning against the buggy, his ankles crossed. With the warmth of the day, he'd rolled the long sleeves of his shirt up to his elbows and pushed the straw hat back on his head. She blinked, thinking him the most handsome man she'd ever seen.

Ruby was already sitting quietly in the back of the buggy, a perpetual smile on her face.

Beneath the brim of his hat, Jakob watched his mother and Abby. From his calm exterior, he appeared to be patiently waiting for them. But Abby sensed a nervous energy in him. No doubt he was eager to return home.

"We better go. I don't want to keep Jakob waiting any longer," Naomi said.

Abby agreed. She hurried past Naomi and climbed into the back of the buggy with Ruby. Ever considerate, Jakob reached to help her, but she pretended not to notice and quickly sat beside the little girl. Ruby leaned against her. Unable to resist the girl's open affection, Abby lifted her arm around her slender shoulders and cuddled the child close to her side.

Jakob helped his mother. Naomi gave him a sweet smile and patted his arm. When she sat back, Abby heard her breathing heavily, as though she couldn't catch her breath. It had been a hectic morning. No doubt the woman needed a rest from her busy day.

Jakob rounded the buggy to climb into the driver's seat, then took the leads and clicked his tongue. As the horse moved into a quick trot down the street, Abby wished that things could be different somehow. But Jakob loved his wife. He didn't want her. And longing for something that could never be would only bring more discontent to Abby's heart.

Chapter Four

That afternoon, Abby carried the heavy rag rug from the main living room outside to the backyard. Swinging it up, she struggled for a moment to get it draped over the strong rope line that stretched between two wooden poles. Picking up a wicker rug beater, she pounded the rug for several moments. Clouds of dust wafted into the air. Bright sunlight streamed across the yard, highlighting the flower beds where yellow tulips and daffodils were just starting to bloom.

Thirty minutes. That's how long she had before she'd need to pull two cherry pies out of the oven. She'd set the timer on the front porch, so she'd be sure to hear it when it rang. Just enough time to get some house cleaning done.

Ruby was inside with Naomi, helping dust the furniture. To ease Naomi's workload, Abby had insisted on mopping the wooden floors herself. Soon, Reuben would be home from school. She was eager to hear his comments over the special note she'd tucked into his cookie bag. Hopefully the message had made him happy.

Tugging on the rug, she adjusted its position and smacked it several times in different places. She coughed and waved a hand in the air to disperse the dust. The sound of horses drew her attention, and she faced the south pasture. On the opposite side of the barbed wire fence, Jakob sat on a disc plow with a two-team hitch. The moment she saw him, a buzz of excitement pulsed through her body. She didn't understand why, but her senses went on high alert every time he was near.

The two gigantic draft horses pulled the plow with ease. Jakob held the lead lines in his strong hands, his body swaying gently as the blades sliced through the heavy clods of dirt. His straw hat was pulled low over his eyes, casting his face in shadow. He didn't look up as he passed, his focus directed at the dappled Percherons as they plowed in long, even furrows. Abby was amazed that anyone could handle such big horses, but she knew they were nothing more than gentle giants. She had been here only one day and already couldn't help admiring Jakob's strength and hard work ethic. In spite of taking them to the bakery in town that morning, he had plowed half of the fields. Neither her father nor Simon had ever been so industrious, and she couldn't help making numerous comparisons.

As he reached the end of the row and turned the horses, Jakob lifted his head and looked straight at her. Feeling suddenly self-conscious, Abby tugged the rug off the rope line and hurried toward the house. When she returned fifteen minutes later with the rug from the kitchen, Jakob and the horses were nowhere to be seen. She had just enough time to clean this rug before her pies needed to come out of the oven.

"Abby!"

She turned. Wearing a blue work apron over his clothes, *Dawdi* Zeke stood in front of the workshop. He beckoned to her, and she tossed her wicker stick onto the lawn. As she walked toward him, she brushed dust off her long skirts.

"I just finished staining the china hutch. Would you like to see it?" he asked when she drew near.

Abby glanced back at the house, thinking about her pies. She nodded, returning his exuberant smile. "*Ja*, but I only have a few minutes."

"That's time enough." He turned and hobbled into the workshop.

Filled with curiosity, she followed. On the outside, the building appeared to be nothing more than a detached three-car garage the men had built themselves. From references made at supper last night, she knew this was where they made furniture. In addition to the farm and bakery, this was undoubtedly a side business that brought extra income to the *familye*.

As Abby stepped inside, bright overhead lights powered by a gas generator made it easy to see. The air smelled of sawdust and varnish. Along one wall, tall metal shelves were lined with tidy stacks of lumber. The bare cement floors were well swept. A wide broom leaned against the open door along with several garbage cans filled with wood shavings and sawdust.

"We use the shavings as kindling for our fires and nesting material for the chickens. Nothing goes to waste," Zeke said.

Along the far wall, several rocking chairs, oak benches, tables and a chest of drawers were in various stages of completion. At the back of the room, a huge bench stood with plenty of room to work on their projects. Along the entire width of the wall, hooks had been affixed to a fiberboard and held an assortment of clamps, screwdrivers, chisels, drills, hammers, levels, saws, tape measures and other items all hanging in their place. Abby wasn't surprised by the orderliness of the shop. She was fast learning that this *familye* took special care with every facet of their life.

Sitting next to the workbench was an ornate buffet and china hutch. A sparkling mirror had been set into the back of the hutch. No doubt it would highlight any dishes that were put inside on the shelves. The rich brown stain of the wood accented the embellished pilasters and complex detailing of the appliqués. Abby tried not to be impressed by its opulent beauty, but she honestly couldn't help it. She would never own such decorative furniture. It was much too exquisite for a plain Amish home. Too prideful. But she couldn't help admiring the skill that had made the piece.

"What do you think?" *Dawdi* Zeke asked.

"It's…it's nice," she said, trying to find the right words that wouldn't sound too prideful.

"*Dawdi*, I need to sharpen the blades on the plow again. There are too many rocks in that farthest field…" Jakob pulled up short as he entered the shop and saw Abby standing there with Zeke.

Dawdi Zeke turned. "I can help with that. I've finished my work. Does it look all right?"

The older man gestured to the hutch. As Jakob walked over to them, Abby felt the weight of his gaze resting on her. She met his eyes briefly, then they all stared at the hutch. Jakob circled the grand piece of oak, surveying it with a critical eye. Finally, he nodded with approval. "It looks fine. You did a *gut* job covering up all the flaws in the wood. What do you think, Abby?"

The two men looked at her, waiting expectantly for her verdict.

She schooled her features so she wouldn't overly express her awe. "*Ja*, it's fine."

What an understatement. The piece was absolutely beautiful, but she refused to say so. It wouldn't be appropriate. She could hardly believe that a man of Zeke's advanced years and with his trembly hands could do such delicate work.

"*Gut.* Jason Crawley commissioned it for his wife. It's their fortieth wedding anniversary next week. I was worried we wouldn't have it ready in time," Jakob said.

"I've just put on the last coat of stain. We can deliver it to Jason on Tuesday or Wednesday, after you've finished the planting," *Dawdi* Zeke said.

Abby looked at Zeke. "I'm sure Mr. Crawley will be very satisfied with your work."

Dawdi Zeke snorted, resting one gnarled hand on his hip. "All I did was stain the wood. Jakob did all the work. He makes all our furniture now that my hands are so shaky."

Which meant that Jakob had made the furniture in her bedroom, too. And once again, she felt a tad guilty for chasing him out of his room, but was touched by his generosity.

"I stain everything because it's easy work and I need something useful to do. I'm old and not much good at anything else," *Dawdi* Zeke said.

"That's not true. You taught me everything I know and you have an excellent eye for staining. I couldn't do it without you," Jakob said.

Zeke chuckled. "*Ja*, but I've never had your feel for the wood grain. You seem to know just how to cut the wood."

Abby looked at Jakob, impressed by the respect he showed his grandfather. She had thought Zeke built the furniture. "I didn't know you both were carpenters."

"*Ja*, we built the house and barn ourselves. Of course, *Daed* was alive back then and helped," Jakob said in a matter-of-fact voice. "But furniture making is just a sideline we do in our free time. *Dawdi* and my *vadder* taught me. It brings in some extra funds."

Free time? She hadn't been here long, but hadn't noticed any of them ever sitting idle. There always seemed work to do. It had been the same back home in Ohio.

"Someday, Jakob would like to open a furniture shop in town, but he's afraid we wouldn't get enough business for us to earn a living full-time," *Dawdi* Zeke said.

"You won't know unless you try," she said.

Jakob nodded, his ears slightly red with modesty. "We'll see. Maybe in another year. Word will get out and I'll have more customers. I don't want to jeopardize our livelihood until we are sure we can make it through a lean spell. Time will tell."

Yes, time would tell a lot of things. Right now, she had no idea where she might be this time next year. But she knew one thing for certain. If not for the deaths of Jakob's wife and father, Abby believed these people would be very happy. And she couldn't help wishing she could be a permanent part of their *familye*.

"Abby! Your pies are all burnt up."

Abby gasped and whirled toward the door. Jakob

turned and saw Ruby standing there breathing hard, as if she'd run all the way from the house.

"Oh, no! I got caught up in our conversation and forgot all about them." Picking up her skirts, Abby ran outside.

Jakob followed, just in case there was a fire he needed to help put out.

As they approached the back door, billows of thick smoke wafted from the kitchen. Jakob stood back as Naomi pulled the smoking remnants of the blackened pies out of the oven and scurried outside to set them far away from the house. Jakob grabbed the fire extinguisher they kept hanging on the wall in the laundry room, but there was no need. The fire was out and the pies were ruined.

"Oh, I'm so sorry. I lost track of time and let them burn." Abby quickly opened all the windows and propped the door wide, waving her arms to get the smoke to filter outside.

"You should have paid more attention. Now we won't have pie for supper," Reuben said.

The boy stood beside Ruby in the doorway leading to the living room, having just gotten home from school after Naomi went to fetch him in the buggy. In Ohio, the schoolhouse was close enough that the children could walk to school. But here in Riverton, their farms were spread too far apart.

A disapproving scowl creased Reuben's forehead. Abby glanced at him, then ducked her head. But not before Jakob saw the absolute misery in her eyes. Her face was flushed red from the heat of the kitchen or embarrassment, Jakob wasn't sure which. Probably both.

"I'm... I'm truly sorry," she said again. "I can fix

it. I'll go right to work and make new pies. I can have them ready by suppertime."

She hurried over to the cupboard and pulled out a mixing bowl and canister of flour. Not only did she seem jittery, but also frightened. As though there might be horrible repercussions for her failing to watch the pies more carefully.

"There's no need for that. We've got other things to do now. Heaven knows I've burned my share of pies and numerous other dishes in this kitchen, too." Naomi bustled back into the house and took hold of Abby's arm to stop her. With a flip of her wrist, she turned off the oven heat.

Although Jakob couldn't remember his mother ever burning a single thing, he appreciated her kind heart and cheerful support.

Abby stood back and twined her fingers together in a nervous gesture, her eyes filled with uncertainty. She wouldn't look at any of them, staring at the floor instead.

"We don't need pie tonight. Do we, Reuben?" Jakob gave his son a pointed look. They all could see that Abby felt bad enough already. She didn't need a seven-year-old boy to act like a spoiled brat right now.

Reuben hesitated, his face twisted in an ugly glare.

"Do we, Reuben?" Jakob said again, his tone more insistent.

The child heaved a disgruntled sigh. "I guess not."

"We'll have cookies instead. I've always got tons of those on hand," Naomi said in a pleasant voice.

Reuben grimaced, as though the thought of eating a cookie sounded repulsive to him.

"I love cookies, especially chocolate chip. You can

make pie tomorrow," Ruby suggested. The girl walked over to Abby and took her hand in a show of support.

"That's right. You can make pie tomorrow." Jakob smiled with encouragement, hoping to put Abby at ease. He hated that Reuben had made her feel bad. And that's when it occurred to him that she expected them to bawl her out for her mistake. Was that what Simon would have done? And would he have beaten Abby, too? The thought of anyone striking this gentle woman upset Jakob more than he could say.

"Bah! It's just pie. No use getting upset about it." *Dawdi* Zeke waved a hand from the back door, as though brushing it all away.

"Danke," Abby said, her voice a low whisper as she showed a half smile.

With the pies out of the kitchen, the black smoke soon cleared, but the stench remained. Two hours later, they finished their evening chores and gathered for supper. Night was coming on, the air brisk and cool, but Naomi kept the windows open. After prayer, Abby helped serve the meal, setting a bowl of boiled potatoes on the table.

"Abby put a special note in my cookie bag today," Ruby told Reuben.

The boy grunted as he took a huge bite of bread spread with butter and strawberry preserves.

"She put a special note in your lunch box, too. What did it say?" Ruby asked.

Everyone turned to look at Reuben. Abby's eyes glowed with anticipation.

Reuben shrugged, not looking up. "I didn't find any note in my lunch. I don't know what you're talking about."

"You didn't? What happened to it?" Ruby asked.

"I don't know. Leave me alone." The boy gave her a sharp jab with his elbow.

"Ow!"

"Reuben, be kind to your sister," Jakob said.

Abby exhaled a low sigh and blinked in bemusement. She didn't say anything, but Jakob knew she was confused. He had no doubt that she'd included an uplifting message in Reuben's lunch box, similar to the one she had written for Ruby. So what had happened to the note?

"Maybe the slip of paper fell out and was lost when you unwrapped your cookies," *Dawdi* Zeke suggested. The elderly man eased himself into his chair and rested his gnarled hands in his lap.

Jakob glanced at Abby. She was watching *Dawdi*, her eyebrows drawn together with concern. She seemed highly observant and undoubtedly noticed that *Dawdi* was in pain. She nodded at Jakob's comment and took her seat before reaching for a thick slice of bread to butter.

"I said I didn't find a note and I didn't," Reuben insisted. A deep scowl pulled his eyebrows together. He hunkered over his plate and ate in brooding silence.

Jakob sensed his son was telling a fib. He didn't like this open hostility toward Abby, but didn't feel that he could call the boy a liar without proof. Abby hadn't done anything to the child, except try to make him happy. And yet, Jakob had no idea how to get Reuben to stop being so angry at everyone. It wasn't Ruby's or Abby's fault that Susan had died. But Abby was a constant reminder of all that they'd recently lost. A reminder that they'd been happy once. And Jakob didn't understand why her presence impacted Reuben this way. But he did know one thing. He had to do something about it, before the boy grew up to be as heartless and cruel as Simon had become.

Abby closed the door to her bedroom. After cleaning up the kitchen, she'd come upstairs without a light. Standing in the dark, she breathed a sigh of relief. Now that she was alone for the night, she could finally let down her guard. She'd been so eager to win everyone's approval. Writing special notes for the children. Helping with the house chores. Making pies for supper. Trying to win their friendship. She'd failed miserably. Instead of easing Naomi's load, she'd increased the work. No matter how clean the house was, the stench of burned food permeated every room. Maybe tomorrow, she'd ask Naomi if she could wash the curtains. That might help. But what had happened to the special message she'd put in Reuben's lunch for him to find? Maybe Zeke was right and the note had fallen out when Reuben had ripped open his bag of cookies. She'd be sure to make up for it by writing him another note for his lunch box on Monday.

For now, she was exhausted, both mentally and physically. Removing her *kapp*, she laid it on the dresser, then sat on a corner of the bed and brushed out her long hair. She stifled a huge yawn as she stood, pulled the covers back and slid her legs between the sheets. She immediately scrambled out. Something prickly had dug into her feet and calves.

Her heart pounded in her chest as she considered what it might be. Spiders? Frogs? Something else creepy? She shuddered at the thought.

Using moonlight from the window so she could see,

she lit the kerosene lamp and brought it over to the bed. Gathering her courage, she flipped the covers over in one hurried jerk, then jumped back expecting some kind of bugs.

Cracker crumbs!

She peered closer to be sure. Yes! Someone had sprinkled cracker crumbs between her sheets. But who...?

Oh, no. She knew the answer without asking. Reuben must have paid her room a visit. The little rascal. Did he really dislike her so much? And why? She didn't understand. No, not at all.

Sudden anger billowed up inside her. Just wait until she told Jakob what the boy had done. Reuben would be very sorry.

With stiff, sharp movements, she pulled the sheets off the bed, folding them so no crumbs fell onto the floor. She'd tried to be kind to the little boy. To go out of her way to make friends with him. And look how he repaid her.

Clutching the sheets close to her chest, she picked up the lamp and stepped out on the landing. The stairs creaked beneath her bare feet, and she moved more quietly, trying not to disturb Naomi.

Who did Reuben think he was, being so rude to her all the time? She was his elder and he should treat her with respect. In the morning, she would give him a good piece of her mind. Jakob would find out what his son had done. He would deal with the child...

She paused, standing on the front porch outside. The chilly night air helped to cool her anger, and she shivered in her modest nightgown. Opening the sheets, she shook them out on the front lawn. No doubt the chickens and other birds would eat up the crumbs.

She couldn't tell Jakob what Reuben had done. If she did, he might spank the boy. She thought about Jesus Christ and what He'd suffered for her sins. He'd harmed no one, yet His own people had demanded His death. A perfect, sinless man, and yet He'd willingly gone through excruciating pain, first in the Garden of Gethsemane when He'd made the atonement, and then upon the cross when He had died. For her. For all mankind.

Gott's only begotten Son had done that which no one else could do. He'd atoned for her sins so that she might be forgiven if only she would repent. So that she could live with *Gott* again. In all His words and deeds, Christ had set the perfect example. Then how could she show any less mercy to Reuben?

Taking a deep breath, she exhaled, letting it sweep her anger away. She must follow her Savior's example and turn the other cheek.

"Abby?"

She jerked around. "Jakob! What are you doing here?"

He stood at the side of the porch, his hair tousled and his shirt disheveled, as though he'd been awakened from sleep and dressed in a hurry. "I heard a noise out here and came to see what it was. What is that you are shaking out of your sheets?"

Peering through the dark, he eyed the lawn where white speckles of cracker crumbs covered the grass.

She quickly wadded the sheets and held them close against her chest. "It's nothing. My sheets just needed some airing."

Okay, that was true enough. She didn't want to get Reuben into any more trouble. That wouldn't be the Savior's way.

Jakob tilted his head in confusion. "It's late. You're airing your sheets at this time of night?"

"*Ja*, but I'm finished now. *Gutte' nacht.*" Before he could ask any more questions, she whirled around and hurried inside the house, closing the door securely behind her.

Peeking out the window in the living room, she watched as he headed back into the darkness toward the *dawdy haus*. He raked his fingers through his hair, shaking his head in bewilderment. Good. He had no clue what was going on.

Watching him go, Abby realized how comical the situation must seem. No doubt he thought her a very odd woman indeed. She felt suddenly light of heart and had to stifle a laugh. No harm had been done. Reuben was simply a mischievous boy who had decided he didn't like her. The poor boy. He was trying so hard to push her away, which told her that he needed a friend badly right now.

One day, she might tell Jakob what had really happened this night. He'd be disappointed in Reuben, of course. But she sensed that he would also find the boy's actions funny. And she longed to share another laugh with him. To see him smile again. But for now, an idea filled her mind and she knew exactly how she should handle the situation.

Chapter Five

The following morning, Abby got up early and made breakfast for the *familye*. The tantalizing aroma of bacon helped diminish the remaining odor of burnt pies. As she set the table, she decided the smell wasn't so bad anymore.

Naomi wrapped and loaded various baked goods into large boxes for delivery at the bakery. While the muffins baked, Abby helped her.

"I'd like to remain behind today, if that's all right. I'd like to try once more to bake pies for our supper, just to show you that I can," Abby said.

"I have no doubt of your ability." Naomi patted her shoulder. "Jakob will finish the plowing today, then he and *Dawdi* will be taking the hutch into town to Mr. Crawley. Reuben doesn't have school today, but I'll take the children with me. It'll keep them busy and out of your hair for a while."

"*Danke.*" Abby nodded in agreement, thinking this might be wise. She wanted nothing to distract her this time and planned to remain inside the house until she was finished.

"I'll do the mending while the pies bake and then prepare a stew for supper," Abby said.

"Oh, would you? That would make my day so much easier. *Ach*, I'm so glad you're here." Naomi gave her a spontaneous hug.

"It's my pleasure." Abby blinked her eyes fast to keep tears from falling. The woman's gesture touched her like nothing else could, and she wrapped her arms around her shoulders.

Ruby and Reuben entered the kitchen fully dressed and ready for their day. When Jakob joined them moments later, Abby forced herself to act casual, but her heart rate tripped into double time.

Tossing her a knowing look, Reuben slid into his chair. He wore a satisfied smirk, as though he were very pleased with himself. Knowing what he'd done, he actually seemed to welcome a fight. He glowered at her, like a cat ready to pounce on a bird.

Flipping two pancakes in the frying pan, Abby pretended not to notice as she set the serving plate in front of the two children. Contention was not of *Gott*. She was not going to fight with the boy nor say or do anything that might cause friction between him and Jakob. She was the adult here. She could handle this situation well enough. She hoped.

"*Guder mariye*. Reuben, I hope you're feeling well today. And you, too, Ruby." Abby spoke in her most cheerful voice.

"How did you sleep last night?" Reuben asked, his voice low and sly.

"*Ach*, like a log," Abby said. "*Ja*, I had the best night's sleep in I don't know how long. Thank you for asking."

"You did?" Reuben asked, looking slightly taken off guard.

"*Ja*, I did." Abby thoroughly enjoyed the look of confusion on his face. She had no doubt he expected her to react to what he had done to her sheets. But she had other plans.

As the men gathered around the table, Abby bided her time. Most of the food was on the table, and she waited for the prayer to end, then cleared her voice to gain everyone's attention.

"I'd like to thank all of you for your warm hospitality to me," she said. "You've all been so kind. Especially Reuben."

She gazed at the boy steadily, forcing herself not to flinch as he looked up, his eyes widening. Out of her peripheral vision, she noticed Jakob's curious glance as he listened to her.

"Knowing how nervous and lonely I must be and trying to adjust to a strange place and fit in with new people, Reuben has been especially *gut* and generous to me," she continued. "He has been so considerate, going out of his way to welcome me. I especially appreciate the thoughtful gift he left for me last night. It was so hospitable of him."

Jakob stared at her with puzzlement, but *Dawdi* Zeke chuckled, seeming to understand what was going on. Surely he didn't know about the cracker crumbs, but Abby thought the older man was smart enough to figure it out.

Reuben was overly quiet, staring at his plate, his face red with guilt. For a moment, Abby thought he might burst into tears. If nothing else, she'd made him think about what he'd done. If he had a conscience—

and Abby believed that he did—then he'd think twice before purposefully trying to hurt her again.

"What gift did you leave for Abby?" Naomi asked.

"*Ja*, what gift?" Ruby chimed in.

"That's between Reuben and me. Would you pass the potatoes, please?" Abby smiled sweetly as she looked at Jakob. She was determined to love his children no matter what.

Jakob handed her a bowl. "Does this have anything to do with you shaking out your bedsheets late last night?"

Naomi jerked her head up. "What? Why were you shaking out your sheets? I washed them the day before you arrived. They should have been clean."

"They just needed a little airing," Abby said. She ducked her head and began to eat, but she caught Naomi's look of puzzlement. Thankfully, she didn't push the issue.

Everyone became overly quiet and subdued, except for *Dawdi* Zeke. The elderly man grinned from ear to ear as he filled his plate and ate with relish.

"*Ach*, I'm delighted to have you here in our home, Abby," Zeke said. "We've been in mourning too long. You're a surprising and pleasant change. You'll keep us on our toes and do us all a lot of good."

"*Danke*. I hope so," she said, trying not to blush with pleasure.

A happy, buoyant feeling settled over her. She liked how she had handled the situation with Reuben, and it gave her a small bit of confidence. But she sure wished she could somehow get the boy to stop glaring and smile for once.

After they finished their meal and dispersed to their

various activities, Abby rolled out dough and baked her cherry pies. The lattice top was a pretty golden brown.

Setting the pies aside to cool, she then prepared the noon meal. She chopped up meat and vegetables, then let them simmer in a pot. As she sat at the kitchen table, she mended a variety of socks, aprons, shirts and trousers. The rest of the day went by without incident, and at supper, everyone exclaimed over her pie. Everyone except Reuben, of course. Like always, he was sullen and quiet.

"This pie is delicious, Abby. Some of the best I've ever eaten." Zeke glanced at Reuben. "Are you sure you don't want some?"

The boy looked at the pie and fresh whipped cream with such longing that Abby thought his mouth must be watering. Maybe he would change his mind. But no. He shook his head, being stubborn.

"*Ne.* I don't like cherry pie. It's too tart."

Naomi snorted. "Since when do you not like cherry pie? And this pie is as sweet as can be. Just right."

The boy jerked his shoulders in a shrug, but Abby knew the answer. He didn't like that Abby had made the pie.

Zeke grinned. "More for us, then. But just remember, *mein sohn*, it's not wise to cut off your nose to spite your face."

Reuben's eyebrows drew together in a questioning glance. "What does that mean, *Dawdi*?"

Zeke nodded. "You just think about it for a while. I'm sure its meaning will dawn on you sooner or later."

"*Ja*, this pie is delicious. The crust is so light and flaky. Don't you think so, Jakob?" Naomi prodded.

At that moment, the man was helping himself to a

second slice, so he obviously liked it. He lifted his head,
seeming startled by the question. When he looked at
Abby, his features softened, but he hesitated for a moment.

"*Ja*, it's very *gut*. You did well," he finally said.

She smiled, feeling enormously relieved by his
praise. Throughout her life, no one had ever thanked
her or told her she'd done a nice job. Not ever. More
than anything, she wanted this man's approval, and she
wasn't sure why.

Jakob knew he shouldn't stay after supper. He should
have gone to the *dawdy haus* instead. But honestly, he
was in a good mood. He and *Dawdi* Zeke had safely
delivered the hutch to Jason Crawley in town, and the
payment eased some of his worries.

He sat on the couch in the living room, trying to read
The Budget newspaper. They'd lit the kerosene lamps,
and their glow provided a warm, comfy environment.
Since the paper came from Ohio, it was packed with
stories and news of their *familye* members and old life
there. He usually enjoyed reading it to everyone, but
not tonight.

His gaze kept wandering over to where Abby was
laughing and chatting with his daughter. With church
Sunday tomorrow, Abby had overseen Ruby's bath and
was now sitting with the girl on the large rag rug in
the middle of the room. She picked up a brush, preparing to comb out Ruby's long hair. Reuben now occupied the only bathroom in the house. *Dawdi* Zeke was
slouched in a soft, old recliner. Naomi sat nearby, the
click of her knitting needles accompanying *Dawdi's*
soft snores and the ticks from the simple wooden clock

on the wall. The sounds were quiet and comforting, yet Jakob felt distracted.

Sitting behind Ruby, Abby parted the girl's damp hair down the middle, then painstakingly worked each section to free the multitude of snarls.

"Your hair is very fine like mine. I want to be careful so I don't cause any breakage," Abby said.

Ruby held up a spray bottle. "My *mamm* used this for the tangles."

Abby took the bottle and kissed the girl's forehead. "Your *mamm* was very wise. Even I use detangler on my hair."

"You do?" Ruby asked, sitting perfectly still, her chin held high.

"Of course. Long hair tends to knot easily when you wash it."

Abby spritzed the child's hair, holding up one hand to shield Ruby's eyes from the spray.

"Jakob?"

He looked at his mother, who had paused in her knitting. She inclined her head toward the paper he held with both hands. "Aren't you going to read some more?"

"Oh. Sorry." He returned to reading out loud so Naomi could hear. An article about a new schoolhouse they were building in Holmes County.

Naomi paused in her knitting and raised a finger, interrupting him. "Another school? You see how crowded they're getting back east? It was wise of your *vadder* to bring us here to Colorado. Now, we have lots of room for our *familye* to grow."

Jakob nodded, having heard this statement numerous times before. Although his mother missed her own brothers, sisters and numerous other *familye* members, he knew this was her way of justifying her husband's decision to move them west.

He finished the article, then searched for another story of interest. Ruby's laugh drew his gaze again.

"Would you like it braided this time, or just pulled back in a bun?" Abby asked Ruby.

"Braided, please," the girl responded with a decisive nod of her head.

Abby picked up the long strands and began to plait the hair, her dexterous fingers moving quickly from front to back. Finally, she tied off the end with a small rubber band.

"Jakob!"

He jerked, glancing over at Naomi. Seeing her slight frown, he began to read again. In all honesty, he had no idea what he was saying. He couldn't seem to focus tonight and decided he was overly tired.

"Almost finished," Abby said.

Jakob looked up as she twisted the braids onto Ruby's head. She held bobby pins between her lips. When she was ready, she took the pins to secure the hair, then patted the finished product with her palms. Last, but not least, she reached for Ruby's *kapp*. Abby caught his gaze and immediately ducked her head in a shy but endearing glance.

"*Ach!* I can see that if I want to know what's in *The Budget*, I'll have to read the paper myself." Naomi shook her head, her lips pursed together in disgust.

Awakened by her exclamation, *Dawdi* Zeke jerked and gave a loud snort. They all laughed as he blinked his eyes open and gave a deep, yawning sigh. He had no idea that he'd been snoring and they found him so amusing.

"*Daedi*, I'm worried about Amber. She hasn't come to the house for her bowl of cream in months," Ruby said.

Jakob chuckled. "It's only been a week or two since she came around the house, not months."

"*Ach*, it seems like months. I'm worried about her."

"Who is Amber?" Abby asked.

"Our barn cat. She's expecting babies, so I've been giving her cream to help keep her healthy. But she's stopped coming around," Ruby said.

"Perhaps she had her babies," Naomi said.

Ruby gasped in alarm and looked at her father. "But who will help her if she's all alone? What will she eat?"

"Don't worry. She knows what to do and catches lots of mice to eat. She'll show up when she's good and ready. And then we'll start seeing more cats in the barn," Jakob said.

The girl showed a doubtful frown.

"It's late. I think I'll turn in." Zeke gripped the arms of his chair and stood stiffly before shuffling slowly toward the door.

"*Gutte' nacht*," Abby said.

"I'll be along in a few minutes," Jakob called to his grandfather's retreating back.

Dawdi waved his acknowledgment, then closed the door behind him.

"There. *Vas denkscht?*" Abby held up a small hand mirror for Ruby to view her hair.

The girl peered at herself and smiled. "I think it's *wundervoll*."

Abby hugged the child, then gathered up the hair implements. "*Gut*. Now, it's off to bed with you."

"*Ahem!*"

Jakob turned and saw that Naomi had put her knitting away, having given up on his reading any more. He stood quickly.

"I'll take her upstairs," he said.

"*Ja*, it's getting late. Reuben should be finished with his bath and ready for bed, too," Naomi said.

Reaching over, Jakob snatched Ruby up and swung her high. The girl squealed with glee as he tickled her ribs and kissed her sweet-smelling neck.

Abby laughed at their gaiety and he paused, looking at her for just a moment. Finally, he found his voice.

"Um, *danke*."

"*Ja*, *danke*, Abby," Ruby said.

She showed another timid smile. "You're most *willkomm*, sweetheart."

Jakob hurried toward the stairs, carrying Ruby with him. His face burned with bewilderment. For a few minutes, he'd forgotten that Abby wasn't Susan. That after he put his children to bed, he'd have to retire alone. There would be no one there to whisper with him in the darkness as they recounted the events of their day. No one to discuss the kids or planting or share ideas with or seek advice from. Abby was a constant reminder of all the joy he'd lost, and he couldn't help wishing he could regain that happiness. But Susan was gone. He had to accept that he would live the rest of his life without a wife. It would be less painful that way.

Chapter Six

As hard as Abby tried to get out the door before everyone else the following morning, she was delayed when she found her shoes filled to the brim with dirt. No doubt Reuben was responsible. She fumed for several minutes, wanting to rant and scream at the boy, but then she remembered the anger she was raised with and decided to exercise self-discipline instead.

Gripping her patience, she walked outside to the backyard in her stockinged feet. After emptying her shoes into the garden, she smacked them together to get all the little rocks out. By the time she'd tied the laces and raced out the front door, she arrived at the buggy only to discover that Zeke and Naomi were already in the backseat with the two kids. Which meant she would have to sit in the front seat with Jakob.

Again.

She glanced at Reuben, who looked down at her black sensible shoes. A sly grin flashed across his face before he turned away, looking innocent as a newborn babe.

Abby looked at *Dawdi* Zeke. Beneath the brim of his straw hat, she saw a sparkle of laughter in his gray eyes.

"There's no room in the back. You'll have to sit up front," he said.

So, he didn't know what Reuben had done. If she didn't know better, she would think he'd purposefully planned things so that she would be forced to sit next to Jakob. No doubt he'd been told her true reason for coming to Colorado. She could only assume he was matchmaking, but it would do no good. She and Jakob would never marry now.

Standing beside the buggy, Jakob silently took her hand and helped her up. His rough palm was warm against hers, and the slight smile he gave her only increased her nerves. She felt as though he were forcing himself to be solicitous of her. Like she was one of his chores. Although she was grateful he'd agreed to let her stay here, she didn't like being where she wasn't wanted.

She straightened her dark blue skirts, knowing she wouldn't escape notice. New members always garnered interest at church.

Jakob climbed into the buggy, released the brake and slapped the leads against the horse's back. As they pulled onto the main road, even the steady clip-clop of the horse's hooves did nothing to alleviate her worries.

Last night, she'd checked her bed and felt a small victory when she didn't find any crackers or a snake between her sheets. But now, her apprehension returned when she remembered Bishop Yoder's words.

There are not enough women of our faith to marry our young men.

She wasn't interested in being pursued by any men. The thought twisted her insides into knots. She was a stranger here and naturally shy. She didn't know what to say to young men. As an Amish woman, she knew

her duty. To marry and support her husband, raising a
gut familye in the faith. She should encourage the eligible bachelors to pay her court. To get to know them
and choose one to be her life's partner. But she couldn't.
Not ever. And that left her feeling rebellious, hopeless
and unacceptable to *Gott*.

"Oh, *ne*. Look, *Grossmammi*. I have a hole in my
dress," Ruby said.

Abby turned to look over her shoulder. Sure enough,
a large section of seam had come undone in Ruby's
skirt. She tugged on a long thread, then waggled her
fingers through the gaping hole, showing a length of
bare leg in the process.

"Oh, dear. If we return home so you can change,
we'll be late for church," Naomi said, her voice sounding flustered.

"It is too late to return home," Jakob said with finality, giving a light flick of the leads for emphasis.

Naomi looked wilted. "*Ach*, Ruby can't run around
like this, showing her bare legs to everyone. We'll have
to turn around, Jakob."

His jaw hardened, and Abby didn't need to ask why.
This wasn't Ohio where they lived close to their Amish
neighbors and could soon be at church. They were far
enough outside town that they had to travel eight miles
one way to reach their destination. If they turned around
now, they would miss most of the meetings, not to mention the fatigue on their horse.

"Don't worry. I'm sure Mrs. Stoltzfus will have a
needle and thread we can borrow," Abby said. "As soon
as we arrive, I'll ask if there is a private room we can
go to, and I'll quickly mend the dress before our meetings start."

"Of course. Such an easy solution. I'm not thinking clearly today. *Danke*, Abby," Naomi said.

Abby reached back and squeezed the older woman's hand. "You're just overly tired. You worked too hard to get all the cakes and breads over to the bakery yesterday. I'll help you more this next week."

Naomi gave her a smile of gratitude. "Would you mind working with Jakob on the planting tomorrow? Then I would have time to get the laundry done."

Abby felt Jakob stiffen beside her and wondered if he'd rather she stayed in the house. But she was a guest here and resigned to doing whatever they asked of her.

"Of course. I'd be happy to help." Abby smiled, but felt a flutter of unease. Helping with the planting meant she would be working most of the day with Jakob.

"But I usually drive the small wagon," Zeke said.

Naomi pursed her lips. "Not this year. You're not a young man anymore, but I'd like to keep you around as long as possible. You'll rest and help me around the house, and that's that."

Abby glanced over her shoulder and saw Zeke blink in surprise at his daughter. He didn't argue, giving in to common sense.

"Can you drive?" he asked Abby.

She lifted her chin, remembering the eight-hitch team of Belgian draft horses she'd driven numerous times in the fields for her brother. She almost laughed, but felt no humor. And yet, a part of her was grateful she knew how to work hard and was capable of driving a large team.

"Of course," she said.

"*Ach*, the hoppers on the planter aren't big and will

need refilling often. You can drive the small wagon with the bags of seed corn," Zeke said.

"All right."

As Abby turned to face forward again, she caught Jakob's glance her way. He seemed deep in thought as he clicked his tongue and gave another slap of the reins.

When they arrived at the Stoltzfuses' farm, Abby sat up straighter and perused the area. Church was held every other week in a member's home. The rustic house was made of large brown logs, so different from the white frame homes Abby was used to back east. The front lawn and flower beds were tidy and well cared for, a tall elm tree offering shade over the front door.

A group of women stood clustered together, chatting. They waved as Jakob drove to the back where a row of buggies were lined up along the inside perimeter of the fence. A teenage boy drew their attention, pointing to where they should park. As Jakob pulled the horse to a halt, another boy began unhitching the animal, then took it away to graze and water until the *familye* was ready to go home.

Jakob hopped out first, then helped his grandfather and mother. Abby didn't wait before climbing down, then reached inside to help Ruby. The girl held her torn skirt together, glancing around nervously to see if anyone was witnessing her embarrassing circumstances.

"There's *Aent* Ruth and *Onkel* Will." Reuben raced toward a young man and obviously pregnant woman.

Reaching for her basket, which contained a pie and two loaves of bread, Naomi smiled at Abby. "Now you'll get to meet my daughter Ruth."

Holding Ruby's hand, Abby followed Naomi toward the house. Men wearing frock coats stood clustered near the barn. Their mixture of black felt and straw hats indicated that the weather was transitioning from winter to spring. Zeke and Jakob headed that way, shaking hands with Will.

Children raced across the yard. Reuben joined the little boys, their boisterous laughter winning a reprimand from one of the mothers.

"How many families are in your congregation?" Abby asked.

"Nine. We're a small district, but we're growing fast," Naomi said.

Hmm. Abby wasn't so sure. In Ohio, her congregation consisted of thirty families. This definitely was a small district, which could be good and bad.

"*Mamm*, it's good to see you." Ruth embraced first her mother and then Ruby.

Abby caught several curious looks thrown her way, especially from the younger, unshaven men, who were obviously unmarried.

"Look at my dress," Ruby whispered as she huddled next to her grandmother and showed a peek of her torn skirt to her aunt.

Ruth gasped and shielded the girl from view. "What happened! You can't go to church like that."

"I don't know what happened. I must have snagged it on something. Abby's gonna fix it for me," Ruby said.

Naomi made the introductions. "Ruth is my youngest, expecting her first child in a few months."

"Hallo," Ruth said, her nose crinkling as she squinted against the bright sunlight.

Abby returned the young woman's gracious smile and glanced down before speaking very quietly so no one would overhear. "You must be so excited to start your *familye*."

Ruth lifted a hand to rest on her rounding stomach and whispered back. "I am. I'm only five months along, but this baby is so active, I'm thinking it must be an unruly boy like Reuben."

They laughed and Abby's heart pinched at the thought of having her own sweet little baby.

"Come on. You promised to fix my dress." Ruby pulled on Abby's hand, and they all went inside the house.

"Guder daag!" A matronly woman with rosy cheeks and a thick waist greeted them from the kitchen.

"Fannie." Naomi rushed over and hugged the woman, then leaned close and whispered in her ear.

Fannie glanced at Ruby. *"Ja*, we'll get her dress mended in no time."

Naomi smiled in relief. Several other women and a few older girls were bustling about the room, stirring pots on the stove, checking the oven and setting out plates and utensils for their noon meal later on. Naomi introduced Abby to everyone, and they gave her a friendly smile.

"Willkomm. We're so glad to have you here," Fannie said.

"I'm glad to be here." Abby nodded pleasantly, then zeroed in on Lizzie Beiler, the young woman she had met at the bakery a couple of days earlier. Lizzie was frosting a chocolate cake, but Fannie whispered something to her and she handed over her spatula.

"Hallo, Abby. I understand you need a needle and thread," Lizzie said.

Ruby nodded eagerly, looking a little anxious. She

obviously didn't want the meeting to start before her skirt had been repaired.

"*Ja*, if you wouldn't mind," Abby said.

"Not at all. *Koom* with me." Lizzie led them to the back of the house, where she closed a hall door to give them some privacy. It seemed she knew her way around this home with ease.

"Do you live here?" Abby asked, knowing her last name was Beiler, not Stoltzfus.

"*Ne*, but I had planned to live here one day. I'm quite close with Fannie and still come here often." Lizzie's words were slightly muffled as she reached into a cupboard and pulled out a sewing box.

"Are you related to Fannie?" Abby wouldn't be surprised if she was. Many of the Amish in a district were related in some way or another. Aunts, cousins, brothers, nephews. In Ohio, they all lived nearby. But here in Colorado, it wasn't quite the same. Not with its high mountain peaks, deep canyons, wide plateaus and desert valleys that constantly hungered for rain to irrigate crops. Farms were spread far apart, and most of their kin relations had remained back east. They were true pioneers, starting a new life in the Wild West.

"*Ne*, I was engaged to her son, Eli. But he disappeared several years ago, the day before we were to be baptized."

"I'm so sorry to hear that," Abby said.

"He just left without a word to anyone. His parents received a letter from him a week later. He went to Denver, to go to college there."

Abby caught a note of bitterness in Lizzie's voice and couldn't help feeling sympathy for her. "I'm so sorry. That must have hurt you very deeply."

As she assessed Ruby's dress so that she could mend the seam, she remembered what Naomi had said about Eli Stoltzfus breaking Lizzie's heart. No doubt Lizzie had been close with Eli's parents.

"*Ja*, it did. I was baptized without him." Lizzie sat on the bed and threaded a needle before putting a knot in the end. She handed it over to Abby, who also sat and quickly stitched the ripped seam.

"Perhaps you will marry someone else. I understand there are several young men needing brides here in the Riverton area, or perhaps you could find someone in Westcliffe," Abby said, conscious of Ruby standing in front of her listening quietly to every word.

"*Ne*, there's no one here that I'm interested in. And what about you?"

Abby didn't look up from her needlework. "What about me?"

Out of her peripheral vision, Abby saw Lizzie cast a quick glance at Ruby, who was peering out the window.

"Jakob is handsome and single," Lizzie whispered low. "Are you going to marry him?"

Not wanting Ruby to take offense at their conversation, Abby shook her head.

"My father keeps threatening to send me back east to live with my grandparents. He believes I could find someone to marry there, but he hasn't made me go yet," Lizzie said, her forehead crinkled in a doubtful frown.

Abby inwardly shuddered at the thought of returning to Ohio, but for different reasons. She didn't get the chance to ask Lizzie if she wanted to go back east. A knock sounded on the door, and Naomi poked her head in.

"Are you ready? They're about to begin the meeting."

"Just finished." Abby bit the thread with her teeth and smoothed the dress to study her handiwork. "It's as good as new."

Ruby hugged her tight. "*Ach, danke*, Abby."

Abby breathed the girl in, enjoying her sweet innocence. "You're welcome."

"*Koom* on, you three," Naomi urged.

Ruby bolted toward her grandmother while Abby quickly restored the sewing box to order. She followed Lizzie outside and into the yard. The married women were lined up by age beside the barn. Naomi took her place among them as they filed inside. Through the wide double doors, Abby saw that the married men were already sitting together on hard backless benches. The unmarried women filed in next, and Lizzie took Abby's hand as they scurried forward. As they paraded down the aisle, Abby was conscious of people watching her. Finally, the unmarried men and boys joined them. One tall young man with bright auburn hair and piercing blue eyes smiled wide at Abby, and she looked away, making a pretense of straightening her apron.

The men sat together on the other side of the room, facing the women. As Abby tidied her skirts, she looked up. Her gaze locked with Jakob's from where he sat across from her. He quickly looked away, focusing on the bishop, who stood at the front of the room. The auburn-haired man continued to stare openly at her, leaning across a row to whisper to Jakob. The two spoke together for a moment and Jakob's gaze lifted to her, then he responded to the auburn-haired man. She had no doubt they were discussing her, and she didn't like it. No, not one bit.

The *vorsinger* called out the first note of the opening song in a loud, elongated voice. The congregation joined in, singing in German from the *Ausbund*, their church hymnal. Without the accompaniment of musical instruments, they drew each note out in a painstakingly slow harmony.

Abby knew the words by heart, but she faltered. The auburn-haired man kept watching her until she became so uncomfortable that she squirmed on her seat. Feeling suddenly miserable, she looked up and caught Jakob's eye again. He looked down, focusing on the floor, and she felt even worse. He must find her so distasteful that he couldn't even stand to look at her.

"The man with the red hair is Martin Hostetler," Lizzie whispered for her ears alone. "He watches all the unmarried girls. He's twenty-three and wants to get married so bad, but he's too pushy. I'm kind of glad you're here so he'll have someone else to bother instead of me."

"Gee, thanks," Abby said, trying not to smile.

Lizzie laughed low. "Just ignore him. That's what I always do."

Abby tried. She really did. But as she watched the ministers file out of the room to discuss who should preach to them, she wondered if she should have pleaded a sick stomach and stayed home today. Between Reuben's open dislike of her, Martin's rude gawking and Jakob's obvious discomfort with her presence, she wondered if perhaps she should have remained in Ohio.

"Please say you'll go to the singing with me tonight. I'll drive you home in my buggy afterward."

Jakob tried to pretend he hadn't heard the invitation, but he couldn't help it. Martin Hostetler stood in front of Abby, no more than a stone's throw away. She held a plate of schnitz apple pie she'd retrieved for *Dawdi* Zeke. Martin had cut her off as she headed across the front lawn.

Zeke sat in a chair on the lawn, deep in conversation with several other elderly men. Martin had been dogging Abby's heels ever since they'd ended their meetings and started lunch. As she helped serve the noon meal, Jakob noticed how easily she fit in with the other women, but she was overly quiet and skittish around the men. Especially Martin, who wouldn't seem to leave her alone. No doubt he was delighted to find an attractive single woman in their midst.

"I'm sorry, but not today." Abby turned toward *Dawdi* Zeke, but Martin tugged on her sleeve, holding her back.

"Why not? Jakob said you're not attached to anyone. Why won't you go with me to the singing?" Martin persisted.

The singing was a venue after Sunday meetings where young single adults could socialize with one another. Afterward, the young man usually took the young woman home in his buggy…the Amish version of dating.

"I… I'm new here and I don't know anyone yet. I think it would be best if I go home with the Fishers this afternoon. Perhaps another time." Her voice sounded low and hesitant, as though she was afraid of angering him.

"*Ach*, how can you get to know any of us if you don't stay for the singing? It'll be fun. You must stay. I insist," Martin said, taking a step closer.

"I… I don't…" Abby didn't finish her sentence.

Her face flushed red, a blaze of panic in her eyes. She backed up against the elm tree and hunched her shoulders, looking small and helpless.

Subdued.

"*Ahem*, excuse me." Jakob interrupted them in a polite voice. "I think Naomi is looking for you, Abby. She needs you in the kitchen."

"*Ach!* I should be helping her, not standing here visiting." She glanced at Martin. "I won't be able to join you tonight, but it was nice to meet you. *Mach's gut.*"

She spoke so fast that Martin looked startled for a moment.

"Uh, maybe another time." He waved at her already-retreating back.

She hurried toward the house. Jakob followed, walking beside her, just in case Martin decided to pursue her. A teenage boy bumped into Abby, and she jerked back.

"Excuse me," she said.

He looked mildly embarrassed before racing off with his friends.

Abby kept going. At the side of the house, she slowed her pace and took a deep inhale.

"Are you all right?" Jakob asked.

"*Ja*, I'm just a little nervous around crowds of strangers."

"I hope it was all right for me to interrupt you and Martin," he said, almost positive that she had wanted to get away from the man.

"*Ja*, I'm glad you did."

"He wasn't bothering you, was he? I know Martin can be a little forceful, but he means well," Jakob said.

She paused at the door leading into the kitchen. "*Ne*, I'm fine. *Danke* for rescuing me," she said.

"I'm just returning the favor. *Danke* for helping my *mudder*. You're right. She's overly tired. You've been a great benefit to her." He spoke low, for her ears alone.

Abby leaned slightly closer and gave him a conspiratorial smile. "You're *willkomm*, although helping Naomi is easy. She's so kind. I wish…"

Again, she didn't finish her thought.

"You wish what?" he pressed.

"Oh, nothing."

He let it go, but a part of him wondered if she was going to say that she wished she'd had a mother like Naomi.

"How old were you when your *mamm* died?" he asked instead.

"I was six. I don't remember her very well. Just bits and pieces, really. I know she loved me, because I remember her comforting me once after my *vadder*…" She shrugged.

After her father did what? Beat her?

"Life must have been difficult for you growing up," he said, trying to imagine what she'd been through.

She met his eyes, still holding the plate of pie. "I guess it does no good to pretend with you. You already know the truth."

"*Ja*, I know."

"You…you won't tell anyone, will you?" She peered askance at him, as though she'd done something wrong and was embarrassed by it.

"Of course not. It wasn't your fault. Remember that time when I broke the stick over my knee?"

She looked at the ground, not replying.

"I can understand why you're uneasy around men," he said.

She whipped her head up, biting her bottom lip. "Is it that obvious?"

"Only to me, because I know what happened. And I'm sorry for it."

"Don't be. It wasn't your fault either," she said.

And yet, a part of him wished his *familye* hadn't moved away. That he could have stayed in Ohio and been there to intercede for her more often. It seemed he'd always been her protector of sorts. For some reason, it came naturally to him. But if he hadn't moved to Colorado, he never would have met Susan. Never would have known the exquisite love they had shared; never would have had his two beautiful children. Or at least, he didn't think so.

"You must be very angry at your *vadder* and Simon," he said.

She released a long sigh. "I was when I was very young, but not anymore. Simon is what my *vadder* created of him. He didn't know anything else. But the anger has to stop somewhere, so why not with me? Besides, the Lord has sustained me through it all. In my loneliest moments, He has been there beside me."

"You're not angry at *Gott*?" he asked.

"*Ne*, why should I be? I found comfort knowing He was there. And though I don't always understand His plans, He has brought me here to Colorado, where I can have a fresh start."

Jakob caught the conviction in her voice. He couldn't imagine ever reprimanding this woman, even when she was a mischievous child. If anyone tried to hurt Ruby, he'd be furious. And yet, anger wasn't what *Gott* expected from him. Even after losing Susan and his father, Jakob knew he should forgive *Gott* and turn the other cheek. He should have more faith.

"Will you take this to *Dawdi* Zeke for me? I didn't get the chance, and he's expecting it." She held up the pie.

"Of course." He took the plate from her hands, watching as she turned and slipped into the house.

A feeling of compassion swept over him, but something else, as well. Respect and admiration.

"*Hallo*, Jakob."

He turned. Bishop Yoder stood behind him, still wearing his frock coat.

"Bishop." Jakob nodded respectfully.

"Did you enjoy the meetings today?"

"*Ja*, very much." Which was true. Jakob loved being with people of his own faith. But honestly, he could remember very little of the sermons. His thoughts had been centered almost entirely on Abby.

The older man jutted his chin toward the house. "I couldn't help noticing that you were just speaking with Abby."

"*Ja*, she just went inside to help my *mudder* in the kitchen."

"How are things working out with her living in your home?"

"*Gut*. She is a great help on the farm."

"Have you reconsidered a possible marriage with her?"

Jakob blinked. He hadn't expected the bishop to be so blunt. "I'm afraid nothing has changed. I still love Susan. I can't consider marrying another woman anytime soon."

Bishop Yoder lowered his head for several moments,

as though thinking how to respond. Then, he spoke in a soft, kind voice. "Before He was crucified, the Savior gave His apostles a new commandment that they should love one another. That commandment extends to us, as well. The Lord's capacity to love was absolute, unconditional and unrestrained. As we treat one another with service, compassion and respect, our love increases. It isn't limited, and it never runs out."

Jakob was speechless. What was the bishop saying? That if he treated Abby with service, compassion and respect, he would love her? That might be true, but he couldn't love her as a man should love his wife. Not a romantic love. When Susan had died, Jakob had felt bewildered, confused and frightened. He was stuck in limbo and couldn't seem to move past her memory.

"Would you still have married Susan, even knowing that you would lose her one day?" the bishop asked.

Jakob nodded without hesitation. "Absolutely."

"Then would you say that loving and being with her even for a short time was worth the pain of losing her?"

Again, Jakob wondered what the bishop was getting at. He didn't like to play mind games. "*Ja*, I would do it all over again, even knowing that I would lose her one day."

"She would want you to be happy, Jakob. Don't be afraid to love again," the bishop said.

Afraid? Jakob wasn't afraid. Not really. Okay, maybe a little bit. He was afraid of loving and losing again. He couldn't go through that trauma a second time, and he didn't want to put his children through it either.

The bishop glanced to where Martin stood conversing with several young men his age. "I also noticed Abby speaking with Martin Hostetler. I know he is eager to find a wife, and he seems very interested in her."

"*Ja*, he asked her to stay for the singing time with him, but she declined."

Jakob felt a bit defensive. He didn't want Abby to spend time with the other man, but that wasn't fair. She was young and pretty and should have some fun. She deserved all the joy this world could offer. And Martin was a nice enough man. He deserved to be happy, too.

Bishop Yoder shrugged. "She is still new here, but that will soon change. One day, some smart young man will realize that she's worth it, too."

Jakob caught the hint, but it didn't make a difference. Not for him. Abby would make some other man a fine wife. A kind, patient man she could love and grow old with.

He thought it was ironic that she didn't blame *Gott* for the sadness in her life. Instead, she relied on the Lord. Her faith sustained her. In contrast, Jakob's faith had faltered. Losing his wife and father had devastated him. He'd felt abandoned and lost. Angry even. Perhaps he could learn some valuable lessons from Abby's humble heart. But marriage to her? Definitely not.

Chapter Seven

The next morning, Abby stepped out onto the back porch and picked up the wire basket they used to collect eggs. Sunlight streamed across the yard, chasing the chill out of the spring air.

Inside the house, she could hear Naomi humming as she sorted laundry. Jakob had driven Reuben to school in the buggy. As usual, the boy had scowled deeply when he discovered that Abby had prepared his lunch. Once again, she'd written an uplifting note and hidden it in his sandwich wrapper where he was sure to find it. Hopefully it would help soften his heart toward her.

Crossing the yard, she headed for the chicken coop, swinging the wire basket beside her. She would get the barn chores done before she needed to help Jakob plant the field corn.

As she passed the barn, she heard a faint sound, almost like the cry of a child. She looked up. The door to the hayloft stood wide open, and she thought Jakob must be airing it out after the long winter. Soon, the fields would be burgeoning with newly planted corn and hay. Tomorrow or the next day, she would plant carrots, beets and peas. Each vegetable did well in cooler climates. She'd have to wait a bit longer to plant tomatoes and squash.

The sound came again and she paused, listening for a moment. Hmm, she must be imagining things.

Continuing on her way to the coop, she let herself inside. The musty smell of chickens and dust made her nose twitch. She gazed through the dim interior, noticing that all but one hen had vacated their nests. The remaining chicken gave a disgruntled cluck and tilted its head, staring at Abby with its dark, beady eyes.

"You're a slowpoke today. But don't worry. I'll give you some extra time before I take your eggs," Abby promised with a soft laugh.

The hen clucked again, as though in agreement. Abby searched the other nests first, placing the white and brown eggs carefully in her basket. She worked quickly, removing any wood shavings from the nests that were particularly dirty and replacing them with fresh straw. When she was finished, she looked at the mother hen and rested one hand on her waist.

"Aren't you finished yet? Or are you going to stay there all day?" Abby asked.

The red hen just stared back at her.

Moving gently but quickly, Abby lifted the hen and removed the eggs from her nest. The hen barely noticed, and Abby smiled with satisfaction.

"I'm all done. I'll see you later this evening, and I hope you're off the nest by that time."

With her basket filled, Abby stepped outside into the sunlight and closed the door. As she secured the latch on the hen house, she heard the strange sound again. A faint *mewl* that died off quickly. Definitely not from a child. More like a little animal. But where was it coming from?

There! She heard it again, more softly this time.

Entering the barn, Abby set her egg basket aside on a high shelf. Dust motes floated through cracks in the walls, the faint sunlight filtering through the dim interior. A subtle rustling came from the hayloft. Abby gazed up at the long, arching timbers curving across the ceiling like the skeleton of a giant whale's rib cage. Even her father's barn in Ohio wasn't this large and spacious. She couldn't help being impressed by Jakob's construction skills.

A tall ladder reached up to the loft. Lifting her skirts away from her ankles, she stepped on the bottom rung and started to climb. Her skirt got twisted around her shoe and she lost her footing. Gripping the side of the ladder, she caught herself just in time and untangled her skirt.

"Ouch!"

Several splinters from the rough timber had dug their way into her fingers. As she reached to pull them out, she lost her balance and fell backward.

Strong arms suddenly wrapped around her. For just a fraction of time, she felt a solid chest at her back and a warm cheek pressed against her own.

"Oh!" She jerked away so fast that Jakob stumbled and grabbed for the ladder to catch himself.

He looked at her, his eyes wide with surprise. "Are you all right?"

She breathed heavily, trying to catch her breath. "*Ja,* I'm fine."

But no, she wasn't. Not really. She felt mortified by the physical contact they had shared.

"Are you certain? You seem flustered. I was only trying to save you from a bad fall," he said.

"I'm sorry. I guess I've developed quick reflexes. I learned at a young age to be on my guard."

He accepted her admittance without comment, but she could tell from his expression that he understood. Living with her father and Simon had taught her to duck fast at a moment's notice.

"Let me see the damage," he said.

She didn't fight him as he took her hand in his, perusing her injury with infinite tenderness. The skin on his palms was roughened by hard work, but his fingers were warm and gentle. Using his blunt fingernails, he plucked out two of the splinters.

"I'm afraid I can't get the last one out, but *Mamm* has a pair of tweezers in the house that you can use," he said.

He released her hand and she folded her hands together, looking down. *"Danke."*

As she glanced at him, her entire body heated up as hot as Naomi's woodstove. She lifted a hand to her face where she still felt the warmth of his cheek. He stood in front of her in his worn work clothes, looking strong and handsome, yet completely harmless. She followed the movement of his hand as he reached up and rubbed his beard.

"What were you doing up on the ladder anyway?" He glanced toward the loft.

"I… I heard mewling sounds and wanted to see if Ruby's barn cat was up there." She took another step back, trying to calm her racing heart. She told herself she didn't need to fear this man, but the jittery instinct to run and hide was difficult to resist.

Jakob shook his head, his eyes creased with stoic sorrow. "I'm afraid Amber is gone."

"Gone where?" she asked, remembering that Amber was the name of Ruby's cat.

"I found her on the side of the highway this morning on my way home from taking Reuben to school. She'd been hit by a car. I just buried her so the children wouldn't see."

"Oh, *ne*." Abby covered her mouth with one hand, her heart filled with sadness. She'd seen how vehicles whizzed by on the road, moving so fast that the drivers could barely notice anything in their path. It reaffirmed Abby's preference for buggies and horses, which moved at a calm, sane speed.

"Will you tell Ruby that her cat is gone?" she asked, her voice wobbling slightly.

"*Ja*, both *kinder* will have to be told. Ruby lives on a farm and understands such things, but I know she'll be upset."

Abby agreed, but didn't get the chance to say so. The mewling sound came again, such a pitiful, weak cry that they could have easily missed it if they'd been talking at that precise moment.

Jakob tilted his head, his gaze lifting to the stacks of hay above. "I just heard it, too. I wonder..."

Without finishing his thought, he set his foot on the bottom rung of the ladder and hurried up. Abby waited below. Was it possible that Amber had her kittens up there? When Abby thought about the babies without their mother to care for them, a sense of urgency swept over her. She took a deep inhale and held it for several seconds. When Jakob reappeared, she let it go.

"What did you find?" she asked.

He didn't reply as he climbed down. When he reached the bottom, she noticed he gripped the ladder with one hand, his other hand held close against his chest.

Safely on his feet, he turned and revealed two baby

kittens so small that he could easily hold them with one hand. A miniature head with teensy ears poked up, showing white fur with one yellow and one gray spot on top. The second kitten had yellow and gray stripes. Both babies peered at her with large blue eyes. Completely defenseless and adorable.

Abby reached to pet them, unable to stop herself. "*Ach*, how precious. How old do you think they are?"

"Their eyes are open, but they're wobbly when they walk. I'd say they're about two weeks old, which fits with when Amber stopped coming to the house at night. No doubt she's been busy tending to her babies."

Abby's maternal instincts kicked in. "They're weak. Who knows how long it's been since they were fed last."

"*Ja*, if they don't eat soon, they won't make it. Babies this young can't last long without food."

"You're right. Please, let me help them, Jakob. They'll make good barn cats and catch lots of mice. I can take care of them and finish all my chores, too. They won't be any trouble at all, and I'll keep them out of your way. I promise." She peered at his face, awaiting his reaction.

His forehead crinkled in confusion. "You don't need to defend them to me, Abby. Of course we'll take care of these babies. Do you expect me to just let them die?"

She realized her mistake. This was not her brother she was talking with. "*Ne*, of course not. I... I wasn't sure what you thought."

"I would never do anything to hurt these kittens, unless I couldn't prevent it."

Of course not. He wasn't cruel, like Simon. His reassurance bolstered her courage and she took the white kitten from him, cuddling it close to her chest. "Does Ruby have any doll bottles?"

"I don't think so." He turned, searching the barn until he found a wooden crate.

"What about a medicine dropper? I can feed the babies with that," she said.

"*Ja*, I believe we have a small dropper. And some old towels we can put in the bottom of this crate."

"Would Naomi mind if we take the kittens inside the kitchen where it's warm? The best place would be right next to the woodstove," she said, hoping she wasn't pushing his patience too far.

"*Ne, Mamm* wouldn't mind at all. In fact, I think she'll be happy that we found Amber's babies."

Carrying the crate and striped kitten, he headed toward the house with Abby following behind. She snatched up the basket of eggs along her way. As they crossed the yard, she was touched by Jakob's kindness. Simon would have yelled and screamed. He wouldn't have wanted to be bothered by a couple of orphaned kittens. He would have even forbidden her to care for them. She knew, because it had happened once before, and she'd been heartsick over the loss.

Even though Jakob had been kind to her, Abby kept forgetting that he was of a different caliber from her brother. And for just a moment, she wished things could be different between them.

"*Ach*, the poor dears," Naomi cried when she found out what had happened.

"It's a blessing that you found them in time," *Dawdi* Zeke said, peering over his great-granddaughter's shoulder.

Ruby snuggled the white kitten close to her pinafore,

her eyes filled with tears. "You won't let them die, will you, *Daed*?"

"We'll take *gut* care of the babies, but their lives are in *Gott's* hands." Jakob handed a dropper he'd found in the medicine cabinet to Abby after removing the final splinter in her finger using his *mamm's* tweezers.

She'd already placed a pan of goat's milk and a little Karo syrup on the stove to warm. After washing the dropper and sterilizing it, she handed it to Naomi. The older woman cuddled the white kitten in the crook of her left arm. The poor animal was too weak to even struggle. After sucking milk into the dropper, Naomi introduced it to the kitten's mouth. At first, the baby resisted and milk dripped onto its fur. Naomi persisted and the kitten soon caught on. It suckled the milk greedily. They all stood around, watching with amazement. Finally, the baby's stomach was round and taut. The kitten yawned, its pink tongue curling back in its little mouth.

While Abby cleaned and sterilized the dropper a second time, Zeke took the full kitten and placed it gently in the nest of warm towels in the crate beside the stove. The baby curled up and almost instantly fell asleep.

"See there. That's a good sign," he said.

"We'll need something more than a medicine dropper to feed these hungry babies. I think we need to go into town to the feed and grain store and see if we can buy a couple of nursing kits. I've seen them there before," Jakob said.

Abby handed the cleaned dropper to Naomi. "I can pay for whatever we need."

"You'll do no such thing," Naomi said as she took the striped kitten from Ruby. The baby mewed pathetically. "We will buy the nursing kits, although I think it'll take all of us to keep these newborns fed. I suspect they'll need to eat every hour or so for the time being. They're very young."

"How do you know what to feed them?" Ruby asked Abby, watching with wide eyes as her grandmother fed the baby.

"My sister-in-law taught me. We found an orphaned kitten on our farm once…" Abby's voice drifted off, a sad look in her eyes.

Jakob wondered if the kitten had died. Something about her voice and the way she'd begged him to let her care for the babies led him to guess that Simon hadn't been too supportive. It would be foolish to let an animal die if you could do something to save it. On a farm, all the animals served a purpose and helped with the prosperity of the place, even barn cats. But Simon wasn't the type of man to care, which might account for why his farm had never done very well.

"Goat's milk won't be enough. It will only tide the babies over until we can go into town and buy some kitten formula at the pet store," Abby said.

Ruby looked at her father, the ribbons on her *kapp* bobbing with her head. "Can you go now, *Daed*? We have to get the babies some *gut* food or they'll die."

Jakob smiled, wanting to reassure his daughter. "Don't worry. I'll go this afternoon, when I pick Reuben up from school. The goat's milk will work fine until then. In the meantime, I need to go outside and plant corn. But I'll return in time to go into town."

Ruby threw her arms around his waist and hugged him tightly. *"Danke, Daedi."*

He kissed her cheek, delighted by her tender heart.

She was so much like her mother. Over the top of her head, he saw the gratitude shining in Abby's eyes. For some reason, he wanted to prove to her that he wasn't like her brother. That he was a better man than that.

Without its sibling and mother's warm body to keep it company, the white kitten began to cry. Abby picked it up and held the baby close.

She giggled. "Its fur tickles my nose."

"Let me see," Ruby said.

Abby lowered the kitten so that the girl could rub her face against its fur. Ruby squealed with delight, and they all laughed. Jakob stared at Abby, mesmerized by the way her smile made her blue eyes glitter.

"It has a yellow spot on its head," Ruby said.

"*Ja*, it's the same color as your *mudder's* daffodils. Maybe that would be a good name for the kitten," Abby suggested.

Ruby nodded. "*Ja*, I'll call this baby Daffy. *Mamm* called her daffodils the daffies."

"Daffy." Abby said the name, as if trying it out on her tongue. "It's perfect. I like it."

"So do I," *Dawdi* Zeke said.

"Reuben can name the other kitten," Ruby suggested.

"That sounds fair," Naomi said.

Jakob watched them all. Abby's eyes glowed with happiness. Sunlight filtered through the window, highlighting wisps of golden hair that had come free of her white *kapp*. He was surprised that she would suggest they name one of the kittens after Susan's flowers, but he was fast learning that Abby was both generous and compassionate. She didn't seem to feel threatened by Susan's memory at all. And her laughter did something to him inside. Something he didn't understand. When they'd been out in the barn and she'd confided how she'd acquired fast reflexes, her admission reaffirmed his desire to shield her from harm. There was no way he could ever refuse her request to care for the kittens. In fact, he wondered if he could refuse her anything.

"I'd better get out to the fields," he said.

"I'll come help," Abby said.

"No need yet. Bring the smaller seed wagon out in a couple of hours. By then, I'll be ready to refill the hoppers."

She nodded, reaching for the eggs she'd gathered. He knew she would clean and put them in the well house, to keep them cool. Naomi would use many of them for her baking, but they would sell the remainder to the country store in town. Another cash crop that brought funds into the household.

"I'll help out here. I may be shaky, but I can still hold a baby kitten," *Dawdi* Zeke said. A deep smile creased the elderly man's face as he watched the striped kitten sleep.

Abby filled a basin with warm water, and Jakob forced himself to turn away. He longed to stay right here and enjoy this quiet interlude with his *familye*, but there was work to be done. He couldn't spend the day ogling baby kittens with Abby.

Chapter Eight

In exactly two hours, Abby hitched up Tommy, the *familye's* chestnut gelding. Naomi was hanging laundry on the line and had a batch of bread in the oven. Abby waved as she pulled away from the barn.

Jakob had already stacked bags of seed corn in the back of the small wagon. His thoughtfulness pleased her. Simon would have made her lift the heavy bags.

As she headed toward the fields, she could see Jakob driving four Belgian draft horses hitched to a four-row planter. Standing on the platform, he wore his straw hat as he glanced over his shoulder often to ensure the seed corn was dispensing correctly. With his strong hands holding the lead lines, he moved the big horses at an even pace, the furrows long and straight. As her wagon bumped over the uneven ground, she couldn't help admiring Jakob's muscular back and arms.

She pulled off to the side of the field, leaving him enough room to turn his team around. When he reached the end of the column, she noticed a perplexed frown on his face.

He pulled the Belgians to a halt, then hopped down

and went to peruse the machinery. He bent over and fidgeted with one of the seed units for a moment, then released a low huff of air. He stood straight and shook his head, holding something in his hands.

Abby jumped down and joined him.

"Is something wrong?" she asked.

He whipped his hat off and wiped his brow with his forearm, then held up a chain that was blackened with oil. "*Ja*, one of the drive chains broke. This is a new field and very rocky ground. I can't finish planting until the chain is replaced."

She could see the frustration etched across his face. No doubt he was eager to finish the planting, but that might not happen today.

"What can I do to help?" she asked.

He glanced upward at the position of the sun. "It appears we'll be going into town now. Things might move faster if you rode with me. While I get the replacement chain, you can get the nursing kits and formula for the kittens. Then we can pick up Reuben from school on the way back. If I can get the chain replaced today, I can finish planting tomorrow."

She paused, surprised that he would invite her to ride into town with him. No doubt Ruby would prefer to remain at home to tend the kittens. But Abby quickly reminded herself that this was just work. Jakob needed her help, nothing more.

"Of course I'll go. I'm happy to help," she said.

He walked around the corn planter so he could unhitch the team. She didn't need to ask why. It would not be prudent to leave the horses standing out in the hot sun while they made the long trip into town.

As he undid the chains on the tug lines, one of the

horses thrust his left hind foot back, striking Jakob on the back of his lower leg. It happened so fast that neither of them saw it coming.

"Oof!" The man dropped to the ground like stone, his straw hat falling off his head.

"Jakob!" Abby raced to his side, frightened that he'd be trampled by the horses.

She pulled on his arms until he was a safe distance away from the giant Belgians. He lay flat on his back, his eyes closed, a grimace of agony on his face as he pulled his injured leg up toward his chest.

"Are you all right?" She touched his pale cheek with one hand, praying that he wasn't injured seriously.

"*Ja*, I… I think I'm all right." His voice sounded tight and breathless as he struggled to sit up.

She helped him, her gaze lowering to his leg. "*Ne*, you're hurt."

Gritting his teeth, he rolled up his pant leg and rotated his calf to show an ugly red mark in the shape of a horseshoe across his flesh. It was swelling right before their eyes.

"You're going to have a nasty bruise," she said.

"*Ja*, Billy clipped me good this time. He has a nasty habit of doing that. I was in too big a hurry and let my guard down," Jakob remarked, breathing heavily.

"Can you stand?" Abby asked, reaching her arm around to support his back. She caught his scent, a subtle mixture of horses and Naomi's homemade soap made with coconut oil.

He nodded and gritted his teeth as he stood with effort. When he tried to put weight on his injured leg, a guttural groan came from his throat. He faltered, holding on tight to Abby.

"It might be broken," she said.

"Heaven help us if it is. I've got to get these fields planted. I can't be laid up right now." His voice sounded roughened by fear and pain.

Abby didn't need to ask why. They had a few days' leeway, but if they didn't get the crops planted, they would have nothing to harvest and no livelihood for the following year. Other men might be able to help, but their Amish community was not large and everyone was busy planting their own fields.

"Don't you worry," she said. "No matter what, we'll take care of it somehow. If nothing else, I've planted fields on my own before. I can do it again."

For some reason, she wanted to reassure him. She knew how it felt to be desperate and alone, and she didn't want Jakob to feel that way when he was in pain.

He jerked his head up in surprise, a jagged thatch of hair falling into his eyes. "Your brother made you do the planting alone? Without his help?"

She couldn't resist showing a wry smile. "*Ja.* Knowing Simon, are you really so surprised?"

He pursed his lips with disapproval but didn't respond. With her aid, he hopped over to the small wagon, and she helped him pull himself into the seat. After retrieving his hat, she scampered up beside him and drove them to the house. Within minutes, she'd raced inside to tell Naomi what had happened. They asked Ruby to stay in the kitchen, to watch the kittens. There was no sense in making Jakob hobble into the house if they had to take him to the clinic in town. He remained in the wagon while Naomi inspected the burgeoning bruise. It had spread and was already turning an angry black color.

"That mean ole horse. You ought to get rid of him, Jakob. He nearly broke your *vadder's* arm once," Naomi said as she gently touched the tight skin with her fingertips.

"Billy isn't mean—he's just skittish. He's still the strongest horse on the farm and we're not getting rid of him," Jakob replied between gritted teeth.

"*Ach*, I still wish you'd trade him for another, gentler horse," she said.

Jakob didn't reply. His jaw was locked, his hands clenched. Abby could tell he was in terrible pain, yet he spoke with complete calm, his voice soft and even.

"Do you think his leg is broken?" Abby asked.

Naomi shook her head. "There's no way of knowing for sure. It could have just bruised the bone, or torn the muscle. With the fields needing to be planted, we can't take the chance. You better drive him into town for an X-ray."

Without a word, Abby unloaded the heavy bags of seed corn from the back of the wagon. The gelding certainly couldn't travel quickly into town while pulling such a heavy load. She had just finished the chore when Zeke appeared from the *dawdy haus*.

"What's going on?" he asked, shambling over to them.

They quickly explained.

"Why didn't you call me to help unload the seed corn from the wagon?" Zeke asked Abby.

"There was no need. I'm strong enough," Abby said. It hadn't been easy, but she knew the work would hurt him much more than it would hurt her. She didn't want to do anything to endanger the elderly man's health.

"I'll bring the Belgians in from the field," Zeke said.

"*Ne*, I'll fetch them," Naomi said. "Abby will take Jakob to the doctor and pick Reuben up on their way home. You stay here and help Ruby with the kittens. If it starts to rain, gather in the laundry."

Since there wasn't a cloud in the sky, Abby doubted the laundry hanging on the line was in any danger of getting rained on. Naomi seemed to know that the simple chore gave Zeke something to occupy himself.

Naomi took off toward the fields before Zeke could argue. As he hobbled toward the house, Abby could hear him grumbling something about getting old, losing respect and being consigned to women's work.

Women frequently drove large teams of horses while their men baled hay. But Naomi wasn't young anymore either, and Abby hated to make her bring the draft horses in from the field. But Naomi had given them no choice. And Abby couldn't help wondering why everyone seemed to want her to go with Jakob instead of letting Naomi drive him into town.

Taking the leads into her hands, Abby slapped them against Tommy's back. Jakob braced his wounded leg against the seat, but his stoic expression told her that he was hurting. To take his mind off the pain, she distracted him with chatter.

"*Danke* for letting us care for the kittens. They'll grow fast and we'll be able to wean them within a few weeks," she said.

"I knew it was important to you. We couldn't just leave them in the hayloft. They would have died," he said.

"*Ja*, there have been times when I've felt alone and helpless, just like those babies. It was you who came to my rescue once," she confessed.

He reached over and squeezed her hand, so suddenly and unexpectedly that she almost gasped.

"Don't worry. We'll do all we can for them. This has been a challenging day, but it'll get better," he said.

She stared at him, surprised at his optimism. He had been injured and was in pain, yet he was comforting her. No accusations. No anger. Just a gentle reassurance.

Looking away, she puzzled over his comments. She was uncertain of his motives. He didn't want to marry her, yet he was always so supportive. A fog of emotions swirled around inside her mind. She trusted and respected this man. He was someone she considered a good friend. But if she wasn't careful, her feelings could easily grow. And loving Jakob would only cause her more grief.

Although the next few hours rushed by for Jakob, it wasn't without considerable discomfort. Abby drove him straight to the only clinic in town. When the horse had kicked him, he'd been blinded by pain so intense that he could hardly breathe. Now, a throbbing ache had settled into his calf, as though his leg were about to explode. He'd feel better if he knew for sure it wasn't broken.

While he received X-rays and an ice pack for his calf, Abby hurried over to the feed and grain store. He'd given her the money and explicit instructions as to the replacement chain she should buy. And when she returned, he was pleased to discover that she'd obtained exactly what he needed to make the repair. She'd also purchased two nursing kits and kitten formula. Thankfully, his leg wasn't broken, but the muscle and surrounding tissue were badly bruised. The doctor advised him to stay off his feet for at least a week, but that wasn't going to happen. The pain would pass, but they had to get their fields planted as soon as possible. Such was the life of a farmer.

On their way home, they stopped and picked Reuben up from school. He stared in silence as Jakob explained all that had transpired throughout the day. As they drove home, Jakob saw the boy casting quick glances at Abby, as though he were seeing her for the first time.

When they arrived home, Abby pulled up out front of the house. With Naomi and *Dawdi* Zeke's support, Jakob limped up the cobblestone sidewalk he'd laid with his own hands years earlier. Glancing over his shoulder, he watched Abby drive the wagon to the barn. Reuben stayed with her, not needing to be asked to help un-hitch the horse. The boy's shoulders were tense and he wore a heavy frown, but he didn't say a word. Jakob was relieved to see that his son understood his duties in spite of his personal feelings for Abby. A short time later, Abby and the boy rejoined the rest of the *familye* inside the kitchen.

"Reuben helped me feed and water the horses. I'll do the milking as soon as we've given the babies some kitten formula," Abby said, setting a brown paper sack on the countertop.

"I'll help with the milking," *Dawdi* Zeke said.

"Danke." Sitting in a chair at the table, Jakob had propped his injured leg on another chair to elevate it. Naomi had prepared a fresh cold compress for him. He felt slightly unmanned to turn his evening chores over to Abby, his son and his elderly grandfather, but he was beyond grateful for their willing attitudes.

"I don't know what we would have done without you today," Naomi said to Abby.

"It's the least I can do. You've been so kind to me."

"I'll help with the milking, too." Reuben spoke in a quiet voice.

Jakob noticed the tenderness in his son's eyes as he held each of the kittens.

"I named the white baby Daffy because she has a yellow spot on her head that matches *Mamm's* daffodils. Abby suggested it," Ruby said. "*Dawdi* thinks she's a girl. You get to name the other kitten. *Dawdi* thinks he's a boy."

Reuben picked up the striped baby, his eyes filled with tender awe. "He's so small. Look at his tiny whiskers. And his claws are so small and sharp. He looks like a little tiger."

"Tiger," *Dawdi* Zeke repeated. "That's a perfect name for a barn cat. No doubt he'll be a good mouser."

Reuben grinned from ear to ear, obviously pleased by the name he'd chosen.

Jakob felt a bit woozy from the pain pill the doctor had given him. Naomi kept urging him to go to the *dawdy haus* and lie down, but he delayed a little longer. Today could have ended in tragedy, and he had a lot to be grateful for. It felt so good to be in the safety of his own home, surrounded by his *familye*. All was well. And yet, something had drastically changed between him and Abby. He wasn't certain what it was and he didn't understand it at all, but he sensed that their relationship had deepened somehow. Surely he was imagining things.

"May I feed Tiger?" Reuben asked Abby in a cautious tone.

She turned from the stove, where she had just heated and filled one of the small bottles from the nursing kit with kitten formula. For just a moment, her eyes widened in surprise, and Jakob realized this was the first time Reuben had addressed her politely.

"Of course you may." She dribbled several drops of milk on her wrist, then nodded at Reuben. "The milk is ready."

"Why did you do that?" the boy asked, indicating her wrist.

"To make sure the milk isn't too hot for the baby's mouth," she said.

Jakob watched as she showed his son how to hold Tiger in the crook of his arm. When she touched him, Reuben tensed but didn't push her away. He jerked when the baby latched on to the bottle a bit ferociously, and they all laughed.

"I can see these kittens have quickly regained their strength. Unless something unforeseen happens, I think they're going to be all right," Naomi said.

"*Ja*, thanks to Abby," Jakob said, unable to deny a warm glow of happiness inside his heart.

"It's a good thing she heard the babies crying and went looking for them in the barn, or we wouldn't have found them in time," *Dawdi* Zeke said.

Reuben glanced at the woman he hadn't yet been able to accept. Abby smiled at him, her expression one of tolerance and compassion, but his face held a skeptical frown. When he gazed at the tiny kitten he held in his arms, his eyes glimmered with love. No doubt he was enamored by the babies.

Once Tiger had eaten his fill, Abby fluffed the towel in the bottom of the wooden crate. Reuben laid Tiger beside Daffy. The two kittens curled together, sharing body heat. And without any warning, Reuben threw his arms around Naomi's waist and hugged her, his face pressed against her side.

"*Danke* for saving the kittens." Reuben's words were muffled against his grandmother's apron, but they all heard him nevertheless.

"You're *willkomm*, but I've done very little. You should be thanking Abby," Naomi said.

The boy looked up at Abby, his eyes filled with doubt. He didn't say a word, just frowned with skepticism.

"You're most *willkomm*, sweetheart," Abby responded anyway.

The boy moved away, brushing at his eyes. If Jakob weren't feeling so fuzzy, he would have thought his son was crying. He was disappointed in the boy. Even a pair of orphaned kittens couldn't convince Reuben to finally become friendly with Abby. Regardless, the kittens had been therapeutic to the grief-stricken *familye*. They had laughed and enjoyed feeding the babies so much. Abby had made a difference in their lives, and Jakob was grateful for her soothing influence in his home. But she still wasn't his beloved wife. Jakob knew it, and so did Reuben. Abby wasn't Susan, and she never would be.

Chapter Nine

"Are you sure you're up to this?" Abby watched dubiously as Jakob limped over to the corn planter.

It sat exactly where they'd left it the day before. As promised, Naomi had brought the draft horses in right after Abby had driven Jakob to the clinic in town. Now, morning sunlight gleamed across the bare ground, highlighting the dark, fertile soil. The day wasn't too hot or cold, but just right for planting.

"It must be done," Jakob said.

Although he was still young, Reuben had joined them in the field. The boy hefted the red toolbox out of the wagon and carried it over to set beside his father on the frame of the planter. Naomi had wanted to help, but Jakob adamantly refused. She wasn't a young woman anymore and the task would be too much for her. Besides, her help wasn't necessary. Not with Abby there.

Jakob reached to open the box but nearly toppled over in the process. He didn't cry out as the movement jarred his leg, but Abby saw the pain written across his face. He wasn't up to this chore either, but he was resolute. No amount of pleading had convinced him to stay in the house. And Abby had to admire his tenacity. He was a man determined to take care of his *familye*.

"Tell me what you need and I'll hand it to you," she said, wishing she knew how to make the repair.

"I'll help, too, *Daed*," Reuben said.

As promised, they all worked together. Jakob stood leaning against the planter, resting his weight on his good leg. Abby placed a socket wrench in his hand, and he loosened a couple of bolts on the sprockets. It took some effort as the bolts were very tight, and Abby was grateful for his strength.

Within minutes, they had the new chain threaded and Jakob tightened down the bolts. When he finished, he turned, stumbled and fell heavily against her.

"Daed!" Reuben cried.

Abby didn't think before wrapping her arms around him, an automatic response. The man grunted, reaching for the planter to steady himself. If Abby hadn't caught him, she knew he would have gone down.

While Abby supported Jakob's right side, Reuben supported his left.

"I think you're finished being on your feet today," Abby said.

"But the planting… I have to get it done," Jakob argued, sounding out of breath.

"We'll get it done, but you will do no more than sit in the wagon and supervise. Reuben and I will do the planting. You're in no position to argue, so don't fight us. Right, Reuben?" She looked pointedly at the boy, seeking his support.

The boy gave a decisive nod of his head. "Right. It's no good to fight us, *Daed*. We only have your well-being in mind."

The boy sounded so grown up. Abby looked away, hiding a satisfied smile. Thinking it would draw them closer, she'd purposefully tried to get Reuben on her side. Her ploy had worked, and the boy grinned at her as they helped Jakob into the wagon. She'd brought a heavy quilt along to elevate and support his leg.

Now that he was off his feet, the man breathed with relief and took the leads into his hands. He drove Abby back to the barn, where she hitched up the Belgians with Reuben's help. The boy was small, but he knew what to do and was a hard worker. They soon had the draft horses back in the field and hooked up to the corn planter.

"You'll need this." Jakob held out a level to her.

Abby reached up and took the instrument, knowing what it was for. She placed it on the main tool bar of the planter, noticing the bubble was off-kilter. Again, Reuben helped as she made a few adjustments. They pushed, grunted and adjusted the air pressure until the bubble inside the level was even.

"The disc openers were working perfectly yesterday, but you better check them again," Jakob called.

Abby nodded and did as asked. The disc openers were set at an angle so that they would open a furrow for the corn seeds to drop into. The angle was about two inches, and she figured that was perfect.

She glanced at Jakob. "They're good."

"Check the gauge wheels, too," he said.

She did, just barely able to turn them. "The down force is good. I think we're ready to begin."

"Just one more thing. The closing wheels," Reuben said.

Running to the back of the planter, he inspected the

wheels. His bare feet sank into the soft soil as he ensured that each set of wheels was angled properly so
that they would close the furrows of dirt over the seeds.

Since he was still quite young, Abby joined him.
Seeing that all was in order, she asked his opinion, hop-
ing to build his self-confidence. "What do you think?
Are they good?"

Reuben nodded, looking very serious and mature for
his age. "All is well. We are ready."

"Very *gut*, Reuben. You're so clever to remember to
check the closing wheels," Abby praised him.

Reuben beamed as he joined her on the driving platform. With Jakob sitting safely in the shade at the side
of the field, Abby took hold of the lead lines. She immediately felt the horses' tremendous strength pulling on
the lines. Looking forward, she gazed at four chestnut
rumps and flaxen tails, which were attached to a total
of eight thousand pounds of horsepower. She'd driven
draft animals before, but each horse had a different per-
sonality. She didn't know these Belgians at all, except
that Billy was skittish enough to badly injure a fully
grown man. And here she was, a mere woman trying
to command all of this strength with nothing more than
the tone of her voice and a strong tug on the lines.

"*Ach*, there's no time like the present," she murmured
to herself.

Gathering her courage, she slapped the leads against
the horses' backs.

"*Schritt!*" she called, wishing her voice wouldn't
tremble so much.

The horses stepped forward, and a lance of joy
speared her heart. Reuben gripped the support bar that
extended across the platform. He gazed ahead, seem-

ing eager for this adventure they had undertaken. But Abby wasn't. She knew how much they were depending on this harvest. She was desperate not to disappoint Jakob, nor let the *familye* down.

"Haw!" she called.

Lifting her head higher, she tugged on the leads. She almost laughed aloud when the Belgians turned left, just as she'd directed them. She did her best to line up the planter with Jakob's last finished row. Then she lowered the long marker bar. The armature extended out from the planter and traced the next row. She kept glancing at it, to ensure she drove the team straight and created long, even furrows.

Within an hour, she learned that Sally was inclined to jackrabbit starts, but Scottie was a calming influence next to her. Boaz stood on the far right side. He was fast, but he wasn't coming around into the turns as well as Abby would have liked. She slowed the team down a bit to give him time to catch up to the horses on the inside. And Billy might be skittish, but he was the strength of the team. He stabilized the planter, his strong muscles bunching as he pulled nice and even.

The work took all of her concentration, but she was still highly conscious of Jakob watching them from the wagon. She'd expected him to nod off and nap, but he sat straight and tall, his injured leg resting on the bunched-up blanket, his glimmering eyes on the planter. When she turned the team to head the other way, she could almost feel his gaze boring a hole in her back. A memory of Simon watching her with a critical eye rushed over her, along with the fear of his disapproval and a possible beating. She didn't believe Jakob would hurt her, but she felt nervous anyway. She wanted to do a good job for him. She told herself it was because she didn't want him to make her leave, but deep inside she knew it was something more. In spite of his rejection of marriage, she still wanted to ease his mind and make him happy.

By late afternoon, Jakob was worried. At midday, Abby had insisted she was doing fine. Reuben had eaten his bologna-and-cheese sandwich with them in the field, but then returned to the house with *Dawdi* Zeke. The boy's shoulders had slumped with weariness, but Jakob was pleased with his efforts. He was learning to become a good, hardworking man.

Now, it was late afternoon and Jakob was anxious about Abby. He looked to where she sat on the bench of the planter, still driving the team. Her spine was stiff, her head held high, but her arms lagged. Pulling against those big horses all day was enough to make anyone's muscles ache. Throughout the day, he'd tried to help her refill the hoppers but was embarrassed when his leg gave out on him and he almost dropped a bag of seed on the ground. She'd saved him just in time, taking the heavy weight of the bag against her own slender body. Though she hadn't uttered one word of complaint, she must have been absolutely tuckered out. In spite of her determination, she didn't have the strength of a man. He hated to push her so hard, especially knowing how Simon had abused her. Jakob certainly couldn't fault her work. Not when they almost had all of the corn planted.

Correction. *Abby* almost had the corn planted. He'd done nothing but sit in the shade and watch her work. In spite of the long rest, his leg throbbed unbearably. And no wonder. A horrific black-and-red bruise surrounded his entire calf and extended down his ankle to his foot and up to his knee. No doubt the blood pooling was the cause of the swelling and pain. In spite of the cold compress *Mamm* had sent for him at noon, it would take time for the wound to heal.

If he and Abby could just make it through the evening milking, they could both rest. *Mamm* would undoubtedly have a hearty meal prepared for them, if they weren't too sick and tired to eat it. He longed to retire but wouldn't leave Abby's side as long as she stood out in the baking sun, doing his work.

"Hallo!"

Jakob turned. *Dawdi* Zeke was driving their smallest wagon toward the field with a stranger sitting beside him. Both men wore straw hats and black suspenders, so Jakob knew their guest was Amish.

Shading his eyes, he tried to discern who the stranger was. Then, he groaned.

Martin Hostetler.

No doubt the man was here to see Abby. Jakob should be glad that one of their faithful members was interested in her. His thoughts toward Martin were uncharitable. He shouldn't mind having the other man here, but he did.

Pursing his lips, Jakob waved to get Abby's attention. After a moment, she saw him and called to the team. When she noticed Zeke and Martin, she paused for a moment, then kept on going.

Hmm. That was an interesting reaction. Jakob wasn't certain if she recognized Martin and wanted to avoid him, or if she was simply eager to finish the last column of planting. A few more minutes and she'd be done.

"Look who came to visit," *Dawdi* Zeke said as he pulled up next to Jakob.

"*Hallo*, Martin." Jakob tugged on the brim of his hat, determined to be polite.

"Hi, Jakob." Martin's gaze riveted over to Abby. She'd turned the horses and was heading toward them, her head bowed slightly as she concentrated on holding the horses in a straight line.

With the giant Belgians as a backdrop, she looked so small and frail sitting on the planter. But Jakob had learned she had a strong will and fortitude. Abby was a survivor. A good woman who would stand beside a good man against the storms of life. Jakob just didn't think Martin was the right man for her.

"What brings you all the way out here?" Jakob asked.

"I heard you got hurt and wanted to see if you needed any help," Martin said.

The man scanned the vast field. The rows weren't all perfectly straight, but they were planted and ready for growth. Since she was driving a strange team of horses, Jakob thought Abby had done an outstanding job and he couldn't have asked for more.

"As you can see, we've almost got the work done, thanks to Abby," he said.

"She's a strong little thing, isn't she?" Martin said, a wide smile on his face.

No, not really. At least, not physically. But Jakob didn't say that. Considering Abby's petite height and build, he didn't think she was strong at all. But her determination made up for a lot of what she lacked in physical stature.

"You could have asked me to plant your fields. It would have been easier on Abby," Martin said.

"*Ja*, but you have your own fields to plant," Jakob said.

Normally, Jakob would have contacted the bishop to see who in their district might be able to help out. The Amish assisted each other whenever there was trouble, but they had only nine families in their congregation. And honestly, Jakob didn't want Martin here, mainly because the man was interested in Abby. As far as Jakob was concerned, no one was good enough for Abby.

Wait a minute! Where had that thought come from? Jakob wasn't sure.

"I would have made the time. My *vadder* and I finished planting our fields five days ago. I could have helped you out," Martin insisted.

Hyperactivity came to Jakob's mind. He wasn't surprised that Martin had finished his planting days earlier. He just hoped their sprouting crops didn't get caught by a late freeze.

"*Danke* for the offer. We'll keep you in mind if we need help planting our hay," *Dawdi* Zeke said.

Jakob just nodded, forcing himself to smile. No one could accuse Martin of being lazy or unkind. The man was definitely a hard worker and an amazing horse trainer. One of the best in the state. He was Jakob's brother in the faith. It wasn't Christian for him to feel uncharitable toward the man. But he did. Which didn't make sense. He'd never had any problem with the man before…

Before Abby came. Too bad Martin had shown up just as they were finishing.

"She's an amazing woman, that's for sure. Some wise man should marry her while she's still eligible. It'd be a shame for her to leave us," *Dawdi* Zeke said.

Jakob jerked his head around and stared at his grand-

father. He sensed that the elderly man was digging at
him, to get him to propose to Abby. But he couldn't.
Not if he wanted to remain loyal to Susan.

They talked for the next few minutes. Or rather,
Martin and *Dawdi* Zeke talked. Jakob just listened and
nodded when appropriate. And when Abby pulled the
horses up, Martin waved both of his hands over his
head. Other than a nod of the head, she paid him no
heed and kept on going.

"Schtopp!" she called to the horses.

She'd reached the end of the column and raised the
marking bar. She was finished, and Jakob breathed a
long sigh of relief.

Still pulling the planter, the Belgians plodded over to
the men. The horses had worked hard today and were
undoubtedly eager for their comfortable stalls in the
barn. They'd earned their supper tonight.

"Hallo, Martin," Abby said, her voice sounding un-
enthusiastic or tired, Jakob wasn't sure which. Maybe
both.

"Hallo!" Martin smiled wide, his buoyant greeting
making up for anything that Abby's lacked.

Her face looked pale against cheeks rosy from the
sun. Now that her burden was over with, she hunched
her shoulders and flexed her arms, as though they
ached.

"I'm sorry I didn't stop right away. I knew if I did,
I wouldn't feel up to finishing the field today. And it
had to be done now," she said.

Again, a blaze of guilt speared Jakob's chest. He'd
pushed her too hard today, but she'd been a stand-up
woman. He'd counted on her and she hadn't let him
down. Spunky and dedicated, just like Susan had been.

Thinking about his wife just then made him feel grouchy for some reason. He told himself it was because his leg was throbbing, but he knew it was something more. Something he didn't fully understand.

"I think I'll head back to the house," Jakob said.

"Me, too," *Dawdi* said. "Martin, why don't you ride back to the house with Abby? You can drive the Belgians and it'll give you two a chance to talk alone."

"*Ja*, I would like that." Martin eagerly hopped out of the small wagon and climbed up to sit beside Abby.

She readily handed over the lead lines to his capable hands, but she didn't look too eager to be alone with him. She stared at *Dawdi* as if he were abandoning her.

"See you back at the house," *Dawdi* said.

Jakob slapped the leads against the horse pulling his seed wagon. *Dawdi* followed behind.

Abby watched them go. Her gaze followed Jakob for just a moment, her eyes filled with some emotion he couldn't name. A pleading look he found both frustrating and endearing. He hated to leave her alone with Martin, but it couldn't be helped right now. She was a fully grown woman and would need to choose whom she married. If she wasn't interested in Martin, she would have to tell him so. Jakob had nothing to do with it. It was up to her.

When Jakob reached the main yard, he pulled the seed wagon up in front of the barn. *Dawdi* Zeke was right. Abby was amazing and should marry and raise a *familye* of her own. He'd thought that he was her protector. That he was doing a great service by keeping her safe. Yet, she'd done nothing but help him and his *familye* since she'd arrived. It wasn't right for Jakob to hold her back. He had to let her live her own life. And yet, he didn't want her to leave. Not ever. But how could he embrace her without being disloyal to Susan? Thinking about another woman made him feel like he was betraying his wife and the love they had shared, the children they'd had and the plans they'd made together.

No matter how he looked at the situation, he just couldn't see a way out. Not without losing Abby or Susan for good.

Chapter Ten

Abby slipped silently out of the bathroom. Dark shadows clogged the hallway, the moon gleaming through the window at the top of the stairs. The floorboards creaked beneath her bare feet and she paused, not wanting to disturb the sleeping children. It was late, but she'd been so grimy after planting the corn that she'd desperately needed to clean up.

Wearing a heavy bathrobe, she longed to crawl into bed and sleep for a zillion years. She couldn't remember being so tired. Even Martin Hostetler's incessant chatter at supper hadn't bothered her. He'd stayed rather late, sitting with her on the front porch and sipping a glass of lemonade as they listened to the chirp of crickets. She'd been too exhausted to participate much in the conversation, but she couldn't begrudge his presence. Not when he'd been such a huge help with the evening chores. He'd unhitched the draft horses and tossed them some hay while Abby ensured they had plenty of fresh water. Then he'd unloaded the unused bags of seed corn and stacked them in a tidy corner of the barn.

Jakob had hobbled out to the barn, intending to assist. His leg was so swollen that Naomi had been forced to slit the trouser leg up to the knee. All he could do was sit on a bench and gaze helplessly while she and Martin milked the cows. As she had worked, she'd felt Jakob watching her. A couple of times, she'd looked over at him, to assess his discomfort. The last thing she wanted was for him to collapse and have Martin help her get him back to the house.

He'd glanced away, seeming embarrassed to be caught staring. From the tense lines on his face, she could tell his injury was still hurting. No doubt he was relieved to have the work done. And she was so glad to be a part of that accomplishment. To make him pleased and reassured.

She hoped Martin wasn't too disappointed in her. She'd been exhausted. When he'd finally been ready to leave, she'd walked him to his buggy. Beneath the moonlit sky, he'd asked if he could court her. Feeling no attraction for him, she'd turned away and told him the truth. That they could never be more than friends.

"Someday, you'll find someone special," she'd said.

"I hope so." He'd shown a half smile but no malice as he turned and got into the buggy and drove away.

Now, Abby lit a bright lamp and set it on the tall chest beside her bed. She jerked the blankets back, not even caring if Reuben might have put cracker crumbs between her sheets. At this point, she was drained enough to sleep through a nuclear explosion. Just a few more minutes and she could close her eyes and rest.

Her body trembled like gelatin. Several times throughout the day, she'd feared the Belgians might pull her arms out of their sockets. For the most part, the horses were gentle beasts, but they were so strong. By late afternoon, it had taken every ounce of willpower to keep tension on the lead lines. It had taken a lot of exertion to direct the horses where she wanted them to go.

She laid her bathrobe on the foot of the bed. Dressed in her modest flannel nightgown, she pushed the sleeves down over her shoulders. Reaching for a pot of aloe vera cream she'd made herself, she popped the lid and kneaded the salve into her skin with slow, purposeful strokes. The ache was bittersweet. Though her muscles were stiff and sore, she felt a deep satisfaction for what she had completed. She'd earned Jakob's, Naomi's and *Dawdi* Zeke's respect. The seed corn was in the ground. Her efforts had been worth it. Tomorrow, she'd turn on the irrigation sprinklers in the morning and help Naomi with the baking in the afternoon. All would be well.

"Abby, are you still awake?"

She turned and gasped. Naomi stood peering around the slightly ajar door. The woman's eyes widened in surprise, and Abby didn't need to ask why. She scrambled to pull the sleeves of her nightgown back over her shoulders. With it settled into place, she faced Naomi.

"Abby! Those scars. What happened to you?" Naomi stepped into the room and reached to touch Abby's arm, but she drew away.

No, no! Naomi had seen what Abby had tried so hard to hide. Her cheeks flooded with heat. She didn't want anyone's pity. She felt ashamed, as if she'd done something wrong. Like she should run away. But she wouldn't do that ever again. She was a grown woman now and lived here in Colorado. She was safe. She didn't need to hide anymore.

Or did she?

"*Ach*, it's nothing," she said. "Just some old scars

from an accident years ago. I'd almost forgotten about them."

Or at least, she'd tried to forget. And to forgive. It was what *Gott* would want her to do after all. To let the atonement wash away her pain and grief. And her anger. Now that she was an adult, she was determined to be happy. To put the sad times behind her. She'd tried so hard to let go of her ire. It was only at moments like this that the past abuse she'd suffered still haunted her.

Brushing off her morose mood, Abby reached for her comb to part her hair down the middle. She smiled, acting like nothing was wrong. "I still can't believe we got the corn planted today."

"*Ja*, it was a big job. We are ever in your debt." Naomi stood beside the bed and folded her arms, her forehead crinkled in a frown of concern. "Land's sake, child. Those scars don't look like nothing to me. Are there more? I couldn't see your back. It looked like the scars went all the way down. What accident could have caused those horrible marks on your skin?"

So much for her attempt to distract Naomi. Shaking her head, Abby forced herself to concentrate on her hair. Fearing Naomi might see the agony written in her eyes, she refused to meet the older woman's gaze. "I fell, that's all. It's a bad memory I'd rather forget. Please let it go."

Naomi opened her mouth, as though she wanted to say more. She must have changed her mind, because she pursed her lips instead. "I'm worried about you, that's all. If anyone hurt you, they should be dealt with."

Abby turned and rested a hand on her arm. "What's done is done. *Gott* has taken care of me. There's no need to worry. I'm fine now. Really, I am."

The older woman continued to scowl, not looking convinced at all. Abby forced herself to relax. To think about the many blessings in her life. She didn't need to live in the past. Not anymore. She could be happy now and made a conscious choice to feel joy instead of fear and pain.

"Was there something you wanted to speak with me about?" Abby asked, trying to keep her tone light and not let her hands shake as she brushed out her long hair.

"*Ja*, but I can't remember what it was now. I guess I'm getting old and forgetful." Naomi gave a soft laugh and waved her hand in the air.

"*Ne*, you just have a lot on your mind. But I'll help you with the baking. I've got to figure out how to move the sprinkler system first. Jakob said it's not difficult and he'll show me what to do."

"He's right. It's not hard at all. I've moved the sprinklers many times. If he keeps his leg elevated, he can ride out to the field in the wagon with you and coach you on what to do."

"Then all is well." Abby set the brush down and came to embrace the older woman.

Naomi hugged her back. "*Danke* for what you did today. You're such an asset to us. I'm so grateful you came to stay here."

Abby froze. The burn of tears caused her to blink several times. For a few moments, she felt overwhelmed by emotion. No one had ever said such wonderful words to her before.

"*Danke*. That's the nicest thing anyone's ever said to me," she whispered.

Naomi drew back and smiled tenderly before patting Abby's cheek. "I'm only speaking the truth. I don't know what we would do without you. Now, you rest."

The woman turned and left the room, closing the door softly behind her. Abby bit her bottom lip, sinking down onto the bed. She'd been so worried about coming here. Colorado was a different place. In Ohio, she'd never had to move heavy sprinkler pipes to water their crops. When she'd first arrived in Colorado, she'd been so worried that Jakob wouldn't remember her, or really want to marry her. Part of her fears had come true. There would be no wedding. Not for her. Which meant she had no permanent home. She didn't belong anywhere. Not really.

And then a thought occurred to her. What if Jakob found someone else to wed? Abby couldn't stay here if he took a new bride. He'd want his room back, so he could set up housekeeping with his wife. The children would have a new mother. The *familye* wouldn't need her any longer. She'd be in the way, like a sore thumb.

She'd have to leave eventually. But where could she go? Everyone in her faith expected her to marry. And if she did that, she would never be a free agent. Never in charge of her own happiness. But she believed it was what *Gott* expected. To raise her own *familye*.

Instead of pushing him away, maybe she should have encouraged Martin Hostetler more. He wasn't bad-looking. He was nice enough and a hard worker, but she could never bring herself to marry him. Not even to provide herself with a permanent home. In spite of Naomi's comforting words, Abby felt as though her situation here at the Fishers' farm was temporary. She couldn't stay here forever. Jakob could decide to marry someone else one day, and then she'd be in the way. She must find a stable place to live. A place to belong forever. And yet, leaving this farm scared Abby more than anything else she'd faced. Because now that she was here, she never wanted to go.

Nine days later, the swelling in Jakob's leg had gone down enough that he could walk without wincing. The bruise had faded to an ugly yellowish-brown, with the hoof print still outlined clearly across his flesh. The injury could have been so much worse. He'd been blessed and thanked *Gott* for taking care of him and for sending Abby to them.

As usual, he awoke early to do the morning chores. No matter how exhausted he was, his body clock always woke him up at the same time every day.

After washing and dressing, he opened the door to the *dawdy haus* and stepped outside. The night shadows embraced him. Joe nudged his leg with his black nose, and Jakob patted the dog's head. The animal accompanied him silently as he crossed the yard toward the barn. The early morning air wasn't as chilly as it had been a week ago, and he was satisfied that there would be no killing frost to destroy their crops. Any day now, the corn would begin to sprout. A feeling of anticipation swept over him. He couldn't wait to see the fields burgeoning with new growth, which would turn into tall green stalks. He had Abby to thank for their bounty.

As he passed the house, he wondered if she was up yet. Usually she beat him to the barn. A light glimmered in the upstairs bedroom where she was staying. That meant she was still inside, moving slower than usual. He hated to work her so hard. He dreaded the thought that she might think he was just as bad as Simon. If he could finish the milking before she arrived, it might alleviate her load today.

As he entered the barn, the prospect of being alone with Abby brought him a feeling of excitement. He had to remind himself that Martin Hostetler wanted to court her, even though she wasn't interested in the man. She didn't know it, but word had spread quickly of her polite rebuttal. Her lack of attraction both pleased and disappointed Jakob. Marriage would mean that she'd have to leave, and he didn't want her to go. His desires were purely selfish, and he was ashamed that he resented Martin. In the past couple of weeks, he'd grown too accustomed to Abby's presence here on the farm, yet she deserved so much more.

Inside the barn, the scent of animals and fresh straw filled his nose. He lit a lamp and tossed feed to the cows. While they munched contentedly, he set a milking stool beside one of the black-and-white Holsteins. Bucket in hand, he eased himself onto the stool and leaned his head against the animal's warm side as he began his morning ritual. He'd moved on to the second Holstein when Abby slipped into the barn.

"*Guder mariye*, Jakob," she said, her face glowing with a shy smile.

"Good morning, Abby. You slept late today," he said.

A glaze of doubt filled her eyes, and she twined her fingers together in front of her. He had learned that this was a nervous gesture she did whenever she feared retribution.

"I'm sorry. I… I'll get up earlier in the future," she said.

He snorted and spoke softly, so she would know he

wasn't angry. "*Ach*, no need to fret. I think you could use a rest. No one can fault how hard you work."

Her tensed shoulders relaxed just a bit, and she retrieved a clean bucket and stool. Sitting beside the cream-colored Jersey, she started milking. The *whoosh-whoosh* sounds of the milk spraying into the buckets had a calming effect, and they didn't speak for several minutes.

"Are you helping *Mamm* bake pies today?" he finally asked, knowing tomorrow was Friday and bakery day.

"*Ja*, and a strawberry swirl sheet cake with white icing. Sarah Yoder said it's a special order. One of the *Englischers* wants it for their daughter's birthday party tomorrow evening. Naomi is going to decorate it with clouds and balloons. It'll bring in double the normal price."

Not that it would cost the *Englischer* a lot. They charged only what was fair, never allowing greed to enter into the equation. That was one reason the bakery was so popular among the *Englisch*. Their prices were so reasonable.

"*Gut.*" He chuckled, then paused before broaching the question on his mind. "Abby, I'm sorry to pry, but there's something I'd like to ask you. It's rather personal."

"What do you want to know?" she asked.

She kept milking, barely looking up…a sure sign that she wasn't as skittish around him anymore. In fact, he thought they were becoming good friends.

He took a deep inhale, remembering what Naomi had told him several days earlier. Even now, he still felt furious and tried to remember that *Gott* expected him to be patient and kind no matter what. "Did Simon or your father beat you with a whip or a strap?"

She jerked, so suddenly that the Jersey cow shifted her weight restlessly and swung her large head around to look at Abby with round, dark eyes.

Abby stared into her bucket, her bent head appearing so sad and forlorn. At first, Jakob thought she was still milking, but he couldn't hear the *whooshing* sounds anymore. He'd upset her with his question, but he had to know. He resisted the urge to stand and take her into his arms and comfort her.

"Why…why do you ask?" she said, her voice sounding small.

He shrugged. "*Mamm* mentioned that she'd seen some old scars on your shoulders. You told her they were from an accident, but she said the marks looked like someone had whipped you. She's just worried about you. So am I."

There. He'd admitted it to her. No taking it back. And yet, the confession came so easily, which surprised him. He told himself that he cared about this woman the way he cared about all of *Gott's* children. That was all. And yet, he knew what he felt for Abby was a bit more than that.

"It's over and done with. I'd rather not discuss it now," she whispered.

So. Maybe they weren't as good friends as he had hoped. But her response answered his question well enough, although he still didn't know what had happened, or if it had been her father or Simon who had beaten her. And though it no longer mattered, he wished she would confide in him. He sensed that bottling up what had happened inside herself would prevent her from healing fully. She needed to let it out. To talk about it with someone who cared. He was just glad that she was far away from the people who had once abused her. All Amish tried to follow the Savior's loving example by shunning acts of violence. For this reason, he didn't understand how Simon could be so cruel to his sister yet still call himself a man of faith.

She returned to her milking, ignoring their conversation. From his angle, he could see the backs of her arms flexing rhythmically as she milked the cow.

"Are you going to the singing with Martin on Sunday evening?" Jakob purposefully changed the discussion by addressing another uncomfortable topic that was weighing heavily on his mind.

She missed a beat in her milking, and the Jersey stomped a foot in agitation. "I… I don't think so."

He hesitated, wondering what he should say. A part of him knew it wasn't good for her to hide out here on the farm. She should mingle with others of their faith. But another part of him didn't want her to socialize with other men. He was being selfish again.

"I don't want to interfere, but Martin is a *gut* man. You should go with him," he said, forcing himself to be magnanimous.

"He…he comes on a bit too strong for me," she said.

"*Ja*, but he means well. You always know where you stand with Martin. He is strong in his faith and would be a good provider to whomever he marries. The more time you spend with him, the more you'll get used to him."

She looked over her shoulder at him with a doubtful glint in her eyes. He didn't want her to leave anytime soon, but her welfare and happiness meant more to him than his own self-seeking desires.

"I've already told him I'm not interested in being anything more than friends," she said, turning back to her work.

The Jersey jostled against her and gave a mournful *moo*, as though eager to be finished with this chore. Abby patted the cow's side in a reassuring gesture.

"That is too bad. You're young and should have some fun. You won't know if you really like him unless you go with him more," he suggested.

"I... I'd rather not."

Jakob read between the lines. Abby didn't trust men and feared Martin might be assertive like her father and brother.

"If it helps, I have never heard anything bad spoken about Martin or his *familye*. His *mudder* and sisters always seem so happy that I don't believe he or his *vadder* treat them unkindly," Jakob said.

Abby looked up, her eyes wide and filled with suffering and angst. Then it was gone and she smiled, hiding her inner feelings. But he knew the truth and longed to comfort her. To tell her she was safe now. But the moment she left his home, he would no longer be able to protect her. And that's when he realized he didn't know much about Martin Hostetler either. Not really. Martin had come from Indiana. Jakob's *familye* had not known the Hostetlers before they moved to Colorado six years earlier. He thought they were good people, but how could he really know what went on inside the walls of their home when no one was watching? It would require a leap of faith on Abby's part.

"I'd rather take it slow. I may never marry at all," she said, her voice sounding noncommittal.

He jerked his head up, blinking at her in surprise. Not marry? Ever? The idea was alien to him.

"You should marry. It is what *Gott* would want."

"I know you really believe that. I do, too. Or at least, I used to. I'm not so sure anymore."

Hmm, he didn't like the sound of that. No doubt she felt that way because of him. She'd come all the way to Colorado, thinking he would become her husband. She didn't seem to want Martin or any man, which left her with few options. But marriage was a way of life to the Amish. *Familye* was everything to them. Jakob couldn't accept anything different. And yet, how could he fault Abby when he was shunning marriage for himself?

"Of course you will marry one day. Until that time, you have a home here for as long as you want it," he said.

Again, she showed a doubtful frown, but didn't say anything. The Jersey gave a low bellow and lashed out with her back hoof, striking Abby against the shoulder. The woman cried out and toppled over her stool, lying on her back on the hard-packed ground.

"Abby!"

Jakob scrambled off his stool and crouched over her. She groaned, reaching to clutch her injured shoulder. She breathed hard, her eyes closed.

"Are you okay?" he asked, grateful the cow hadn't struck Abby's head.

She nodded and opened her eyes, rubbing her shoulder. Gazing up at him, she released a whimsical laugh. "You and I make quite a pair. We keep getting kicked by the livestock. At this rate, we'll both be black-and-blue before long. Bishop Yoder will wonder what's going on here at this farm."

He chuckled, enjoying her sense of humor. Considering her past, it was good that she could laugh about the situation. The flash of worry he'd felt had left him shaking. He didn't want to worry about this woman. Didn't want to care.

But he did.

Leaning over her, he pulled several pieces of straw away from her white *kapp*. Her wide blue eyes met his, and he felt lost in their depths. Captivated. Drawn closer until he kissed her, a gentle caress that deepened for several moments. She lifted a hand to rest against his chest, just over his heart. He breathed her in, then remembered who he was and who she was and that she was not Susan. He jerked back, his face heating up with embarrassment. They gazed into one another's eyes with startled wonder. And Jakob felt a new awareness sweep over him. Abby wasn't just a girl from his past. She was now a beautiful woman.

"Jakob," she said his name, so softly that he almost didn't hear her.

Reality crashed over him and he felt awful for what he'd done, as if he'd taken advantage of her. "I… I'm sorry, Abby."

He hurried to his feet and helped her stand, then moved away and folded his arms. He couldn't meet her gaze. Couldn't face the disloyalty he felt toward his wife. He'd taken vows with Susan. He'd promised to love her until the day he died. Never once had he been tempted by another woman.

Until now.

"That was wrong of me. A lapse in judgment. It won't happen again," he said.

He bent over and picked up his milk bucket, eager

to give his hands something to do. Abby was overly quiet, and he wondered what she was thinking. He already knew she didn't trust men, and he'd just given her a reason not to trust him.

"Is your shoulder all right? Maybe we should ask *Mamm* to put a cold pack on it for you," he said, trying to ease his guilt.

She nodded, looking flushed and embarrassed as she moved her shoulder carefully to test its soundness. "It's fine. I suppose I'll have a bruise, but it'll be all right."

A long, dark silence followed as they gathered up the milk pails and headed toward the house. They didn't speak, didn't acknowledge what had transpired between them. Jakob thought that was best. But no matter how hard he tried, he couldn't forget what had happened. Nor could he deny that he had feelings for Abby. He was definitely attracted to her, but that wasn't enough. Not for him, and not for her. Because deep in his heart, he didn't believe he could ever love her the way he loved Susan. And after everything Abby had been through, she deserved for someone to adore her. But that someone couldn't be him.

Chapter Eleven

Abby took a deep inhale of fresh air before tucking a strand of hair back inside her *kapp*. Gazing at the wide-open sky, she squinted at the noonday sun, enjoying its warmth on her face. A couple of weeks had passed since Jakob had kissed her in the barn. A couple of weeks that made her feel jittery every time he was near. They hadn't spoken about the incident since then, and she thought perhaps she'd imagined it ever happened. Now, she wished that she could forget.

Soft clods of dirt broke beneath her feet as she walked along one wide furrow of the cornfield. Shifting the wicker basket she carried to her other hand, she thought about Jakob's and Reuben's lunches tucked inside. Later that afternoon, she would plant tomatoes. Hopefully she would have lots of beans, peas and corn to put up in bottles in August.

A mild breeze ruffled the green sprouts growing in long rows of the fertile field. Like any farmer, seeing the verdant color of the new plants brought Abby a deep sense of joy and satisfaction. She paused a moment, waiting for Ruby to catch up. The girl hopped over several rows, then came running in her bare feet. The edge of her purple pinafore apron rippled in the wind.

"There's *Daed* and Reuben." Ruby pointed toward the south corner where Grape Creek bordered the fields. Clutches of purple wild iris grew along the banks.

Jakob's father had been wise to buy this farm. It came with deeded water rights and spring-fed water for the livestock. The creek twined its way across their property. Very handy for watering their garden and front lawn.

Correction. This was Jakob's property. Funny how she felt as though she belonged here, because she didn't. Not really. And yet, Abby had done so much work here that she couldn't help loving this land and caring about the *familye* that lived here.

She followed the long row to the end, conscious of Ruby skipping behind. Skirting the edge, she couldn't help noticing Jakob. And without a word being said, her cheeks flushed with heat as she again remembered the brief kiss they'd shared.

No! She shook her head, refusing to think of what had happened that day. It would only make her long for things that never could be.

Dressed in gray broad fall trousers, a blue shirt, suspenders and work boots, Jakob straddled the irrigation gate. His head was bowed as he scooped mud, sticks and grass out of the creek with a shovel. He slopped the black muck against the outer bank, then dug out some more. No doubt the irrigation ditch was clogged.

Back east, they had much more rainfall to sustain their crops. But here in the West, there was a reason they called the life-sustaining water "liquid gold." Without it, Jakob's fields would dry up to dust.

If all went well, they would harvest the corn in the fall. And then the wedding season would begin. Abby dreaded it. She'd come to Colorado planning to marry. Though she was determined to carry on, she couldn't help feeling slightly disillusioned. Okay, more than slightly. If she were honest with herself, it had been a huge disappointment.

"Now?" She heard Reuben ask. Neither he nor Jakob were aware that Abby and Ruby had arrived with their noon meal.

"*Ja*, let it go." Jakob stood back and nodded, looping his free hand around one of his suspenders.

The boy grunted as he tugged on the metal gate. It finally gave with a low grating sound. A rush of water sped past them, soon filling the small ditch. Tossing his shovel onto the opposite bank, Jakob reached for a hoe and directed the water down a number of corn rows. The cracked earth greedily soaked up the moisture as it sped forward along the furrow.

Abby watched in fascination. On her brother's farm in Ohio, they'd used gravity irrigation for the garden and pivot sprinklers for their soybean crops, but they didn't have to water nearly as often as they did here in the West. At supper last night, Jakob had indicated it would take hours each day for him to water their thirsty crops. And Abby knew an inch of water could make all the difference in doubling their production versus reaping just enough to barely subsist on.

"*Daed*, we brought your food," Ruby called in a cheerful voice.

Jakob looked up as he pulled several weeds out of the ground and smiled at his daughter. "And just in time, too. I'm ravenous."

"Me, too," Reuben said. He smiled at his sister, but the disapproving frown slid into place when he glanced at Abby.

Jakob's gaze shifted to Abby, and she looked away, feeling suddenly flushed with heat. He removed his straw hat and wiped his forearm across his forehead. Abby stood next to him, trying not to notice how his slightly damp hair curled against the back of his neck.

"The crops seem to be doing well. Every row has sprouted," she said. Which meant she had planted the seed properly.

He nodded, a smile curving his handsome mouth. "*Ja*, and I'm finding very few insects that will harm the corn. We should have a bumper crop this year, but I may need to use an herbicide next year to keep the weeds down."

To emphasize his point, he gave a jerk of his hand, pulling another weed out by the roots before tossing it aside.

"After I've planted the garden today, I can help weed," she offered.

"I'll help *Daed* with the weeding," Reuben said, his jaw hard as he lifted it slightly higher.

"I'm sure you're a big help to your *vadder*," she said, trying not to rile the youngster. She still felt bad that her mere presence seemed to rankle the boy so much.

"I think there are enough weeds for all of us to pull." Jakob chuckled and tossed another one aside where its roots would dry up in the sunshine. "Let's sit down." He gestured toward the bank by the creek.

Ruby took the basket from Abby and plopped down before opening the lid. "Wait until you see what we brought you."

She pulled out a cloth and laid it across the coarse grass, then removed several plastic containers. She grunted as she popped the lid of one and held the dish up for inspection.

"Chocolate cream pie. Yum!" Reuben said.

"*Ja*, Abby made it and I helped."

At the mention of Abby's name, Reuben scowled and looked away. Abby didn't understand. Sometimes the boy would smile at her, then seem to catch himself and frown instead. During meals or as they were working around the farm. Almost as though he were fighting against himself and purposefully trying not to like her.

"You helped?" Jakob looked pleasantly surprised.

"She did. I couldn't have done it without her," Abby said, noticing how the girl beamed.

"That's nice. No doubt you'll be as good a cook as Abby and *Grossmammi* one day." Jakob's voice was filled with complimentary thanks.

"*Ja*, it was easy. Just mix a box of pudding. But Abby also adds cream for more richness. She taught me how," Ruby said.

Abby sat near Reuben, hiding a smile of amusement. Ruby had quoted her words verbatim, speaking as if she now knew a special secret. But honestly, it had been fun to teach the girl to make a cream pie. Even Naomi had watched with a critical eye as Abby had stirred in the cream. The older woman had then commented that it was a clever way to add in a richer flavor to the pudding mix.

"The pie is for after lunch. First, we should eat something more nutritious." Abby reached into the basket, then handed each of the boys a ham-and-cheese sandwich.

Reuben peeled back the wrapper, and a small slip of

paper fell out. Although the children were now out of school for the summer, over the past weeks, Abby had continued putting uplifting notes in his lunch. She also left a special message around the house for Ruby to find each day. While Ruby was delighted by the kind messages, Reuben continued to deny ever receiving them.

The boy picked up the note and Abby held her breath, thinking he might finally read and comment on it. Instead, he crumpled it in his fist and let it fall to the ground. Jakob and Ruby were busy with their own food and didn't seem to notice.

Abby's heart plummeted. She released a low sigh of frustration, thinking she might never win the boy's approval.

Sitting beside her brother, Ruby plunged her bare feet into the cooling water of the creek. Reuben soon thrust his feet in, too. Between bites of her own sandwich, Ruby chattered nonstop about how tall the corn sprouts were getting and how big the kittens were growing. Since he loved both topics as much as the girl did, Reuben didn't seem to mind her constant babbling.

"We're gonna have a bumper crop of corn, that's for sure," Reuben said, quoting *Dawdi* Zeke.

"We're gonna have a bumper crop of kittens, too," Ruby said.

Reuben munched on some potato chips before tossing a few blades of grass into the swirling creek. "*Ja*, I think Tiger is the biggest."

"That's because he's a boy," Ruby said. "*Grossmammi* says the babies will soon be big enough to live in the barn, but I'd rather they lived in the house with us."

Taking a bite of food, Abby covered a low chuckle.

"Why do you think that's funny?" Jakob whispered, leaning toward her with a conspiratorial glance.

Abby spoke in a quiet voice so Ruby wouldn't hear. "I think Naomi is tired of the kittens running around the kitchen and making messes. They've gotten big enough to climb out of their box and are constantly underfoot. Soon, they'll be all over the house. She is definitely ready for them to live in the barn."

He released a low laugh, then nodded and spoke loud enough for Ruby to hear. "Once they are old enough, the babies will live in the barn."

Ruby frowned over her shoulder at her father. "But I don't want them to get hit by a car like Amber. I want them to stay inside with us, where they will be safe."

Although Reuben was silent, his eyes also showed a glint of concern.

"We can't lock them up forever. Animals need to be free to live their life and be happy. Imagine how you would feel if I locked you in the house all day and night," Jakob said, his voice gentle but firm.

"I wouldn't like that at all," Ruby said.

"Neither would I," Reuben said.

"But *Daed*, they might get hurt if they live out in the barn…" Ruby spoke in a slightly whining voice.

"The cats will live in the barn. *Gott* will look after them, just as He looks after us," Jakob said, his tone hinting that there would be no more discussion on the subject.

As Abby expected, Reuben refused to eat the pie she'd made. Ruby had no such inhibitions and chewed with relish. Reuben glanced at her several times, a look of hunger in his eyes, but he didn't ask for any. Both children seemed overly quiet. Abby figured out why when she heard Ruby whisper to her brother.

"Do you really think *Gott* will protect the kittens if they live in the barn?"

"*Ja, Daed* said so and that's *gut* enough for me. Stop worrying about them," Reuben said.

Abby was impressed. Although Reuben hadn't seemed to accept his mother's death and he kept his distance from her, she knew the boy had a tender heart and trusted his father enough to accept his faith in the Lord. Even without their mother's aid, Jakob was doing a good job raising his children.

Ruby seemed to be rather gloomy now, fretting over the babies. Seeing her downcast expression, Reuben suddenly kicked his foot, splashing water on her.

"Hey!" Ruby kicked back and the two children were soon engaged in a water fight. With the heat of the day, it didn't matter. The water would cool them off.

"You can't catch me." Ruby hopped up and took off toward the corrals.

"*Ja*, I can." Reuben chased after her.

Their laughter filled the air as they let off some energy before returning to their chores.

Abby glanced over to where Reuben had dropped the note she had tucked into his sandwich, but it was no longer there. She shrugged, thinking it must have blown away.

Watching the children run, she smiled at their gaiety. "I wish Simon had played with me like that when we were young."

The moment she said the words, she regretted them. Jakob turned her way, having heard her comment. She'd tried to keep her past life private and didn't want to reveal more than she must. But Jakob already knew almost everything, so it didn't really matter anymore.

"Why do you think he wouldn't play with you?" Jakob asked.

She shrugged. "I fear he learned very early from our father to…"

She bit her tongue, trying not to speak the words.

"What did Simon learn from your father?" Jakob pressed, his voice soft but insistent.

Abby tucked the empty food containers back into the basket. "You already know my *vadder* could be quite cruel at times."

Most of the time, actually. She had not one single memory of him ever smiling, and she had no idea what his laughter sounded like. In retrospect, she realized he must have been a very unhappy person. And Simon was just like him. She just didn't understand why. What had made her father so miserable?

Jakob rested a hand on her arm, and she went very still. "Abby. Please talk to me."

She lifted her head, meeting his gaze. He held a purple wild iris in front of her eyes. He'd plucked it from nearby. Abby stared, charmed by his gesture. It was the first time a man—any man—had given her a flower, and she wanted the moment to last. Taking it from him, she brought the velvety petals close to her face and breathed in their sweet fragrance.

"Don't you think Simon came up with some of his meanness on his own? He didn't learn it all from your *vadder*," Jakob said.

She caught the note of disapproval in his tone and hesitated before bowing her head. "I think all of us have the capacity for good and bad, but my *vadder* encouraged Simon through his poor example. You would never allow Reuben to treat Ruby badly. But you've also provided a good example for your children to follow. Simon never had that in our home growing up."

"*Danke* for the compliment. I try to be a good, responsible parent, although sometimes I need to do better. But I can't imagine ever whipping someone with a strap, even if I had seen my *vadder* do it. *Gott* would not approve of such actions. Not ever. Is that what your *vadder* did to you? Or is Simon responsible for the scars my *mudder* saw on your shoulders?" A bit of outrage tainted his questions.

Abby couldn't imagine whipping someone either, and yet it had happened to her. But it was still difficult to open up and tell him.

"I wish you'd confide in me. It might help," Jakob said, his voice soft with encouragement.

She hesitated as memories rushed over her. Normally, she would have said no. But this time, something felt different. Like she finally had a friend she could trust. Someone she could count on, who would never betray her.

She took a deep breath, thinking he might be right. For so long, she'd kept the abuse to herself, locked up inside her heart and mind. For years, she'd even blamed herself. But as she'd grown older and attended church, listening to the preachings, she'd learned that *Gott* didn't approve of such violence and anger. He was a kind, loving Heavenly Father who wanted only the best for His children.

For her.

In all these long years, she hadn't spoken about what had happened to anyone. Until now.

Before she could stop herself, it all poured out. Like a valve that had suddenly burst and the steam released in a hurried rush. Her voice wobbled, and she felt the burn of tears. She also felt the anger, the humiliation and the pain that followed. She told Jakob everything. About the whippings, the criticism and being locked in the root cellar when she was bad. Which must have been often, because she'd spent a lot of time in that dark place. She'd felt worthless and ugly inside. And when she finished her story, she stared at the wild iris lying in her lap, letting its beauty remind her that there was still so much to live for. Her hands were shaking, and she gripped them together to stop.

A long pause followed, with just the rustling of the wind to break the silence.

"You know *Gott* would never approve of what your *vadder* and Simon did to you, don't you?" Jakob asked.

No, for a long time, she'd really believed it was her fault. That if she worked harder and was smarter, faster, better, then her father would finally appreciate and love her. Now, she realized that Jakob was right. Her father's failing had nothing to do with her. At the time, spilling the milk had seemed so serious. So negligent. She'd felt horrible for what she'd done. Thoughtless and useless. But what about the times when she'd simply walked into a room and become the target of abuse? And for the umpteenth time, she wondered why her father had always gotten so upset at her. Why had he seemed to hate her so much? She would probably never know.

She took a deep inhale and let it go. "Perhaps *Gott* wanted me to learn from my experience. It has made me a much more compassionate person. For a long time, I thought I could make my *vadder* and Simon love me.

But no matter how hard I tried, they always seemed to despise me. Especially Simon."

"He may not be capable of love," Jakob said, his voice filled with pity.

"*Ja*, and I think it must be because he hates himself. I wish I could have helped him somehow. To make him see how his hatred was cankering him inside and making him and everyone around him so unhappy. But he never allowed me to get close enough to try. I feel so sorry for his wife and *kinder*, because he has turned his anger on them, too." She wiped her damp eyes.

Jakob took her trembling hands into his and squeezed gently, holding them for several moments. "Just as you said, we all have the capacity for good and bad. Simon is in control of his own actions, no matter what your *vadder* did. Instead of protecting and loving you, he made the choice to hurt you. He could have chosen differently. We each have our own free agency to choose."

Abby lifted her face and met his eyes. "*Ja*, you are right. But I can't help wondering. Wasn't I worthy of his protection? Wasn't I good enough to earn his and my *vadder's* love?"

"Oh, Abby." He took her into his arms and held her close.

She knew she shouldn't let him touch her. That she should push him away. But she couldn't do it. Instead, she breathed him in, feeling his warmth surrounding her. His protection. She felt so safe whenever he was near.

Finally, she moved back, feeling hollow inside. He'd been kind, but he loved Susan. They were friends and nothing more. It would be better if she just kept her distance and looked for a new place to live. She couldn't compete with a dead woman for his affections. She could never win his love. And that's what hurt most of all.

Jakob sat back and watched as Abby quickly packed up the basket. She carefully placed the wild iris he'd given her inside, and he wondered if she intended to keep it. He stood, thinking he should help her, but he didn't dare touch her again. He'd listened as she'd told him about her life, her voice an aching whisper. Tears had washed her cheeks, and he'd longed to brush them aside. To ease her pain and see her smile again. But he feared she might take his actions the wrong way. A feeling of love for Abby enveloped his being, but he fought it off. Even though she was gone, he couldn't betray his vows to Susan.

"You are worthy, Abby. You are a daughter of *Gott*. What could be more worthy than that?" he said, hoping she believed him.

She showed an unsteady smile. "*Danke* for listening to a foolish young woman's ramblings. But I'd appreciate it if you'd keep these things just between the two of us."

Her voice cracked and so did his heart.

Of course she didn't want others to know what had happened to her. He couldn't blame her. But he wished there was some way for her to see herself as he saw her. As a lovely woman who was worthy of a man's love. Not because of anything she did or didn't do, but simply because of who she was. If he hadn't already met Susan and given his heart away, he would be free to love Abby…

No! It did no good to think that way. He had married

Susan. He had loved her. He always would. In the short time they'd been together, they had shared so much. A love like that didn't come along twice in a lifetime.

Or did it?

The outline of Abby's *kapp* and sweet profile looked so innocent that he longed to hold her in his arms again. But that would only increase the confusion between them. They were merely friends. It was best if he kept his distance, for both of their benefit.

"You are *willkomm*. And trust that I will not share your words with anyone, this I promise," he said.

A long, swelling silence followed.

She gestured to the bubbling creek. "Do you think we'll have enough water to last the summer?"

"*Ach*, I do. Someday when I've saved enough, I hope to buy a lateral irrigation system. It's expensive, but worth it. A pivot system is easier, but it wastes a lot of good land. A lateral system would cover the entire area of our rectangular fields and give us a much greater yield of produce." He spread his arms wide to indicate the corn and hay fields. "A sprinkler system would make it so that I could devote more time to our furniture-making business. I love farming, but I love working with the wood, too. I really think I could set up a shop and make a go of it in town, as long as I knew my *familye* had its needs met first."

"That plan sounds *wundervoll*. I have no doubt we can make it work."

She shifted her weight, and he sensed that she was restless. Then he realized that he'd just confided his own hopes and dreams to her, too. She was so easy to talk to. So easy to be around.

Glancing toward the house, he saw Reuben trotting

toward them. The boy seemed to know that it was time to return to their labors. Ruby must have stayed at the house with Naomi.

"*Ach*, here comes Reuben. I better get back to work," he said.

"*Ja*, me, too. Naomi will be wondering what happened to me."

She stepped away and he watched her go. Ducking his head, he picked up his hoe and started working with the water, weeding as he moved down each row. He longed to call her back, to ask if she could help with the weeding. They could visit while they worked together and make the chore pass more quickly. The thistle and lamb's-quarter were bad this year. If he didn't remain vigilant, the weeds could crowd out the corn and cause yield loss in their crop.

When he looked up, Reuben stood in another row, hoeing out the weeds. Abby was gone. No doubt she was inside the house, helping *Mamm* with the baking, washing laundry, scrubbing floors or tending to the kittens.

"Why don't you like Abby?" he asked his son.

Reuben jerked his head up, a surprised look on his face. "I… I just don't."

Jakob leaned against the handle of his hoe, choosing his words carefully. "She's done nothing to hurt you."

"I know." Reuben looked away, a guilty flush staining his face.

"Then why are you so sharp with her? Why won't you eat any of the delicious pies she makes?"

"*Mamm* made pies, too," the boy said.

Ah, yes. And no doubt the youngster thought no one could make pies as well as his mother.

"Is that it? You think Abby is trying to take your *mudder's* place?" Jakob asked.

The boy gave a belligerent jerk of his shoulders. "I don't know."

Jakob stepped across the row and placed two fingers beneath the boy's chin before lifting his head to meet his eyes. "*Mein sohn*, you have been given a great gift. You remember your *mudder* so well. You know how much she loved you and you loved her. Don't you?"

Reuben answered fiercely, his eyes suddenly damp. "*Ja*, she loved me and I loved her."

"And no one can ever take that love from you. But Abby never really knew her *mudder*. She has lived her entire life believing that no one loves her."

The boy's brow crinkled. "What about her *vadder* and *bruder*?"

Jakob shook his head sadly. "Not even them."

"But why? Your *familye* is s'posed to love you no matter what."

How innocent his son was. How sweet, loyal and impressionable. But Jakob was unwilling to betray Abby's confidence.

"It doesn't matter why. Until she marries, she only has us. I'm positive if she had lived, *Mamm* would have been good friends with Abby. She doesn't want to take your *mudder's* place. She just wants to live and be happy and accepted. It's okay for you to be nice and like her. Can you do that?"

The scowl remained firmly on Reuben's face, but his eyes filled with uncertainty. Jakob could tell the boy wanted to agree, but something held him back. A deep loyalty to his mother's memory. Jakob didn't want to force Reuben to comply. That would only lead to resentment and hate. The Savior always remained calm. He showed respect and taught truth, letting people decide for themselves if they would follow Him. Jakob would rather win his son's compliance through gentle persuasion and a genuine desire to do what was right.

"Think about it," Jakob said. "The Lord taught us to be fair and just. To be kind and loving. I know you will come to the right decision."

He returned to his work, leaving Reuben to consider his words. And that's when a thought occurred to Jakob. He was such a hypocrite. He told his son that it was okay to like Abby. That she couldn't take his mother's place. And yet, Jakob couldn't seem to accept his own advice. He'd been kind to Abby, but he didn't want to get close to her. Because doing so made him feel disloyal to Susan. But recognizing this flaw didn't make it any easier for Jakob to change how he felt. He couldn't love more than one woman. He just couldn't.

He thought about Abby leaving one day, and an immediate melancholy gripped his heart. She'd come to his *familye* at the worst possible time in their lives, after they'd lost two key members of their *familye*. In spite of that, his children seemed happier with her here. Regardless of his stubborn insistence not to like her, even Reuben was calmer. Their farm was prospering during a time when his injury could have forced them to sell their land. With Abby's help, Naomi didn't look as exhausted all the time. And because he didn't have to do the heavy work, *Dawdi* Zeke's back pain had finally eased. Jakob knew they had Abby to thank. She had done the work of two. They would definitely all feel the loss if and when she finally left.

Chapter Twelve

The following week, Abby was outside taking clothes off the line when the rattle of a horse and buggy caused her to turn. Lizzie Beiler waved, the strings of her white *kapp* blowing in the wind.

"Guder daag," Lizzie called.

"Guder mariye," Abby returned, surprised to see her friend all the way out here.

Abby dropped a clean bath towel she had just folded into the laundry basket and walked out to meet Lizzie. She glanced up, noticing a cluster of gray storm clouds congregated just overhead. They might open up and rain by afternoon, but she'd have the laundry gathered in before then.

"What brings you all the way out to our farm?" Abby asked in a pleasant tone once Lizzie had stepped out of the buggy.

"I wanted to visit, so I brought you an apple cake." Lizzie reached inside the buggy and lifted out a basket covered with a clean white cloth.

"Ach, that's kind of you."

"Has Jakob recovered from his injury?" Lizzie asked.

"Almost. He's doing fine now. Come inside and I'll make you a cup of herbal tea."

Abby linked her arm with Lizzie's as they walked toward the house. A light breeze brushed past them, causing several leaves to scatter across the front yard.

"I also must confess I wanted to see how you are doing." Lizzie cast her a sideways glance.

"I'm fine, all things considered," Abby said.

"Any good news to report between you and Jakob?" Lizzie spoke low.

Abby didn't pretend not to understand. "*Ne*, there will be no wedding for Jakob and me, if that's what you mean."

Lizzie shrugged. "I won't give up hope yet. You two are ideal for each other."

Abby hid an inward sigh. "I'm afraid he is still mourning his wife, and I can't fault him for that. But honestly, I've been too busy to think much about it."

Which was partly true. The thought that she would never marry was rarely far from her mind, but she couldn't do anything about it, so she pushed it aside.

"And what about you? Have you heard from Eli yet?"

Lizzie shook her head. "*Ne*, and I don't expect to. He's been gone so long, I'm sure he's forgotten about me and moved on with his life."

Abby felt disheartened by this news. Both she and Lizzie had loved men who didn't want them. It was a sad state of affairs.

They stepped inside, where they were greeted warmly by Naomi. Soon, they were all gathered around the kitchen table, laughing and enjoying cups of peppermint tea and slices of Lizzie's apple cake. They saved a slice for Reuben and the two men, who were out in the barn mending the leather harness. With little Ruby listening in, Abby was grateful they could talk only about general topics. She feared if Lizzie pressed her much more, she might burst into tears and confide all her fears and broken dreams to the woman. Although it felt good to have a friend who cared about her, she was kind of relieved when Lizzie left a half hour later.

As Abby walked Lizzie outside to her buggy, she didn't mind when the other woman squeezed her hand. "If you need to talk, I'm always willing to listen. Take care of yourself."

"*Danke*, I will. And you, too. *Mach's gut.*" Abby tried to smile, but inside she started trembling. She didn't understand why thinking about Jakob and her dashed plans of having a *familye* of her own should bother her so much, but it did.

Resolved to exercise more faith in *Gott*, she waved as Lizzie drove away. Then she picked up the wicker basket filled with clean clothes and carried it upstairs to the children's room. After setting it on the floor, she slid open Reuben's top dresser drawer. She stared at the melee of clothing strewn around inside. What a mess! It looked like an eggbeater had been in here.

Shaking her head, she started folding each item into tidy piles. She laughed to herself, thinking that kids could be so chaotic. She'd spent a large part of the morning mending the *familye's* garments and wanted to get everything put away before Reuben caught her in his room. If he knew she'd darned his socks and mended his torn shirt, she feared he might refuse to wear them.

Bending at the waist, she lifted the repaired clothing and tucked it into the drawer. To make more room, she pushed the other clothing aside…then paused. A flash of white caught her eye. She reached to the farthest back corner of the drawer, and a pile of papers wrapped with a rubber band crackled as she pulled it forward.

Her notes! The uplifting messages she'd written and put in Reuben's lunch over the past weeks since she'd arrived. But what were they doing here?

She gaped in confusion, remembering all the times he'd denied receiving them. Even the note he'd thrown on the ground the day she'd confided in Jakob was here, spread carefully as if to remove the wrinkles from when he'd crumpled the paper in his fist. The wind hadn't blown it away after all. Reuben must have picked it up and kept it. Which meant that throwing it on the ground was all for show. But why? He'd made it clear that he disliked her. That he wanted nothing to do with her. So, why had he kept her notes?

"What are you doing in my stuff?"

She whirled around and found Reuben standing in the doorway. Dressed in his plain trousers, shirt and suspenders, he looked like a smaller replica of his father. His gaze took in the open drawer and the slips of paper she still clutched in one hand. And like a giant storm cloud moving across the sky, his face darkened.

"Those are mine. You have no right to go through my things!" he yelled, his cheeks flushing with embarrassment and anger.

Before she could explain, he rushed at her, knocking her backward. She cried out, her hands clawing at something, anything, to stop her fall. In the process, she dropped the papers. They rustled to the floor as she bounced against Ruby's bed. Reuben gathered the notes up and tucked them inside his waistband before leaning over her. Abby's natural instincts kicked in, and she lifted her arms to protect herself.

"What are you doing in my drawer? You're not my *mudder*," the boy yelled.

He didn't strike her, and she lowered her arms. He stood in front of the dresser, stuffing the clothes back inside with stiff, furious movements. He released a low sob, and that's when she realized he was crying. The notes had obviously meant more to him than he'd let on. Otherwise, he wouldn't have kept them. But he didn't want to admit it.

Because she wasn't his mother.

She stood and walked to him, moving nice and slow. In the past, her inclination whenever she faced physical conflict was to run from the room and find a safe place to hide until it blew over. But now, she forced herself to be brave. To put this motherless boy's needs before her own.

"Reuben, I didn't mean any harm." She spoke in a soothing tone. "I just found the notes when I was putting your mended clothing away. I'm sorry. I didn't mean to pry."

He slammed the drawer closed, then brushed at his eyes. "You don't belong here. Why don't you leave?"

Ah, that hurt, like a knife to her heart.

"I can't," she said.

Finally, he faced her, his eyes red with resentment and tears. "Why not? Why do you have to stay here?"

"Because I have nowhere else to go." She said the words simply, making no apology.

His little jaw quivered, his face filled with misery. "Why can't you go back to Ohio?"

She looked away, not wanting to explain. "There's nothing there for me anymore."

He sniffled again. "But they're your *familye*. We're not."

"I know, but you've been *wundervoll* friends. Why did you keep the notes I put in your lunches?"

He hesitated. "Be...because I liked them. They made me feel *gut*."

He hiccupped and hid his face behind his hands, as if the admission was shameful to him.

"Then why did you say you never saw them?" She spoke gently, trying not to frighten or anger him. Determined to get at the crux of the problem.

"Because you're not my *mamm*, and I don't want her to think I don't love her anymore."

Finally. Finally, they were getting somewhere.

"Reuben, I don't want to take your *mudder's* place. I know how special she was to you. But I doubt she would ever think that you don't love her just because you were friends with me. And I wish I could bring her back to you. But I can't."

He leaned against the top of the dresser and buried his face against his arms. His shoulders trembled and he made little gasping sounds, telling her that he was crying again. Her heart went out to him. He'd lost so much, and she longed to ease his pain.

She stepped closer and rested a hand lightly against his back, fully expecting him to thrust her away. But he didn't. Not this time.

"Reuben, your *mudder* will always be a part of you, no matter what. You can take joy in that. You'll meet many people throughout your life, but no one can ever take her place. Not me, not anyone."

He lifted his head and blinked at her, a large tear rolling down his cheek. "Do you…do you mean that?"

"I do. I don't want you to forget your *mudder*. Even though she died, I certainly haven't forgotten mine. I just want to work and live here for the time being. I just want to be your friend."

"Friends?" he reiterated, wiping his nose on his sleeve.

She nodded. "*Ja*, I'd like that very much."

"Would I have to stop loving *Mamm* just because I decide to like you?" He peered at her with a bit of distrust.

She realized he must be struggling with guilt. That he believed it would be disloyal to his mother if he accepted her. Maybe Jakob was struggling with the same problem.

"Absolutely not. Liking me has nothing to do with loving your *mudder*. We're two separate individuals. And the amazing thing about love is that it's infinite."

"Infinite? What does that mean?" he asked.

"It means immeasurable. Boundless. You see, love can grow and expand within our hearts and never run out. Think about how our Heavenly *Vadder* loves all of His children. That's a lot of people to love, isn't it? But *Gott's* love never ends. It just keeps growing and encompasses everyone. And just like Him, we can love more than one person. But loving someone else doesn't mean that you have to stop loving your *mamm*. It doesn't change the relationship you had with her. Not ever. That's why love is so amazing and beautiful."

The boy gave a slight shudder, his forehead creased in thought. And then he threw himself against her, his tearstained face pressed against her abdomen as he hugged her tight.

"I'm sorry, Abby. I like you. I do. I want to be friends.

But my *mamm*…" His desperate words were muffled against her apron.

She held him close, brushing a hand through his tousled hair. Her heart melted, a full, powerful sensation filling her chest. "There, it's all right now. We are *gut* friends. I like you, too."

In fact, she loved this boy, but didn't dare say so. Not right now, when their relationship was so fledgling. Perhaps in time.

He drew back and brushed at his face again. He gave her a wan smile. "I'm sorry for putting cracker crumbs in your bed."

She arched one eyebrow. "And filling my shoes with dirt?"

"*Ja*, I'm sorry for that, too."

She laughed, reaching out to playfully buffet his shoulder with the palm of her hand. He laughed, too.

"I know. I forgive you. But I'm glad we can laugh about it now," she said.

"It wasn't very nice of me. I can't believe you didn't tell *Daed* what I did."

"What good would it have done to get you into trouble with your *vadder*? I knew you were just feeling threatened and that you missed your *mudder* more than you could stand."

"*Ja*, I miss her every day. But I won't do anything like that to you ever again. I promise," he said.

"*Gut*. I'm so glad. I always knew you were a kindhearted boy."

"You did? But I've been so mean to you. How did you know?"

"Only a tenderhearted person could love his *mudder* the way you do. I'm sorry I made you worry."

He shrugged. "You're just looking for a home of your own. I'm sorry I wasn't more welcoming. You're our guest and I should have been kind."

She smiled to show him that all was forgiven. They looked at each other for a moment, and she breathed an inward sigh of relief, so happy to be rid of the animosity between them.

"*Ach*, I'd better get downstairs. Naomi is probably needing my help with the baking," Abby said.

She picked up her basket, giving him one last smile of reassurance. He grinned back, showing a tooth missing in front.

As she headed toward the door, she heard a scuffling sound on the landing. She reached the threshold just as the door to Naomi's room was closing, which seemed odd. Abby thought the woman was downstairs in the kitchen, baking bread. Maybe Naomi had come upstairs for something.

Thinking nothing of it, Abby hurried on her way, feeling suddenly light of heart. She was so grateful that she and Reuben had finally become friends. That they had agreed upon a truce and he could finally accept her. If only Jakob could do the same, she'd be a happy woman indeed.

Jakob stood inside his mother's room and leaned against the closed door. Whew! That was a close call. Abby had almost caught him eavesdropping on the landing. He'd been downstairs when he heard Reuben yelling and had come up to see what the trouble was. When he'd arrived, he'd heard his son crying and then the boy's apology for being so mean to Abby. The boy had mentioned something about putting cracker crumbs between her sheets and dirt in her shoes. Jakob was mortified at the extent of his son's hostility. But why hadn't Abby told him about it? Why had she suffered in silence? She'd told Reuben that she didn't want to get him into trouble. But what about Abby? Jakob felt horrible that his son had done such things to her, yet her patience and kindness was inspiring.

Instead of criticizing the boy, she'd offered soft words of forgiveness and reassurance. In spite of her upbringing, she'd shown compassion when she could have been cruel. She could have let Reuben squirm for a while and think about his hostile actions. But Jakob had learned that Abby wasn't that way. She was quick to forgive, her bright blue eyes shining with empathy. Quick to offer solace for an aching heart. Her charity toward his *familye* impressed him. In fact, he'd never met anyone like her. Not even Susan had been so forgiving. And once again, Jakob was grateful for her gentle kindness toward his *familye*.

According to the book of I Corinthians, charity suffered long, was kind and envied not. It was not puffed up with pride, anger or vengeance. Because charity was the pure love of Christ, it took love to a higher level. A level that transcended earthly life and became eternal. It saw beyond the moment and rose to the level of the Savior. Yes, *charitable* described Abby perfectly.

Opening the door to his mother's room, Jakob peeked out to find that he was alone. Stepping onto the landing, he closed the door silently behind him, then hurried down the stairs. Avoiding the kitchen and the women he thought were working there, he crossed through the living room and walked outside onto the front porch.

Love is infinite.

Abby's words filtered through his mind. She'd told Reuben that loving someone else didn't mean he had to stop loving his *mamm*. In his heart of hearts, Jakob knew what Abby said was true. Yet, it still confused him. He had loved Susan so much that he thought he never could love someone else.

Correction. He still loved Susan with all his might, mind and strength. But now, he had to reevaluate his feelings. If he believed the scriptures and what Abby said, he should be able to keep loving Susan and still be able to love another with the same deep sincerity he'd felt for his wife. But how could that be? How could he give his heart to someone else when he was still so in love with Susan? Maybe he didn't have to stop loving his wife in order to love and find happiness with another woman. It was something to think about.

Crossing the lawn, he headed toward the backyard. As he rounded the corner of the house, he came up short. Abby was bent at the waist, digging in the garden. He would have slipped away to the barn, but she stood straight at that moment, saw him and waved. Her graceful fingers were caked with mud from pulling and cleaning radishes. With swift proficiency, she laid several of the red roots in one of the muck buckets she used for collecting vegetables. A basket sat nearby, filled with fresh lettuce and beet greens. As he drew near, a stray wisp of golden hair framed her flushed face and an endearing smear of dirt marred her delicate chin. Like the day when she'd planted the corn, she didn't seem to mind the dirt. In fact, she seemed perfectly at ease working with the earth.

Pulling several more radishes, she smiled up at him. "Since this is my first time growing a garden in Colorado, I'm not sure if it's doing well or not. There are so many vegetables I could grow in Ohio, but Naomi said they won't do well here."

"*Ne*, we have a much shorter growing season. We don't have as much water and we're at a higher elevation, so we get the frost sooner."

He glanced at the long rows filled with verdant green plants burgeoning in the fertile soil. Naomi had basically turned the garden completely over to Abby. Not a weed was in sight, and she'd been diligent about watering regularly, too. Again, he thought that she would make a perfect farmer's wife. Even her tomato plants were loaded with round, green fruit, attesting to the bountiful harvest they'd soon have…if they didn't get an early freeze. No one could fault her efforts.

"In spite of the growing difficulties we face here, your garden is doing very well," he said.

Her garden. It wasn't Susan's garden anymore. And somehow that no longer bothered him.

Using the back of her hand, she brushed the stray hair away from her face, then tossed a perplexed frown at the row of celery she'd tried to grow. Because the plants required lots of water, the stalks were dry and small. But Jakob knew that wasn't Abby's fault.

"Everything is doing well except for that." She gestured with disgust at the plants. "Naomi warned me not to try to grow celery here, but I wouldn't listen. I thought if I gave it lots of water and attention, I could make it work, but this soil doesn't seem to hold the water very well."

The Amish loved celery, using it in many of their food dishes. It was a sign of prosperity, and they grew extra for the wedding season. He knew it must be a disappointment to Abby that it wouldn't flourish here in Colorado.

She tilted her head, an accepting sigh escaping her full lips. "I guess I'll just have to get used to the difference. I miss the gardens I could grow in Ohio, but I've never seen anything more beautiful than the tall Rocky Mountains and the wide Arkansas River."

She gazed toward the East where the Sangre de Cristo Mountains stood like a great sentinel guarding the valley. With the lush green and purple mountains as a backdrop, she looked beautiful and lonely standing there. A plain woman with no makeup and frills, yet Jakob thought he'd never seen a more beautiful woman in all his life. A powerful urge swept over him to take her into his arms and hold her close against his heart.

"Don't worry. We can buy whatever celery you might need at the store in town," he said.

"I suppose so, but it's not quite the same as growing your own," she said.

He couldn't take his eyes off her. He stared at her sweet profile, suddenly yearning to make her happy, to see her smile and hear her laughter again.

"Maybe next year, we can plant some celery along Grape Creek. Wild asparagus grows well along the creek banks, so why not celery?" he asked.

That thought gave him pause. Next year, if she was still here.

She rested one hand at her waist and gazed at him in awe. When she spoke, her voice was filled with wonder and delight. "Do you really think so? It would be *wundervoll* if I could make celery grow here. I don't mind going out to the fields to tend it if it means we can grow our own."

A surge of admiration swept over him. Nothing seemed to intimidate Abby. So hardworking and energetic. So eager to try new things.

"All we can do is try," he said, a hard lump suddenly clogging his throat.

"*Ach*, I may not be here next year, but if I am, we'll give it a try," she said.

He hated to hear his own sad thoughts spoken aloud, but he couldn't fight the truth. If Martin Hostetler had his way, she'd marry him and be living at his farm next year. And Jakob didn't want that. No, not at all. Which brought him to what was really troubling him this afternoon.

"Abby, I overheard part of your conversation with Reuben a little while ago." He made the confession before he could change his mind. And once again, he thought how easy it was to confide in her.

Her eyebrows drew together in a doubtful frown. "You did?"

"*Ja*, I had come upstairs when I heard him yelling, but then I didn't want to interfere. I realized it was a big moment for the two of you."

"*Ja*, it was," she said, smiling with satisfaction.

"I just wanted to say that I appreciate what you did for my son. I've spoken to him many times about his *mudder*, but nothing I've ever said has sunk in. You've been kind, and I'm grateful. Maybe he can finally start to heal now."

And maybe he could heal, too.

"You're *willkomm*. I just hope I really helped him see that he doesn't have to forget his *mudder*. She'll always be a part of each of you," she said, her voice very quiet.

"I know it hasn't been easy for you either, moving to a strange land, expecting to marry and all."

He paused, waiting for her to speak. Wishing she would say something to make this easier on him. But she didn't say a word. Just gazed at him with those dazzling blue eyes and an indulgent, noncommittal expression on her face.

"If...if I can have a little more time, I think perhaps I might be able to..." A yell cut him off before he could finish his thought.

"Jakob! Abby! *Kumme inwennich*."

They both turned and saw *Dawdi* Zeke waving urgently from the back porch, asking them to come inside.

"What is it?" Jakob called, taking a step toward his grandfather.

"Bishop Yoder is here. He says it is urgent that he speak with both of you."

The bishop was here? Not an odd occurrence on any given day. Bishop Yoder frequently called on the *familye* in the early evening for no apparent reason. Jakob knew the man did the same with other members of their congregation. It was the bishop's way of watching over his flock, seeing to their needs and ensuring they were living their faith. But what could be so urgent that the bishop would show up here in the middle of the workday?

As he and Abby walked toward the house, Jakob wondered what could be so important that Bishop Yoder had to speak with both him and Abby right now. A bad feeling settled in the pit of Jakob's stomach. Deep down, he knew that the bishop's visit did not bode well for either him or Abby.

Chapter Thirteen

Dawdi Zeke held the door open for her as Abby stepped inside the kitchen. The fragrant aroma of fresh-baked bread enveloped her. Six loaves sat cooling on the table and would feed the *familye* for the week.

Setting her basket of vegetables on the counter beside the sink, she waggled her dirty fingers at Zeke. "I'll just wash up first, if that's all right."

"Of course. Come in when you're ready." The elderly man nodded and disappeared into the other room.

Picking up a bar of homemade soap scented with vanilla, she washed her hands. A heavy weight settled across her chest. What could Bishop Yoder want to see both her and Jakob about? Whatever it was, she didn't think it could be good. She found herself wishing that people would just forget about her and leave her alone. She was happy here at the Fishers' farm and longed for the time and freedom to thrive. But some innate sense warned her that the bishop was about to upset her life once more. She didn't know why or how, but she knew her life was about to make another drastic change.

She spent extra time cleaning the dirt out from under

her short fingernails. As she lathered her skin, she was highly conscious of Jakob standing nearby, waiting for her to finish. She longed to confide her fears to him, but didn't dare. She had told him enough already and didn't want to get any closer to him.

"Are you all right?" he asked, his voice sounding subdued. Maybe he also sensed that something was about to change.

"*Ja.*"

But no, she wasn't. Not really. Ah, she was being silly. The bishop had probably come for a routine visit. He'd probably summoned her and Jakob simply because they were part of the same household and he wanted to visit with the entire *familye*. She was worrying about nothing.

Finally, she rinsed and Jakob handed her a towel to dry her hands, then accompanied her into the living room. He startled her when he rested his hand against her left shoulder blade for just a second, waiting for her to precede him into the room. His touch was gentle and warm, increasing her awareness of him. But it also brought her some small comfort. His presence made her feel safe somehow.

Bishop Yoder sat on the sofa, his straw hat in his hands. Naomi sat across from him in her rocking chair, nervously twisting her black apron strings around her fingers. *Dawdi* Zeke sat in his battered recliner. But where were the children? If this was a routine visit, Ruby and Reuben would be here, too. Since they were absent, that meant this was not routine at all.

"*Ach*, here they are," Naomi said. She patted her *kapp* and showed a nervous smile.

"*Hallo*, Jakob. *Vee gehts?*" The bishop stood and greeted him with a handshake.

"*Gut*, we are all well. *Danke*," Jakob said.

"And you, Abby? *Vee gehts?*" The bishop took both of her hands in his, looking deeply into her eyes.

Abby saw a mixture of sympathy and concern in the man's gray eyes...a combination that once again put her on edge. What was going on?

She showed a half smile. "I am well, *danke*."

"*Gut. Gut.*"

With the niceties over, they all sat and the bishop took a deep inhale, as though resigning himself. Then, he reached into his hat and pulled out what appeared to be an envelope.

"I received a letter from Abby's brother this morning," he told them.

Abby's thoughts scattered. She sat up straighter, her pulse beating madly against her temples. Although she'd written to him several times, Simon had not replied once in all the weeks she'd been here.

"Wh...what did Simon have to say?" she asked, her voice wobbling. She clenched her hands together in her lap to keep them from trembling. She didn't understand why she should be upset by this meeting. Simon was far, far away and could no longer hurt her. Right?

Bishop Yoder cleared his throat, looking intense and uncomfortable. "He has demanded that you return to Ohio at once."

Naomi gasped. "What? But why?"

The bishop met Abby's gaze. "He claims that he didn't know where you had run off to, and as the patriarch of your *familye*, he feels responsible for your well-being. He is appalled that you are staying here in

Jakob's home without benefit of marriage, and he demands your immediate return."

"But…but that's not true. Simon knew where I was going, otherwise how would he have known where to write to you?" she said, feeling outraged that her brother would lie about such a thing.

"He claims that a member of our district wrote to tell him that you were here and that you were unmarried," Bishop Yoder said.

"That might be true, but I've also written to Simon several times. Although he's never written back. He has known very well where I have been," she said.

The bishop studied her face, as though searching for the truth there. "He said that you had run away in the middle of the night. He is eager for your return."

Dawdi Zeke *harrumphed* at the implication. Naomi's eyes widened in outrage. Abby understood the allegation full well. With his letter, Simon was claiming that she'd betrayed him and her *familye* by leaving home in secrecy. That she had lied to the bishop and the Fisher *familye* when she'd told them that her brother knew where she was.

"*Ne*, it isn't true. He knew everything. I have never lied to him, nor to you. Not once," Abby said, the heat of outrage and embarrassment flowing over her entire body. How dare her brother discredit her like this to Bishop Yoder and the Fisher *familye*. It was offensive, cruel, shameful and…

Evil.

"May I see the letter?" Jakob asked humbly, holding out his hand.

The bishop passed the envelope to him. Everyone seemed to hold their breath as he opened and scanned the pages. His face remained passive, but Abby noticed that his shoulders had tensed. As he read, his jaw hardened like granite and his eyes narrowed. While other people might miss the signs, she knew him well enough to realize that he was upset by what he read, but endeavored to maintain his self-control. Finally, he tucked the papers back inside the envelope and returned it to the bishop.

"It states that, since Abby is not married, she must return to Ohio," Jakob said.

The bishop nodded. "*Ja*, that is correct."

"*Ach*, that alone tells me that he knew Abby's purpose in coming here. He knew that she planned to marry me."

Bishop Yoder looked at Abby. "I understand that Martin Hostetler has been courting you quite seriously."

Abby almost snorted. Not once had she gone out with Martin, and she found it almost comical that his few visits to the farm and their conversations at church could be called a serious courtship. Martin might be interested in her, but she wasn't interested in him. And that was that.

She shook her head. "I'm afraid that is rather one-sided, but I still want to remain here. Please don't make me go back. Please."

Okay, she'd resorted to begging again. But at this point, she'd do anything not to return to the harsh life awaiting her in her brother's home.

"I'm sorry, Abby," Bishop Yoder said. "But your *bruder* is the head of your *familye* now that your *vadder* is gone. If you were married, things would be different. But as a single woman, you must respect Simon as the patriarch of your home. You must obey him and return to Ohio."

No, no! She didn't want to obey her brother. She longed to make choices for herself, to escape the domination of any man. Surely *Gott* did not condone the abuse she had suffered. Surely it was wrong. But even as she thought these things, she knew it was no use. She did not believe that *Gott* approved of her brother's actions, but neither did He approve of her disobedience. He would want her to bear her burdens humbly and meekly, with long-suffering and no murmuring.

Blinking back tears of disappointment, she bowed her head in submission. In her heart, she was willing to suffer anything as long as she could retain her relationship with *Gott*. If she had to return to Ohio, then the Lord must have something else in mind for her. She had to believe that. She must! Because nothing was more important to her than her faith. She must wait upon *Gott's* will.

"What if Abby were to marry right now?" Jakob asked.

Abby lifted her head and stared at the man, wondering what he was saying. If he suggested she marry Martin Hostetler just to keep from going back to Ohio, she couldn't do it. Not only was she not interested, but Martin also deserved to wed a woman who truly loved him.

Bishop Yoder shrugged. "Then her first duty would be to remain with her husband. Do you have a proposal in mind?"

A long silence followed, weighed down by a morose confusion. Abby held her breath, wondering what Jakob would say. She didn't know what to think at this point. Nor did she dare hold out any hope. She loved

Jakob. She always had, since they were children. She loved him, but he didn't love her. It was that simple. He had made it clear on numerous occasions that he still longed for his dead wife. That his heart was too full of memories of Susan to make any room for another. Loving Abby was an impossibility. Nothing could save her now. Not even Jakob. She had no choice but to return to Simon in Ohio.

"I will marry Abby." Jakob said the words before he could change his mind.

Her low cry of surprise sounded like a shout in the quiet room. He knew his proposal startled her, but he wouldn't take it back. Not when he knew the abuse she would be subjected to if she returned to her brother. His conscience wouldn't allow him to do that. Not when he knew that he could prevent it. Even if they had a marriage in name only, it would be better than sending her away. He couldn't do that. He couldn't.

"Oh, Jakob! How *wundervoll*." Naomi clasped her hands together in an exclamation of joy.

Dawdi Zeke grinned and nodded with approval, his spectacles sliding down his nose. "*Ja*, it's the right thing to do. I wholeheartedly approve."

Even Bishop Yoder smiled. And now that Abby had made friends with Reuben, Jakob believed his two children would be delighted, too. Marrying Abby would fix everyone's problems. It would bring stability to his home. She'd already become a member of the *familye*. They should make it permanent and official. She could stay here and she'd be safe. It was the right thing to do. Wasn't it?

"May I speak with Jakob in private, please?"

Jakob turned to see Abby sitting primly with her hands folded in her lap. Her back was stiff, her neck straight, a calm yet resolute expression on her face.

She stood and turned toward the door without waiting for anyone to speak. In automatic response, Jakob followed her outside, wondering what she was thinking. What if she refused his proposal? Surely she wouldn't do such a thing. Not when she knew the alternative.

Outside, he expected her to sit on the front porch, but she kept going. Down the stairs, across the green lawn and toward the fence line bordering the cornfield... where no one could listen through open windows and eavesdrop on their conversation.

Beneath the spread of a hackberry tree, she finally stopped and turned to face him. Lifting her chin two inches higher, she locked her gaze with his.

"Do you love me, Jakob?" Her words were spoken so quietly that he almost didn't hear.

He paused, his mind churning. He loved Susan. He always would. But did he love Abby, too? Did he?

"This is what I wanted to talk with you about earlier, when we were interrupted by the bishop's visit," he said. "I... I have come to care for you a great deal, Abby. In fact, I want you to stay here, with my *familye*. I don't want you to leave."

She shifted her weight and folded her arms. "I know you care for me and that we are *gut* friends. But since I came here, my feelings have changed. I don't want to be second-best. I want more from the man I marry. Do you love me?"

"Abby, I... I need more time. I've caught glimpses of how it could be between us, but I still don't know," he said, wishing he could make sense of his feelings.

He knew he didn't want her to leave. That he was desperate for her to stay. Yes, he'd overheard Abby telling Reuben that he could love his mother and still be friends with her. Jakob's common sense told him that he could do the same with Susan. He could love both her and Abby. But a deep part of Jakob's heart wouldn't let him make that leap.

"*Ne*, Jakob. If you loved me, you would know in here." She placed the palm of her hand against his chest.

Her touch was warm and gentle, setting his heart to racing. He longed to pull her into his arms and offer her some reassurance. He was physically attracted to her. He enjoyed being with her. But did he love her?

"I want to marry you, Abby. To make a *familye* with you. I don't want you to go. In time, I believe I would—"

She shook her head, interrupting him. "*Ne*, Jakob. We are out of time. As tempting as your offer is, I will not accept a pity marriage. Not from you and not from any other man."

He snorted. "Believe me, my offer is certainly not out of pity, Abby. Any man would be blessed to marry you. I'm very aware of how beautiful and superb you are. Against great adversity, you have followed the rules of the *Ordnung* all the days of your life. Your faith inspires me to be a better man, to do more *gut*. You're everything I could ever want in a wife. It's me who should throw myself on your mercy. I'm the one who is so deficient."

And he sensed that she could help him find the answers. Today, he'd felt as though he were on the cusp of discovering something transcendent about himself, but Bishop Yoder had interrupted them. Now it was as if he couldn't wave away the fog so he could see what was hidden so clearly in his own mind. It had been there, then it was gone and he couldn't find it again. He didn't even know what it was he felt for Abby. She was unique. His feelings for her were so different from what he'd felt for Susan. He only knew he was desperate for her to remain here with him.

"You are very kind, and I thank you for your offer," she said, showing a sad little smile.

"But...?"

"But a marriage without love would not be *gut* for either of us. When I finally wed, it will be to a man who adores me. A kind, generous man who puts me above all others, except *Gott*."

"I do, Abby. I mean, I will do all of that."

She scoffed. "You care for me like you do all the members of our congregation. Like you would a neighbor or dear friend. But not as a wife. Not as a cherished partner to toil and live each day of our lives together. If we wed, you would eventually come to resent me. You would feel trapped. And I would feel like a castoff. Like a second-class burden no one else wanted. I couldn't live like that, Jakob. I'm not asking you to give up your love for Susan, but I am asking you to love me just as much as you loved her. Can you do that?"

Here it was. He blinked in confusion, wondering if he could. It was a novel idea to him. How could he love both women equally at the same time?

"I... I don't know. You are both so different, yet you are both so *wundervoll*. It's like comparing wheat to corn. I want both of them, but I married Susan first and still feel loyal to her."

She laughed and it was so good to see her smile again, but not like this.

"Only a farmer would make such an analogy," she said.

"*Ach*, I am a plain man and I make no apologies for it. It is who I am, who I will always be. You would need to accept me for who I am, just as I must accept you."

"You don't need to apologize, Jakob," she said. "You are a *gut* man of faith, and any woman would be honored to accept your marriage proposal. One day, I hope you find what you are seeking."

He couldn't believe what she was saying. "Are you turning me down, then?"

"Yes, Jakob, I am."

He stared at her, stunned to the tips of his scuffed work boots. Not because she was refusing him, but because she fully knew what would happen if she did. "You would rather return to Simon and his abuse than to marry me and remain here in Colorado with my *familye*?"

"*Ne*, of course not. I would love nothing more than to stay here. I love Naomi and Zeke. And I adore Ruby and Reuben. But I would rather suffer Simon's abuse than live here and love you, yet know in my heart that you don't love me in return."

She loved him? That was a startling realization. It touched a deep part of his heart. Knowing that she loved him, he wanted even more to protect her. To not hurt her ever.

What he felt for Abby was powerful. They were close friends. Weren't they? But was friends enough for marriage? Were his feelings as strong as what he had felt for Susan?

His love for Susan was still in the present, wasn't it? He still loved her. And yet, his feelings had changed somehow. She was the mother of his children. He had cherished her. But now, Abby was here in his life and Susan was gone.

A blaze of frustration scorched his senses. He wanted to give Abby what she asked for. To love and cherish her as a man should love and cherish his wife. But he was so afraid. What if he couldn't do it? What if it wasn't in him to love more than one woman that way? And if he did, how could he stand the pain if he lost her the way he'd lost Susan?

"Let's not make any decisions right now," he said. "I will ask Bishop Yoder to delay your return to Ohio a little longer."

She was silent for a moment, considering his words with a perplexed frown. The corners of her eyes crinkled as she squinted against the bright spray of summer sunlight. In spite of working outside with him each day, not a single freckle marred her smooth complexion. He remained perfectly still, holding his breath. Giving her time to consider his suggestion. The wind rustled her skirts, whipping them against her slender ankles.

"I don't think more time will make any difference for either of us," she said. "We both know what we want, and neither of us can have it. She's not coming back, Jakob. You know that, don't you?"

Abby's words struck him like a fist to the face. Yes, he knew it, but maybe he was just now starting to accept it.

"I will return to Ohio where I belong," she said with finality.

"*Ne*, I will ask the bishop for more time before he replies to your *bruder. Gehne mir!* We'll go now and tell Bishop Yoder of our request."

To keep her from refusing, he reached out and took

her hand in his, pulling her gently with him toward the house. She didn't fight him, and he was relieved. Her agreement meant everything. This was the best solution. It would buy them more time together. And tomorrow, he would take her for a buggy ride in the afternoon, just the two of them. He would court her. Hold her hand. Maybe even kiss her. They would have time to get to know each other on a romantic level.

Time to convince her to marry him.

Inside the house, he quickly made his request to the bishop. *Dawdi* Zeke remained stoic, his bushy eyebrows pulled together in a frown. Naomi looked worried, too, but Bishop Yoder nodded his assent.

"I would like nothing more than to have Abby remain here within our community," the bishop said. "I will delay in responding to your *bruder* for a brief amount of time. But then, Abby will need to go back."

Abby stood silently holding her hands together in front of her. She didn't speak, nod or move a muscle. Her eyes were wide, her face ashen. And that's when Jakob felt the futility of his request. Time would make no difference. It wouldn't change anything between them. Nothing would, and he realized he'd have to face up to it.

Chapter Fourteen

"Do you want me to cut some more wood?"

Jakob paused as he sanded a piece of cedarwood and looked at *Dawdi* Zeke. Standing inside the workshop, the elderly man indicated a neatly stacked pile of wood scraps on the other side of the workbench.

"*Ne*, I think we have enough cut already."

Jakob glanced at the row of birdhouses lining the tall shelf. He and *Dawdi* Zeke supplied the hardware store in town with an assortment of birdhouses, feeders and wishing wells, selling them on consignment. Tourists loved the gaily painted fixtures, which were another source of income for them. And they were easy to produce, made from scraps of wood left over from larger projects. If Abby helped *Dawdi* Zeke paint, they might be able to sell them in some of the neighboring towns, too.

Abby. He'd thought of little else since Bishop Yoder had left over two hours earlier. Beneath the warm glow of kerosene light, he rubbed his fingers along the grain of the wood, feeling for any rough edges. He needed time to think. To come up with a plan. Some way to protect Abby from her brother. But nothing came to mind.

"What are you gonna do about Abby?" *Dawdi* Zeke asked.

Hmm. Jakob had to give his grandfather credit. The elderly man hadn't said a word about her since the bishop had left. But now, *Dawdi* seemed to be growing restless.

After wiping the surface of the wood with a tack cloth, Jakob shook it out. A small cloud of dust made him cough. "I'm not sure yet. I hope she will stay here and decide to wed me."

Dawdi Zeke picked up a brush and dabbed red paint on the top of a miniature roof. "*Ach*, no doubt she's feeling like she'll always be in second place if she marries you."

Jakob didn't ask why. He knew *Dawdi* was right, but he didn't want Abby to feel that way. She deserved better than that. She was so wonderful that he wanted her to feel happy and secure in their marriage, not as if she were a last resort.

"She's made it clear that she won't marry a man who doesn't love her," Jakob said.

And that was the crux of the problem. Jakob couldn't love her. If she died the way Susan had done, he couldn't face that loss again. Neither could his children. So where did that leave them? Nowhere!

Dawdi Zeke nodded. "I can understand her feelings. My second wife felt the same way."

Jakob jerked his head up, his mouth dropping open in surprise. He'd known since he was a toddler that *Dawdi* Zeke had been married twice, but he had no idea his grandmother felt second-best. "You mean my *grossmammi* felt like that?"

"*Ja*, for several years, until I convinced her differently. My first wife was Maddie. You never knew her, she died long before you were born. She had auburn hair and the prettiest hazel eyes you ever saw. She died of pneumonia when she was only nineteen years old. She was four months along with our first child."

Jakob's heart wrenched with sadness. Although he'd known about Maddie, he hadn't realized she was expecting a baby. His grandfather's story reminded him that he wasn't the only one who had lost a beloved wife and unborn child. In spite of his sorrows, Jakob had so much to be grateful for. He just had to look for the good and count his many blessings.

"*Ach*, I'm sorry, *Dawdi*."

"There's no need to be sorry. Maddie is with the *gut* Lord now. She's happy and content, and I hope I'm worthy to see her again one day," *Dawdi* Zeke said.

The elderly man was silent for a few moments and a faraway look filled his eyes, as though he were remembering back to his youth.

"There was a time when I didn't think I could stand the loss," he said. "I was barely twenty years old at the time. It took a long thirteen years before I could move on. I was thirty-three before I wed again. Helen, your *grossmammi*, was the *mudder* of my seven *kinder*. We were married sixty years. She was so talented, sweet, kind and sensible. A hard worker who loved *Gott* more than anything else. Her faith meant everything to her. I came to depend on her and loved her like I've never loved anyone in my life, and I miss her every moment of every day."

"But if you loved Maddie so much, how did you let your heart come to love my *grossmammi*, too?" Jakob asked.

Dawdi Zeke shrugged. "Over the years, I missed my Maddie. If she had lived, I have no doubt we would have been married all our lives. But then I wouldn't have known Helen and the joy we shared. Now, I'm a very old man, but my heart still feels young when I think about the two women who shared my heart. Even though they were so different, I loved them equally. I could never choose between them. And now that I face meeting *Gott* soon, I can't say that I would change a thing. He knew what I needed to make me grow in faith. I faced a lot of pain losing Maddie, but He's never deserted me. Not once."

Jakob thought about his grandfather's words for several moments. "But when you loved Helen, didn't you feel disloyal to Maddie?"

Dawdi Zeke tilted his head, his bushy gray eyebrows drawn together in confusion. "What for?"

Jakob thought it was obvious, but explained anyway. "For loving another woman."

"Ne!" *Dawdi* Zeke waved a hand. "I loved both women at different times. There was nothing wrong in that. I loved them, just as *Gott* loves them. I couldn't choose between the two. My Maddie wouldn't have wanted me to go on living my life alone and unhappy. It's *Gott's* plan that we wed and raise a *familye*. That's what makes up eternity. Our *familye*. And if I hadn't loved and married Helen, I never would have had *kinder*. I wouldn't have you."

Jakob had never thought about that. What if he was supposed to marry Abby and have more children with her? If he let her go, he might be letting her down. He might be letting *Gott* down, too.

Dawdi Zeke gave him a gentle wink. "I understand what you're going through, *mein sohn*. I truly do. You want to love and be loyal to Susan, but that won't help Abby. She needs you now. Don't wait thirteen years to learn the lesson I learned. Be at peace. Don't forget your faith. *Gott* has a plan for you. When we think all is lost, sometimes He can surprise us. Let Susan go now. Hold on to your faith and Abby."

As his grandfather stepped away, Jakob found it suddenly so easy to feel the older man's confidence in *Gott*. To feel so light of heart. He'd loved Susan, but now she was gone. She was at peace, but he hadn't been. Not for months.

Jakob thought about after the Sermon on the Mount, when the Savior left in a boat. He was awakened by his disciples to find a great storm waging around them. That was how Jakob had felt since Susan died. His heart and mind had been in constant turmoil, battered by doubts and fear. But Jesus was the Prince of Peace. He had calmed the angry storm and taught a powerful lesson. That when we have faith and rely on Him, we also can have peace no matter what storms life throws our way.

Christ's example spoke with strength to Jakob now. And suddenly, it was so easy to hand his burdens over to the Lord. To let go of his anguish and doubts. To rely on Christ, his Savior and friend. He would go forward in faith, confident and firm in his trust that *Gott* would show him the way. No longer would he be afraid.

He paused, that thought filling his mind. He wasn't afraid anymore. In fact, the possibilities suddenly seemed endless. He'd been holding back his feelings for Abby out of guilt and fear of losing her. But that had to change.

Glancing at the open door, he saw the dark sky filled with shining stars. Abby was probably asleep by now. Too late to seek her out and talk to her. And he could hardly wait for tomorrow.

That night, Abby read a bedtime story to Reuben and Ruby. She almost cried when both children cuddled up with her so they could see the pictures of the book. The fragrant smell of Naomi's vanilla soap wafted from their clean skin. Reuben slipped his hand over her arm and laughed at her attempts to lower her voice the way Jakob did. It seemed as though there had never been even a smidgen of animosity between them. When she finished the tale, Reuben climbed over to his bed. Abby tucked both children beneath their covers and kissed them each on the forehead.

"Have you been to your room yet this evening?" Reuben asked expectantly.

Abby gave him a quizzical look, wondering why he would ask such a thing. Hopefully he hadn't filled her clothes with thistles, or put soap in her hairbrush. They were beyond such childish pranks now, weren't they?

"*Ne*, why do you ask?"

He looked away, his cheeks flushing red. "No reason. I was just wondering."

Ruby stifled a wide yawn, her eyes drooping as she spoke in a sleepy, contented voice. "You'll never leave us will you, Abby?"

Abby froze, her heart squeezing hard. She didn't know what to say. The children weren't yet aware that

Simon had summoned her home. They didn't know she would be leaving soon.

"*Ach, Mamm* left us. Everyone leaves eventually," Reuben said, his voice a bit begrudging.

"But your *mudder* didn't want to go," Abby said quietly. "Her body just gave out. She would have stayed with you forever if she could."

"How do you know?" Ruby asked.

Abby tickled the girl's ribs, making her giggle. "Because that's what *mudders* do. I feel the same way about you and Reuben. I'd stay with you forever if I could."

"*Daed* says *Mamm* and our baby *bruder* are with *Gott* now," Ruby said.

Abby nodded. "*Ja*, that's right."

Reuben peered at her, his wide, dark eyes seeming to look deep into her heart. "But you won't leave us. Not for a long time until you're very old. Will you?"

Abby took an inhale to steady her nerves. She didn't want to make promises she couldn't keep, but this conversation was breaking her heart. "I can't promise that, *liebchen*. None of us can promise to stay. But you know I'll always love both of you, don't you? I can promise that."

"*Ja*, and I love you, too," Ruby said, yawning again. "Tomorrow, *Grossmammi* said we're going to take the kittens out to the barn so we can get them used to their new home. Do you really think they'll be okay out there?"

Relieved to change the topic, Abby nodded. "I do."

"But what will they eat? They don't know how to catch mice yet. They'll be lonely out there in that big old drafty barn."

"They'll learn soon enough to catch mice, and they

can curl up in the warm straw. Hunting will come naturally to them. And you can keep an eye on them to ensure they're not going hungry. If they are, you can give them some scraps from the kitchen to eat."

The babies had gotten so big since Abby had found them in the barn weeks earlier. They had grown fast, but Abby wouldn't be here to watch either the cats or the children grow into adulthood.

Tomorrow. Tomorrow she must leave. No matter how long the bishop delayed corresponding with her brother, she couldn't stay here any longer. She appreciated Jakob's efforts on her behalf, but she'd spent enough time with him that, if he didn't love her now, he never would. Staying longer would only exacerbate the situation. It would be pure torture, building up all of their hopes only to have them dashed. And in the end, she would have to return to Ohio anyway. It would be better to leave now than to spend more time with Jakob, knowing he could never love her. Her heart couldn't take that. Not anymore.

"Rest now," she said. "*Gott* will take care of you no matter what happens in your life. You just need to have faith and all will be well."

She blew out the kerosene lamp and left the door slightly ajar. Ruby rubbed her eyes again and Reuben rolled over. Abby peered at them through the dark, listening to their soft even breathing for several moments.

As she crossed the landing to her own room, she had to blink back tears. Never before had her faith been put to such a test, and she wondered what *Gott* had in store for her. She didn't want to leave, but knew if she refused, she could be censured by the church. She might even be shunned, which meant that Jakob and his *familye* couldn't speak or eat with her, nor take anything from her hand. She didn't want to put Bishop Yoder or the Fishers in that uncomfortable position. What would it accomplish, except to create more heartache for them all?

Pulling back the covers to her bed, she fluffed the pillow. A white scrap of paper fell to the floor. Picking it up, she read the words scrawled in childish handwriting: *You smell like apple blossoms.*

Folding the note, she closed her eyes and held the paper close against her heart. Tears squeezed from between her eyelashes. Now she understood why Reuben had asked if she'd been to her room this evening. She had absolutely no doubt that he had written this message and was wondering if she'd seen it yet.

She hadn't realized that she smelled like apple blossoms. It must be the homemade lotion Naomi had given to her. But the fact that Reuben had noticed and thought to comment on it touched her heart like nothing else could.

Once she was gone, who would write uplifting notes to put in Reuben's lunch pail? And who would comfort Ruby if one of the kittens went missing or got hurt? Naomi, *Dawdi* Zeke and Jakob would do all they could for both children, but Abby could hardly stand the thought of leaving them. Not now. Not when she loved them so much. Not when she still loved Jakob. Finally, for the first time in her life, she felt wanted and needed. Like this was her home. But it couldn't be helped. Nothing was going to change Jakob's heart. She had to leave.

The following morning, Abby was up early. As quietly as possible, she packed her battered suitcase. Its contents included the note Reuben had hidden beneath her pillow, a picture Ruby had drawn of the baby kittens scampering across the yard and the wild iris Jakob had picked for her in the cornfield. None of them would ever know how much she treasured these simple things or how much their gestures of kindness meant to her.

Stowing her suitcase under the bed where no one would see it, she went downstairs to do her chores. It was still dark outside as she crossed the yard to the barn, the crisp air filling her lungs. She found her wire basket for collecting eggs sitting on a bench just inside, filled with a bunch of silver lupines.

Her stomach did a myriad of flip-flops. Jakob must have picked the flowers for her, but it didn't mean he loved her. Still, his gesture touched her heart.

Lifting the bouquet, she pressed it to her nose and inhaled deeply of the sweet fragrance. She would add several of the violet flowers to her cherished possessions.

A flash of white caught her eye. Plucking it from the basket, she discovered a note addressed to her. As she opened it, her heart thudded and her hands shook like aspens in the wind.

Abby,
I'm sorry I missed you this morning. I left early so that I can finish my chores in time to take you for a buggy ride this afternoon. Mamm will take the kinder with her to the quilting frolic, so you won't need to watch them. Please plan your workday so you can be ready to leave with me around noon.
Jakob

Abby's pulse tripped into double time. No one had ever left her a message like this before. No one had ever gone out of the way to plan a buggy ride with her. Martin Hostetler didn't count because she'd told him "no" several times. It was so tempting to stay and spend an enjoyable afternoon with Jakob, but his note was what convinced her it was time to go. She detected no affection in his words. No words of endearment. Nothing to indicate he was excited to spend the afternoon with her. He'd even signed the note simply with just his name. No emotion. No love.

She must not be sucked into false hope. Over the past few months, she'd spent plenty of time alone with Jakob, and he still didn't love her. Nothing would change with a bunch of flowers and a buggy ride, but she was grateful that he had at least made the effort. She didn't blame him. In fact, she admired him for his honesty and his loyalty to Susan. She just wished he could find room in his heart to love her, too.

Today, she would leave. *Dawdi* Zeke would spend most of his time inside the workshop. Naomi would take the children with her. Jakob was already out in the fields watering and weeding the crops. He wouldn't be back for hours. By the time the *familye* returned home, she'd be gone. It was a nine-mile walk to the bus depot in town, but she could make it. She'd leave a letter of explanation and go. It would be easier this way. No tearful goodbyes. No guilt or recriminations. They'd just quietly get on with their lives.

Tucking Jakob's note into the heel of her shoe, she hurried with her work. Thirty minutes later, she was back in the kitchen and greeted Naomi and the children with a cheerful smile and a kiss.

"*Danke* for your sweet note. It made me feel so happy," she told Reuben.

He smiled, looking suddenly shy as he took his seat.

The tantalizing aroma of sausage and cornmeal filled the air. As she spooned scrapple into their bowls, they didn't seem to notice anything different. It was just another ordinary day. And yet, Abby felt like crying.

"Did Jakob tell you that the *kinder* will be going with me to the quilting frolic this morning?" Naomi asked in a pleasant tone.

"*Ja*, he left me a note." Abby turned away so no one would see the tears in her eyes. She didn't want the woman to know that she wouldn't be here when Jakob returned. That she'd probably never see any of them again.

"I wish you could join us, but there will be plenty of time for you to attend other frolics another time," Naomi continued, seeming almost buoyant at the thought.

Abby didn't respond. No doubt the woman was eager for her eldest son to marry again. And why not? The Amish were taught to cherish their children. They valued *familye* second only to their obedience to *Gott*.

As she set a plate of warm biscuits on the table, the kittens mewed at Abby's feet. They wanted their breakfast, too. Looking up, she locked her gaze with *Dawdi* Zeke's. He hadn't picked up his spoon to eat and was watching her quietly, his gray eyes narrowed with shrewd intelligence. Did he know what she planned? Oh, she hoped not. Running away seemed dishonest somehow. She loved the elderly man and hated to do anything to lose his respect.

Turning away, Abby quickly filled a saucer with cream and tiny pieces of sausage. If this was the last time she would get to feed the kittens, she wanted to make it a good meal for them. She set the dish on the floor beside the stove and petted the two babies as they ate ravenously, their long tails high in the air.

Within an hour, Abby had washed the dishes and swept the floor, and was standing on the front porch, waving goodbye to Naomi and the children. Tears clouded her vision as she blew them a kiss. As predicted, Zeke had disappeared into the workshop. Now was her chance.

Hurrying inside, she ran upstairs to retrieve her suitcase and the letter she'd written late last night addressed to the entire *familye*. In the kitchen, she placed the envelope in the middle of the table, where it was sure to be seen. After picking up the basket of food she had prepared for her journey, she opened the front door cautiously. She peered out, making certain *Dawdi* Zeke wasn't around. When she didn't see him, she scurried toward the main road, eager to put some distance between herself and the farm.

From past experience, she figured it would take three hours to walk the nine miles, which would put her in town around noon. That was roughly the time when Jakob would be ready to collect her for their buggy ride. If her memory was correct, a bus would be departing at one thirty. She'd be tired, but she could rest once she'd bought a ticket and was safely on her way to Ohio. But as she walked along the dusty road, she couldn't help feeling that all was lost.

Chapter Fifteen

"**W**hat do you mean Abby is gone?"

Jakob stood outside the barn and stared at his *familye* in disbelief. He'd returned home early from the fields, dusty and smelling of sweat. He didn't want Abby to see him like this and was eager to go to the *dawdy haus* so he could clean up before their buggy ride. In fact, he'd thought about nothing else all day long. Talking to her. Being with her.

"She's gone," *Dawdi* Zeke said again. "She left a letter for us on the table in the kitchen. She's walked into town, planning to board a bus back to Ohio today at one thirty."

One thirty? Jakob glanced at the azure sky. He didn't own a watch, but he knew from the position of the sun that it must be almost noon.

"Go after her, *Daed*. You have to bring her back." Ruby stood beside Naomi, rubbing her tear-drenched eyes.

Reuben sniffled as he held *Dawdi* Zeke's hand. "*Ja, Daed*, go and get her. Hurry, before she's gone forever."

"*Ach*, Jakob. Don't let her leave," Naomi said.

A cold, sick feeling settled over Jakob. Abby was gone. She'd left without saying goodbye.

"But why? I thought we had more time. I left her a note this morning. Why would she leave without telling me?"

Dawdi Zeke shook his head. "You know why she left. Do I have to explain it again?"

No, Jakob knew. He'd always known. But he'd been in denial. He thought he could stave off the inevitable, but Abby was smarter than him. She knew they couldn't go on the way they had been. Their relationship had to move to the next level, or die.

And that's when the truth washed over him with the force of a tidal wave. He loved Abby. He always had, but he'd been so fearful. Afraid of loving and losing her the way he'd lost Susan. But now, he knew that he wanted to be with Abby. To hold her close and have more children with her. To plan for the future and grow old with her.

To marry and love her all the rest of his days.

Yes, he loved her. He could admit it now. When he'd written the note to Abby and planned the buggy ride, he'd wanted to be near her but hadn't understood how he felt. Now, an overwhelming love enveloped him and he didn't push it away or try to ignore his feelings. He loved her; he was certain of it.

The revelation was like a thunderous epiphany. It came on so strongly that he couldn't deny it any longer. Something he'd always known deep inside, but just couldn't bring himself to admit. But it was there now. It had taken root within him and was growing fast. The fledgling, thrilling love that made him hopeful, expectant and anxious to be with her.

And now, he may have lost her for good.

He glanced at the buggy Naomi and the children had used to go to the quilting frolic. It was still hitched to Tommy. Reaching for the tugs on the harness, he spoke over his shoulder.

"Does anyone know when she left? Do I have time to ride into town before she's gone?"

He spoke in a rush over his shoulder, removing the harness hitched to the horse.

Dawdi Zeke helped him, pulling on the girth belt. "I suspect she left right after Naomi and the *kinder* went to the quilting frolic, but she would have been on foot. You've got to go after her, Jakob. Tell her the truth."

Jakob paused. Turned. "The truth?"

"*Ja*. That you *lieb* her. It's time you finally admitted it."

Yes, it was time. A flash of panic rushed over him. Not because he loved her. Oh, no. He felt the panic of dread, that he was about to lose something more precious than gold. He had to hurry, to get to town before the bus left. He couldn't let Abby go. Not now. Now when he'd finally realized how he really felt about her.

He turned toward the barn, intending to retrieve the only saddle they owned. There was no need. Reuben had gone after it for him, grunting as he half carried, half dragged the heavy leather toward the horse.

"*Danke, sohn.*" Jakob lifted the dusty apparatus easily and swung it and a horse blanket up onto Tommy's back. Although the Amish were good horsemen, they rarely rode horses. Not for recreational purposes, anyway. But this was an emergency.

The horse sidestepped, not used to being ridden. Jakob persisted, figuring he could move much swifter if he rode astride instead of driving the buggy. But that meant that Abby and her luggage would have to ride behind him on the way home. Right now, it couldn't be helped. He didn't care about anything except reaching her before it was too late.

The bus was delayed. Some kind of engine failure.

Sitting on a hard chair inside the terminal, Abby glanced at the clock on the wall. Almost two o'clock. Jakob, Naomi and the *kinder* would have returned home by now. They would have found her note on the kitchen table. They'd be upset, wondering and wishing and crying. But it was best to get it over with and move on.

Someone coughed and she glanced over to where two *Englisch* women sat nearby, their heads bent close together as they discussed this delay. Another woman comforted her crying toddler while her husband checked his wristwatch, then shook his head with annoyance. Other passengers sat around, too, waiting inside the air-conditioned terminal instead of outside in the baking sunshine. Occasionally one of them looked at her, their curious expressions telling her they thought her plain appearance was rather odd. They all seemed as anxious as Abby to get on the bus and leave town.

Her battered suitcase and small basket sat beside her on the floor. She looked at the clock again, wishing Harry, the conductor with the blue name badge pinned to his shirtfront, would give them another update. If they couldn't get the bus working, she couldn't go back to the Fisher farm. She hated the thought of spending the night here and worried about what she would do.

Turning toward the door, she adjusted her black traveling bonnet and blinked. Jakob stood in the doorway, looking out of breath as he stared directly at her.

Through the wide windows, she saw Tommy standing with his head down, blowing hard, his reins tied to the bike stand out front.

"Oh, *ne*."

She buried her face in her hands, her cheeks burning as hot as kerosene. If only the bus hadn't broken down, she'd be long gone now. What could she do? She didn't want to face him. It was too humiliating. Too sad. Too…

Someone touched her hand. She looked up into Jakob's eyes. In a glance, she took in his dusty clothes, his slightly damp hair and sparkling dark eyes. For a moment, she thought she saw relief pass over his face, but she must have imagined it.

"Hallo," he said, but he didn't smile.

"Wh…what are you doing here?" She couldn't move. Couldn't breathe.

"I came to bring you home where you belong."

His words confused her. Why would he come after her if he didn't want her? He could just let her go, and no one would ever blame him for it.

"Folks," Harry called to get their attention. "I'm real sorry for the delay. We had an oil leak, but a new bus has just arrived. If you'll give us a few more minutes to fuel up, we'll be ready to leave soon. You can line up out front and we'll take your luggage now."

The passengers breathed a collective sigh of relief and started gathering up their things. A few more minutes and Abby would be on the bus, leaving behind her hopes and dreams of a happy life.

"I… I don't understand." No doubt he was feeling guilty, so he'd come after her. She didn't want to make it worse.

"I came for you. It's that simple." He sat beside her.

Feeling embarrassed, she stood and he did, too, following her every move.

"Jakob, you don't need to worry about me. I'll be fine, really. We aren't getting married, and that's that. There's no need to feel guilty about this."

"The only thing I feel guilty about is hurting you. But I didn't come here because of that. I came because I love you."

What? She shook her head, thinking she'd heard him wrong.

He held out his hands in a pleading gesture. "Just hear me out, Abby. Please."

She glanced toward the door, realizing she had only minutes before they would be boarding the bus. But she couldn't turn her back on him. Not now, not ever.

"When I learned you were gone, I couldn't stand to lose you. Last night, *Dawdi* Zeke helped me understand what I've been feeling. I've waited all day to tell you. That's why I planned a special buggy ride, so we could be alone. But then I got home and found out you had left."

"*Dawdi* Zeke?" She felt beyond confused. She hoped Zeke hadn't talked Jakob into marrying her.

Jakob quickly told her about Zeke's two wives. It was a touching story, but Abby didn't see how it could change anything between them.

"It wasn't until I spoke with him that I realized the truth. I love you, Abby. I always have. I just couldn't see it. My heart was too crowded by fear."

Oh, how she wanted to believe him, but she couldn't. Not without real proof. "Fear of what?"

He took a deep, settling breath, his expression serene and...happy. "I was afraid that if I let myself love again,

I might lose you one day and it would hurt too much. And then I realized I was losing you anyway. I could let you go and avoid the pain, but I also would never know the exquisite joy of loving you. And I couldn't live without that."

"Oh, Jakob. Please don't say such things." She shook her head, her eyes filling with tears.

"It's true, Abby. I really mean it. Love comes with risks. But then I remembered my faith. *Gott* knows we won't grow without opposition in our lives. He wants us to live by faith. And how can I do that if I never need Him?"

"But what about Susan? You still love her."

"*Ach*, I do. And I think you wouldn't want me if I didn't. But I remember overhearing you speaking to Reuben the day you found your notes in his drawer. You told him that love can grow inside of you without reaching capacity. That love is eternal. It has no end. It just goes on and on. And right now, it has encompassed my heart. I love you, *liebchen*. Please, say you'll be mine forever. Because I can't go home without you."

"*Ahem!* Excuse me, miss, but the bus is boarding now. If you're going to Ohio, you better come now." The conductor stood in the doorway, waving at Abby.

A look of pure panic filled Jakob's eyes and the color drained from his face. He glanced between the conductor and Abby, as though his whole world were caving in on him.

"Please, Abby. Don't go." His voice sounded hoarse with emotion as he took her hand in his, looking deep into her eyes. "I understand now why my *vadder* wrote to you. He knew I needed you to heal my shattered heart. The bus must have broken down for a reason…

to keep you here until I could arrive. *Gott's* hand is in this, I just know it. Stay and marry me. Please. Make me the happiest man in the world."

She hesitated, feeling torn. Wanting to believe him, but not quite daring to do so.

"If you go, I'll be forced to follow you to Ohio," he said.

She blinked in surprise. "You'd do that?"

He nodded. "I'll never give up until you accept my proposal. And believe me, you don't want me to meet up with Simon again. I believe in living a simple life without violence, but meeting with your *bruder* might push me to the breaking point. I won't allow him to hurt you again. And I mean it. I can't imagine living without you. I love you so much…"

"You'd really resort to violence if you saw Simon again?" She could hardly believe what he said. It was unthinkable, and yet the thought of Jakob defending her against her cruel brother touched her heart like nothing else could.

He looked down, his face flushed with shame. He nodded, staring at the floor. "*Ja*, I'm afraid so. *Gott* would be disappointed in me and I'd probably be shunned, but I'm afraid I might do Simon bodily harm if you go back to him. If my *familye* hadn't moved to Colorado when we were young, I would never have met Susan and would have married you years ago. I loved you even then, and I can't lose you again."

"Oh, Jakob!" Tears streamed from her eyes. She didn't even try to hold them back. "I… I love you, too. I have ever since I was a girl. That day you took the stick away from Simon and broke it over your knee, you were my knight in shining armor. I thought you were going to hit Simon, but you didn't. And in my eyes, you could do no wrong."

"Um, excuse me, but are you coming or not?" The conductor called to them again, sounding a bit irritated.

Jakob looked at her and waited, his face creased with hope and despair all at the same time. But she had to give him credit. He didn't answer for her. He waited, letting her decide for herself.

Abby shook her head, her heart near to bursting. "*Ne*, I'm not going. Would you be kind enough to reimburse my ticket instead?"

The conductor jerked his head toward the ticket office. "Sure. Just see Judith at the front counter and she'll help you with that."

Abby nodded and then she was in Jakob's arms. He held her close, gazing into her eyes with so much love and adoration that she wasn't sure she could contain it all. This was her dream come true. All she'd ever hoped for. To be wanted and needed.

To be loved.

"*Ach*, you've made me very happy. I love you so much," Jakob said.

"And I love you."

He kissed her and she was almost ashamed to admit that she didn't care who might see them. Almost. At this point in their relationship, she figured they'd both earned the right to a little show of romantic emotion.

When he released her, he smiled wide as he kept hold of her hand and picked up her suitcase and basket with his free hand. "Come on. Let's return your ticket, then stop off at Bishop Yoder's place on our way home. I want to receive his formal approval and let him know that we'll be holding a wedding at our place in the next couple of weeks."

"But that won't be enough time to invite Simon."

"*Gut.* I think it's best if he's not here. I don't want to give him the opportunity to interfere in any way."

Neither did she. "Do you think Bishop Yoder will agree to our marriage so soon?"

He nodded. "I do. He understands what is at stake. I believe he'll agree."

She smiled, unable to hide the exquisite joy radiating from her heart. "*Ach,* Naomi may not like it. We're not giving her much notice to plan the feast."

As they walked toward the ticket counter, he shrugged his unbelievably wide shoulders. "Don't you worry. She will be thrilled. And we'll help her."

"I doubt Simon will like it very much when the bishop writes to tell him that we have been married."

"I don't care what Simon doesn't like. He isn't a part of our lives anymore."

Yes, finally. Finally, she was well and truly free of her brother's abuse. Knowing Jakob was absolutely right, she didn't argue one bit. She waited patiently as he redeemed her ticket, then took her outside. He tied her suitcase and basket to the back of the horse, then helped her climb up behind him on the saddle.

As they rode down Main Street and headed out of town, she wondered what Bishop Yoder would say when he saw them riding together like this.

Wrapping her arms around Jakob, she spoke against the back of his neck. "It's not very modest of me to ride astride behind a man who isn't my husband."

He patted her arms, which were crossed in front of him. "I'm your betrothed now, which is almost as *gut* as being your husband. Before anyone can chastise us, we will be married. And Bishop Yoder will be too delighted by the news of our wedding to question our method of travel today. Especially when I explain the urgent reason why it couldn't be helped. When I'm old and gray, I'll tell our *kinder* that you were my runaway bride."

She snorted. "You make it sound so dramatic."

"It was, until I found you at the train station. I almost lost you. And now, I'll never let you go."

Accepting his word on the topic, Abby laid her cheek against his back and squeezed him tighter. It would do no good to argue the point, especially when she knew he was right. She'd achieved her fondest dream. She had Jakob's love. At that moment, nothing else mattered in the world except the two of them. The good Lord had brought them through. He'd brought them together. And that was all they needed.

* * * * *

AMISH COUNTRY AMNESIA

Meghan Carver

To readers of Amish fiction
and stories that explore the miracle of faith,
and to readers of suspense and stories that
keep you up at night with a chill up your spine.
I pray you find this a compelling blend of both.

So teach us to number our days,
that we may apply our hearts unto wisdom.
—*Psalms* 90:12

Chapter One

Jedediah Miller jerked to the left on the snowmobile, barely skittering it around a stand of barren trees and praying for a fork in the trail up ahead. His hands slipped inside his gloves, and he hitched up his grip on the handlebars. Those two men were following too closely for safety or common courtesy.

On the other side of the trees, his two pursuers edged closer. Jed's heart thumped stronger under his snowmobile suit, and he leaned into the machine, urging it to go faster. A small hill quickly approached, and he flew over it, the skis losing contact with the ground for a moment. As he crashed back down, adrenaline beat through him, his pulse speeding to the thrum of the snowmobile.

The rev of the snowmobiles behind him pushed him on, to a speed that he was sure was not intended for the trail. A speed he wasn't sure he could manage much longer. These guys drove like professionals, but he was only a casual snowmobiler, saving it for his time off. Trees zipped past him on both sides, and he would have admired the quiet stillness, the hushed beauty of a winter in northern Indiana, the gentle snow-covered hills and the barren trees reaching for every bit of sunshine possible in the muted sky, if not for the two jackals behind him and their mad race.

A *crack* pierced through his concentration, and by instinct, he ducked down on the seat.

They were shooting at him now.

Bark flew off a tree as he whizzed past, a few bits bouncing off his windshield. Apparently, these two weren't good shots, at least when they were going at an outrageous speed on snowmobiles. Judging from the closeness of that tree trunk, though, Jed was sure they could hit their mark when they were at a standstill. Determination to survive drove him on.

He ventured a quick look behind him. Was it Jimmy the Bruise on one of the snowmobiles? His two pursuers were wearing all the protective gear, including helmets and tinted goggles and snowmobile suits completely zipped up. Not an inch of skin or anything identifying was showing, not even Jimmy's telltale purple-and-blue birthmark. All of their gear was black, as well, a rather standard color for snowmobilers. That bit of information wouldn't help at all.

A shiver ran down his arms at the thought of the man at the head of the counterfeiting ring. A nasty birthmark wound its way around the man's neck and down his arm. Being on the police force had brought Jed into contact with a lot of different people, but there was no getting used to a guy who looked like that. No matter how long he lived, Jed would never forget the look of that dark splotch that appeared to hold the man's throat in a vice grip.

Jed had seen that mark plenty of times in the past

twelve months of undercover work that had taken him from Fort Wayne to Indianapolis to Cincinnati and back to Fort Wayne. It had been a harrowing experience that still haunted his dreams, both in the daytime and at night, but it was going to pay off. In just a few weeks, his testimony in court would put the counterfeiters behind bars, at least most of them. Jimmy the Bruise and another had gone missing, escaped from police custody.

A third shot pinged off the back of his snowmobile. The case would fall apart without Jed's testimony. If they could kill him, the counterfeiting ring would get off easy and be back in business within months. Only Jed could put them away for good.

It was time to lose these two yahoos. Without backup available, he couldn't apprehend them. He wanted to kick himself for forgetting his phone that morning. But at least he could try to save himself and the valuable testimony he possessed. Then he would call for a search of the area. There were only so many places to hide in and around the heavily Amish community of Nappanee, and he couldn't imagine that any Amish would shelter two people as prone to violence as these were. Jed tossed up a prayer for the safety of any of the peace-loving Amish who might come into contact with these two thugs.

He inhaled as deeply as he could with the restrictions of his helmet. Fresh oxygen infused him as he leaned his body weight forward on the snowmobile to increase the speed. What was supposed to have been a restful week off in the stillness of northern Indiana had suddenly morphed into a deadly chase. Jed allowed a brief thought of what his life might be like without the danger or violence of being a police officer, but the snowmobile shot up another ridge and brought him back to the present.

A small pocket of evergreens stood ahead, to the side of the trail. At the last moment, just at the edge of the grove, he leaned left and gripped the handlebars, shooting behind the trees and off the trail. The snow wasn't as packed here, but he increased the throttle, urging the machine to go faster. He wound through the trees, dodging boulders, but the two men continued behind him. At least the shooting had stopped, but that was probably just because they needed both hands on the handlebars to stay in a forward motion.

He searched his memories of the area frantically. Where could he hide? It had been years since he'd been here. And he was limited in where he could go because of the snowmobile. Plowed roads were definitely not conducive to a vehicle that ran on skis. So, he couldn't lead them to a sheriff's office, and he certainly didn't want to take that violence where there might be people.

A small stream burbled to his right, large rocks and snow-covered foliage on either side, and he leaned left to steer the snowmobile away from the water. Even though the sound of their engines told him they were fast approaching, he dared another glance back. They were too close. Much too close for safety.

He faced forward again as the machine arced to the left. A tree rushed up in front of him, and he jerked the snowmobile to the right. But another tree rose up in that direction. He pushed his body to the side to steer the machine away, but it was too late. The fiberglass front of the snowmobile crumpled into the solid trunk of the tree, killing the engine. Jed couldn't control his body, and like a rag doll, he pitched forward. His helmet hit the windshield, and his head slammed against the inside of the helmet.

Pain shot through his frontal lobe. Lightning seemed to flash behind his eyes. Lifted from the seat by the impact, he soared forward and to the right. The limbs of the tree and the snow-covered underbrush flew by. He landed in the bushes on his back, snow falling on him and brambles tearing at his nylon suit. Pain coursed through his body as he rolled over just in time to see his snowmobile burst into flames.

He jerked off his goggles and helmet and gasped for air as the cold bit at his skin. Despite the snow that had fallen on him, he was still exposed in his gray snowmobiling suit. Surreptitiously, moving only his eyes, he looked toward the boulders at the edge of the stream. He would be better camouflaged among those rocks.

His two pursuers had finally stopped, but just a few yards from his wreck. Jed couldn't see their eyes through their goggles, but from the tilt of their helmets, he surmised they were watching the fire.

In an army crawl, lifted up only on his elbows, Jed inched toward the rocks around the stream. Aches ricocheted through every inch of his body. The closest boulder seemed miles away, moving at that speed, but it was his only hope.

Suddenly, one of the men turned, appearing to survey the area. Jed buried his face in the snow and froze. There was something about a face and, in particular, eyes that always seemed to draw attention, and Jed determined that he would not be found out simply because he couldn't look away. He waited for what seemed like an eternity, praying for safety and courage and survival, his muscles taut. When nothing happened, he slowly lifted his head, just enough to be able to scan the area.

The men still sat on their snowmobiles, watching as Jed's machine burned. If there was anything Jed had learned in twelve months of undercover work, it was patience. He could wait there, lying in the snow, as long as necessary.

After a few minutes, the men turned around to look behind them. Jed grabbed his opportunity.

Still lying nearly prostrate, he scuttled toward the rocks and catapulted himself over the closest grouping of boulders. He landed on his back on an unyielding surface, and a sharp rock caught the side of his head on the way down. A fire of pain shot through his skull, and he reached up a hand to touch a warm, sticky spot. The sky swirled and danced unnaturally above him until all went black.

Sarah Burkholder stood at the kitchen sink, her hands immersed in the warm soapy water, and stared out the window at the snow-covered barn. An apple pie rested on the counter, its aroma of cinnamon and nutmeg filling the roomy kitchen. The pie would be a welcome addition to supper.

The mechanical whine of a snowmobile had not been far off that afternoon, the noise an unwelcome intrusion into her normally peaceful world. Her home was miles from the snowmobile trail through the state park, but it sounded as if a rider had left the beaten path. She would be glad when he stopped his racing and returned to the park.

An envelope propped on the windowsill drew her attention. Her mother's careful handwriting scrawled

Sarah's name and address across the front. Sarah had read it so many times that she almost had it memorized. In no uncertain terms, her mother had urged her to return to live with them in Lancaster County. She had written that they could sell at the market together, and Sarah would be supported and encouraged by the love of her family. Her real point in writing, it seemed, was to tell her of one particular widower who had been asking after her.

Sarah rubbed the back of her hand across her chin. She remembered the man her mother had mentioned in her letter. He was nice-looking enough, and kind. But there never had been a spark between them. Still though, would it be better than being alone? Did *Gott* only grant one love in a lifetime?

The fresh dilemma swirled in her mind. Should she continue to teach school in the Indiana Amish community she had grown to love? Or should she return to Lancaster County, to Pennsylvania and the family she had left behind? A tear escaped and trickled down her cheek at the memory of her husband. Life had changed drastically in that one terrible moment, and not for the better.

Even though she had committed to teaching for the entire school year and did not need to decide for a while, she promised herself she would pray during the winter break and seek the will of *Gott* for her future.

She dried her hands on a nearby towel and then dabbed the corner of her apron to her eyes.

How could it have been *Gott*'s will that her husband die in that buggy accident? That was best for her? For their daughter, Lyddie?

Ach. That was not the Amish way, to question the authority of *Gott*. Another tear overflowed, and she lifted the apron again. *Father, if Thou be willing, remove this cup from me. Nevertheless, not my will, but Thine, be done.* At least she had Lyddie, the joy of her life, although the poor child was growing up without her *daed* and at only six years old.

Where was Lyddie anyway? She had been instructed to stay close to the house and barn today.

Sarah retrieved her heavy winter cape and bonnet from the hook near the door and stepped out onto the back porch. The noise of other snowmobiles was a little louder outside, but then they moved away. She inhaled deeply, the winter air slicing through her lungs, and savored the return of the stillness.

But she still needed to find Lyddie. With snowmobiles around, the child ought to stay closer to home. Most of their *Englisch* neighbors were mindful of those in the Amish community, but Lyddie still had chores to complete, as well. The floor needed to be swept and the eggs gathered.

She walked to the end of the porch, her gaze sweeping from the barn to the tree line. "Lyddie!" But there was no telling if she was in earshot.

Sarah stepped back inside and changed quickly into her heavy snow boots. She would have to go searching on foot.

As Sarah pulled the door closed behind her, the child broke from the trees, followed closely by Snowball, their brown-and-white malamute. A look of alarm held fast on her face as she ran as best she could through the snow, a few blond curls that had struggled free from her *kapp* flying behind her. "*Mamm*! A man. An *Englischer*! He is hurt. He has been attacked." Lyddie gasped for breath as she skidded to a stop in front of her mother. The dog barked as if to urge Sarah to help, then turned and faced back toward the woods.

Sarah's hand flew to cover her mouth and then migrated south to cover her heart as if it could still the wild beat at Lyddie's news. An attack? She prayed the child was mistaken.

Lyddie pulled at her mother's hand. "*Mamm*. We must help the man."

"*Jah*. We must." She paused. "In case it is needed, hitch the sled to Snowball."

Lyddie ran to the barn to retrieve the sled she had rigged to hitch to the large snow dog. Sarah stepped back inside to grab a quilt, and when she returned to the porch, daughter and dog were ready to go. With no idea what she might find, she at least wanted another way to supply warmth.

Sarah pulled her cape about her and stepped out to follow her daughter. "Show me where he is."

She followed as Lyddie led Snowball and retraced her tracks in the snow, babbling like the brook in springtime about hiding in the trees as the snowmobiles came closer and watching two snowmobiles chase another snowmobile and the man who then did not move. The dog bounded alongside, strangely quiet, as if she knew her barking could draw unwanted attention. After hiking for several minutes, Sarah felt the acrid odor of smoke fill her nostrils.

She pushed Lyddie faster, clumping behind in her snow boots, as they followed the sight of a thin plume of gray smoke rising from over another hill. *Gott, have mercy.*

They crested the hill, and Lyddie led her through some trees and into a tiny clearing next to the creek.

Sarah knew it well. Some wild raspberry bushes grew not far away where they would pick berries in the heat come August. But now, everything was covered with the white blanket of winter even as more snow fell.

At the site, Sarah gasped. *How could anyone have survived that?* A red-and-black snowmobile had crashed into a tree, and flames rose from its crumpled form. She rushed forward, the heat warming her face. Instinctively, she held out an arm to hold Lyddie back from the fire.

She turned toward her daughter, not taking her eyes from the wreckage. "Lyddie, where is the *Englischer*? Show me."

The girl moved past Sarah's arm and skirted around the flames. She held out a hand to Snowball and he sat, then she headed for some boulders at the edge of the creek bed. "Here. He has not moved."

Sarah surveyed the area. With what Lyddie had said about the man being attacked, she didn't want to risk any danger on their part. But all seemed still and silent there in the woods.

On the other side of the boulders, a man in a gray snowmobile suit lay with a fine layer of snow on him. A gash on the side of his head trickled a bright red flow of blood. A little bit of blood had dripped onto his shoulder and the rock where he had apparently hit his head. His snowmobile suit was torn in a couple of places, but other than that, he appeared well. His eyes were closed as if in sleep, but Sarah flew to his side. She kneeled on the snow next to him and pulled down the collar of his protective jacket to feel for a pulse. His heartbeat was strong. She released a breath she hadn't been aware she was holding. The man was still alive. She lowered her head and turned to listen for his breath. It was even and steady. She then gently felt every bone, but each felt solid and unharmed.

So far, everything had checked normal, but he still had not reacted to her touch.

She prodded his shoulder, lifted his hand, rolled his ankle. "Hello? Can you hear me? Can you wake up?"

He remained unresponsive.

A chill shook through her. Whether it was fear or the cold did not matter. She needed to be careful of her surroundings, for her sake, for the sake of her daughter and for the sake of this unknown man. But she also needed to get him to warmth and shelter to treat his wounds.

She shook her head, a desperate attempt to understand human beings. What kind of person would allow an injured man to lie in the snow and not care for him? Obviously, not a good one. Lyddie had said that there were two on snowmobiles chasing the man. She had even mentioned a gun in the hand of one of the pursuers. Had they hoped to kill him? Thought he was dead?

Sarah stood and looked back to the site of the accident and what was left of the tracks in the snow. Thankfully, all remained quiet. But what if the attackers returned? Lyddie had said they had driven off and out of sight. But if they were evil enough to leave a hurt man here, a man who appeared to be dead, what would they do to an innocent Amish woman and her daughter? There were no other footprints besides their own and a couple of sets of prints near where the snowmobiles had stopped. It seemed as if they had dismounted but then left again. There were also no other snowmobile tracks, but the falling snow was quickly filling in everything. Soon, there would be no visible signs of any human presence left.

The best thing to do would be to get the man to the house immediately. To safety. A neighbor had a telephone in his barn for business, but the neighbor was farther from here than the distance to her own home. If his pursuers did return, Sarah did not want to be there, exposed, nor did she want the injured man to be, whoever he was.

"Lyddie." Sarah kept her voice to a loud whisper. "Bring the sled. There." She pointed to a path around the rocks.

As the dog brought the sled, Sarah leaned down to the man. "My name is Sarah, and my daughter, Lyddie, is here." Could he hear her? She had no way to know, but she needed to try. "You are injured, and I am taking you to my house. We will load you on the sled."

Lyddie led Snowball to pull the sled until it sat alongside the man. Squatting down, Sarah put her arms under the man's shoulders and instructed Lyddie to get him by the ankles. "We will move you now," she said to the man, then nodded to Lyddie, and together they swung him onto the sled, then tucked the quilt about him.

The man moved his head from one side to the other, a low groan issuing from his lips, but his eyes did not open.

With Lyddie's encouragement, the dog strained against the harness to haul the sled. Sarah grabbed the handle and helped to pull through the snow, as well. As the hum of snowmobiles sounded again in the distance, Sarah urged the dog to haul faster. Safety behind her locked doors was close, and her hands perspired within her gloves at the thought of being out in the woods if those men returned.

The man continued a low groan off and on through most of the walk back to the house. At the back door, Sarah released Snowball and rubbed her ears, conveying her gratitude for the dog's help. The stranger had moved in the sled, so Sarah leaned down and shook his shoulder again. "Can you hear me? We are home, and I need you to stand and walk inside. Can you get up?"

When he didn't stand, Sarah grasped one arm and put Lyddie on the other. Together, they pulled him to a sitting position. That movement seemed to awaken something inside him, for he stood, leaning heavily on them. With his eyes mostly closed, he staggered into the house as Sarah guided him into the downstairs guest bedroom. He was not overly tall, but his solid form filled out his snowmobile suit, and Sarah knew she would never be able to get him up the stairs.

As he lay down on the quilt, his head thrashed and his eyelids fluttered as if with some internal struggle. His eyes opened suddenly, and she gasped to look into such vivid green eyes. He startled, grabbing toward his hip as if reaching for something, a harsh and intense look on his face.

She jumped back, clutching her skirt.

Perhaps he was the dangerous one after all?

Chapter Two

An eerie quiet filtered through his mind, a stillness that felt foreign and uncomfortable. With what felt like great effort, he opened his eyes only to find more darkness, softened slightly by moonlight coming through a window. Before he could form a coherent thought or try to lift his head, the darkness consumed him again.

His next sensation was a sharpness in his temple. Without even opening his eyes, he knew it was daylight. He released his eyelids to a slit. Bright sunshine streamed through windows on either side of the bed.

He lifted a hand to his forehead, trying to locate the source of the stabbing pain. His hand came into contact with what felt like a bandage, but the hurt seemed to come from all over his head. Just the act of moving his arm made him aware of an aching soreness that consumed his entire body. Shading his eyes, he opened them further.

The walls around him were a stark white. Light blue curtains hung at the windows, but they were thin enough that they did not block the light very much. He was in a bed, covered with a colorful quilt, a wood armoire standing against the wall across from him. Near the door, a young girl with a blue dress and white cap on her head sat in a straight-backed chair, reading a book. She must have noticed his movement, for she looked up and their stares locked. Her mouth formed a perfect O of surprise, and she dashed from the room.

Before he could try to sit up, the girl returned with a young woman who wore a similar dress and cap.

The woman pressed her lips together as if concerned, and tiny crinkling lines formed around her eyes. But her gaze radiated warmth and care. "How are you?" Her voice was quiet and calming.

She pulled the chair up to the bedside and sat, her hands clasped in her lap. Her face seemed to be completely devoid of makeup, and yet a beauty radiated from her that he hadn't seen in… Well, he couldn't remember when.

He cleared his throat, trying to summon his voice. His mind was a complete blank, yet a sense of discomfort, danger even, seemed to hover over him. How was he? "I'm… I'm sore."

"I am glad to see you are awake. I bandaged the cut on your forehead last night." She fluttered her hand up to the side of his head. "May I check it?"

He nodded. She peeled back part of the bandage, her touch a whisper against his skin. "It has stopped bleeding. That is *gut*." She stood and stepped to the window, lifting the curtain to look out. She stood there a moment, surveying, a frown creasing her brow. But as she returned to the chair, she seemed to force a small smile. "Now. Introductions. I am Sarah Burkholder. This is my house. And this," she motioned the girl forward, "is my daughter, Lyddie."

She looked at him, expectation etched around her eyes and mouth.

But his mind was blank, a black hole of nothingness. He closed his eyes to block out any distractions, including the woman's pretty face and the sweetness of the little girl, and searched for any information about who he was. What was his name? What was his job? What had happened yesterday that landed him here in this home? And why did he have such a pervasive feeling of danger?

He had no idea.

He opened his eyes to find the woman still watching him, waiting for an answer. "I don't know."

Confusion flitted across her face. "You do not know your own name?"

He thought again. "No."

"Where do you live?"

Again, he searched and came up blank. "I don't know. Here? With you?"

"No. Not here." She giggled, a musical sound that calmed him. "What is your job?"

"I don't know. What can you tell me about yourself? Where is your husband? Where are we? How did you get me here?"

She held out a hand. "In good time. First, I will send Lyddie to fetch the doctor."

At a nod from her mother, the girl ran out of the room. A few moments later, an exterior door slammed.

The woman settled herself again on the chair. "My husband was killed two years ago when a car hit his buggy. We are near Nappanee in Indiana, in the home my husband built when we moved here. We are Amish."

She gestured to her dark blue dress, her white apron, her starched *kapp*.

"Yes." Somehow, he knew the word *Amish* and had a vague inkling of what it meant. That's why the girl went running for the doctor. There would be no telephone in the house.

"Lyddie and I brought you here on a sled pulled by our malamute, Snowball. I did not see it, but she told me that you were chased by two men on snowmobiles. You crashed into a tree. I think you hit your head on a rock by the creek."

"What about the two men?"

"They left you. They must have thought you were dead." She paused, clearly thinking through her next words. When she spoke again, it was haltingly. "I do not like to bother the sheriff. He is…not friendly to me. To our way of life. But I will contact him if you wish."

"No!" He struggled to sit up in bed, ache consuming his body. Where did that vehemence come from? A dark foreboding invaded his mind when he thought of law enforcement, and he clutched his head in an effort to calm himself. "I… I can't explain it. I don't know why. But no, don't bring the police into this. Not yet." Maybe if his memories returned and he could figure out who he was and what sort of situation he was in, then he could involve law enforcement. "I wouldn't know what to tell them anyway."

She laid a hand on the quilt as if to calm him. "I will respect your wishes. But you need a name. Are you sure you cannot remember your own?"

"My head aches so terribly that it hurts to try to remember anything."

"May I call you John?" She tilted her head, and one

side of her mouth quirked up. "John is a good Bible name meaning *Yahweh is gracious*. Would you not agree that the Lord has been gracious to you, saving you from worse harm?"

Something pinged in his brain. "Yes, the Lord has been gracious."

"You are a religious man? You believe?"

A comfortable warmth filled him as she asked the questions. "I don't know for sure, but I think I do."

"That is *gut*. But also, you are a *John Doe*. Is that not what the *Englisch* call a person with no name?"

"How do you know that?" This beautiful Amish woman whose presence soothed him was certainly a mystery.

She ducked her head, the top of her *kapp* catching the sunlight. "I love to read."

As if to change the subject, she stood and crossed the room to the armoire, pulling out an Amish-looking pair of trousers and shirt as well as a pair of suspenders. "Your clothes need to be laundered. You may put these on for the time being. They belong to my brother, but he left them here after his last visit."

A whistle sounded from another room, and she laid the clothes at the foot of the bed.

"That is the kettle. I will bring you some herbal tea. Chamomile. It will help relieve your headache and your muscle soreness. Do you like tea?" She stood and moved to the door.

Did he like tea? He had no idea, but the lovely Sarah was so kind and so accommodating that he would drink just about anything she could bring him. A nod would have to suffice to show his agreement, as a spasm of pain shot through his head.

Why couldn't he remember anything? Who was he? Why was he there, in the Amish countryside, and who were the two men from yesterday? A blankness settled over him, but it was cloaked in darkness as the overwhelming sensation of danger returned, and he feared not only for his future but also for the future of the beautiful widow who sheltered him.

Sarah dropped the bag of tea leaves into the cup and slowly poured the boiling water over it. She inhaled deeply of the soothing scent, in need of some calming herself after the events of the prior twenty-four hours.

A shiver threatened her, and she returned the kettle to the propane-powered stove top before she stepped to the window to survey the yard again. Her sleep had been fitful the night before, her dreams filled with burning snowmobiles and strange men come to harm her and her daughter.

Who was this man in her spare bedroom, and what sort of danger had he brought to her peaceful household?

For what must have been at least the tenth time, she mentally retraced the events of yesterday. It certainly had looked from the snowmobile tracks like this man in her house was the one being chased. But did it follow, then, that he was innocent? Good? She had no way of knowing, and it seemed, neither did he. Did it matter? She had a Christian obligation to help those in need.

As she watched, the doctor's car pulled into her drive. Lyddie flew out of the passenger side and toward the kitchen door. *Ach*, the child would be so excited about a ride in the car she would chatter of nothing else for days. The tall, thin Dr. Jones unfolded himself from the driver's seat, retrieved his black bag from the back seat and approached the door as Lyddie waited for him. The hair around his temples sported more gray than the last time Sarah had seen him, and a pair of glasses perched on his pointed nose.

He stepped inside the back room, and Sarah rushed to hang up his coat. "Dr. Jones, *danki* for coming."

"Hello, Sarah. I'm always glad to visit my Amish friends and keep up the traditions of my father. Family and community are important to some of us Englishers, as well." A teasing twinkle sparkled in his eye. He looked pointedly at the remains of the apple pie on the stove top.

"Would you like a piece of pie before you go? I would not want you to leave hungry." The banter was as old a tradition as the house calls, but Sarah relished her friendship with the doctor.

"If you insist." He smiled with warmth and touched her shoulder before he turned toward the downstairs bedroom. "Now, Lyddie tells me you have a man in there who was in a snowmobiling accident yesterday?"

Sarah filled him in on the details she knew, few as they were, including the man's apparent amnesia, as she led him into the room and pointed him to the chair at the bedside. John had changed into the Amish clothing, creating quite a change in his appearance, and was resting on top of the quilt.

"Dr. Jones, this is John. At least, he has agreed to be called by that name. I gave him my brother's clothes to put on." She turned to the patient. "John, this is Dr. Jones."

John attempted a smile, although it looked painful, and shook hands with the doctor. "You make house calls? I didn't know anyone did that anymore."

Dr. Jones laid his black bag on the bed next to John and opened it. "My father made house calls, so I choose to continue that practice, at least with the Amish. They have a bit more difficulty in getting to the office than other folks. And there's never a poor return on being neighborly."

As the doctor retrieved his stethoscope from his bag and instructed John to unbutton his shirt, Sarah stepped out to finish making the tea and shooed Lyddie upstairs to her room to work on her stitching. She took as long as she could and then grasped the tray and stepped toward the door. "May I come in?"

"Yes, that's fine."

She entered the room to find the doctor slowly moving an instrument back and forth in front of John. He followed it with his eyes but without moving his head. But when he spotted her, her breath hitched as his green eyes smiled at her.

The doctor placed the instrument back in his bag and snapped it shut. He stood and moved back to allow Sarah to place the tray on the bedside table. "Your patient seems quite well, Sarah. You bandaged that nasty cut on his head quite admirably, and it should heal nicely. Apart from that, a little soreness and his memory loss, I would say he is in fine shape. I don't see any problems."

"That is *gut*."

He held up his hands in caution. "However, my ability to examine him is limited here. I would suggest that as soon as he feels able, he get to the hospital for an MRI and a thorough examination." He pulled a small bottle from his bag and placed it on the table. "Here is some acetaminophen, in case your chamomile tea doesn't relieve the pain like he wants. However," the doctor turned to John, "you should take it only as a last resort. Allergies to acetaminophen are rare, but because you can't remember your medical history or what medicine you might be allergic to, we don't know how this might affect you."

"What about my memory, Doctor?"

"Well, amnesia is a tricky thing, and we medical professionals still don't know much about it. Your memory will most likely return in time. How long I cannot say."

John shook the doctor's hand and thanked him for coming, then accepted the cup of tea from Sarah.

Dr. Jones looked at Sarah and nodded toward the kitchen, and she stepped in front to lead him there. As she approached the pie, he laid a hand on her arm. "Can you wrap it to go, please? I have an appointment and can't stay."

"*Jah*, if you wish."

As she packaged two slices of the apple pie, he stood close enough that he could keep his voice low. "I admire you for taking this stranger in and caring for him. But I want to warn you, as well. I know you have, at least, a rifle for hunting. You should keep that close for protection for you and Lyddie. Just in case. If you don't need protection from this stranger, then you might need protection from whoever caused the accident yesterday."

She handed the pie to him. "*Danki*, doctor, but you know that is not the Amish way. I will trust *Gott* for His protection and His guidance."

Dr. Jones grasped his bag in one hand and the pie in the other, and Sarah moved to open the door for him. "I knew that would be your answer, but I felt the need to say it." He paused, then looked her in the eye. "One more thing. I think I see a bit of resemblance between John and Mary Miller. There's something about his eyes that makes me think of her."

"*Mammi* Mary? The widow who lives over on Wood-bridge Road?"

"Yes, but maybe it's nothing." He stepped outside. "I'll pray for you and for the stranger, and don't hesitate to contact me if you need help."

Sarah closed the door gently behind him and then turned the lock until it thudded into place. The rifle? It still rested in its place on top of the cabinets. She kept it cleaned and in good working order, but it had not been used since before her husband was killed.

No, there it would stay. She would trust *Gott* and His protection.

But a wiggle of worry wormed itself down her back. Who was this strange man? Had he brought danger with him? Had she willingly brought into her house a wolf that she had dressed in Amish clothing?

Chapter Three

John helped as best he could in cleaning up their simple breakfast of sticky rolls and scrambled eggs, but his skills were so lacking that he figured he hadn't done much kitchen work before. His shoulders sagged at the thought of how long it might take to regain his memory.

Sarah was jittery as she quickly washed the dishes and laid them out on a towel to dry. Between keeping an eye on him and jumping up to look out the window, she barely sat for the meal. He hoped his presence wasn't too upsetting to her, but how could it not be? She didn't know him, and yet here he sat, completely dependent upon her goodness. What kind of man was he? Could he be trusted? Was he honorable? Neither of them knew.

As she laid the last glass on the drying towel, he ventured a suggestion. "I think we need to head back to the scene of the accident. Or was it an attack? It's frustrating not even to know what happened yesterday." He rubbed a hand over the knot in the back of his neck and took a deep breath. "If I could just remember—something, anything—I might know what to do next. But there could be something at the site to help me remember. Fill in some of the emptiness. It's a good time to look because of the bright sunshine. If there's any clue there, we should be able to find it."

Lyddie ran for her heavy cape. "*Mamm*, may I take Snowball and the sled?"

Sarah turned from the sink to her daughter, her eyes wide. "It has not yet been decided." She set her worried look on John. "Do you think it is safe?"

What *did* he think? With this amnesia, his mind felt like it couldn't think, or at least it was difficult to think. "You said there was no one there when you found me. And obviously, no one has found us here. To be completely honest, I don't know. But it seems that it should be, and I don't have any other ideas for how to figure out who I am or where I'm supposed to be. I think this is my only chance."

"*Jah*. I think you are right." She hung up the towel and headed for the stairs. "I will put on an extra pair of leggings for warmth, and we shall go. Lyddie, same for you. And we will take Snowball but not the sled. John, what do you think?"

"Yes, the sled could get in the way, but the dog could be helpful in staying alert."

A few minutes later, John had bundled on a heavy wool coat and hat that Sarah had in the barn, and they set off toward the site of his snowmobile crash. The sunshine made the snow sparkle, but it did not add any warmth to the day, and he pulled the coat closer around him. Snowball frisked about, her white tail curled up over her back. John had no doubt that the dog would sniff out danger before he saw it. But John still couldn't help constantly scanning their surroundings for anything remotely suspicious.

As he crested the top of the ridge, John got his first good look at the snowmobile. But all that remained were charred parts and crumpled fiberglass. A whisper of smoke half-heartedly rose from the wreckage, but it was not enough to mark their location to anyone nearby. He held out an arm to stop Sarah and Lyddie. He listened for a full minute, but the only sound close by was the panting of the malamute.

He skidded down the slope and stopped next to the debris. Would it summon up any memories? The vinyl seat remained intact, and he tried to picture himself sitting on it, his hands on the handlebars. His snowmobile suit was gray. He knew that because he had seen it. But nothing dislodged any memories.

"Spread out a bit," he instructed Sarah and Lyddie. "Look for anything that might be the least bit helpful."

Sarah circled around the creek bed, where she had found him the day before, her head bent to the task. Lyddie followed behind her mother, overturning a few rocks. She wandered toward the woods, picking up sticks and throwing them into the trees, and then returned toward John. Her full blue skirt swished against her black snow boots, and snow that had fallen from the trees rested on her shoulders and *kapp*. Snowball followed her faithfully, sniffing in her footsteps.

The child was adorable, but John forced himself to return his gaze to the remains of the accident site.

"Look! I found something!" Lyddie's squeal of delight drew him quickly to her side. She bent to the ground and retrieved from the snow a piece of metal that reflected the bright sunshine.

The snow quickly brushed off of the edges, and she handed it to John. "What is it? What does it say?"

Sarah appeared at his side, her breath puffing in small clouds. "It is the badge of a police officer."

"Fort Wayne Police Department," John read. "Is that far from here?"

"It is over an hour by car." She shrugged. "We pay a driver and go to shop sometimes. Is this yours?"

"I don't know. It could be mine. Or it could belong to one of the men who Lyddie says attacked me. Let's keep looking. Maybe there's some identification."

As Sarah and Lyddie pushed snow away from the debris, questions pinged in John's mind. Could the badge be his, thrown off him in the wreck? What about a weapon? Was he a police officer?

Ten minutes of thorough searching yielded nothing more.

John examined the badge in his hand, trying to force himself to remember. "So, I could be a police officer. Or maybe I'm not. There's no way to know if this badge belongs to me because there's no name on it, just a number, and I don't remember any numbers. I suppose it could have been thrown off me in the wreck, but if I am a law-enforcement officer, then where is my weapon?" He pulled off a glove and rubbed his temple. A dull throb began to echo through his head. *Or am I the criminal the police were chasing?*

"This does not help with any memories?" Sarah gazed at him with eyes crinkled and warm with tenderness and compassion.

Before he could answer, Snowball perked up her ears and uttered a low growl.

Lyddie dropped to the snow next to her, a mittened hand on her back. "What is it, Snowball?"

"Shh." John held out his hand to silence them. He

listened intently, straining against the growing thrum of the headache. A machine was approaching. A snowmobile?

"Could it be someone to help?" Sarah kept her voice to a whisper.

John shook his head. "No way to know. But we need to get out of here. I can't explain why, but I don't want us here when the snowmobile arrives." He nodded toward the woods. "Into the trees. Quickly."

He grasped Sarah's hand to lead her, and he was instantly warmed by her touch. Sarah threw him a startled look but did not draw away. She urged Lyddie toward the woods and called for Snowball to follow.

Several feet into the tree line, John made sure Sarah was tucked behind a large cottonwood. He looked back toward the clearing just in time to see a snowmobile emerge from the far side. A glance back to Sarah revealed that she had grabbed hold of Snowball's collar. Lyddie stood on the other side of the dog, her hand resting on the dog's head as if to keep her calm.

It would have to do for now. Their movement through the trees, to head for Sarah's house, would only draw attention to them. And since they could never outrun a snowmobile, it was best to hide.

John crouched behind another tree and turned his attention to the approaching snowmobile.

The driver pulled up to within a few feet of the crash debris. He killed the engine and then dismounted. He wore a typical snowmobile suit, black with white trim, and he appeared to be a thick man underneath. But since the man wore a helmet and goggles, John could not tell anything more about him.

The man surveyed the accident site, then picked up

a stick and poked at the debris. When he seemed satisfied, he dropped the stick and slowly scanned the surrounding area.

Snowball continued to pant, although the sound was so quiet that John had to strain to hear it. Lyddie put her hand over her mouth and clamped it shut. John wanted to tell her that the dog would not take kindly to that, but he didn't dare whisper or leave his hiding place. The dog pulled her head away, a low whine issuing forth as she shook her muzzle free.

John dared a peek around his tree. The man had taken a couple of steps in their direction. He had removed his gloves and tucked them in a cargo pocket and was working on his goggles and helmet. John's gut clenched at the possibility of being discovered, but all he could do was wait.

With his head cocked, the snowmobile driver stared at the trees, a look of deep concentration on his face as if he were listening. Had he heard Snowball whine? It could have sounded like a wild animal, and yet there weren't many animals out in the winter. John turned back to Sarah and Lyddie just in time to see Sarah move to correct the girl, probably for holding the dog's mouth shut.

As she reached out a hand, Sarah seemed to lose her balance, and she wobbled out from her hiding place.

Helpless where he was, John watched the man's stare zero in on Sarah as she leaned out. She immediately grasped the trunk of the tree and pulled herself behind it, but not before a loud inhalation escaped.

John's heart beat wildly against his rib cage, and he swallowed down bile as his stomach churned at the look of evil on the man's face.

* * *

Sarah's gasp seemed to echo through the empty woods. She shot her hand up to cover her mouth, but it was too late to stifle the sound.

He had seen her.

Whoever that man was that radiated evil intent, he now knew they were there.

But just as startling was the blue-and-purple bruise mark around the man's neck and on his hand, peeking out from the cuff of his jacket. Even in the midst of her fear, a small wave of sympathy rose for the man with such a birthmark. Her gaze flew to his eyes again, and the sympathy quickly disappeared at the malice she saw there.

She clutched at what felt like safety—the solidness of the tree trunk. Her feet felt mired in the deep snow and the boots. She could not run if she tried.

Lyddie stood from kneeling next to the malamute and looked at Sarah, her eyes wide with questioning and fright. The girl was just trying to be helpful, but it could get them all killed.

Gott, help us!

But in that moment of desperate prayer, Lyddie's whisper filtered in.

"*Mamm*! That is the man! I saw him yesterday!" Even through the mitten, the point of her finger was unmistakable. "See his neck and hand? Scary!"

"Lyddie!" Her whisper came out more harsh than she intended. She needed to have a talk with her daughter about kindness and compassion when others looked different, but now was not the time. "Get back!"

As Sarah grasped Lyddie's shoulder and pulled her behind the tree, she snuck another glance through a few fall leaves that still clung to several branches. The man's eyes were wide, and a small smile snaked across his lips as if he understood the situation. Perspiration dampened her brow despite the cold of the winter day. She struggled to even her breathing and remain calm, but her breath continued to puff out in short spurts.

She looked at John, and he simply held a finger to his lips to indicate she should remain quiet.

At the very least, the man had to know now that she had been around the site of the crash and, most likely, knew something about John. He knew that she was involved.

If there was any doubt of the man's knowledge of her, it was all erased as he drew a weapon out of a cargo pocket and pointed it at her.

Her breath hitched. She clutched at Lyddie and Snowball, both to protect them and to keep from collapsing.

He slowly approached the tree line, each step an ominous crunch in the hardened snow.

"Sarah." John's whisper filtered through the panicked haze in her mind. She forced her gaze away from the gun to see John motioning for them to run deeper into the woods.

Somehow, she moved her head enough to nod her assent.

With a death grip on the arm of her only child, she turned to run. Her heavy winter boots felt glued to the ground, too bulky to move, but she clunked along for a few steps. The weight of her despair sank her farther down into the ground. How could she possibly outrun a bullet at her slow speed? *Gott* was always there, she reminded herself, and she begged for His protection.

The cracking sound of a gun firing rang in her ears.

Would she feel the pain of death? Or would she just suddenly find herself in the presence of *Gott*? Who would care for Lyddie?

A strong force—a hand—pushed on her back. Strong enough to push her down. She landed face-down in the snow, her hand still on Lyddie, who fell next to her.

Lyddie turned to look at her, fear contorting her face.

"I love you," Sarah mouthed.

Then she closed her eyes, praying that her death would be quick and painless.

Chapter Four

John kept his hand on Sarah's back, waiting for a second gunshot to ring out through the silence of the snowy woods. Sarah's back hitched and spasmed underneath his touch with her shallow and uneven breathing. The terror she must be feeling, a gun pointed at her and her only child, must far surpass his own fear. He wished he could take it away, but he could only provide a human connection and pray.

The quiet of the winter afternoon echoed around them in between the swooshing of his heartbeat in his eardrums. What must have been only seconds of waiting for death seemed to stretch into eternity.

Where was the gunshot? What was their would-be killer waiting for?

The squeal of car tires broke the silence. John jerked his hand away from Sarah in surprise. They must be close to a road. The sound of a car missing traction on gravel hit his ears, and he turned his head just enough to see the man return to his snowmobile.

Sarah lifted her head out of the snow, the arch of

her eyebrows telegraphing the question of their safety to John.

Were they saved? Or was that the man's reinforcement, come to seal their fate?

He nodded *no*, hoping she understood his message not to move.

The man paused to look back at Sarah and Lyddie.

John tucked his head down, fearing that to make eye contact would only further anger his aggressor. A grunt sounded, and the slip of a nylon snowmobile suit in motion slid past John's ears.

Another squeal of tires reverberated through the woods. John snuck another glance behind in time to see the man tuck his weapon into a cargo pocket. The man quickly hopped on his snowmobile, revved it and took off through the trees in the direction of the road.

John let out a breath and forced himself to release the tension in his muscles.

"He has gone, John?" Sarah was still staring at him.

He nodded. "I believe so."

Remaining on her stomach, she scooted to Lyddie, scooping her into her embrace. The two lay together, and John watched her comfort her child, her hand stroking Lyddie's arm and brushing hair away from her face.

Had he had a mother like that? He stretched through his mind for a memory until an ache pinged in his forehead. No images or feelings surfaced. His life remained a void.

He passed a hand over his forehead and retrieved his hat from the snow a couple of feet away. With the danger gone, at least for the moment, they needed to get to the shelter of Sarah's house.

"Sarah," he whispered. "We need to go."

She turned to him and swiped away tears with her mitten. She nodded and got to her knees, then helped Lyddie before she stood.

"*Mamm*, are we safe?"

Sarah looked long at John, but all he could do was shrug. He wasn't going to lie, and he honestly didn't know if they were safe. All he knew was that they shouldn't stay there.

She put an arm around Lyddie and simply said, "We need to get home."

"May we have hot chocolate?" The girl's lower lip trembled.

Sarah seemed to force a smile for her child. "*Jah*. For sure and for certain."

"Ready?" John waited for an affirmative nod from Sarah and then turned to lead them back toward the house.

He stepped forward at a brisk pace, checking to make sure Sarah and Lyddie were following all right. Their big problem was the snow. More was coming, but until it covered their tracks, John didn't want to lead their would-be killer right back to Sarah's house. He detoured farther into the woods, stomping his feet and spreading the snow out. He circled around a tree and then a grouping of bushes and then another tree.

John motioned to Sarah. "Stay directly behind me. We don't want to leave three sets of prints in the snow, now that he—whoever *he* is—knows that there are three of us."

"*Jah*," Sarah agreed.

Whatever shelter of brush was available, John led them behind it. If the snowmobiler did return, John didn't want to be caught out in the open. Farther and farther from the crash site they marched, and all was quiet.

The huffing and puffing had become more pronounced behind him, and John himself could use a breather. He slowed his pace to allow Sarah and Lyddie to rest.

Several minutes later, they emerged from the tree line and into the yard. Sarah and Lyddie headed straight for the back door, untying their winter bonnets and shaking the snow off their capes before they entered.

John remained outside and surveyed the edge of the property. All seemed untouched. The snowmobiler had certainly gotten a good look at Sarah, but that didn't automatically mean that he knew where she lived or where to find them. Could they be safe now?

Sarah's home looked like all the other Amish homes in the area. Two stories with an attic rose whitewashed above an immaculate yard, at least what he could see under the snow. Red paint adorned the large barn, a striking contrast against the winter whiteness. He imagined that in the spring flowers would stand in neat rows, and he pictured Lyddie and Snowball playing on the green grass in the yard. Sarah's home was orderly inside and out. John wondered if the cliché "A place for everything and everything in its place" had originated with the Amish.

At the back door, John removed his hat and hung it on a hook. He secured the lock and stood for a moment, letting the warmth of the woodstove-heated home seep into him. Sarah busied herself at the counter, scooping cocoa powder into three mugs. Her face was rosy from the snow, and her natural beauty shone forth, framed by the rich brown of her hair.

Steam began to pour out of a kettle on the stove top. "Come. Sit. It will be ready in a jiffy." Sarah motioned him to the table, her hand trembling. "You need good food. Comfort food with nutritional value. To heal, *jah*?"

He crossed the kitchen to her and grasped her hands in his. Perhaps that would stop the shaking. "You were scared. Are scared. You don't have to fix a meal."

"I do, *jah*. When I am scared, I cook. When I am worried, I cook. When I am happy, I cook. It soothes."

He nodded his understanding and lowered himself to a chair.

She busied herself at the countertop, cutting thick slices of what looked like homemade bread. "You like tuna salad? Chicken noodle soup, also?"

Did he? He had no idea, but the simmering concoction in the pot on the stove top gave off an incredible aroma. "Um, sure."

As she continued the lunch preparations, John let his gaze wander the open living room. It was so quiet he could hear the satisfying squish of tuna salad being spread on bread, Lyddie's soft whisper as she sounded out words in her book, even his own breathing. He tapped his finger on the table, not surprised that he could hear it thumping on the wood. The silence was unnerving and yet pleasant at the same time. A man could do some serious thinking in that sort of solitude. But did he want to?

A side table with a lamp on top and a lower shelf filled with books and newspapers next to a plush blue recliner caught his attention. "Do you read much?"

"*Ach, jah*. I love to read. Lyddie and I visit the library on a regular schedule."

"What's your favorite?"

"I read all kinds. Cooking books, quilting, books about faith, even the good romance novels. Without television or a computer, I have more time for reading." She glanced at him while stirring the soup. "Do you enjoy reading?"

Did he? He picked up the book resting on the table, something with forgiveness in the title, and held it in his hands. It felt sturdy and comfortable there. He lifted it to his face and inhaled the scent of the paper, closing his eyes to try to picture himself somewhere, anywhere, with a book in his hands. But his mind was a blank. "I don't know, but I hope my new self, whoever I am now, likes to read."

Sarah nodded, a shy smile on her face. "Why not just decide that you do?" She placed two plates on the table and returned to the counter for the third. "Would you like a chocolate-chip cookie after lunch? Cookies are always a help in distress, *jah*?"

"Jah," he agreed, the foreign word a tingle on his tongue.

Distress. He had certainly brought plenty to this peaceful and peace-loving Amish household. It was all his fault, and what made it worse was that he had no idea why he was in trouble. Would prayer help? Perhaps. Was he a believing man? Maybe. Something stirred in him at the idea of praying to an almighty God. He bowed his head, but all he could summon was *Lord, help.*

The sound of Lyddie dropping a book on the floor startled him out of his attempt. She picked it up and settled herself on the sofa, apparently prepared to read until the refreshments were ready. John looked again around the room. Plain white walls, graced only by a calendar and clock, and a lack of knickknacks did nothing to detract from the warmth and welcome of the home.

Was all safe now? It was a question at the forefront of

his mind, although there wasn't much else crowding the space in his brain. It was also the question he supposed Sarah would ask soon. How he would answer he had no idea, except that it seemed the man on the snowmobile had seen only Sarah and Lyddie. Perhaps he might just think they were curious about the wreckage.

But at least for this moment, he would sit still and be calm and recuperate. He didn't know anymore what future moments would hold just as he didn't know what past moments had held, so he would live right now, in this moment of warmth and light and safety.

"Lyddie, come quickly," Sarah called. The two joined John at the table, and Sarah and Lyddie bowed their heads for silent prayer. John bowed his head and tried to thank God for the food and the warm home, looking up again after Sarah said *amen*.

The child ate quickly, and Sarah suggested she go to her room to practice her stitching. The two hugged for a moment, and Sarah tucked a stray curl behind Lyddie's ear. As the girl passed John, she impulsively reached out to hug him. Her squeeze was tight and fast, and it infused John with a fondness that didn't feel familiar to him.

As soon as Lyddie was gone, Sarah turned piercing eyes on John. "Who was that in the woods, and why was he shooting at us?"

Both valid questions. Questions for which he had no answers. "I wish I knew, but I can't even remember my own name. I certainly can't remember anyone else's name." He shrugged his shoulders. "I have no idea who that man was, but he seemed only to see you and Lyddie. Being at the site of the accident probably didn't help us."

"And you were dressed in the Amish clothing. Would that not help hide you?"

John thought back to what he had on. "Yes, I had an Amish coat on. My hat, which looked Amish, had come off, but it was nearby. But, I don't have the beard that most Amish men have." He scruffed his hand over his jaw. "Just a little stubble. Still, though, that could be enough to disguise me."

"Are we in danger?" Sarah hugged her arms around her middle.

He couldn't answer *yes* or *no* to that question. But he could advise caution. "I'm not sure. But we need to be careful. Even though I have no idea who that man was that shot at us, and he didn't see me, he saw you. I'm grateful he was scared off by that car that drove by." He would be back, though, just at a more opportune time.

Sarah's hands trembled as she picked up her plate and glass and placed them in the sink. "Will he be able to find us here?"

She glanced around her home, the one she had shared with her husband, the one that held so many memories with Lyddie. Was there a threat right outside the blue-shaded windows, a threat that would come bursting through and alter her life?

"You don't know him, right?"

"No, I have never seen him."

"Then he's probably not familiar with the Amish around here. At least not to the point where he knows who you are and where you live." John stood and carried his plate to the sink. "I think we're all right for now."

For now. But John's memory was gone. He didn't know his name or his occupation or even what sort of person he was. Could she trust him to be vigilant? To be protective if necessary? To know what to do?

She ran water in the sink and added soap while John continued to clear the table. At least he was a helpful sort. What woman wouldn't appreciate that? And so far, he had been courteous and thoughtful.

He placed the last dish on the counter and smiled. "Do you have a cloth? I'll wipe up the table."

Ach, he was handsome, too, with that dark brown hair that seemed to stand up in all directions and his green eyes the color of fresh grass in the spring. He was the opposite of her blond-headed Noah, but now that he was dressed like a proper Amish man? She would need to guard her heart carefully.

She handed him a dishcloth and plunged her hands back into the hot water. How could she ever think that way about him? First of all, her husband, the love of her life, had passed just two years ago. How could she be untrue to his memory? And second of all, John was an *Englischer*. An outsider. She would never agree to be unequally yoked. How could she be so selfish as to even consider John? *Gott* had allowed her husband to be killed in the buggy accident. Thus, it must be *Gott*'s will that she be alone. She would embrace the will of *Gott*, no matter what misery may come her way.

John returned the cloth to her, and she rinsed it and hung it over the faucet. "Your last name, Burkholder, is it a common Amish name?"

"Are you wondering how easily this bad man might be able to ask around and find us? But how would he know my name?"

He stuffed his hands in his pockets, stretching the suspenders. "Just trying to figure it all out."

"Burkholder is somewhat common in northern Indiana. But not so much, yet, that we all need nicknames like in other Amish communities where there are multiple men with the same name."

"Do you have family nearby?"

She retrieved a clean drying cloth from a drawer and prayed to *Gott* that she wouldn't need it to dry her tears. "I grew up in Lancaster County in Pennsylvania. My husband, Noah, thought the area was becoming overcrowded and moved us to Indiana for more job opportunities and land to build a house and barn. So, no, I do not have family nearby. My family remains in Pennsylvania, although they do come to visit from time to time."

"Have you thought of moving back?"

She eyed the letter from her mother that still rested on the windowsill. "Yes." That was all the answer she could summon.

He leaned one hip against the counter, and the fresh smell of the woods in winter wafted toward her. "What about a telephone? What would you do in case of an emergency?"

She twisted the towel in her hands. Sarah had never thought herself isolated, but when this *Englischer* started asking his questions, doubts began to ping in her mind, especially with no husband handy. "Since we are close to the edge of the state park, the area is heavily wooded. We are on the outskirts of the Amish community, and neighbors are scarce. My husband preferred the seclusion. There are some *Englisch* houses on the main road, but they are quite a distance, especially in the snow, and they are in the opposite direction of our church district. Our closest neighbor has a telephone in his barn for his business, but he is a couple of miles away. I can use it when I need it, and then I pay my part of the bill to him."

"You never thought of having your own phone?"

"My husband and I talked about it, for our barn, but it did not seem that necessary since the neighbor had one." She glanced at him as he pulled back the window blind a fraction of an inch and glanced out. "That must seem odd to you."

John turned to her with a wry chuckle. "Everything seems odd right now."

Of course it does. How could she be insensitive? Her troubles were nothing compared to what John was going through. "Our church district is currently considering cell phones, just the old kind that flip open. No internet. But it has not yet been decided."

"Any chance that'll happen soon?"

"No. A new rule needs to be approved unanimously, and some are still doubtful. It could take a long time." She stacked the plates in the cabinet and hung up the towel. "I cannot think what I would need it for, except maybe emergencies."

John opened his mouth to answer, but the sound of her gravel driveway crunching under the tires of a car that had turned into her lane kept him silent.

Should she duck out of sight? Turn off the lamp? Her mind felt paralyzed, and all she could do was grip the edge of the countertop as she watched John peer through a slit in the curtain.

It must have been only a second before he turned to her. "It's the sheriff's car."

The sheriff? The man who had never been helpful but only trouble for the Amish? Was he here for John? Did that mean that John was a bad guy…or a good guy?

She spun to scan the room. Lyddie remained upstairs, the best place for her right now.

Sarah stared at John, waiting for an instruction. But he sat very still, as if not wanting to show his own alarm. Perhaps he was trying to think of what to do.

He jumped to his feet, and she stepped back, startled at his sudden movement. With a look toward the back door, he said, "Step out the back way and meet him in the driveway around the front. Be friendly, but don't let him in the house. Just in case." He pointed to the window near the front door. "I'll be concealed right behind that curtain, and I should be able to hear everything that's said. Can you do that?"

With a nod, she grabbed her cape from the hook and slung it over her shoulders. A glance back as she opened the door revealed John at the window already, pulling the curtain aside. "You'll be fine." He coupled the encouragement with a grin.

She had no idea whether he truly felt that way or not, but it was good to hear.

Outside, she stepped carefully off the porch and inhaled deeply of the cold air, letting the chill cut through her lungs. It revived her, and she prayed for *Gott*'s help as she stepped toward the Sheriff's vehicle. "Sheriff Jaspar. What can I do for you?"

The sheriff stepped forward from his driver's-side door, a tall, lanky man whose uniform hung on him. He pushed his wire-rimmed glasses farther up on his nose, although they seemed nearly embedded in his eyes already. "Mrs. Burkholder, isn't it?" He quickly adopted a quizzical look.

"*Jah*. That is correct."

"There's been a report of smoke in the area, and I'm making the rounds, just checking it out."

Sarah tightened her arms closer to her under her cape and snuck a glance at the front window. John's snowmobile crash had created lots of smoke. "Is anyone burning their rubbish?"

The sheriff stepped closer, so close that Sarah could see the little pattern on the rim of his glasses. "No. Not that I've found yet. And it's not the smoke from a fireplace or woodstove. Curious thing, really, and awfully close to your house."

Sarah took a small step backward. She desperately needed some distance from the man but didn't want to antagonize him. "I have only my heating stove."

Jaspar closed the gap between them. "Shall I come in and make sure?" He laid his claw-like hand on her arm.

A loud gasp escaped her and echoed through the winter silence. Before she could respond to the sheriff, the front door flung open. John stepped out, one hand fisted around his suspenders.

The sheriff turned to see who it was and immediately stepped back from Sarah. His gaze seemed to travel up and down John's height and back and forth the width of John's shoulders. He took another step back.

"Sarah?" John's intensity pierced her, and she nodded slightly to indicate that she was all right. He probably didn't dare to speak any more, not with his *Englisch* accent.

Sheriff Jaspar straightened his hat and then nodded at John. "Is this your brother? I've heard you have family in Pennsylvania that come to visit on occasion."

She wouldn't lie, but she did not see the need to tell the whole truth either. "*Jah*, I have family in Lancaster

County." She fluttered her hand to her throat and swallowed hard. "He is visiting for a while."

The sheriff seemed satisfied as he edged back toward his car. "Well, I have a deputy looking into the smoke, as well. No need to worry, but let me know if there's any trouble." A roguish smile crawled across his face. "I'll keep you up-to-date."

She raised a hand in goodbye and quickly joined John at the front door. He opened it for her, and she stepped inside while he remained outside, his hand on the knob of the open door, staring hard at the sheriff as he backed out of the drive.

Her hands shook as she removed her cape and turned away from the door to sink into a chair at the kitchen table. John closed and locked the door then lowered himself into a matching chair.

The cape draped over her lap warmed her quickly, but she couldn't stop the trembling. She glanced at John, but he stared at the wall, seemingly lost in thought. "You are exposed now. You have been seen."

A few moments passed, then he tore his gaze from the straightforward direction and looked at her. There was a hard edge to his expression, yet it was tinged with compassion. "I couldn't just leave you out there with him. I saw everything through the window."

She smoothed out the tablecloth with the palm of her hand. "The sheriff is new and does not know how to get along with the Amish. What can I do?"

"Depending on what he finds out about the smoke that's been reported, you can pack your bags and prepare to leave."

"Leave?" Her hands seemed to act independently,

and she found herself smoothing more of the cloth at a furious rate.

"Yes. We need to think about where we might be able to hide, just in case there is danger." He paused. "I've wondered if I should just leave. Perhaps you would be safe again if I was gone. But the problem with that is that he has seen you. He pointed his weapon at you."

"But the sheriff, if he finds what caused the smoke, could find the men who chased you. Perhaps we should help him and tell him what happened."

He clasped her hands in his. "But you don't trust the sheriff, and after what I saw and heard just now, I agree with you. That's not the proper behavior of a law-enforcement officer."

"Then perhaps we can contact someone else. I can hitch up the buggy and we can drive to the telephone." Her hands were warm in his, and she had no desire to leave her home, whether it be to hide or to seek help. She wanted just to stay here, with John holding her hands. How long had it been since a physical touch had communicated such comfort?

"I'm just not sure who we can trust." He removed a hand from hers and ran it through his hair. "I'm not sure of anything. And I don't want to make the situation worse."

Sarah glanced around the room and listened to the sounds of her only child playing in the room above her. She had a responsibility to the girl as well as to everything she and her husband had worked for. The sheriff was involved now, but did that make her feel any safer? The only man who had proven that he had a protective nature was the man sitting at her table. But he couldn't even remember who he was. What if, when he regained his memory, John was one of them?

Chapter Five

John needed two things. He needed a breath of fresh air. And he needed to remember.

Well, he needed a few other things, as well, like confidence that he had the instincts to protect the woman and her child, an assurance that all would end well and another piece of that amazing apple pie.

As Sarah had busied herself with baking something—he couldn't remember now what all she had said she was making, but apparently it was like therapy for her—he had tossed on the coat and, after a look around the yard to make sure there was no trouble, headed to the barn to explore a bit.

He swung the door open and stepped into the warmth, filling his lungs with the scent of hay. With the door closed behind him, he searched the nooks and crannies of his mind to see if the scent of the barn felt familiar. Was he a farming man? An outdoors enthusiast? An animal lover?

Nothing came into his mind. It was as blank as a washed blackboard.

In different circumstances, the loss of his memory

could have been an interesting opportunity to remake his life. The disappearance of his memories included not only the good ones but also the bad ones. Was he at odds with someone in his life? With no memory of it, he could approach the relationship with a fresh perspective.

Under these circumstances, though? In the house was a woman and her daughter who needed his protection from danger he had brought to their doorstep, no matter what he could or could not remember. Three lives depended on him.

A tabby cat mewed and rubbed against his legs. He bent to scratch it between the ears. Was he a cat person? He had no idea, but this one sure was cute. A mouse skittered along the wall, and the cat crouched down, its fur standing at attention along its back. The cat crept toward the mouse and pounced, catching it under its paw. John watched the cat play with and torment the mouse for a moment. When the cat took the mouse into its mouth and sauntered away, John wandered farther into the barn.

The sheriff had not been reassuring in the least bit, and that drove John to search for something—anything—helpful. Weapons? Although he wasn't sure what, or if he would know how to use it if he found anything. Hiding places? But how complex could a barn be? Anyone familiar with living in the country would know where to look. Memories? He grinned to himself at the irony of looking for memories in a new and unfamiliar place.

Sarah had made it clear that the Amish were a nonviolent people, so he didn't expect to find any weapons in the barn. It didn't have to be a gun, though, that could provide some defense. Perhaps a tool would do.

A door stood to his right. He had to push hard on the latch to get it open, and the hinges squeaked as he pushed. Clearly, it hadn't been opened in a while.

Large windows let the afternoon sunshine spill in, dust motes dancing in the still air. A large wooden table filled the middle of the space, and the other walls were filled with shelves of tools and piles of wood. He had found a woodworking shop, and it looked as if nothing had been touched for quite some time.

He wandered toward a board that lay on the bench and ran his hand over the smooth wood. Someone had taken quite a bit of time to sand it well. A stack of rough-cut lumber sat on a shelf to the side, but he knew better than to run his hand over the wood full of splinters. It looked to be oak, but he had no idea how he knew that.

A block plane lay on a shelf, and he hefted it in his hand, the smooth and worn handle resting in his palm. It felt right there, but it wouldn't do much good as a weapon. Did he have a woodworking background? Confusion riddled his brain, yet it mixed with the pleasure of knowing that something felt right to him.

A child's step stool rested on the workbench. Stain had darkened it to a rich brown, and a can of polyurethane sat nearby. A brush rested on top of the can. It looked as if that was all that was left to finish the stool.

He picked up the brush and turned it around in his hand. A sense of satisfaction filled him, a pleasure in craftsmanship.

He was learning a little bit about himself already, in just these few minutes spent in the barn. Apparently, he liked to work with his hands. Had he learned about woodworking in a high school shop class? From his father? An image flashed through his mind, so strong and so startling that he closed his eyes to block out distraction. It was the vision of hands using a brush on paper. Were those his own hands? Strident voices had filtered in from another room, but what were they discussing so fervently?

He opened his eyes and looked down at his hands as he held the brush. Were they the same? Who were the people, and what were they arguing over? He closed his eyes again to return to the memory, but it was gone. Only a vague unsettled feeling of wrongdoing lingered.

His hand closed in a tight grip over the paintbrush. Why couldn't he remember? Whatever it was, whatever had been right there, even for a split second, seemed crucial. But why? John threw the brush on the table and took a deep breath.

Anger wouldn't solve anything.

"John?" Sarah's sweet voice filtered through the stillness of sawdust and afternoon sunlight and dancing dust motes.

"I'm in here." He quickly straightened the can and the brush. Why did he feel like a child who had been caught with his hand in the cookie jar?

Sarah appeared in the doorway, the light blue of her dress fairly glowing in the sifted sunshine. Upset stretched across her face.

He stepped to her, his heart beginning a worried thump. "What's happened? I said you should stay in the house with the doors locked."

"All is well inside." Her gaze swept across the room and came to rest on the little stool. "What are you doing in here? With that?"

"I…uh…" John glanced back at the stool, which

now seemed to incriminate him in some way. When he turned back, Sarah's eyes puddled with tears. "I was looking around. This looked like it might be the right size for Lyddie."

"Jah." She swiped at her cheek. "It was to be for Lyddie. This was my husband's workshop. I haven't been in here since he died."

The reality of the situation slammed him, and he gulped in air. Her husband had been a carpenter, and the stool had been his project at the time of his death. "I'm sorry. I didn't know."

Sarah walked to the workbench and fingered the edge. "My husband made furniture, the Amish furniture that *Englischers* love so much, for stores in the big cities like Indianapolis, Chicago, even Cincinnati and Louisville. This was where he worked."

He had overstepped his bounds and hurt her. Being in here was difficult enough for her, but to see him with one of her husband's projects, a project for her daughter? How could he make it up to her? Make it right?

"I'm sorry." He would say it a dozen times if that would help. "You've done so much for me. I wanted to do something for you."

She nodded, then covered her face with her hands. Her shoulders shook, and John saw a tear escape.

He longed to close the distance between them and comfort her, but did he dare? How would she receive it? Would it only make the situation worse?

Sarah gave up trying to hide her tears and hugged herself instead, but how much better that comfort would be if it were a strong man's arms around her. Reassuring. Soothing. Consoling.

Ach, but *Gott* had taken away her husband. That had been His will. So be it. But how she suffered since his death! Still, though, had not the bishop just preached about *Gott* comforting in sorrow? About praising Him through the difficult times? Well, she would obey. A verse sprang to her mind as she rubbed her hands over her arms. *Blessed be God, even the Father of our Lord Jesus Christ, the Father of mercies, and the God of all comfort.*

Jah, blessed be *Gott*.

John apologized again, breaking her reverie. The look of misery on his face matched the misery she felt in her heart. He stepped toward her, seemingly unsure of what to do next.

"It is all right," she whispered into the space between them.

Despite the cold outside, it was warm in the barn. John had removed his coat and rolled his sleeves up. He reached out and touched her gently on the forearm, then withdrew his hand as if he felt the same zing on his skin as she felt through her sleeve.

As Sarah sniffed the last of her tears, she watched John return the tools to their places. The muscles in his forearms rippled as he hefted the large can of polyurethane and placed it on the shelf with some other containers. Of course, she had been treating his wounds and changing the bandage on his arm where he got cut on the rocks. But that was simply medical care of an injured person. Now, to see him standing solid and in good physical condition, he was strong and handsome.

Guilt stabbed her in the heart. *Gott* would never want her to be unequally yoked with an *Englischer*. She had no business looking at him as anything except a fellow human being who needed some help temporarily. Maybe she did need a husband and her daughter needed a father. For sure and for certain, she wanted to be married again and have more *bobblin*. Many more babies.

But if that was the will of *Gott*, He would bring her the right husband in His time.

John pushed the little step stool to the center of the workbench, then turned to her. "Is that better? I don't want to be the cause of any further difficulties. I won't come in here again."

Sarah swiped one last rogue tear from her cheek, the twisting of her heart slowing. The scent of wood and sawdust filled the barn, but it seemed also to waft particularly from John. It was the scent of hard work and masculinity.

It was the scent of misery.

This dance was difficult, and John didn't know the steps.

With everything back in its place, Sarah seemed to calm a bit, but John still wondered if he should comfort her further. How would he be received? And what was this attraction he had for this beautiful plain woman?

He touched her upper arm, gently, questioningly, and she simply smiled. *"Danki."*

She turned and strode into the main part of the barn. John followed and closed the door securely behind him.

"Did you find what you were looking for?"

John chuckled. "I'm not sure I know what I'm looking for. Just exploring."

"Would you like some coffee? To warm you?"

One of the horses whinnied, and the cat returned to rub against the hem of Sarah's long skirt.

The door burst open, and John bounded in front of Sarah. His pulse throbbed in his arteries at the rush of adrenaline. He had allowed himself to be lulled into a sense of security, in the warmth and comfort of the barn. But he needed to be alert at all times.

Frigid air slammed into his face. Lyddie stood in the doorway, a caped and bonneted silhouette against the light outside. "*Mamm*? I came downstairs, and you were not there."

Sarah pulled Lyddie into a hug. "I am sorry, little one. I was out here with John."

The girl looked up, her round cheeks framed with blond wisps of hair, her *kapp* like a beacon of innocence over it all. John's heart twisted within his chest at the sight of mother and daughter. He longed for the love and acceptance of family. Did he have it and just not know it?

Lyddie stepped away from her mother, an adorable and impish expression gracing her face. "May I have a snack?"

"We just had lunch. Are you hungry again already?"

Mother and daughter stepped toward the door, ready to return to the house.

"Just a minute." John lunged toward the closest stall and dodged a flick of a horse tail. A pitchfork rested against the wall, waiting for the next time for chores. It would have to do for now, with nothing else available. He hoisted it in his hand, the solid wooden handle fitting snuggly in his palm. "Let me check outside first. Just to be safe."

He sidestepped around the pair and pulled his coat on. He surveyed the yard but without stepping completely outside. The winter wind whipped around the side of the house, stirring the snow into a whirlwind that skipped over the frozen ground. Mournful gray clouds now filled the sky. A storm was approaching quickly.

John led them across the yard and back to the house, the pitchfork pointed forward. He wasn't sure how he might explain that to the sheriff if he returned, but he would figure something out if necessary. His continual scan of the area didn't reveal any present threats.

But that didn't mean they weren't there, in the shadows, biding their time, waiting for the opportune moment.

Inside the house, he locked the door and leaned the pitchfork against the wall.

At the ready.

Just in case.

Chapter Six

The afternoon had brought only more cloud cover, and sunset had seemed to come early. Flurries of snow had begun as Sarah had returned to the barn to bed down the two horses, Thunder and Lightning, for the night. Now, as Sarah looked out the small barn window, fat, fluffy flakes of snow traipsed down to add a fresh layer. Snowball panted at her side, ready to go wherever she went.

John stood at the door. He had been waiting patiently, helping as he could, and now was ready to escort her back to the house. With pitchfork in hand, he had prowled the perimeter of her property to make sure all was safe. The farming implement remained at the ready, but with no present threat, he seemed a little more relaxed. "Done?"

"Jah." She turned back toward the hayloft. "Lyddie! Time to go back to the house!"

The six-year-old clambered down the ladder as Snowball left Sarah's side to prance around at the bottom, her tail conveying her enthusiasm.

Sarah's heart beat the staccato rhythm that had become her new normal as John opened the door and surveyed the yard. There was nothing normal about it, though, and she prayed to *Gott* that this danger would be over soon.

"Is all well?" She peeked over his shoulder, inhaling the scent of sawdust and wood, but all she could see was the serenity of a snowfall on a winter's night.

"Seems so."

For now. That's what he wasn't saying.

"I'm trying my best to remember. So that I can get back to my life and get out of your way." He stepped out into the snow, and Snowball ran in front, her nose turned up to the snowflakes. "I'm sorry for all this."

"*Jah.* It will come in time."

"If I had any idea of who had attacked us earlier, I might be better able to know how we could defend ourselves. But I don't know who he is or what he wants."

There it was again, the talk about self-defense. Sarah put her hand on his arm. Perhaps the gesture would help calm him. "You know that self-defense is not the Amish way."

"I know. I know. I know what you've already said. But I'm not Amish, and I'll defend myself, and you and Lyddie, if necessary."

Sarah removed her hand and stuffed it in the pocket of her cape, checking on Lyddie to make sure she was following behind. An ache rose to throb in her chest, but she refused to examine why a wave of loneliness invaded her soul. She was Amish. John was not. She forced her thoughts to stop right there.

He would do what he needed to do, and she would do what she needed to do. In the end, she would be grateful if her life was spared, and the life of her daughter. But if it was *Gott*'s will that her time had come, she would do her best to accept it graciously.

Snow gathered on their shoulders, on John's hat and Lyddie's *kapp*, as Snowball bounded alongside. The animal licked her hand as if trying to reassure her.

Halfway there, Snowball's exuberance came to a halt. A branch snapped to their left. The malamute's ears stood at attention, and then she began a low growl as she eyed the tree line. John swung out his arm to stop them. They stood like statues, listening and squinting into the darkness. The pitchfork pointed toward the sound.

The ache in Sarah's chest increased with her heart rate. A thousand different scenarios raced through her mind. Was this what John had been afraid of? Had the man in the snowmobile suit, with the scary bruising and the gun, finally found them? And the worst question of all—how would a pitchfork protect them against a bullet?

"To the house." John's strident whisper broke the silence. "Quickly."

Sarah grabbed Lyddie's hand. Together, they picked up their skirts and galloped toward the back door as quickly as their winter boots would allow. John followed close behind, his hand at the small of Sarah's back, urging her along.

At the door, John pushed her and Lyddie inside along with Snowball. "I'll check around. Lock the door, and don't open it until you see me."

She nodded her assent and closed the door behind him. Lyddie dropped to her knees to hug the dog. Desperate to do something with her hands, Sarah unfastened her cloak while she watched through the window as John disappeared into the darkness. A few moments later, his face appeared in the pane. She quickly unlocked the door for him.

As he hung his hat on the peg, Sarah locked the door behind him. He leaned against the wall and rubbed his temples. "Nothing. I saw nothing."

Sarah inhaled a large breath to clear away the anxiety. "Is your head hurting again?"

"A little." He hung his coat on the hook and resumed massaging his forehead.

"Why not sit down for a spell? Perhaps it will ease your headache. If you can feel better, it will help us all."

He nodded. "Maybe, but I'll be right in there—" he pointed toward the recliner in the living room "—and you call me if you need anything."

"*Jah*, I will."

As he retreated to rest, she instructed Lyddie to set the table. With her cape and bonnet on the hook, she quickly washed her hands and peeked into the propane-powered oven at the chicken she had put in before she had gone to care for the horses.

A couple of years ago, Sarah had doubted the choice of a malamute as a farm dog. Everything she had read indicated that they were not good guard dogs, often licking the hands of strangers rather than growling a warning. But her husband had wanted a strong dog, a work dog, and the malamute breed was nothing if not strong. Of course, once Lyddie had held the soft, furry puppy, the decision was made.

So, Snowball's warning outside had been a surprise, but perhaps not helpful in the end. They had feared an intruder when it had probably only been a deer searching for food. Now, Snowball settled into her bed on the back inside porch.

The chicken had browned nicely, and Sarah stood to lift the lid of the pot on the stove top. Chunks of potato simmered in the gently bubbling water. She retrieved a fork from the drawer and speared a piece of potato against the side of the pot. It resisted a little too much, but a few more minutes would finish them.

Unsettledness dogged her, and she licked her lips to ease the dryness as she reminded herself to keep a steady hand when taking the chicken from the oven. If only John were sitting at the table, would that ease her? It seemed that he had been there with his calming presence for a lot longer than just a couple of days. But that's all it had been since Lyddie had led her to the man bleeding into the snow near his wrecked snowmobile. She glanced at the table, eyeing what she had begun to think of as *his chair*. But she wouldn't bother him. He needed his rest, especially with his headache. Rest was always helpful in recovery, and she prayed that included recovery of memories.

She paced to the front window and peered out. But when she saw nothing but more nothingness, she pulled the curtain closed and double-checked to make sure the window was completely covered. She tested the lock on the front door, the cold of the metal sending a chill into her fingers. Her path took her through the living room, and John shifted in the chair as she passed. At the back inside porch, an attached but enclosed entryway without coverings on the windows, Snowball lay on her bed in the corner, raising her head for a petting when Sarah stepped in.

Lifting her long skirt out of the way, she crouched down to scratch behind the dog's ears. The malamute seemed almost to smile as Sarah spoke to her in her doggy voice. "Are you comfy, Snowball? Is it nap time? Are you tired from all your guarding?" She arranged the blanket around her, gave her one last scratch on top of her head and pushed herself to standing.

In the kitchen, Sarah thrust her hands into the oven mitts that rested on the countertop and removed the lid of the pot of potatoes into the sink. As she hefted the pot to carry it to the sink to drain the potatoes, Snowball whined from the back inside porch. Normally, she would not have noticed, but since John had arrived, her senses had been on full alert. Snowball had not been acting like herself either, which gave Sarah pause.

Still holding the pot, she approached the door to the porch to check on the dog, a reassuring sound on her lips. But as she entered the doorway, a man's scowling face stared in from the window.

She froze, her hands gripping the handles of the pot. Her heart took up an instant beating against her rib cage, as if trying to break free.

The man seemed to be looking to her side. He had not seen her.

Gott, help!

Before she could think to move, the doorknob rattled. The man's face pointed toward the doorway. His stare caught her. She looked straight into the most evil eyes she had ever seen.

What should she do?

A split second later, the door flung open. A malicious winter wind swirled around her. As the man reached in toward her, a crowbar in his hand, she turned the pot up and heaved the contents toward him. The water and chunks of potato hit him squarely in the face and chest. Water splattered on the floor, and chunks of potato bounced against her shoes.

The man let loose a cry of agonizing pain. Sarah stepped back but held on to the pot, her mind reeling to figure out what she should do next. With his eyes shut in pain, he continued to advance through the porch toward Sarah.

John scrambled from the chair and made it to the doorway to the back porch as the man emitted a second shout of agony. He quickly assessed the situation—the man clawing at his eyes, obviously in great pain and unable to see, and the Amish woman with the gut instincts to use a pot of boiling water as a weapon.

With both hands, John pushed the man back out the door. The intruder stumbled away, one hand on his face and the other hand out in front like a blind man trying to feel his way. He emitted a string of words that John was glad Sarah could not hear. Living a sheltered life as the Amish did, she may not even have known what they were.

John rushed back inside and locked the door. Sarah had returned to the kitchen, placing the pot in the sink and then standing, staring as if in shock. Lyddie peeked from behind the doorway, her eyes wide and her hands worrying the ties that hung loose from her *kapp*.

Not for the first time, John felt a desperation for a telephone. There was simply no way to summon help, except for hitching up the horse and buggy. But what help would he summon? The lack of knowledge was more crippling than the lack of a phone.

"That was good thinking on your part, Sarah." As he approached, she turned, her eyes puddled with unshed tears.

"*Gott*, forgive me. But I was so scared. I... I just reacted."

He laid his hand on her forearm and squeezed, a gesture he hoped conveyed his appreciation in her actions that had protected them all. "He'll be helpless for a while. His eyes were turning bright red and beginning to swell. But it's just a matter of time before he's back, probably with a vengeance."

Lyddie shrank against the wall. Snowball finally had emerged from her bed and came to Lyddie's side to lick her hand. "*Mamm*, are we going to die?"

Something seemed to shake free in Sarah, and her eyes focused on her daughter. Without heed to the windows or doors, she rushed across the kitchen and dropped to her knees in front of Lyddie, gathering her in her arms. "*Ach, liebchen*. We have John to protect us."

Both females looked to him with pleading eyes. John felt helpless enough on his own, with no memory and all experiences erased from his mind. But he couldn't let down this mother and daughter. Perhaps now was a good time to start praying. From what he had heard from Sarah over the past days, even though he didn't know who he was, God still knew everything about him, even down to the number of hairs on his head.

He embraced them both and impulsively planted a kiss on the girl's forehead. Then, taking a few steps backward, he grabbed the pitchfork from its resting place near the door, tossing up a prayer for protection and guidance. "Right. We need to get out of here. Whoever that was at the door, he'll be back. There's no way to tell how soon. It just depends on how much the boiling water hurt him and how soon his vision returns."

Sarah nodded, the tiny lines around her eyes seeming to ease a bit as John spoke. "A friend in a neighboring church district was canning last fall when the boiling water bubbled and burst up into her face. She was blinded temporarily, but she said the pain was intense. This water had cooled a little, and I do not think enough water hit him in his eyes to blind him permanently."

"Okay. So, pack a bag, Sarah, quickly. Grab the essentials. A change of clothes. Your toothbrushes. I don't know yet where we're going or how long we'll be gone."

He looked to Lyddie. She raised her head from her mother's shoulder, a crease on her cheek from the tie of Sarah's *kapp*. "Lyddie, get whatever your mother will allow you to take. Not too much. Just, perhaps, a favorite doll or a blanket."

The two stood and began to move toward the stairs, but John had one last instruction. "Turn out the kerosene lamp. We'll work in darkness. If he returns before we can leave, I don't want him to be able to see in. I'm going to grab some water and snacks. Be back down here in two minutes."

A quick peek out the window revealed that their attacker had not yet returned. John set the pitchfork aside and retrieved some bottles of water and little bags of snacks. Was he surprised that the Amish would buy prepackaged food? They shopped at the grocery stores just like everyone else. Whatever he thought, he didn't have time to examine it now. One thing he did know about the Amish, or at least about this Amish woman, specifically, she was resilient. She might be scared or worried, but she wasn't crumbling. Strength and resolve adorned her. Her unwavering faith in God only added to her beauty.

Sarah and Lyddie returned quickly. With John leading, they dashed across the yard to the barn. Snowball followed, pushing snow around with her muzzle as she trotted behind. By the moonlight that filtered in through the barn windows, Sarah hitched Lightning to the buggy and tied Thunder to the back.

"Will we move faster if we leave the second horse here?" John couldn't remember knowing anything about horses. He would have to rely on Sarah's expertise now.

"I cannot leave him alone in the barn." Sarah hitched up her skirt and climbed into the buggy after Lyddie. "Not with that bad man on the loose. And no one will be here to care for him."

John only nodded and swung up into the buggy as Sarah gave a *tch-tch* to the horse. She called for Snowball, and they pulled out of the barn and into the empty yard, the malamute trotting alongside.

"The snow will muffle the sound of the horse and cover our tracks, *jah*?"

"Yes. It should."

The moonlight cast eerie shadows across the landscape, and snowflakes flittered down from scattered clouds. A shudder involuntarily coursed through him. Where would they go from here? Was there anybody out there who cared? In the unnerving quiet of the lonely night and with his memory erased, it didn't stretch his imagination to think that they were the only three people left on the face of the earth.

A tiny window at the side, about the size of his face, allowed him the smallest of views. Another window about the same size afforded a view out the back of the buggy. The light of the moon reflecting on the snow provided ample light as Sarah guided them onto the road. John peered through his window, trying to see behind, and strained to hear the slightest sound a car might make if one approached. At his instruction, Lyddie kept to the back corner of the buggy, away from the window. As she clutched her blanket and doll, John longed to wrap his arms around the adorable girl and soothe her, but she would be safer if he maintained his vigilance.

With all quiet out his side, John turned to Sarah. She held the reins loosely, but the skin was tight across her mouth. At least they had what Sarah had called the storm front on the buggy to keep the snow from pelting them in the face.

He spoke quietly. "Where do you think we should go?" He tapped the brim of his hat. "For obvious reasons, I'm drawing a blank on what our options are outside of your house."

She forced a small grin, but the tightness remained. "The Amish take care of each other. We believe the Bible calls us to live in community together. There are plenty of families who would take us in."

"That may be true, but I don't want to bring danger to them."

"*Jah*, you are right."

"To have someone innocent hurt because of my problems that I can't even remember? That's unacceptable. It's terrible enough that you and Lyddie have been dragged into this."

Sarah chewed on her lip. If their situation hadn't been so dire, if he could just remember who he was, if she wasn't Amish and he wasn't *Englisch*, it could have been romantic, a buggy ride on a moonlit, snowy night. But there were too many *ifs* to let that thinking continue.

"But we need to stay somewhere, if just for the night. I cannot let Lyddie sleep in the buggy. And it is cold."

She pushed some loose hair off her forehead with one hand. "My friend Katie would let us in any time of the night."

"Does she live nearby?"

"Near enough. It will take some time, but I would not have suggested it if we could not get there with Lightning and the buggy."

He peered out the window again and then returned to face Sarah. "How do you know her?"

"She is also a widow and has twin three-year-old girls, Ruth and Rebekah. She struggles on her own." Sarah paused and swallowed hard. "Like I do. We help each other out with chores. I was supposed to drop Lyddie at her house in the morning to help with her twins while I sold my and Katie's goods at the market."

"Okay. If you think that's best."

Lyddie had fallen asleep by the time they reached the friend's house. There had been no sign of their attacker, but Sarah had said she was sticking to the back roads. It had taken a little longer, but perhaps they had been safer.

John waited in the buggy with Lyddie as Sarah knocked on the door.

The young Amish woman answered quickly, and Sarah and her friend had a hushed conversation. A few minutes later, Katie disappeared and then returned with boots and her cape. She opened the barn, and Sarah hopped back into the buggy to drive the horses inside.

"What was her reaction?"

"She was surprised, but of course we are welcome to stay."

"Did you tell her everything?"

"*Jah*. She has met the new sheriff also and agrees that he is not helpful or friendly to us."

John sagged against his seat. So even though law enforcement seemed to be involved, investigating the cause of the smoke, it probably wouldn't help. He continued to be on his own, struggling to remember and find a resolution to the situation with a deadline he couldn't quite grasp looming closer. "If I didn't think you were in danger, I would just leave and take the danger with me."

"I cannot just let you loose. You do not know who you are or where you belong. Where would you go? *Ach*, no. I will take care of you until you are well."

Katie unhitched the horses and settled them in stalls, Snowball tagging along into the warmth of the barn. As Sarah carried her bag, John pulled Lyddie from the back of the buggy and settled her against his shoulder, carrying her into the house. The girl was a comfortable weight in his arms, and the ache for a family returned. He pushed it away as quickly as it arrived. As he settled them into the spare bedroom, Sarah and Lyddie said good night.

In the dark of the living room, John spread his blanket on the couch. He would be the only one on the first floor, protecting them all by sleeping closest to the only entrances to the house.

He toed off his shoes and laid down, pulling the quilt over him. The tick of the clock tocked against his ear, in time to the worries that ricocheted through his mind. For now, they were safe, and all was well.

For now.

But what would tomorrow bring?

Chapter Seven

Sharp sunlight struck Sarah in the face. A peek through one eye revealed that a tiny crack in between the curtain and the edge of the window was the culprit. She raised an arm to cover her eyes and collided with the form in the bed next to her.

"Ow, *Mamm*." Lyddie's mop of blond curls, unrestrained by her prayer *kapp*, stirred in closer. The quilt moved across her, pulling nearer to Lyddie.

Sarah inhaled deeply of the chilly morning air and exhaled slowly, letting her mind absorb all that had happened in the last forty-eight hours. For a moment upon awakening, she had not been able to identify where she was or how she got there. Was that how John felt all the time? Her heart pounded within her at sympathy for the man whose life had been erased, and she took a moment to utter a silent prayer for the restoration of his memories.

She hugged Lyddie tightly and then eased out of the bed. *Jah*, she had been tired. But if the sun was that bright and that high already, the day was disappearing while she lollygagged in bed.

But it was beginning well, safe and warm and with, she was sure, a hot and hearty breakfast soon. Maybe fresh-baked biscuits with a dollop of apple butter, eggs with cheese and bacon, juice, milk, coffee. How could a day not feel like a fresh start with that kind of nourishment at the beginning?

She gently eased the straight pins through the fabric to fasten her skirt to the bodice, then twisted her hair into its customary bun and fastened on her prayer *kapp* with bobby pins. How would the day end, though? Here at her friend's house? At home? Or at another location?

The fresh aroma of coffee forced the musings from her mind. She would take life one day at a time and recite to herself the verses from the psalms that had comforted her in both her move from Pennsylvania and her husband's death. *So teach us to number our days, that we may apply our hearts unto wisdom... O satisfy us early with Thy mercy; that we may rejoice and be glad all our days.* However many days she had left—and considering their present dangers, it seemed to be fewer and fewer—she would rejoice and be glad.

Her task for that day, in addition to keeping herself and Lyddie alive and well, should have been to get her goods to the market. Despite the help of the students' parents, her teacher salary just wasn't quite enough. The parents were generous with foodstuffs and firewood. Every week, it seemed, a pupil would bring a basket of apples or a fresh loaf of bread. But if she'd learned anything in the past few days with John, it was that the future was not certain. Any little bit of money saved would provide extra security. But her current circumstances did not allow for normal activities.

Leaning back over the bed, she rustled Lyddie. "Time to awaken, sleepy."

Lyddie groaned but began inching her way toward the edge of the bed.

In the kitchen, Sarah found John with the newspaper in one hand and a cup of coffee in the other. Katie stood at the stove top, a spatula in hand.

"That smells delicious." Sarah retrieved plates from the cupboard and quickly set the table. "Scrapple? Did you make it last night?"

"Jah." Katie nodded toward the stairs. "Will Lyddie be up soon? We are almost ready."

Sarah nodded.

The paper crinkled, and John looked toward the frying pan. "What's scrapple?"

Sarah smiled at her friend. "It is *wunderbar* for breakfast, made of pork scraps boiled down. Then we thicken the broth with flour until it is a paste. Add some seasoning and chill through the night in the loaf pan."

"In the morning, we fry slices in the skillet." Katie gestured toward the slices sizzling in the pan.

As Sarah poured milk for the children, Lyddie appeared on the stairs, a huge smile stretched across her face. "Scrapple? *Danki*!"

Breakfast passed quickly, and the pork dish won John's hearty approval. As they cleared the table and washed the dishes, Katie pulled Sarah aside. "I have been watching John. You said he does not know anything about himself. But do you not think he looks like *Mammi* Mary?"

Sarah inhaled sharply. "The doctor said the same."

"She is at market this morning, selling her baked and jar goods. Perhaps you should go see her."

"*Jah*, I will talk to John."

At the sound of his name, John approached from the living room with a detour to peer out the window. "Talk about what?"

"Both Katie and Dr. Jones have said that you resemble Mary Miller. She is an elderly widow without family in the community and like a *grossmammi* to me. She is not my real grandmother, but she could be. I wonder if we should go see her, if she might have some clue to your identity. She has been in Nappanee for a long time. She is at market this morning."

Katie turned to Sarah, thought knitting her brow. "Did she not have family that left the Amish church? What happened to them? I think she has mentioned something about Fort Wayne, but I just cannot remember."

John stroked the stubble on his chin and walked first to the front window to look out and then to the enclosed back porch to peer into the yard. "Yes, let's go. The market will be crowded, right? We should be safe there, in a public place."

"And the market may help you remember. There could be something familiar there, something you see or smell or hear. The doctor said that even health professionals do not understand much about amnesia, so anything could be helpful."

"Perhaps." But he didn't look hopeful.

Her friend laid a comforting hand on Sarah's arm. "But I will keep Lyddie while you go, *jah*? It will be better for her here."

"*Jah*. Lyddie will help with the twins, so you can get your work done."

"I will pray that you and John find some answers."

"Pray for our safety, as well."

John donned his coat and hat, and Sarah hugged Lyddie long and hard. "Be helpful. Be careful," she said, although she knew her daughter did not need the admonishment.

As Sarah tied the strings of her winter bonnet under her chin, John checked outside. When he was satisfied that all was secure, they stepped quickly to the buggy.

Sarah hitched her skirt and stepped up to the buggy seat. Her friend held out a dried-apple pie to her. "For *Mammi* Mary. Every conversation goes better over a piece of pie."

Sarah shifted her foot against the brake and clucked to Lightning. The buggy jerked forward. "*Danki*, Katie. 'Tis true. We will see you in a little while."

She hoped, but would they?

As her friend waved goodbye, Sarah faced forward and turned the buggy onto the road. "*Mammi* Mary makes the best hot cider in all of northern Indiana. She may have a thermos of it at market."

As Sarah guided Lightning, she warmed inside, but was it from the handsome man next to her or the thought of hot cider with lots of cinnamon?

If only it could be a leisurely drive. But John wouldn't allow himself to relax back into the seat. Instead, he repeatedly checked every window for approaching vehicles, whether automobile or snowmobile, his hand gripping the edge of the seat.

He was fairly certain he wasn't Amish, but he didn't know exactly what kind of life he had lived before the attack or the speed at which he conducted it. This pace, though? Being able to see the tree limbs burdened with snow and rabbit tracks in the fields? The clip-clop of the horse in front? He wished it could be tranquil. Rather, it was frustrating, being out in the open with no real option for a speedy getaway. He leaned forward on his seat and stuck his head out for a good look around. All was clear for that instant. But what would the next minute bring?

So far, amnesia had been equal parts disconcerting and comforting. He had had moments of panic, of sweaty palms and racing heart, not knowing who he was, where he lived, who his relatives were. Did he like asparagus? Had he had a good childhood? Were Christmases warm and enjoyable or lonely and agonizing?

But it was also oddly comforting. Whatever bad memories he had had, they were gone. Had he had an argument with someone? A falling out? A difficult moment? It was now all erased. He had a fresh beginning in front of him. He could be whoever he wanted to be.

His nose began to tingle from the cold, and he rubbed a gloved hand over it. This riding in an open buggy was not for those who easily chilled. Sure, they had the storm front, and a couple of heavy blankets were available in the back if he wanted one. For sure and for certain, as Sarah would say, the Amish were a hearty bunch. Yes, they were peaceful, but they had endurance.

He checked the windows again and listened carefully. The hum of a car engine sounded faintly in the distance. Through the side window, he scanned the horizon, but a small hill rose up and prevented much visibility. John's fists clenched as he waited for the vehicle to appear.

"A car?" Sarah's voice held a tremor of something. Apprehension?

"I think so. Just keep driving. Is there a turnoff coming up? Anywhere to go?"

"No. Nothing."

The humming became louder, and as the vehicle crested the rise, the sound became more of a rumble.

John pressed his face to the cold glass to see what was coming. A moment later, it slowed as it approached. A delivery truck with the name of a popular beverage passed the buggy, veering around them and into the other lane to make a wide berth.

Sarah's exhalation matched his own. Relief filled him, and John turned forward to see that she slumped against the seat. The sooner they arrived at the public marketplace to see *Mammi* Mary, the better.

They rode in silence, and Sarah's lips moved occasionally. He continued his vigil through the windows but needed a distraction. He hated to interrupt what was probably prayer, but a little more information about their destination would also be helpful.

He waited for a pause in the movement of Sarah's lips, a waiting that was not unpleasant as he studied her pert nose and the way her eyelashes fell gently on her pink cheeks. She must have sensed him watching, for she turned and narrowed her eyes at him. *"Jah?"*

"I just was wondering about *Mammi* Mary and how she came to be like a grandmother to you."

"Each church district is close. Close together in where they live and close together in relationship. That is one of the best benefits of being Amish."

"Right. I understand that. But you talk about her as if you have a special relationship with her."

"I guess I do. She is also from Lancaster, so we have that in common. Her husband died many years ago, and she has no other family. I think there was a child, but she does not speak of him or her."

"So, you're both alone here in Indiana?"

"Jah." She paused to swallow. John wanted to kick himself. Was it sadness that clogged her throat? "I have suggested that she move in with me, but she will not. She says that she is hoping I will marry again."

Now it was John's turn to swallow hard. "Marry? A nice young Amish man?" He didn't want to examine why that thought bothered him.

"Jah. Must be Amish."

John turned to stare out the window again, unable to think of a reply that wouldn't embarrass him.

Another car approached and drove around them, slowing as it passed. John held out his arm to motion her to lean back and watched for the people to come into view. Sarah's hands perspired in her gloves, and she tightened her grasp on the reins. As the car pulled forward, a young girl in the back seat held up her cellular phone and pointed it at them.

Sarah flung a hand to her face as she whispered to John, "Cover your face."

He immediately looked away and raised a hand to cover his eyes, nose and mouth. As the car passed on, John sagged back. "Not very polite, taking our picture like that, but at least they weren't the guys who are after us." He swiped his hand over his forehead and then straightened his hat. "Does that bother you?"

"We are used to it. And what *gut* purpose would that serve, being bothered?"

"None, I guess."

"And see? They thought you were Amish. The clothing helps you fit in."

"But it isn't really my own, just like the name John isn't mine. For the sake of safety, though, I'll keep both the name and the clothing."

As they approached an intersection just a mile from the market, Sarah spotted a buggy coming from the right, followed closely by yet another buggy. Amish traffic was getting heavier as they neared the market. She glanced over at John. He had his arms crossed over his chest, even as he continued to survey the area and examine each vehicle that came into view.

Sarah pulled on the reins to halt Lightning at a four-way stop. After passing through, she turned to John. "You should drive."

He sat up straight. "What? Drive the horse and buggy?"

"*Jah.* We are getting more traffic, and it will look wrong if I am driving. It will draw attention to us." The very thought of drawing the wrong attention compelled her to check from side to side.

"I don't know anything about how to drive a horse and buggy."

"I will show you. It is not difficult." She suppressed a smile at the anxiety on his face. "You will learn quickly, I am sure. At the very least, you need to hold the reins in your hand, so we look like everyone else."

"Okay. But you know the last thing we need is a runaway horse and a buggy accident. Just stay close."

Sarah studied him for a moment. He was awfully cute when he was nervous. And she would definitely stay close, for as long as he wanted her. "It would be worse if those bad men found us again, *jah*?" That sobering thought brought her attention back to the task at hand.

John didn't answer, which was probably wise, considering the tension of the moment. "So, what's first?"

"The first rule to remember is to never let go of the reins. You are in charge."

He nodded solemnly and held his hands to mimic hers.

"See how Lightning's ears are flicking back? He is listening for you to tell him what you want him to do."

"Do I need to tell him something now?"

"No, he is fine." Would John be fine, though? For being such a strong and protective man, he looked as skittish as a colt. "You will be fine, too. Just sit up straight and place your feet on that low front board to brace them." Sarah tapped the toes of her boots against the board.

At the sound, John glanced down and then arranged his feet on the board just as Sarah had hers. He would do well, being such a quick study. "Okay. What now?"

"Now you take the reins. Hold them between your middle and third fingers. Like this." She held her hand out to demonstrate.

With John holding his fingers in the proper position, Sarah placed the reins in between his fingers. As she released them into his grip, her hand swept across his, and she felt what was probably a jolt of electricity at the touch of his hand. She had never felt electricity or had electricity, but that was how the novels described it. Was that what this feeling was? It was a tingle that instantly *ferhoodled* her. It scared her, so maybe she should let go of his hand. But it also made her want to hold on because it thrilled her.

It must have been only a second or two, that touch. But she forced herself to let go. He was, after all, supposed to be the one driving the buggy.

John's skin burned where she had touched him. Soft, gentle Sarah.

It didn't last near long enough, and she jerked her hand away as if stung. Cold invaded suddenly, and he shivered in the vacuum left by her withdrawal.

Back to business. That's what his attitude should be. That's what his attitude should have been all along. It was not his business to be smitten by this sweet and soft yet surprisingly resilient Amish woman.

He gripped the reins with a ferocity that matched the tension he felt. This not-knowing had been interesting at first. A bit of a relief, really, as he realized that he couldn't remember bad memories either. But now he was at his wit's end. He had just enough information to know that there was something important—something bad—lurking in the recesses of his mind. But what was it? And how could he dredge it out?

"See? You are doing well." Sarah's voice brought him back to the present and the important task of driving the horse and buggy safely to market.

Something about her voice made him turn to her, and a gentleness seemed to radiate from her.

Would the market help him remember? Smells? Sights? Sounds? If he knew what would trigger a memory, he would remember already and wouldn't need to trigger the memory. It seemed to be a vicious circle. And if he was a man of faith, then shouldn't prayer be a part of his life?

"*Ach*, John, mind the horse."

He shook his head to clear away the fog of thoughts to see that with a lack of attention to his driving, he had allowed Lightning to slow and wander off the side of the road. "I'm sorry. What do I do now?"

"Just cluck your tongue like this, and keep a light touch. *Tch-tch*, Lightning." The horse flicked his ears and headed back toward the road, picking up his pace. "He knows what to do, but he appreciates encouragement."

John adjusted his grip on the reins. "What did you say?"

A quizzical look shot across Sarah's face. "Just now? You mean about Lightning being a good horse? He knows what to do. He just needs encouragement from time to time, reassurance that he is on the proper road."

"Kind of like people."

"Jah."

The sting of angry heat in his chest reduced to the slow burn of conviction.

He knew what he needed to do with this faith he claimed, but could he? Perhaps with some encouragement. The statement Sarah had made seemed to have some truth about it, but how could it when he didn't seem to know anything, especially what to do next?

Was anything he was thinking making sense? With so many holes, he wasn't sure it was. But one thing he would do on trust, as a blind man stumbling with his hands out.

He would trust God more, and ask His guidance in the future.

Chapter Eight

Sarah was pleased with John's skill in driving the buggy, and she only took the reins back to guide Lightning through the back parking lot of the Commons Market. She tied the horse to the hitching post at the side of the large, long building and grabbed the dried-apple pie for *Mammi* Mary.

Caution was always wise, but was John overdoing it? They had escaped the night before, but nothing had happened since. Perhaps the bad men had given up their search? *Ach*, did bad men ever give up, though? John had paused as she secured the horse and buggy, looking carefully around the parking lot and the doorway, his face a mask of alertness and care.

Inside, the Commons Market was a bustling business with rows and rows of vendors hawking their wares. Surely, they were safe in there, with so many, many people milling about. She had been in the market on many occasions, looking for a friend and completely unable to find her in the crowd. They could disappear in here without difficulty.

John let the door close slowly behind him as his eyes grew wide. "Is it always this busy?"

"No. Sometimes, it is busier." She pointed to a vacant table. "See? Some vendor booths are empty in the winter. In the summer, we sell fresh produce from our gardens. Some sell fresh flowers, both in pots and in arrangements. But now, it is mostly preserves we put up back in the fall."

"Amish goods just taste better than those from the grocery store?"

Heat crept into her cheeks. "That is not for me to say. But *Englischers* tend not to stock up, and they are always looking for someplace to go so they can get out of the house. Word gets out, especially now with the internet, so there are tourists as well as the locals."

"How do you know about the internet?"

"I have seen it here. *Englisch* vendors and customers with their little computers. It is not something I would ever want, even if the bishop did allow it. It seems rather intrusive. Too controlling of their time." She led him through an aisle past a couple of vendors, and then turned right down another long aisle.

"It looks like you could find anything you wanted in here. From this spot, I see sewing materials, big barrels of candy, clothing, furniture, knickknacks that look handmade, spices. There's even a guy over there selling sandwiches."

"*Jah*, it can be overwhelming."

He stood for a moment, looking around, probably surveying for any threatening people but also trying to take it all in. Considering the quiet of the Amish life he had been living for the past few days, it perhaps seemed like a lot of noise all at once. Market days were interesting because they were different, but they were often also too much for Sarah, requiring a strong cup of chamomile tea and an oatmeal cookie in the quiet stillness of her home at the end of the day.

"It's so busy, I would think it would be difficult to find someone in here."

"*Jah*, I have had that problem before." It was bolstering to have a man around again to be helpful and look after her, and this man was comforting enough that she gave voice to her worries. "So, you believe we would be hidden in here? Safe inside the crowd?"

"Yes, but let's find Mrs. Miller as quickly as possible. Okay?"

"*Jah*, I would like that." Balancing the pie in one hand, Sarah removed her winter bonnet and straightened her white organza *kapp* as they walked down the long aisle. She turned to find John staring at her.

He cleared his throat, his cheeks brightening into a light shade of pink. "So, um, not all the vendors here are Amish?" He turned his gaze to the others as they passed by the booths.

"A lot of us are Amish, but some are not. Some dress as Amish just to attract buyers." She motioned a few tables down. "We're almost there."

"That's not right. Doesn't it bother you?"

"What *gut* would come of being bothered? I trust *Gott* to sell my goods when I'm here and to provide for me and Lyddie."

Sarah slowed as she approached a booth on the right filled with jar goods, loaves of bread and berry pies. A weight lifted from her shoulders as she spied the elderly woman in the lavender dress and starched white *kapp* organizing her jars. In the past, whatever had been wrong, *Mammi* Mary had been able to soothe with a kind word or a comforting touch or a hot drink. Sarah prayed that would be the case today, although her problem this time was quite a bit larger than any others she had had.

John's heart ached within him at the notion of having such a peace with life's events as Sarah seemed to have. He yearned for that, but how did one achieve it? Especially with an utter lack of memory? But the chatter and commotion of the market around him wouldn't allow his thoughts to develop that idea any further.

Sarah stopped at the edge of a booth where the elderly Amish woman was setting jars on a shelf with her side turned to them. "*Mammi* Mary," Sarah called softly.

The woman turned slowly and squinted in their direction for a moment. She then raised her hand in greeting, a large smile lighting her wrinkled face.

"*Wilkom.* Come. Come."

John caught the pie as Sarah thrust it at him. He watched *Mammi* Mary open her arms to Sarah, and as Sarah returned the hug, a sudden pain struck his temples. He stared at the elderly woman's face, visually tracing the wrinkles that lined her pale skin, startled at the blue of her eyes, and the instant headache lessened to a dull ache.

Slowly, he approached, looking up and down the aisle. This visit was important to Sarah, and could, perhaps, be important to him. But he didn't want to linger too long. It might increase the chance for their danger to be brought upon this woman.

Sarah turned to retrieve the pie, a wide and beautiful smile lighting her face, and then handed it to Mrs.

Miller. "Katie made this pie for you, *Mammi*. Dried
apple."

"And you brought it. *Danki* to you both, *liebchen*."
She gestured to usher them farther into the booth and
away from the crowds. "Lyddie is with Katie this morning?"

"*Jah*. She is helpful with the twins."

"*Gut*." But as John approached, Mary looked hard at
his face, her sharp gaze piercing him. An odd expression lit her features. Curiosity, maybe? But surely she
would have had many interactions with the *Englisch*,
especially here at the market.

He stepped in closer, behind Sarah. As Mrs. Miller
took the pie, she continued to stare at John.

"*Ach*, I am sorry for my slowness." She gestured
Sarah toward a door in between her booth and the neighboring stall. "You know where the vendors' break room
is. We can have our visit in there. Let me ask my neighbor to watch my tables, and then we will have introductions."

Sarah led the way into the small room and placed
the apple pie on one of two tables. A kitchenette stood
against the far wall. It was empty of other vendors and
had no other entrances, but seemed secure. A small
window was covered with a light calico curtain. He
stepped to it quickly and lifted the curtain just enough
to peek outside. It looked out onto the parking lot filled
with horses and buggies, but not a single person was in
sight. He allowed himself to breathe deeply, but the infusion of fresh oxygen did little to calm him.

Following Sarah's lead, John removed his coat and
hat and draped them over an empty chair. The door
opened, and *Mammi* Mary entered, motioning for them

to sit at the table. John chose a chair that faced the door, the hairs on the back of his neck standing upright as Mrs. Miller appraised his Amish clothing and then fixed her stare on his chin, which sported only the shortest of whiskers.

Sarah spoke first, although she seemed rather affected by Mary's stare. "*Mammi* Mary, this is John. He was in a snowmobiling accident near my house, and Lyddie and I are caring for him until he is well." She paused. "Until his memory returns."

John extended his hand but quickly withdrew it as Mary continued to stare at him. "It's a pleasure to meet you, ma'am."

"Call me Mary, as Sarah does." It seemed to be difficult, but she tore her gaze from John and looked back to Sarah. "What do you mean, *until his memory returns*?"

"We are not sure what happened. He had an injury on his head, but it could be the trauma of the accident. He cannot remember anything."

John absently touched the bandage that remained on his forehead and just nodded his agreement.

"Nothing?"

"No, nothing."

Sarah continued. "Both Dr. Jones and Katie said that he looked like you. We hoped you might have some information that could help John remember."

Mary shook her head in sympathy, then stepped toward the kitchenette. "Let me get us some cider." But as she retrieved three mugs from the cupboard, poured cider from a thermos and carried the mugs to the table, she continued to stare at him. "Do you remember your name? Is it really John?"

John sipped his cider. "I don't know what my real name is. Sarah suggested she call me John."

"Where are you from?"

"I don't know. I would guess somewhere in northern Indiana since that's where I am now. But I suppose I could have traveled here from a great distance, also." He shrugged and took another sip. "That's not helpful, is it?"

Sarah smiled at him, but Mary continued peppering him with questions. "What is your occupation?"

"We found a badge from the Fort Wayne Police Department at the crash site, but I don't know if it's mine or not." Should he tell her that he wasn't sure who on the police force was trustworthy and who wasn't? He looked to Sarah, but she didn't give any sort of indication that he should tell more.

Mary lifted her hand to her mouth, her eyes wide and eyebrows raised. "Is there anything you know about yourself?"

"The only thing I think I know is that I like to work with wood. Or at least I know something about woodworking. I discovered that in Sarah's barn yesterday."

"So, you are not Amish even though you wear Amish clothes? You do not have a beard, and yet you are not shaved."

John looked down at his shirt and fingered one of the suspenders. "Sarah let me borrow these. I don't think I'm Amish, and yet the Amish don't seem completely foreign to me. I don't know why."

Sarah leaned forward to rest her forearms on the edge of the table. "John got some blood on his clothes, so I let him wear my brother's." She caught his glance and then cut her eyes sideways. What she was saying wasn't untruthful, but neither was it the entire story. She certainly had never indicated just how much danger they were in. But Sarah knew Mary, and he didn't. He would trust her judgment. Perhaps she was protecting her elderly friend.

Of the three mugs of cider, only Mary's remained untouched, yet she stood and excused herself, going to stand at the small sink. John shifted in his chair to see her better from the side. She had raised a wrinkled hand and pressed it to her cheek as she stared at the wall.

"Mammi?" Sarah cast a worried glance at John, then pushed her chair back.

Before she could stand, Mary seemed to wipe an eye, then returned to the table, lowering herself heavily into the chair.

John rubbed his forehead, being careful of the bandage. What was his role here? Should he say something? Comfort in some manner? Perhaps he should just excuse himself to check outside and leave the women alone.

He started to push his chair out, but Sarah grabbed his hand. Apparently, she wanted him to stay.

He settled in his chair again, and she withdrew her hand from his and instead pulled Mary's hands together into both of hers. *"Mammi,* are you feeling all right today? You look as if you are seeing a vision."

Mary sighed. "I am, Sarah. The *gut* doctor and Katie were right to send you to me."

She drew away from Sarah and lifted John's smooth, strong hand in her wrinkled and spotted ones. "I think you are my grandson, Jedidiah."

Chapter Nine

"I'm what?"

"You're my grandson. And your name is Jedediah. Jedediah Miller."

John shoved back his chair with a loud scraping sound and ran a hand through his hair. The shocking news propelled him to pace the room. It was ten steps from the table to the edge of the kitchenette. Ten steps back.

A pulsing began in his head, not exactly the pound of a headache, but the tight feeling across his forehead he had come to associate with trying to summon a memory.

His shoe squeaked on the linoleum floor as he spun back to the women who sat at the table, both now staring with wide eyes at him. "Jedediah? That's my name?" It did not feel familiar on his tongue or sound right in his ears. The old woman must be desperate for connection with a family member or seeking attention or…or *ferhoodled*, as Sarah would say. Confused.

"Are you sure, *Mammi* Mary?" Sarah's sweet voice

that lilted with the accent of her Pennsylvania German seemed to approach him as if through a tunnel.

"For sure and for certain, Sarah. As sure as I am sitting here."

John stopped midstride, his attention and his thoughts no longer under his control but focused on this woman who said she was his grandmother. "Why do you think so?" It must just be speculation.

"You look exactly like my son. The spitting image, I believe the *Englisch* would say. The last time I saw you in the flesh, you were five years old and in the back seat of the Amish taxi, waving goodbye as your *daed* and *mamm* drove away from their family and their faith." A stray tear wandered down the older woman's cheek.

His feet continued him on the path between the kitchenette and the table. Shouldn't he be glad, thrilled even, to have some answers, finally? In a way, he was. But there were no memories associated with this information. He couldn't remember a father or mother, an Amish upbringing or leaving in a taxi. Maybe if there was some connection to a memory, it would be easier to believe.

"*Mammi*, what else can you tell us about John? About Jedediah?"

One thing did seem sure—he liked the sound of his name, whatever it was, on Sarah's lips.

Another thought pierced him, a thought that ricocheted around his aching skull. Did the man who was after them know his real name? He listened at the door, but all he could hear were the common sounds of a marketplace. He crossed to the window to peer outside, but all was calm there, as well.

Mary finally lifted her mug and sipped her cider.

Whether or not John was finding any answers in her revelation, apparently she was discovering some satisfaction.

"Your parents' names are David and Miriam Miller." Mary's voice was calm and soothing. "They left years ago, and I have not seen them since. However—" Mary leaned forward and lowered her voice "—when my daughter-in-law, your mother, Jedediah, mails me notes about my grandson, I keep them in a special place."

"You have letters from my mother?"

Mary sipped again, slowly. "This is my family. I love my son, my daughter-in-law, my grandson. My life has not been the same since they left."

John bent himself into a chair across from the woman who claimed to be his grandmother. "So, I'm Jedediah? And I grew up here?"

"Jah." She spread her arms as if to encompass the countryside. "Indiana. Since you were five years old."

A thought pinged in his brain. "So, is that why bits and pieces of the Amish life seem familiar to me despite the amnesia?"

"Jah, I 'spect so."

"Jedediah, huh?" He tried it a couple more times to see how it felt on his tongue. It wasn't bad, but it wasn't familiar either. "Isn't that an Amish name? Or at least a Biblical name?"

Sarah clasped her hands, a grin reaching across her beautiful face. *"Jah.* That is a good, strong, Biblical name. It is a popular Amish name. It means *beloved of the Lord."*

John pressed the heels of his hands to his temples, a vain attempt to suppress the dull ache and revive more memories. "There's a memory in there somewhere. It's a struggle." He exhaled slowly. "I think I may have been called Jed."

"That is short for Jedediah, *jah*? That would be the shorter, *Englisch*-sounding nickname."

Mary ran a finger over the handle of her mug. "Perhaps your parents gave you that name when they left the Amish church."

"Didn't you say my mother sent you letters? Do you still have them?"

Bolting upright, Mary gasped. "*Ach*, I did. Where is my mind?" As she stood, she paused with a stricken expression and ran a gnarled hand over John's. "I am sorry. It is hard to imagine what you must be struggling with in your loss of memory. Let me get the letters. I hide them in a compartment of my money box since no one gets in there except me. It is my most secret place."

John could barely sip his apple cider before she was back, a small stack of envelopes in her grasp.

The paper of the oldest envelope had yellowed slightly, and the faded postmark reflected a date nearly twenty years earlier. The letter was brief and conveyed the simple message that they had settled and all were well. John held it with the tips of his fingers, but as he studied the meticulous handwriting, it was the same as it had been for the past few days. No memories emerged. Not a single one.

Apparently, he had played baseball, second base, and done well in school. A twelfth birthday party had been a particular delight filled with friends and pizza and bowling. His mother had sent a total of five letters over the years, and he sorted through them, noting the growth and development of a person who Mary had said was him. The tone of each letter was stiff and formal, as if written to a stranger.

The last letter was dated just a few months prior. He stood to pace the room again, reading it carefully. "So, I have no brothers or sisters, and I'm not married? It's just my parents and me?"

"*Jah.* That is what the letters seem to say. Something as momentous as another child or a wedding would have been mentioned, I am sure."

A memory flung itself into his mind, and he staggered backward with the force of it.

He was a police officer. Was that his badge that they had found at the crash site? Fuzziness surrounded the memory, but he was sure he was law enforcement. Was he from Fort Wayne, the city on the badge? The memory receded, and he was left without any idea. The letters didn't contain a return address, and the city and state of the postmark were too faint to read, so that didn't help either.

Another memory, this one stronger, pushed him to drop into a chair. A prickling sensation crawled up his arms and seized his chest. He was in danger. They had found him out, and the only end that would satisfy was his elimination. But who were they?

John forced himself to take several deep, cleansing breaths. Panic wouldn't serve any of them right now. He closed his eyes to try to bring the memory closer to his consciousness. *They* were criminals. But not all. One, at least, was someone who masqueraded as being on the side of good and right.

But who?

He opened his eyes to find Sarah and Mary watching

him. Mary's lips moved silently. Could she be praying for him, even then?

"It's just too fuzzy." He shrugged an apology. "I know I'm a police officer, just as we suspected, but I can't remember where or what my last activities were, right before the crash."

Sarah reached a comforting hand to him. "Anything you can remember is helpful."

"It also seems that there is something important coming up soon, but I have no idea what." He swallowed, hesitant to give the next bit of information. But after what they had been through, Sarah was not unaware. "The danger is great."

"*Jah*, we knew that already."

"I just can't remember any more than that. So much is still missing." He squinched his eyes shut again to try to summon up images. Who were the criminals? What was their criminal behavior? And what did it have to do with him?

He pictured the police badge they had found in the snow. *Shield.* The word zinged into his mind. That was what it was more properly called. But he could summon no recollection of wearing a uniform or handling a weapon or even who his colleagues might have been within the department. There was at least one officer who was not completely on the up-and-up. But who? And were there others?

The void engulfed him, a black hole that had swallowed all his memories. He was unable to pull out anything further.

And just like that, his head began to pound, right behind his eyes. He wouldn't be able to remember anything else now.

He grabbed his mug and took another long pull on his cider, but it only soured as it hit his stomach.

"Are you well? Are any more memories returning?" Sarah's gentle voice soothed him more than the cider ever could.

"I feel a headache coming in. And no. No more memories. I'm a police officer, and I'm in trouble, both from a criminal ring of some sort and from someone or some people within the police department. That's all I can remember." He scrubbed a hand over his face. His glance fell on the clock. "What about the market? *Mammi* Mary needs to return to her booth, and I'm not comfortable staying in one place much longer. We need to change our location."

"Just a few more minutes. I have a question for *Mammi* Mary, John, if you will allow me." A sheepish look graced her face.

He nodded and spoke the question that was probably on both of their minds. "If you're my grandmother, then why am I not Amish?"

Sarah returned the nod. He had asked her question.

"You are short on time, so I will keep this sad story brief." Mary sighed and shifted in her chair, fingering one of the ties that dangled from her prayer *kapp*. "The Lord only blessed me with one child. Your father, David. We were unusual within the Amish community. Amish families typically have lots of children. But I savored every moment with him. As children do, David grew up and met a lovely young Amish woman. Your mother, Miriam. Your *grossdaadi*, your grandfather, and I had known her most of her life and loved her like our own. It was not long after they married, and they welcomed you, their first *bobbeli*. A beautiful baby boy."

Sarah turned to smile at him, and John felt a blush rise to his cheeks. "It sounds like everything was fine then. What happened?"

"When you were four years old, your *mamm* had another baby. A little girl. But as sometimes happens, the *bobbeli* was born with problems. Your father, a good Amish man, hitched up the buggy and went for the telephone to call for help. But help did not come fast enough. The baby died."

A pain rose in his chest, surprising him with a sudden heartache for a sister he never knew. Mary's eyes stared at the door as she seemed to relive those days.

"As soon as the funeral was over, your *daed* packed up your *mamm* and you, and you left in the Amish taxi. He was so bitter over what he thought *Gott* had done to him that he would not speak to us. He just left." Mary ran her hand over the smooth surface of the table, multiple emotions running across her face as she seemed to fight to keep control. "I have not seen him since."

Silence fell over the room, grief enveloping John, although nothing that Mary had said seemed familiar to him. He listened closely for anyone approaching the break room, but there was no one. Now that he had just the slightest bit more information, he needed to be even more vigilant for their safety.

"What about your husband? My grandfather?"

"He died years ago, not long after your father left the Amish community. The doctor said it was a heart attack, but I believe his heart was broken by the loss of his family." Mary passed a hand over her forehead as if trying to wipe away the difficult memories. "Because of David's disdain for the Amish way of life, I do not have much information about you. Like I said,

I would assume that if your mother had had any more *bobblin*, she would have written when she sent information about you."

"So, I'm an only child." Not that he could remember any siblings, but a new feeling of loneliness invaded him.

"Can you remember if you were raised with any faith? I have not been able to tell from your mother's few letters what their standing is with the Lord. They left here so bitter and angry that I expect they rejected *Gott* altogether."

"I'm just not sure. I think I believe. It seems right to me. But clearly, I'm not Amish. Not anymore."

A skim through the letters tantalized him, but it only seemed like he was reading about a stranger. His mind had no recognition of the person in the notes. Memories were there, he knew, but they were just beyond his mental grasp.

Sarah picked up one of the envelopes and studied the careful manuscript.

What he did know, though, were three things. First, he wasn't married according to the letters, but still, he was beginning to care too much for his own comfort about the beautiful Amish woman who, even now, smiled as she looked at the letter. Second, the feeling of danger was real and intense. And third, the sooner he could remember, the sooner this could all be over, and he could return to his life.

The question was, would that be for better or for worse?

His name was Jedediah.
Sarah's heart swelled within her, and she wanted a

piece of paper and a pencil to doodle that name in the margins like a silly school girl.

Jedediah was a *gut* name.

But no. She absolutely must stop her thinking from going in that direction. John had just stated an obvious truth.

Clearly, I'm not Amish.

She glanced over at him as he hooked a hand into one side of his suspenders, deep in thought. The green of his shirt complemented the vivid green of his eyes. *Ach*, he was handsome in his Amish clothing. For sure and for certain.

He might look Amish on the outside, but on the inside he was *Englisch*. Raised that way. Living that way. *Jah*, the look on the outside was important to a girl. But just as important, even more so perhaps, was the inside. A man's standing before *Gott*.

His *gut* qualities made for quite a long list. Many qualities her own *daed* and *mamm* would approve of.

"Jedediah Miller." It was a whisper as she examined the envelope.

A warm hand rested on her sleeve. "What is it?"

She looked up into John's eyes, questioning and probing like she had a startled look on her face. She probably did.

Mammi Mary pushed her chair back and stood, the sound of the scraping against the floor breaking the connection with John.

Of course, it was foolish to think that he might consider returning to the Amish. She shouldn't even entertain such a notion. His family had left the Amish church, and he had an important position within the *Englisch* community.

She stood and moved next to *Mammi* Mary at the sink. "Let me wash those mugs, *Mammi*. You probably need to return to your booth."

Mary placed the cups in the sink and stepped toward the door. "*Danki*. I hope I have been helpful. Stop to say goodbye before you leave."

The cold water of the faucet hit her hands as John opened the door for *Mammi* Mary, bringing her back to the present day. Mary said *danki* for holding the door, and Sarah turned back to the sink, refusing to look at John. *Ach*, his Amish clothes looked so natural on him.

But his caution as he opened the door invaded her daydream, a reminder of their danger. Not that she could forget that her life was at stake. Once he remembered who he was and returned to his job in his world, an event that surely would happen soon, he would be gone. Gone back to his police officer job that required the carrying of a weapon and an everyday potential for danger.

And she would probably move, with Lyddie, back to Lancaster County and marry the man her mother had found for her. An Amish, peace-loving, nonviolent man who would never use a gun, except, maybe, to hunt for food to feed his family.

If John was committed to his job that involved violence, then he would never have any interest in becoming Amish. If she was committed to remaining within the Amish church, the only church and community she had ever known, then she would never have any interest in becoming *Englisch*. It was a tangle for them both.

A tangle?

Sarah shook her head to clear her thoughts, the white starched ties of her *kapp* swinging back and forth. There was no tangle. There was simply danger, evidenced by

John's hesitation at the door and his careful look outside. When it was over, John—*Jed*—would leave.

It was better that way. Was it not?

With a promise to stop at *Mammi* Mary's booth on their way out, Sarah placed the mugs back in the cupboard and then lifted the curtain on the window just enough to check on Lightning. Dark clouds filled the sky and threatened overhead, and she was grateful that her church district drove enclosed buggies with storm fronts to hold back the wind and snow and keep at least a little of the cold out. It might make the upcoming drive a bit more comfortable.

A shudder coursed through her, but it wasn't anticipation of the cold this time. Gratitude for the enclosed buggy filled her for another reason—safety. She refused to let her mind wander to the targets she and John would be in an open cart.

She turned back to the table to see John—*Jed*—fidgeting with the edge of the pie. Was he nervous about what he had learned? Did it not sit well, his name and occupation?

"Was it a *gut* thing that we came here to see *Mammi* Mary? You know who you are now, *jah*?" Surely to discover one's true identity after a case of amnesia would be a relief.

"Yeah, it was good. But I wouldn't say I know who I am. I have a name and an occupation, but nothing more. And even the name and occupation don't feel familiar or right to me."

"Perhaps in time they will grow more comfortable."

Silence grew between them before John answered. "Maybe."

"What about your *mamm* and *daed*? We could contact them."

"You didn't notice? There were no return addresses on the letters. But I can look for a David and Miriam Miller in Fort Wayne as soon as I have access to a computer." He rose to check out the window, leaning near her to peer out the window from her direction. Was it truly just last night that she had thrown the boiling water in the face of the intruder and then run from her house? It was only a matter of time before he found them. That was the reason for John's caution.

Ach, he was so close. His scent of wood and sawdust tickled her nose. She needed a distraction from him, and fast.

As he pulled away and returned to his seat, she cleared her throat. The last thing she wanted was to sound choked up or emotional over him. "What about your name? Do I call you Jedediah now? Or do you continue with John?"

He looked at her and shook his head as if he couldn't believe he was in a situation that required such a choice. "Neither feel right. But I've become accustomed to *John* over the past couple of days. And it might be safer. Keep me incognito until I can remember more. Assuming the guys who are after us know my real name, I wouldn't want them to hear you call me Jedediah and figure it out. It could put us in further danger."

"But you are in my brother's clothing. That is not disguise enough?"

Her brother's clothing. That's all he was doing, wasn't it? Playing dress-up?

"I don't know if it's disguise enough, but I don't

want to take a chance." John glanced at the clock, but he couldn't remember what time they had arrived at the market. "We should move on. We've been here long enough."

A sigh trickled out of Sarah as she lifted the pie from the table and placed it in the refrigerator. "*Jah.* Let us remind *Mammi* Mary of her pie on our way out."

John placed his palms on the table, but as he pushed himself up to standing, his low-grade headache increased. He sank back to his chair, cradling his head in his hands.

The sound of swishing skirts trickled to his ear, and he soon felt a gentle touch on his shoulder.

"Are you remembering something?"

He searched the darkness in his mind, but it was empty. "No, nothing more. But I wish I could. I have the feeling it would help us tremendously if I could just summon up the details."

"But we know your name and who your parents are. You are a police officer. That is something, *jah*?"

"It's not enough, though. There was another police officer in on the criminal activity, an officer higher in rank than I am. But who? I can't contact my own precinct because I don't know who's dirty and who isn't. I wouldn't even know which police department to contact anyway. The shield was from Fort Wayne, but was it mine? Am I with the Fort Wayne Police Department, or is the other guy? Or are we both?" He sat upright and slapped his knee, the sting matching the angry heat that grew in his chest. "And what's coming up? What event? I just wish I could figure out how it all ties together."

Sarah scooted a fraction of an inch away from him, casting him a sidelong glance.

Defeat made him sag against the chair. His temper had gotten the best of him, and he'd disappointed Sarah. She didn't need to say a word. Her body language spoke volumes to him. Anger was much more *Englisch* than Amish.

"*Gott* will do what is His best will for you."

Whether she meant it as an admonition or not, Sarah's quiet statement struck deep to his soul. Was he a believer, as he had speculated? It resonated within him, a yearning to know and praise God. If he was a believer, then God should be taking care of them, right? Certainly, Sarah had just said so. Was He? Was He there, looking at them both?

Look at the evidence. John shifted in the chair. Was that his law-enforcement training kicking in? Or was that the revival of his faith instructing him to count his blessings? It didn't matter where it came from as long as he followed through. He was still alive, even though he could have been killed, apparently a few times over, by now. He had survived the snowmobile crash and the rocks. He had lost his memory and suffered a few scrapes, but he was in safe hands, at least for the moment. He was not in the hands of the bad guys, whoever they were.

So, what next? He was eager for a purpose, a plan that would help him to know and understand where he was going. This indefinitely temporary position in limbo was unnerving at best, maddening at worst. He couldn't traipse about the countryside, hiding from place to place, pretending to be Amish for the foreseeable future, no matter how fetching the Amish woman was beside him.

Chapter Ten

Sarah collected her cape and bonnet from the chair. "We have the information we were seeking. Is it time to go?"

John simply nodded and grabbed his coat and hat. He paused at the door and opened it slowly. Sarah stood behind him, stretching to her tiptoes to see over his shoulder.

"It looks clear."

But as John opened the door further, Sarah gasped to see the crowd of customers gathered at *Mammi* Mary's. It seemed that everyone in the market had decided to shop at her booth.

Mammi Mary turned toward her money box and locked gazes with Sarah. A wide smile pushed the wrinkles aside. "Sarah, can you help?"

Sarah pushed gently on John's shoulder to urge him from the break room. "Just for a few minutes, John? The income is so important, and it is a *gut* crowd."

John agreed, and *Mammi* Mary turned back to her customer. Sarah quickly stashed her outer garments under the nearest table and rose to see a familiar face. "*Wilkom*, Mrs. Granger. How may I help you?"

The customer leaned to the right and seemed to make a deliberate point of noticing John, who stood a few steps behind Sarah. "Good afternoon, Sarah. You're here with a gentleman friend, today?" Her bright red lips that matched her bright red blouse curled into a knowing smile, and the earrings that dangled to her shoulders shook their agreement.

Heat leaped into Sarah's cheeks. It was not the first time someone had tried to make a match, and she knew Mrs. Granger's intentions were honorable. But right in front of John? She needed to downplay the situation right fast. "He is helping to carry the boxes today."

"Mmm-hmm. If you say so." The customer prattled on as she picked up jars to examine the labels. "I shared some of the pumpkin butter with my book club last week, and they just went wild. So, I want some more of that. And my Harold loves jalapeño jelly. I could never stomach the spicy stuff, but he just spreads it thick on a cracker and gobbles it down." She laughed at herself, her earrings bobbling with mirth, as well.

"I am glad you like Mrs. Miller's preserves." Sarah darted a look around, suddenly aware of the number of people there. What if their pursuers were hiding in the crowd? She rubbed her hands together to keep them from shaking.

"Last week, and the week before, and the week before, I looked at the chowchow. And I think I'm ready to try it. Do you have any today?"

Sarah turned to look through *Mammi* Mary's jars on the shelf and found John surveying the crowd. The intensity of his vigilance soothed her somewhat. She found two jars of chowchow and forced her mind on the income that *Mammi* Mary so desperately needed.

Mrs. Granger grasped the jar, her red-painted fingernails a contrast to the yellow of the chowchow. "Now, what is in this? Mary told me last week, but I just can't remember."

"It is a pickled relish. Chopped pickles, seasoned mustard, fresh vegetables from the garden." Sarah placed the other jar of chowchow on the table.

"And what do I do with it?" Mrs. Granger twisted the jar over and around, watching the yellow-orange, thick and gooey substance slosh inside.

"Whatever you want—hamburgers or beans. My little girl likes it on her mashed potatoes."

The customer pressed her lips together as she considered the chowchow. "Okay, I'll try it. And I have these others, as well." She dug around in her sizeable leather purse and brought out two twenty-dollar bills to hand over to Sarah.

Sarah accepted the money and handed it to John, who had appeared at her elbow. "Let me do that." She turned just enough to see that John sported a dazzling smile aimed directly at Mrs. Granger. Had he heard her earlier comment about her gentleman friend? Sarah fisted her skirt, a vain attempt to dry the perspiration that now slicked her palms.

He handed her a paper sack from a pile next to the money box and then turned his attention away.

"He's handsome." Mrs. Granger seemed to be trying to keep her voice low, but it surely wasn't low enough for Sarah's liking. "Will I be seeing him again?"

Sarah gently placed the jars into the bag. All she could manage was a shrug of the shoulders and a glance at the nearest door, longing for a quick exit. The money box creaked open behind her, but where was John with the change?

A touch on the shoulder turned her attention away from Mrs. Granger. "Can you finish this? I'll be back in a minute. Will you be all right here with Mrs. Miller?" John's voice sounded near her ear.

She turned to find John holding the two twenties out to her. His skin had a green tinge, not unlike the color of the money, and he looked rather woozy. "I will be all right. Are you not well?"

He did not answer, just walked toward a nearby vendor.

"John?"

"The flu is going around, Sarah. Maybe he's coming down with it?" Mrs. Granger's comment forced Sarah's attention away from John as he retreated from the booth. "Chicken noodle soup, that's what my mother always prescribed. But you would know that, wouldn't you?" She took up her bag of jar goods. "Harold's waiting in the car for me. Can you believe he prefers to be out there and not in here shopping? Goodbye, dear. See you next week."

As the customer turned toward another booth, all Sarah wanted was to find John and see what was wrong. She turned in the direction he had gone and found him two vendors over, staring blankly at a quilt, still a little green. But with the money box right there and customers still pressing into *Mammi* Mary's booth, she couldn't chase after him.

Mammi Mary needed her, so she helped another customer, keeping John within view. But as the customer finished and turned to go, Sarah found Sheriff Jaspar approaching, another man with him.

Her throat seized her, a lump forming immediately over which she could not swallow. The sheriff? The man with him was a bit taller and looked to be solid strength, with a swagger in his walk that communicated to Sarah that no one should challenge him.

She cleared her throat, as if she could cough up the lump. Perhaps she should just treat him like a customer? She would give Mrs. Granger her jar goods for free if she could just have her back at the booth, rather than these two.

But as the sheriff stopped directly in front of the table, she found her mouth completely dry and unable to form any words. Why did this man strike such fear into her? Or was it the presence of both of them? Whatever it was, the sooner they stated their business and could be on their way, the better.

"Good afternoon, Sarah." A half smile snaked across his fleshy lips.

A shiver slithered up her spine. All she could manage was a nod.

"This is Simon Carlyle. He's a fellow law-enforcement officer. We're looking for someone who's gone missing."

"Well, Jaspar, don't scare the girl." Carlyle's grin portended maliciousness, and his evil tone felt like a hand closing on Sarah's throat. "We're just looking for someone we haven't heard from in a while." His left eye twitched as he spoke.

Well, this was a whole new level of being *ferhoodled*. For sure and for certain, they were looking for John. Otherwise, why ask her? Her hands took on life and fiddled with the jars on the display shelves while her heart threatened to pound out from underneath her apron.

"The man who was at your house. Did you say he was your brother?" The sheriff rested his hand on the weapon in his holster.

She glanced toward *Mammi* Mary, but she seemed to be deeply involved in helping a customer. It took all her energy, but as much as she wanted to, Sarah did not look around for John. Wherever he was, she prayed he was out of sight. He was not her brother, but if she didn't answer the question, was that lying? "He is no longer there, but I thank you for your concern." She held her breath.

The sheriff didn't speak, just stared, his dark eyes boring into her, as though if he waited long enough she would spill out all the information he sought.

The blackness of his stare threatened to crumple her, even as a muscle around her eye began to spasm. She was desperate for John's return to help her, and yet she didn't want to put him or *Mammi* Mary in harm's way.

What should she do?

The scent of it overwhelmed him, a mixture of ink and paper and a metallic odor that John could nearly taste. A hint of throbbing began at his temple, but this time it was coupled with a wave of nausea.

It was the money. The two twenty-dollar bills that Sarah had handed him. Even after he had given it back and walked away, as far away as he dared with their pursuers possibly lurking nearby, the odor tickled his nose, clinging to him. But why was it affecting him so?

A memory lurked. Its elusiveness irritated him like a scratchy tag on a new shirt. He couldn't quite reach it, and he knew that if he could just get ahold of it, he could rip it out.

He had stumbled two booths over, far enough away he wouldn't have to answer questions from customers but close enough that he could keep an eye on Sarah. He held his fingers to his nose. The scent lingered on his skin. A tsunami of lightheadedness passed over him, but he powered through it, looking up at the ceiling to steady himself.

The customer with the bright red blouse had left not long after John, and so John had studied the booth around him. He picked up a small wooden sign, stained a deep brown, that had been painted with the phrase Plain & Simple. The wood had been sanded but it was still rough enough to scratch at his hand and pull him away from the agony of a lost memory. A basketful of dolls in Amish dress but without faces rested nearby. Snowmen made with socks and colorful buttons filled another basket.

John surveyed the booth and the area beyond it as the booth's operator helped a customer with an armful of purchases. The operator accepted the bills from the customer, and John felt fixated on the stack of ten-dollar bills in her cash box. That memory, whatever it was, hovered near the edge of his mind, tantalizing in its closeness yet completely out of his reach.

If he closed his eyes, would that help? If he blocked out all distractions and tried to summon one single image connected with the odor of the ink and paper of the money, could he remember? Would his mind be able to connect the dots as to why the aromas brought such strong sensations?

He lowered his eyelids, letting the darkness consume

him. The noise of the market around him still filtered through, but with effort he could ignore it. The vivid green of a twenty-dollar bill floated in the blackness, but nothing else. Maybe it had nothing to do with the men who were after him and Sarah. Maybe he was a rich man with the love of money. Or perhaps he was a poor man, constantly in need. Either of those were valid reasons for the effect the bills had on him.

There was no point in pursuing that memory any further. He opened his eyes and turned back to Mrs. Miller's booth, rolling his shoulders as if that could shrug off the disappointment that he couldn't remember anything exact.

But the two men with Sarah weren't customers. When had they arrived? John immediately recognized the sheriff and pushed him to the periphery of his concentration. The other man, though…

A jolt like a stroke of lightning coursed through John, and he nearly staggered from the weight of it. He knew that man.

On instinct, he sidestepped to a position behind a rack of handmade signs. He picked one up and fingered it, hoping he looked like he was admiring the merchandise. At eye level there was a break in between the racks of signs, and John peeked through at the two men. The man with the sheriff was definitely familiar. John knew him from somewhere, that much was certain. But no name or place or relationship came to mind. The clothing was nondescript, dark pants with a black jacket, and his haircut and features, from what John could see, were also unremarkable.

Given that he was with the sheriff and that the sheriff had already proven to be less than helpful, John doubted there was any virtue in his visit to Sarah's booth. But as he stared, the all-too-familiar haze invaded his synapses. Just like with the money, though, no memory would come forth.

He jerked his attention to Sarah. The two men pressed against the table, as close as they could get to her. She stood still, seeming to hold her own against the presence of the men. But the way her hands pressed flat against her apron and skirt, the stretch of the skin around her eyes, the tautness of her shoulders... He needed to get back to her and get her away from the men.

Mrs. Miller was helping a customer at the far end of her stall and didn't seem to have seen the sheriff. Still, though, he needed to protect the elderly woman and draw the men away from her. There was one predictable thing about bad men—they were unpredictably bad.

He returned the wooden sign to the rack and pulled his hat farther down on his head. His short buzz cut was nothing like the Amish bowl style of haircut, and the more the hat hid that fact, the better. One step out of the booth made him feel exposed, but the beautiful Amish woman and her surrogate grandmother needed him. He would not fail them.

As he stepped closer, he could hear their voices and see the man's left eye twitching as he talked. A memory pressed on his temples. The man was lying to Sarah. That was his tell, when his eye twitched. John still couldn't place him or remember his name, but perhaps that would come in time.

For now, his mission was clear. Save Sarah. Draw the men away from *Mammi* Mary.

He continued back toward the booth slowly, acting

like he was looking at the goods for sale on the way. She glanced at him but managed to keep recognition out of her gaze.

With another pull on his hat, he picked up a jar of apple butter and pretended to examine it. Now that he was close enough to hear, he knew that the two men were pressing her for information about the man who was at her house the other day. About him. One leaned in close with a veiled threat, his hand holding tight her forearm.

With what must be muscle memory, his chest tightened, his arms tensed. Was he ready for a fight? Had he been a brawling man? He pushed those questions from his mind and focused on Sarah, who had edged in his direction.

He replaced the apple butter on the shelf and picked up the chowchow. His disguise as an Amish man was only good as long as it lasted. With his best attempt at a Pennsylvania German accent, he asked Sarah about the goods. "Please, what do you put in the chowchow?"

Relief wobbled onto her face as she looked at him. She looked back at the sheriff with a glance and jerked her arm out of his grasp. "Excuse me, Sheriff Jaspar. I need to help this customer."

Without waiting for him to reply, she turned to John. "Each batch is different, *jah*?" She pointed to the jar label, and he prayed that the two men didn't notice the slight wobble in her hand. "This has green tomatoes, some red and yellow bell peppers, cucumbers and onion. Also some carrots and green beans from the garden."

"Sounds *gut*." John scruffed a hand over his chin. He didn't have the beard of a married Amish man, so perhaps he could pass himself off as unmarried? But he did have a few days of stubble, and he had no idea if an Amish man ever had stubble.

As he slowly placed the jar on the edge of the table, he snuck a glance at the man with Sheriff Jaspar. The man was staring at him, fine wrinkles on his forehead creased in recognition. For a moment, their eyes met, and John struggled not to step back from the cold deadness in the man's eyes.

"Jedediah," the man hissed. He snaked a hand out to grasp John's arm.

Forcing himself away from the man's stare, John glanced at Sarah with a small nod. "*Jah*, I will take this." But instead of picking up the jar of chowchow again, he let his free hand knock it off the table along with a couple of jars of canned tomatoes. As the containers fell, he jerked his arm out of the other man's grasp.

The jars shattered as they hit the floor. The many ingredients of the chowchow mingled with the tomatoes to form a sticky, red-and-yellow mess that spread quickly across the cement. The two men jumped back to protect themselves from the bits of glass and goo as a large splotch hit John's leg. The man who had just grabbed John slipped on the edge of the mess, flailing his arms out to steady himself.

"*Ach*, I am sorry," John called loudly as he stepped back. "What a mess!" At his exclamation, a couple of other Amish and a few nearby customers and vendors noticed the spill and rushed to help clean it up. One vendor grabbed a roll of paper towels nearby and inserted himself in between John and the men, ready to drop to his knees and wipe it up.

It was just the muddle he had hoped to create. Well-intentioned folks muscled in to help with the cleanup, brooms appearing to sweep up the glass that had scattered even to other booths. John hated to cause the mess for others to clean up and waste Mrs. Miller's jar goods, but it provided a way out. He dashed around the table and grabbed Sarah's hand, heading for a door marked Exit. At the door, he glanced back at *Mammi* Mary. She nodded at him, an acknowledgment of gratitude for what he had done to draw the men away, and held her hands together as if praying.

Inside the door, though, a hallway appeared before them, but it was better than back to the booth. "Come on," he urged her, and then maneuvered them down the hallway toward a corner. Crates and boxes and folding chairs littered the area.

Halfway down the hallway, Sarah's hand slipped out of his as he rushed on. "Wait!" Her cry of help turned him back to find her skirt hem snagged on a stack of crates. "I am caught." She sought the spot of fabric that had stuck on the wooden edge and tugged, but it remained fast.

"Do I bring the crate?"

"No. It'll slow us down. Let me help." He bent over the offending stack of crates, alternating between frantically trying to loose the material of her skirt that was caught and looking back the way they had come. No matter which way he worked it or how Sarah twisted it, the fabric would not come free.

"Look." Sarah's whisper was laced with panic.

The sheriff and the other man stood at the end of the hallway, the direction from which John and Sarah had come.

They were cut off. Whatever lay around that corner, that was their lot.

With a loud rip, John tore the skirt loose.

Free again, Sarah dashed down the hallway. John followed close behind, spurred on faster as the sound of the men's shoes clumping on the floor seemed to catch up with them.

Around the corner, a door loomed up. John nearly bumped into Sarah as she grabbed for the handle. "Out?"

"Yes. Go!" He reached around her to grab the door and laid a hand on her back to propel her outside. The blast of cold on the perspiration that dotted his face made him gasp, but he gulped in a large breath of fresh air and pushed on.

He quickly assessed that they had come out the side of the building. Pointing the way, he followed Sarah around the closest corner and to the back of the brick building. Just ahead of them, a row of tall arborvitae trees formed a hedge around a Dumpster.

"There." He kept his voice low, but a glance back showed the men had not caught up. "Behind the evergreens."

The stench hit him as soon as he found secure positions for both Sarah and himself. His stomach roiled at the stink of rotting food and whatever else had been placed in the large garbage bin. He prayed they would not have to hide there for long.

A small break in between the trees afforded a protected view of a portion of the parking lot. John leaned forward, the scratch of the evergreen limbs scraping on his face. The sheriff's vehicle pulled into view, and John jerked back, pulling a branch across him. Through the needles, he watched the car cruise by, the sheriff at the wheel and the other man in the passenger seat. They were scanning both sides of the parking lot, but as far as John could tell, they didn't have any idea where he and Sarah had gone.

John slowly pulled the hat farther down over his head and forced himself to return slowly to his spot deep in the arborvitaes. Sarah was watching him with wide eyes, and he put his finger to his lips to signal her to remain quiet.

She was trembling, and he took her hand to steady her as he motioned for her to get down behind the Dumpster. One side of their hiding space was completely open to allow access to the garbage bin.

As he lowered himself to his knees, the sheriff's vehicle stopped, directly in front of their hideout.

Chapter Eleven

John steadied himself against the bin, his heart twisting within his chest at the sight of Sarah. Her lips were blue from the cold, and her hands trembled from fright.

The sheriff and the other man were still there, hovering on the opposite side of the trash bin. The hum of the car's engine buzzed in his ears and pulsed through his arteries.

Running wasn't an option. Even if they could sneak through the evergreens, surely the movement of the branches as they pushed through would alert the men to their presence.

Staying wasn't an option. Even in top physical condition, there was only so long a person could stay squatting on his haunches. Add in the bitter winter cold, and their time was limited.

And now he had to sneeze. The tickle quickly became overwhelming, and he wiggled his nose even though that did nothing to alleviate the irritation.

The vehicle's droning sound began to move away. He hadn't heard a car door, so it seemed safe to assume that both remained in the vehicle that was now leaving. Sarah continued to stare at him, her eyes shadowed with fear, and he cut his view toward the other side of the Dumpster, hoping to communicate with her that he was going to check on the other side. After a gentle reassuring squeeze of her hand, he withdrew from her grasp. On the balls of his feet, he spun toward the edge of the large bin and peered around the edge.

There was nothing there.

He paused, listening intently for the sound of any vehicle. There seemed to be the whine of an engine a way off, perhaps even two. But that could be traffic through the parking lot or from the road on the other side of the building. He stepped from behind the Dumpster, his muscles tensed and ready to flee if necessary.

A few quiet steps took him to the other side of the trash bin and the edge of the building. He exhaled slowly and then peered around the corner.

There it was. The sheriff's car had just reached the other end of the market building and was turning the corner to drive through the front parking lot and, hopefully, to the exit onto the main road and far, far away from Sarah and him.

He ducked behind the corner on the chance that the sheriff might glance that way as he turned. His shoulder bumped something, and he turned to find Sarah standing next to him, her lip quivering.

"I think we're all right." His breath formed a cloud in front of them. "But let's wait another minute."

She nodded and hugged her arms around herself.

"Then let's get to your buggy."

Worry lines crinkled around her eyes. *"Jah."*

John was not a parent, but his heart twisted within his chest as he imagined what Sarah must be feeling, in danger and separated from her only child. He, too, yearned for the sweet presence of the child, a realization that nearly knocked the wind out of him. So far, they were unharmed, but he wanted to check on Lyddie's safety and then move on to a safe place.

Quiet surrounded them, and after another glimpse around the corner showed no vehicles, he ushered Sarah back around the Dumpster and through the arborvitaes. In a few minutes, they had untied Lightning and were back in the buggy. Sarah grabbed a couple of heavy blankets from the back and settled one around her shoulders, handing the other one to John. He pulled it over his back and around front, grasping it in one hand as he held the reins in the other.

"Perhaps the blankets will make us look different than we did in the market, in case the sheriff drives by again." He gave his *tch-tch* to the horse to urge him forward.

"*Jah*. But what if they do not?" Sarah leaned back, as if to hide farther in the recesses of the buggy.

"We'll handle that if it happens. Could they recognize Lightning and the buggy?" The horse twitched his ears at the sound of his name.

"An Amish person would, for sure and for certain. But probably not an *Englischer*. Would they not pay more attention to cars than to horses? And I do not think the sheriff has been here long enough to become familiar with everyone and their animals."

"Yes, I think you're right." No matter what others might think of the Amish, and he certainly had no recollection of what his impressions had been before he hit his head, Sarah was a very bright and perceptive woman. Yes, she would be considered old-fashioned.

Yes, they chose to live differently from the rest of the world. But that didn't mean they were any less intelligent. If anything, her slower pace of life had probably served her well and made her notice much more.

As they drove away from the market, Sarah took back the reins.

"Is there a different way we can return to Katie's house? Just to be safe?"

"*Jah*. But it will take a little longer."

"That's fine. I think that would be the safer course of action."

John was relieved to give up the control of the horse to the person who knew better what to do. Driving an animal to pull a buggy was something that took more skill than he seemed to have at the moment. He peered out the small window and strained his ears for any cars approaching, but the couple of vehicles they did encounter just passed slowly.

"Who was with the sheriff? Did you catch his name?"

"*Jah*. The sheriff introduced him as Simon Carlyle." She glanced at him as if expecting a reaction.

John tumbled the name about in his mind. Were there any connections? He shook his head. "It sounds familiar, like so many other things, but I just can't place it. And I didn't recognize his face. What else did the sheriff say?"

"They said they were looking for someone they had not seen in a while and asked about the man who had been at my house."

"Me." The sour taste of bile coursed upward in his throat. "What did you say?"

"I did not lie." Her voice was adamant, but was she trying to convince him or herself? "I said he was no longer there. That is true. You are not at my house. You are here."

He grinned, that feeling of the simple upward curve of his lips bringing a needed sense of relief, howsoever brief. "That was clever thinking. And I agree. You did not lie." He peered out the window and saw nothing, hoping, in vain, to continue that respite from worry. Whether there was another vehicle there or not, he would still worry...until his full memory returned, and he could fulfill whatever obligation he had that was upcoming, an obligation that he hoped and prayed would end the danger for Sarah and for himself. "This Simon Carlyle was not wearing a police uniform, but that doesn't mean that he's not the dirty cop."

"It does not mean, either, that he is."

"And he wasn't the one on the snowmobile, the one who shot at us in the woods near your house?"

"No. I have not seen him before."

"So, we have no more information now than we did before we went to the market."

"We have the name and face of Simon Carlyle. Perhaps that will come to have meaning for you in *Gott*'s time."

It sounded nice to hear from Sarah's lips, but John was beginning to doubt whether he would ever remember anything more.

The return to Katie's house was uneventful, and relief coursed through John at the sight of it. Inside, after a long hug for both Sarah and John, Lyddie returned upstairs to play with the twins, and Sarah filled her friend in on the basics of their trouble at the market.

Katie quickly fixed mugs of hot chocolate and set out a plate of oatmeal cookies. "For warmth and comforting," she said. "And you must not return to your house but stay here. Whoever these men are, they will not know you are here."

"But the sheriff might. If he does not know yet that we are friends, he could find out by just asking around. And then if he brings that trouble here..." Sarah seemed to swallow hard, unable to finish her thought.

"Sarah's right. We can't stay here, but thank you for offering." John glanced toward the stairs, but only giggling trickled down from the second floor. "The danger has now increased since we stayed last night. I don't want to bring that to you or to any of the Amish community."

Sadness shadowed Sarah's eyes. "*Jah*, we must go. We will take Thunder also, behind the buggy, so you do not have the task of caring for another large animal."

Katie placed a hand on Sarah's arm. "You must leave Lyddie here. With me."

Sarah held her breath for a long moment and then exhaled slowly. "It pains me, but I had hoped you would offer."

An odd sensation coursed through John. He would miss Lyddie's smile and blond curls, and yet he knew they had to consider her safety, as well. Plus, it would be easier to stay safe with just the two of them. "*Jah*, it is the right thing."

Sarah smiled at his use of the Pennsylvania German, but as she turned toward the stairs to call for her daughter, he spied her wiping away a tear. Was she trying to hide her concern from Lyddie and the twins so that they weren't scared? Or was she worried about whether she would see her daughter again?

If John wanted to admit the truth to himself, it was probably both.

Lyddie bounded down the stairs as the women stood from the table.

Sarah seemed to paste a smile on her face as she turned to the child. "Lyddie, John and I need to go out, but you are going to stay here with the twins and Katie. I will be back as soon as I can." She pulled Lyddie into her embrace.

"How long will you be gone, *Mamm*?" The child leaned into Sarah, and John felt a tear spring to his own eye.

"I do not know, *liebchen*." Sarah's voice quavered with emotion.

Katie stepped toward the pair and put her hands on Lyddie's waist to pull her around gently. "We will make fresh cookies and bake bread, and you can play more with Ruth and Rebekah. We will have a *gut* time."

Lyddie paused to study Katie and then turned to her mother for one more hug before she ran for the stairs. Sarah dried her eyes with the hem of her apron as Katie packaged up the rest of the oatmeal cookies and handed them to Sarah. "Where will you go?"

"School is not in session, so we will hide in the apartment that is over the school. We will be warm, and there are some dry goods the parents brought during the fall term. The small barn will house Thunder and Lightning, and we will take Snowball. She will help look out for us."

"Before we go…" John let his sentence trail off, to gather his thoughts. He couldn't trust many people with his nearly nonexistent memory, but he knew the faith of these two women was solid. The memories summoned by the attack at the market were tantalizing, the odor of the ink and paper of the money still tickling him. Desperation to involve law enforcement pounded at him, but if he made a blind call without enough of his memories, he could call the wrong person and get them both killed.

"Before we go," he began again, "could you two pray that my memory returns?"

"*Jah.* We have been praying already."

"What is on your mind?" Sarah pulled her cape around herself.

"I'm struggling to remember something important that is coming, and I feel like I need to remember soon. Prayer is always a good idea, right?"

The women gathered close to John and bowed their heads in prayer, asking the Lord for the return of his memory and the safety of them both as they traveled to a hiding spot.

His shoulder nearly touched Sarah's, and he inhaled deeply to replace the odor of money with her sweet smell of cinnamon and apple pie. He had only good memories of her—her beautiful face as he awakened in her guest bedroom, her delicate hands as she handed him the cup of chamomile tea, the dusting of flour on her cheek as she made pie crust—and he cherished those as a drowning man grabs onto a life preserver. She had been kind and caring and generous from the start. If he were not to recover his memories but were forced to start over, those would be pleasant memories to have at the forefront of his new life.

The unison *amen* startled him from his musing.

"Thank you." John pasted a smile on his face, praying it would encourage the women. "Let's go, then."

Sarah and Katie hugged their goodbyes as John

stepped ahead to the door and checked the backyard. All was clear as far as he could tell, but he would never let Sarah go first.

After one more hug from her daughter, Sarah touched the reins to Lightning's back and urged him down the lane. John sat beside her, blankets at the ready if the cold became too bitter, the malamute trotting alongside. The winter afternoon sun slanted across the yard, casting long shadows over the road. Winter had always been Sarah's favorite time of year—silent snowfalls, sledding, hot mugs of cocoa, warm mittens, cozy quilts. But now? With this danger? A few brown leaves leftover from autumn skittered across the road, startling her and making her look in both directions, as she half expected a bad man to jump out and accost them.

She cut her eyes at the man who sat next to her, the police officer who couldn't even remember his name. He sat tall and strong, keeping vigil over the countryside in all directions. *Jah*, she felt safe with him, but he was still just a human being against weapons that could kill. For not the first time in her life, gratitude for her peaceful Amish life overwhelmed her.

He turned suddenly and caught her staring at him. His green eyes flashed at her, and she adjusted her grip on the reins to hide the trembling in her hands. At least the shaking in her knees was hidden by her skirt and cape. She broke the contact and turned quickly back to the road.

The feeling of attraction wasn't new to her. The memory of her deceased husband enveloped her, and a yearning for that close companionship overwhelmed her. Some days—many days—she felt completely and utterly alone. But her husband had been Amish, and their union was sanctioned by the holy Word of *Gott* and by the Amish church. A relationship with this man beside her could not happen, not without leaving the Amish church, something she was not willing to do.

"What is this apartment like?" The low rumble of his voice sent a shiver down her spine, and she used her free hand to rub her arm, hoping to pass it off as a chill from the cold.

"It is small with only two bedrooms, fit into the attic space of the school building."

"And it's for you since you're the teacher?"

"*Jah*. Because of the amount of land available here in northern Indiana, unlike in Pennsylvania where it is quite crowded, the Amish farms and families are more spread out. Sometimes, a teacher has to travel quite a distance to get to the schoolhouse. Especially for the younger girls, the ones who are not yet married, it is too far to travel every day, back and forth to their family's home. So, the teacher could live in the apartment during the week and then go home to family on the weekend. Also, we will not pass it on our route, but there is a very busy road with only a yellow blinking light at the intersection that most have to cross. It is dangerous in a horse and buggy."

"Are most teachers unmarried?" He shifted in his seat as he turned to check out the back window, and Sarah caught a whiff of his masculine aroma of fresh-cut wood and the wool of his Amish coat.

She swallowed down the dryness in her throat. "*Jah*, I am unusual. But our church district was kind and generous and gave me the position after my husband died so I could provide for Lyddie. I wanted to stay in the house I lived in with my husband. His death was enough to handle already. I did not want that abrupt change of moving to the schoolhouse apartment. And I wanted a more normal home life for my daughter. So, I stayed in our house, and I manage the traffic every day we have school."

As Lightning pulled them over a small rise in the road, the white clapboard schoolhouse came into view. With the exception of only a small barn to the back and side, it stood alone on a large parcel of land. A fence ran along the edge of a tree line, the bare branches scratching and clawing at each other in the wind.

"Is that the school?"

"*Jah.*"

John seemed to study the scene, his fingers scratching across his stubble that was quickly becoming a beard. But only married Amish men wore beards. If they weren't careful, the Amish neighbors might believe him to be a married man, and that would not do for Sarah to ride about with a married man.

"I don't see tracks in the snow, other than what appear to be from animals. I can tell better when we get closer, but at this distance, they appear to have their typical irregular patterns. Of course, Carlyle—you said that was his name, the man from the market?—wouldn't have any reason to come to a closed-up Amish schoolhouse."

Sarah nodded and, a few moments later, got Lightning and Thunder comfortable in the barn. There was very little space for the buggy, so she and John maneuvered it to the back side of the barn. Hopefully, it would be hidden from the road there. She was just grateful that her horses would have warmth and shelter.

She led the way to the back door of the schoolhouse, keeping Snowball close by her side. John followed, using a branch with a few leaves left to try to smooth over their tracks in the snow. The sky was heavy with dark clouds, but that did not always portend a snowstorm.

As they entered the cloakroom, the schoolroom with the empty desks and the cold woodstove visible through the doorway, John turned questioning eyes to her. "When does school start?"

"Soon." Sarah instructed Snowball to stay close outside as she closed the door and then removed her bonnet and hung it up. A scarf and a pair of mittens hung on a hook, probably left by a pupil, and one child's lone lunch box rested on the shelf above the hooks.

John stepped close behind her and peered over her shoulder into a small room adjacent to the cloakroom. "What's in there?"

"All the rooms are connected on the first level. That is our recess room, where we keep our equipment for the children to play with outside. Baseball is very popular with the boys, so we have a number of balls and bats. The girls like to jump rope. A few other things."

She led him through the schoolroom and to the stairs at the side of the building. Upstairs, the entire apartment was visible from the landing. "There are two bedrooms because sometimes there are two or three teachers, depending on the number of students."

John quickly claimed the bedroom closest to the stairs. "To better protect us," he said.

Sarah stepped into the other bedroom. It was comfortably sparse and plain, just like home, and the only wall decorations were a calendar with the wrong month and a clock whose batteries must have died.

Gott, protect us here and keep us from that fate.

But the little space was warmed with colorful quilts draped snugly over the beds and, in the main area, a handsome solid-wood table with four chairs. Sarah placed her small bag on the chair next to the bed and returned to the kitchen. Even though it was still midday, the heavy cloud cover created shadows that slanted across the walls, but it only took a moment to light the kerosene lamp.

In the cupboard, she spied some canned goods and dishes stacked neatly. From the back, she retrieved a couple of quart-size jars of vegetable soup. If she remembered correctly, this soup had been given by a student's mother, a woman who was renowned throughout the church district for her flavorful blends of vegetables and stock and spices. Sarah felt a smile stretch across her face as she found a box of crackers and a jar of peach slices. They would eat well tonight, and nothing could comfort so well as a bowl of steamy, delicious soup.

Nothing except the warm embrace of a strong, protective man.

Ach, she was as bad as a youth in her *rumspringa*. And the only running around she was doing now was to stay away from a couple of evil men who seemed to want John dead.

She shook her head as if that could clear her thoughts and focused her attention on lighting the propane-powered stove. It wouldn't take long to heat the soup, and she pulled a couple of bowls from the cupboard and turned to set the table.

But John had returned from his room and stood so

closely behind her that she bumped into his chest, her voice stuck in her throat. She wobbled, and he caught her by the upper arms, his face perilously close to hers. So close that she could see the various tints of green in his eyes.

He stood for a moment, holding her arms. Could he hear the pounding of her heart or see the longing in her eyes? Having once experienced love, it was difficult to be alone again, especially in her care of her daughter. Here he stood, looking so Amish and handsome in his plain clothing...

"Do you think it's cold in here?"

John's deep voice broke the moment, and Sarah stepped back, the cold seeping in between them as he loosed his grip on her arms.

"*Jah*, it is." Sarah hugged herself and rubbed her upper arms where John's warm hands had been but a moment ago, but the sensation of his touch would not leave her.

John took a couple of steps toward the door, a look Sarah couldn't quite identify on his face. Was he embarrassed? Or was he disappointed that he had interrupted their connection with his question? "I'll light the heating stove I saw downstairs." His voice was rough and felt like sandpaper over her. "There's no telling if anyone will notice smoke out of the chimney, but there's no reason for those men to think that we're here, at the schoolhouse. Besides, I don't think we have a choice. We have to stay warm."

"*Danki*, John. You probably saw the woodpile by the barn. There should be plenty. The parents of the students keep it supplied." She forced herself to look away from his intense green eyes and hugged her arms around herself.

He glanced out the window. "The clouds are heavy, but there's still light to see. But it's overcast enough I should be hidden in my black coat. Be back in a minute."

As she listened to his boots clunk down the stairs and through to the cloakroom, Sarah turned back to the stove. By the time he returned, she had the table set and the meal spread.

As heat began to radiate through the floor, Sarah led them in bowing their heads for the silent prayer. The soup was as delicious as Sarah had predicted, matching the aroma of vegetables and spices that had filled the little kitchen as it heated. But with each spoonful, John ate more slowly. Soon, he laid down his spoon and began to rub his temples.

"What is it? Are you getting another headache?"

"Yes, and they seem to come when a memory surfaces."

"That is *gut*, *jah*? What is the memory?"

"So far, it hasn't been that good. My memories are so incomplete. All I can come up with right now is an image of a woman in a kitchen. I would guess she's my mother, but it's so elusive." He took another sip of soup and held it in his mouth before swallowing. "I think the flavor of the soup is resurrecting it. I don't remember what she looks like. Her face is too fuzzy. There's a feeling of comfort. But..." His voice trailed off as if he was afraid to delve any deeper.

"But what?"

"I feel uneasy when that picture pops into my mind.

If she is my mother, then what is there, in that relation-ship, that troubles me?"

Sarah dabbed a napkin to her lips as she thought. A difficult relationship with one's mother could cause all sorts of heartache. If these were going to be John's memories, maybe he was better off not remembering.

Ach, that could not be. His ability to remember was the only thing that would end this time of hiding and fright.

"You were raised Amish for a few years, but then your parents left the faith. But you also have said that you think you are a believer. Perhaps your unease is because you love your mother, but she is not a believer any longer?"

He rewarded her with a slight smile as he retrieved his spoon. "Maybe you should have been a psycholo-gist."

Heat leaped up her neck and into her cheeks, but was it because of the smile or the compliment? "No. It is just common sense."

"Well, I'm disappointed that I can't remember more."

She grabbed her bowl and glass to carry to the sink. As she turned her back to John, she blinked to hold back a sudden tear that threatened. Of course, she wanted the danger to end, and it seemed that that could only be ac-complished by John's memory returning. But then John would leave. He would go back to his home, wherever that was, and his life, whatever it had been.

And whatever his life had been, it certainly didn't include the Amish or her. Not anymore.

Chapter Twelve

The sun was struggling to break free of the heavy, late-afternoon clouds as Sarah retrieved a quilt from the bedroom. An Amish doll, probably one belonging to a student, rested on the top of the bureau. Sarah choked back the tears that threatened, resolving, not for the first time in her life, to be content with the will of *Gott*. John had said a tender goodbye to Lyddie earlier, a look on his face Sarah couldn't quite decipher. Whether or not *Gott*'s will included John in her life and in Lyddie's life, or even whether it included life at all, she would accept it.

Sarah's breath hitched in her throat. Could they be a family? Lyddie had commented about other girls' fathers and understood, as clearly as a six-year-old could, what had happened to her daddy. But what could Sarah do about it? Right now, Sarah was simply grateful that Lyddie was safe.

A noise thumped from downstairs. Her heart raced momentarily until her mind caught up. John had gone down to the first floor to check on the wood supply for the heating stove. He must be stockpiling logs nearby to get them through the night and the next day. As the wind howled around the outside of the structure, a strong gust slammed into the outer wall, and the entire building seemed to shiver.

Sarah pulled the quilt over her shoulders, as much for comfort as for warmth, and returned to the main room to sit at a wooden secretary that stood in the corner. The drawer held ample paper and envelopes as well as her choice of writing utensils. She selected a single piece of paper and her favorite style of pen and settled in to compose a letter that demanded to be written. That did not make it any more appealing or acceptable, though.

The pen scratched across the paper, and Sarah was glad, again, not to have a telephone. *Jah*, there were times the device was helpful. But in the *Englisch* world, she would pick up the telephone and talk to her mother. And right now, she simply did not need to hear her *mamm* babble on about the virtues of the Amish man back in Lancaster County she had chosen for Sarah. The only man in her thoughts was the man downstairs, caring for her by providing warmth.

She forced herself back to the letter and continued.

Dear Mamm,
Lyddie and I are well, and I pray that you and Daed are, as well.
    I have prayed over your last letter and your suggestion, and Lyddie and I will return to Lancaster County as soon as I can finalize the travel plans.

She had no idea what this Amish man in Pennsylvania looked like now or what he would do to provide for a family, but her mother would surely fill in all the details if Sarah asked.

But she didn't want to ask. She wanted John, the man she couldn't have. To join the Amish church, John would have to give up electricity, telephones and technology. Could he? Or did he not even remember those things? Could he also give up his weapons? Surely, he had many as a law-enforcement officer. Once his full memory returned, would he not want to return to his former life? Doubt flurried over Sarah like a blizzard.

A step sounded behind her, and a floorboard creaked. She turned suddenly, knocking the paper off the desk.

It was John. She had been so engrossed in her thoughts that she did not hear him climb the stairs. The paper rested on the floor, her writing face up. The last thing she needed was to explain that letter to John. She leaned to scoop it up.

"Everything all right?" He rested a hand on the back of her chair.

"*Jah*. Just startled." She folded the letter and tucked it in her apron pocket. "Would you like a cup of tea? To warm up?"

"Sure."

As soon as the tea steeped, they sat at the table, stirring honey into the chamomile-and-black-tea blend.

"I was looking around downstairs, and I counted twenty desks. Do you have that many students?"

"It varies each year, of course. But at the last term, *jah*. Every desk was filled." Sarah swallowed a sip of her tea.

"And what sort of a teacher are you? Are you one of those stern, pinch-faced kinds?" He crossed his arms over his chest and seemed to pull his eyes and mouth together until he was mimicking a harsh frown.

"No. Definitely not." Sarah couldn't help but smile.

"You're a good teacher, then. One who is understanding and helpful. Fun, even, who reads aloud and does crafts and even plays baseball with the boys at recess." He stood and pantomimed swinging a bat and then lifting his skirts and running the bases around the kitchen.

At the sight of him, Sarah laughed out loud, but immediately placed her hand over her mouth. Too much noise might alert someone to their presence. But John's antics brought a lightness to her heart that she hadn't felt since Lyddie had come running out of the woods to tell her a man was hurt. No, even before that. It was a lightness she had not had since news had reached her of her husband's buggy accident.

John returned to his seat and hooked a thumb in his suspenders. His smile slowly faded as he studied her. "How long will you teach? Until a strong and handsome Amish man comes along and sweeps you off your feet?"

The filmy bubble of her happiness popped. It was all a charade, him in the Amish clothing and learning to drive the buggy and taking care of her, just as much as his running the imaginary bases was a charade.

She must have had a sad or upset look on her face, for John seemed to realize what he had said just a split second after Sarah did. She shifted in her chair, and the letter, through the apron, poked her in the leg, a sharp reminder of the plans for her future that did not include John.

Her last two sips were gulped down. She collected the tea cups, not looking to see if John had even finished his, and washed them quickly, setting them on a towel to air dry.

"Would it be all right if I lay down for a few minutes? For a quick nap?" Her voice felt like a mere whisper, but she beat a hasty retreat toward the bedroom. Just before she closed the door, she spied John staring at his hands and what seemed to be profound sadness etched on his face.

A gray gloominess penetrated his eyelids. Images came and went, and a chill felt seeped through to his bones. Grogginess lay heavy over him like an Amish quilt, but John forced his eyes open. He was sitting in a wooden chair, his chin touching his chest, his arms crossed over his middle. But, where was he? He cut his eyes to the walls, but they were plain and white. He rubbed his arms and inhaled the lingering scent of vegetable soup.

Now he remembered, a prickling sensation that poked about in his mind. He had come to the Amish schoolhouse with the pretty Amish schoolteacher just that afternoon.

He jerked upright. How could he have fallen asleep with danger all around? It hadn't been that long since their escape from the market that morning, and although, in theory, they were hiding someplace no one should be able to find them, he didn't know what resources their pursuers had to be able to locate people. He stood hastily, grabbing the back of the chair before it could fall backward. A hurried glance through all the upstairs windows revealed only the snow-covered countryside. Judging by the late-afternoon light, he couldn't have been asleep more than a half hour. At the door to

Sarah's bedroom, he knocked softly. He hated to wake her, but he felt an irrepressible need to know she was still in there, safe.

Quiet footsteps sounded to the door. It opened slightly to reveal Sarah without her *kapp*, her hair slightly mussed.

Sarah was beautiful. That much was for sure and for certain. And she was having a most positive effect on him. She embodied gracefulness and delicacy even as she sipped a cup of coffee, straightened her prayer *kapp* or dabbed at her daughter's mouth with a napkin.

"Is everything all right?" Sarah's eyes were wide with concern.

John shook himself out of his few memories. He needed to concentrate on the here and now. "Just wanted to make sure everything was okay in there."

"*Jah*. I will be out in a minute." She closed the door, and John spun to lean heavily against the doorjamb.

Was he falling in love with her? With Lyddie? Both were valid questions and ones he wasn't sure he could answer. What did love feel like? With nearly all his memories gone and his own given name, *Jedediah Miller*, sounding so foreign on his tongue, how could he know what true love was? The image of her laughing and smiling at his antics earlier filled his mind's eye. That was a memory he would hold on to for the rest of his life. He wanted to stay with her, to continue to get to know her, to soak up her zest for life and love. Yet, could he give up the modern world and join the Amish? Could he be a proper *daed* to Lyddie? If so, it would have to be for the love of Sarah, Lyddie and *Gott*.

As Sarah emerged from the bedroom, hair in place and smoothing her skirt, the hum of a car sounded outside. John immediately locked gazes with Sarah as she tossed him a worried look. From the closest window, concealed by the light blue curtain, John spied a four-door sedan approaching the lane for the schoolhouse. It was traveling too fast and slipping in the snow. As he counted the number of people in the car—two—a flash of memory struck him. His knees began to buckle, but he gripped the window ledge to watch until the car passed their lane and drove out of sight.

Sarah grasped his arm and led him to a chair. "You have another headache. Another memory returning." It was a statement, not a question.

How quickly she had come to know him.

"Yes."

"What is it? I know that you are eager to know more about your life."

"Assuming it's good." He squeezed his eyes shut, trying to summon something out of the darkness. "I remember driving in a car and following a man, I think that man from the market, as he drove to an old warehouse. He was driving that same style of car as we just saw outside."

Sarah brought a glass of water and placed it on the table in front of him, her free hand resting briefly on his shoulder. Whether or not she meant it as a calming comfort, it served that purpose. John felt the muscles in his neck relax as Sarah sat down across from him.

"Remember the doctor said your memory could return in bits and pieces. He also said it was a form of post-traumatic stress disorder."

"I do remember that. I just wish I could remember what is so important that's coming soon. That could end all of this hiding." John's fingers flew, without his conscious thought, to his temples. It had become nearly a habit in the past few days, the rubbing of his forehead when he was trying to remember. Another vision flashed in his mind, and he closed his eyes as it flashed like lightning in the darkest night.

A courtroom. He'd been in one before. Many times, in fact. *Do you swear to tell the truth, the whole truth, and nothing but the truth? I do, so help me, God.* A trial was coming. A couple of weeks, and he would need to take the stand. His testimony was crucial evidence.

But about what would he testify?

Another image flashed, the man from the market. Without opening his eyes, he asked Sarah, "The man at the market said his name was Simon Carlyle? He's the dirty cop." But were there more? He delved deeper, trying to see more of the image. Who was he with? John couldn't remember anyone else.

The snowmobile accident and the man who had returned. The one who had pointed his gun at them. The one who would have killed them all, given the opportunity. The vision in John's mind was as clear as if he was standing there in the snow. The man was called Jimmy the Bruise, and he ran a counterfeiting ring. The odor of the money at the market hit him like a punch in the face, and he felt his hands fist on the table as if prepared to fight back.

But then everything faded.

As suddenly as the images had flashed, they disappeared.

All was black.

He slowly opened his eyes, letting the light in bit by bit, forcing his hands to unclench and rest on the table.

Sarah was watching him, but kindness and warmth and understanding radiated from her beautiful brown eyes.

Not yet had every single memory returned. But it was a lot. "It's time to get the right law enforcement involved. Men I can trust." He now knew who to call. But first, he had to get to a telephone, and keep them both safe along the way.

Chapter Thirteen

As much as she tried to emanate encouragement to John, Sarah struggled to keep her hands from shaking. "The police? You have remembered more, *jah*?"

John had a wild look about his eyes. "Yes. We need to get to a telephone. Where is the closest one?"

"But there is a snowstorm coming." The closest window revealed dark gray clouds hovering near the horizon. "I can tell by the clouds. If we were to get caught out in it..." She didn't finish the sentence, but she didn't need to. He knew exactly what could happen if they were stranded in a blizzard.

"Look. I can't remember all the details yet. But I know that Simon Carlyle, the guy from the market, is a dirty cop. He was extracting payment from a man who goes by the name Jimmy the Bruise in exchange for protection. Jimmy is the man with the birthmark, the head of a counterfeiting ring. He's the one we saw at the snowmobile crash site. I need to testify in a trial coming up soon. And I think I know who to call for help." He stood and grasped her arms. "At the very least, to keep you safe."

John's voice had risen with emotion, and she put a finger to her lips to quiet him.

"What about your friend? Isn't there a phone shanty outside her barn?" He kept his voice low, but an urgency sparked in his eyes.

"Katie? No. That is the opposite direction of home. And I do not want to bring trouble to Katie. She is raising her twins alone, and Lyddie is there. Neither do I want to bring trouble on *Mammi* Mary, but she does not have a phone anyway. And the market is too far away." She returned the glass to the sink. "It is best to head to the neighbor closest to the schoolhouse, a couple of miles down the road. They are out of town, but we can use the telephone in the shanty near his barn. Perhaps the police could find us there?"

"That'll do. How long will it take to get there?"

"Long enough that we should bring the quilts on the beds for warmth. What about our things we brought from my house?"

"Leave them. God willing, we'll come back to collect them." Urgency tinged his voice. "Right now, let's get moving and get to that phone. This storm that's coming is only going to make it worse."

Had that hasty departure from home only been yesterday? Right now, as she pulled the quilt from the bed, it seemed as if her life had been spent on the run. The idea of home had never been so sweet.

Fat flakes of snow began to flutter down outside the window, but that only drove her on. She rushed past the window again on her way out of the room, and the snow had grown from flurries to a steady fall in just those few seconds. That would make the drive that much more difficult and slow, but what else could they do?

She had no reason not to trust John. If he thought they were in danger staying in the schoolhouse, then who was she to say any different? Better to take her chances out in the snowstorm with John than to risk facing a gun in the schoolhouse.

John hastily folded his quilt but couldn't help but stare for a brief moment out the window. Large snowflakes quickly covered the plowed road. It wouldn't be easy going, but he wasn't sure what else to do. With the responsibility for the lovely Amish woman weighing heavy on his shoulders and a come-and-go memory that he couldn't rely on, his resources were minimal. Instinct, really, was all that he had. That and prayer that God would protect and provide.

All he knew right now was that they needed to get to a telephone as quickly as possible.

Strike that. That wasn't all that he knew. He knew that he shouldn't just think about prayer. He should do it. But surely God would understand if he kept his eyes on the weather outside and his feet in motion to the door.

God, there's a vague inkling somewhere deep in my soul that we used to talk to each other a lot. And now you know me better than I know myself, although that has probably always been the case.

We need protection as we travel through this snowstorm, and I need to be able to reach someone trustworthy when we get to that telephone. Please, put a special protection around Sarah. If anyone gets hurt, let it be me.

Sarah's shoes clacked on the wood floor as she emerged from the bedroom, quilt in hand. Tension radiated from the fine lines around her mouth and eyes, but as she caught his gaze, she forced a smile.

The woman truly was beautiful. Her blue dress with the white apron contrasted against the deep brown of her eyes, and even though she didn't wear any hint of makeup, her smile made his heart beat more urgently.

"*Ach*, John, are you *ferhoodled*?"

He cleared his throat. "Um, no. I'm fine. Ready?"

But at the top of the stairs, a muffled sob sounded behind him. He spun back to her to find anxiety in her eyes and tears on her cheeks.

She had been trying so hard the past few days to keep going and stay strong, and now she looked ready to crumble. John rushed to her and gathered her in his arms. She seemed to melt into him, resting her head on his shoulder. Soon, dampness from her tears soaked through his shirt.

"I am sorry for crying on you, John." She touched his shoulder where it was wet.

His hand, as if on its own, found her hair and pressed her to him. "No, no. It's my fault. I'm sorry I dragged you into this. I…" What if something terrible happened to her? As he held her, it became perfectly clear that he cared for her deeply. Did he even want to go back to whatever life he had had if he couldn't take her with him? Before they headed out into the snow and all that awaited on the other side of the door, should he tell her how he felt? "Sarah, I want you to know that I care for you. A great deal. Do you think—"

Snowball barked from the yard below, jerking his attention to the nearest window.

A dark car drove over the ridge and into view, cutting off his question and, indeed, his very thought. His arms stiffened around Sarah, but he couldn't take his eyes from the vehicle. It was coming fast. Too fast.

The driver seemed to hit the brakes too late and slid through the turn into the lane that led to the schoolhouse. John stepped toward the window, one arm still around Sarah, and peered out at the car. There were two people in the front seat, and the one in the passenger seat was definitely not Amish. He couldn't make out faces, but both seemed to have the scrunched sinister look of someone on a mission. An evil mission. A throbbing began in his temple, and he swallowed hard.

He stole a glance at Sarah and saw what he had expected. Fear. "Do you recognize that vehicle?"

"No."

He squeezed her around the waist, praying it would infuse her with courage. "We need to get out of here. Now."

They ran to the door, but the car had turned into the lane. Their time was running out.

What if they had left just two minutes sooner? Would they be safe now? But how could they have gone any faster? They had grabbed their outer garments as soon as he had remembered who to call.

At least the enclosed staircase on the outside of the building was on the side of the school opposite from the lane. Their exit could be hidden if they got down soon enough. He opened the door to the apartment, and the wind whipped up through the staircase with a ferocity that took his breath away. Snow swirled in his face, but there wasn't time to linger.

Taking two steps at a time, John led them down. The dog continued barking as John paused at the open doorway at the bottom and peered around. The door that led into the schoolhouse stood immediately to his right, but it did not look as if it had been tampered with. He strained to hear the thrum of the car over the brutal wind. It was still running, but the engine didn't have the sound of a vehicle in motion. So far, they were ahead of the men in the car, but not by much.

Hesitation could cost them their lives. But should they make a run for the barn, through the open yard? That would be their escape, with the horse and buggy, although a buggy could never outrun an automobile. Or should they seek shelter inside the schoolhouse? But that could be their trap if there was no way out once they entered.

Before he could decide and act, the trim around the door exploded. Sarah yelped as he stepped back, one arm flung up to protect his face and the other arm out to hold Sarah back behind the shelter of the enclosure.

A shot had been fired, and it had missed him by mere inches.

His decision had been made for him. He jerked the door open, and with his back to the yard, shielding Sarah, he pushed her into the schoolhouse in front of him. The wind slammed the door shut behind them.

"Get down." He squatted, and Sarah followed.

They inched toward the teacher's desk at the far side of the room, although John wasn't sure why he was leading them there. He desperately scanned the room, but he couldn't see anything helpful in the old-fashioned wooden desks with wrought-iron legs, the bookshelf, the colorful artwork on the walls. At least the green shades were pulled on the windows, but there was nothing that would protect them from another bullet.

They were trapped and completely at the mercy of their pursuers, just like the mouse in Sarah's barn that the cat had caught. But would their end be the same as the mouse?

Chapter Fourteen

Sarah clutched her full skirt in her fist, desperate to keep from stepping on it as they crept through the schoolroom. She threw up a prayer for Snowball. Her barking outside had stopped, but Sarah had no way to know if the dog had been bribed with a treat or harmed in some way.

John halted, a hand up to pause her. He turned first to the left and then to the right, probably to scan for danger that may have followed them into the school.

Tears threatened, but she blinked hard to keep them at bay. She refused to let them win. *Jah*, it was true that self-defense was not the Amish way. But how often did someone committed to the Amish church and the Amish way of life have her life endangered? Some picked at them from time to time, teased them for being old-fashioned. But threatening her life? It was unheard of, at least in the Indiana Amish communities.

She teetered on the heels of her boots and grabbed a fresh fistful of skirt. What was wrong with running away from danger? Nothing that she could tell. It was human instinct, for sure and for certain.

"What now?" Her voice was such a low whisper that she was not sure John had heard her.

But then he turned to her, and the urgency in his green eyes made her forget everything around her. He didn't respond verbally, but he squeezed her free hand, warmth and confidence and security passing from him to her in his look and in his touch.

As difficult as it was, she forced herself to pull away. To look away. Anywhere but at him. The whole situation was quickly becoming—*jah*, had already become—overwhelming, especially since John's profession that he cared for her. Why did the *Englisch* think they had to voice everything on their minds? Perhaps some things were better left unsaid.

The gloom of the schoolroom seemed to swallow them. As the snowstorm outside intensified, a similar gloom stole over her. She had to admit, if only to herself, that she was falling in love with him, despite what wisdom would advise. But she certainly had no intention of telling him. What would that accomplish?

And especially in the midst of this trouble. She had been ejected from her home out of sheer fright. She had been chased at the market, too afraid to go back to the shelter of her friend's house. And now the shot that she had been fearing for days had actually been fired.

Peaceful. That's what her life had been. Her whole life, up until now, had been lived in harmony with her family, her community, her circumstances. It had not been easy when her husband was killed in the buggy accident, but it had not been like this. Overwhelming. Frightening. Unbearable. She wanted to crumple on the ground and give in. Give up.

Was this the valley of the shadow of death? How did

the rest of that psalm go? She had learned it as a little child in school, but now she couldn't seem to get her thoughts straight.

Lyddie's voice reciting the psalm rose up in her mind, and she could almost feel her soft little hand pressed on hers, a gentle whisper of a touch.

Jah, she would fear no evil, for *Gott* was with them. Wherever they ran, His rod and His staff would comfort them.

Sarah closed her eyes in quick prayer. Her daughter needed her mother to guide her, to protect her, to love her. Sarah would not let her down. She would be strong, if only for her daughter, a *wunderbar* blessing from *Gott*.

John wobbled on his heels, drawing her attention. He looked at her expectantly, but she wasn't sure what he wanted except her trust. He had been a hero, even though he was the injured one. He had protected her, guiding and directing their way to keep them from harm.

But now he looked at her with anticipation imprinted on his handsome face. Just as she needed John to stay strong for her, she needed to stay strong for him. No matter what the future may hold for them, they were in this together, at least for now.

Bobbing forward onto his knees, John grasped her upper arms. She startled, but he squeezed her gently, filling her with encouragement. "You know the school and the area better than I do. How can we get out of here and to that telephone? Can we get to Thunder and Lightning and the buggy? Or is there a faster mode of transportation?"

He was still hopeful, still trying, even though he surely knew the answer. "No, there is nothing faster. We only have the horses and the buggy."

"Okay, we'll do our best. What's the fastest way to the barn?" A door slammed from the front of the schoolhouse. John popped up, turning his head toward the sound, and Sarah followed. "Lead us. Go!"

She turned to the back of the room and maneuvered quickly through the desks. Skirting the teacher's desk, a brief memory of calm and quiet school days with eager students flashed in her mind. A door stood behind and to the side, and she dashed through the doorway, pausing just inside to make sure John had followed.

"The recess room?" John looked around at the baseball bats in their wooden storage box, the shelf of softballs, the pegs with jump ropes and a couple of scarves left behind.

Over John's shoulder, she spied the two men she had seen before as they entered the other end of the schoolroom.

"John!" She kept her whisper low. "They are here."

Sarah took a small and careful step toward the exterior door. She didn't dare to look, but she didn't need to. She knew it was too far away to make a dash for it. Too far away to run to the barn to hitch the horse to the buggy. Too far to get away from the gun he was now leveling at them.

Before John could turn, a bullet shot through the schoolroom. It seemed to stop near her, but nothing exploded this time. A softball rolled off the shelf next to her, but all she could hear as it hit the ground was her own screaming.

Sarah's scream sounded muffled in John's ears as he rushed forward to push her out of the doorway. She held a hand over her mouth, her other hand clutched over her chest.

He didn't have time to pick up and examine the softball that had caught the bullet. Something clicked in him, and survival instincts kicked in as he pushed down on Sarah's back, forcing her to lower herself into a crouch. He apparently had been trained as a police officer. Was that where those instincts originated? Whatever it was, he had to get them out of there, although capture seemed imminent with the advantages in weaponry and transportation their pursuers had.

With his touch on her back, or perhaps because she had run out of air, Sarah's screaming had stopped. In the deathly silence, the slow pound of footsteps ricocheted through the schoolroom. John hadn't been able to turn enough to see the shooter's face before they had rushed for cover. But whoever it was, he apparently thought they were trapped. He thought he had plenty of time to find them and finish what he came for.

He was right.

From his hunched position, John eyed the recess room. He had only a few seconds before the shooter came through the door. His gaze darted about the space, and energy surged through him. Could he take the guy? Maybe, but that wasn't the best course of action with Sarah there. The Amish were nonviolent and didn't want to hurt others. That was fine, and he would restrain himself. But that didn't mean he couldn't set up the possibility of a simple accident.

His gaze caught on the bats resting in a wooden box near the door, the handles leaning against the wall.

That would do.

Silently, he pointed Sarah toward the exit, and she

huddled near the outer door. Then, he scooped up as many baseball bats as he could fit in his arms.

The thunder of the footfalls pounded more closely. He held his breath and trained his vision on the floor in the doorway. Too soon, and his plan would flop. He would end up with a bullet through him. Too late, and he could encounter the same fate.

A second set of footsteps joined the first. Both were there, just on the other side of the door.

He darted a glance back at Sarah. She stood, wide-eyed, her hand on the doorknob. He nodded at her, and she seemed to visibly calm, filling her lungs with air and then slowly releasing it. Where her confidence in him came from, he had no idea, but he wouldn't let her down now.

A boot toe appeared in the doorway. *Now!* He let loose all the bats, giving them an extra push with his arms. They rolled across the wooden floor, bumping into each other and crashing loudly. One immediately landed on the boot toe, and the toe disappeared back through the door into the schoolroom.

"Back up!" An angry voice sounded from the next room.

"No. Forward." The owner of that command seemed to be the one in front, for the toe of the boot appeared in the doorway again, kicking at the equipment. Bats rolled and clunked across the floor, now ricocheting back toward John and Sarah.

Without a sound, John gestured toward the door and mouthed, "Go!"

She pulled the door open and stepped outside, Snowball running to meet her. Snow immediately swirled in. In three steps, John was right behind her. As he closed the door, he checked over his shoulder. Jimmy the Bruise had come through the door and was slipping on the bats, about to hit the floor, his weapon waving wildly. The other, Carlyle, grasped the door frame, desperate to stay upright.

Without looking, he whispered to Sarah. "Get to the barn."

The two continued into the recess room, wobbling over the rolling baseball bats. Jimmy the Bruise leveled his gun at John. Could he duck out the door in time to escape the bullet?

But then Jimmy fell, his weapon waving wildly. It went off, the bullet screaming toward the ceiling.

John slammed the door shut behind him and took off running, as quickly as the gathering snow would allow, toward the barn. Sarah was only a few steps in front of him, Snowball running alongside.

As John caught up with Sarah, the dog's barking quickly turned to a throaty growl. That could only mean one thing. Carlyle and Jimmy had emerged from the schoolhouse.

"Stop!"

John halted and slowly rotated toward the angry voice. Carlyle had his weapon pointed directly at his heart.

Chapter Fifteen

John raised his arms, palms out, as he stared down the barrel of the gun. Slowly, he raised his gaze to the man behind it.

Simon Carlyle. The man from the market. The dirty cop.

"Well, Jedediah Miller at last. You're a hard man to find." A sneer snuck across Carlyle's face. "Are you hiding? Or did you get religion? 'Cause you're going to need it after we're done with you."

John didn't answer. In the silence, Sarah cried out next to him.

She recognized someone, and it drew John's glance to the man behind Carlyle. A nasty bruise-like birth-mark crawled from his hand, presumably through his coat sleeve, and up to his neck. A jolt of recognition coursed through John. This was the same man from the snowmobile-accident site, the one that Lyddie had told them about. It seemed like a lifetime ago now, standing at the wreck and looking for evidence of his identity. But there was no doubt.

It was Jimmy the Bruise, the counterfeiter, with ink

and, soon, blood on his hands if he carried through with his apparent intent to kill them all.

A sudden headache pounded at his temples. He knew by now that meant that more memories were trying to emerge from the haze, but he could only pray that they were memories that would help them get away from these lunatics.

If only he had a snowmobile.

"Stop your yapping, Carlyle, and get it done." Jimmy had stepped up next to Carlyle. "If you don't, I'd be happy to." Jimmy pointed his gun at John, lining him up in a shot that wouldn't miss, not at that close range.

"Not now." Carlyle swung his arm at the bruised man to lower his weapon. "Stop shooting to kill."

Jimmy growled at him but relaxed his arm.

"We've gone over this and over this. If you murder them, execution-style, it could get back to me. And there's no way I'm going to jail for you or with you. We've got to get rid of them in a way that makes it look like an accident. Not just a shooting."

"I don't care." The Bruise released a word that made Sarah cover her ears.

Sarah's movement caused Carlyle to swing his weapon toward her. "Get your hands where I can see them. Amish Boy here may trust you, but I don't."

In his peripheral vision, John saw Sarah raise her palms toward Carlyle. Her lip quivered, but it probably wasn't from the cold. Snow had piled up on their shoulders as they stood listening to their pursuers argue.

"All right, Carlyle, let's get this done. It's no good to draw it out. Just pop 'em."

"No." Carlyle nearly growled at The Bruise. "Look. You may be a criminal worthy of jail, but I am not. I'm an officer of the law, and I plan to continue in this position without even a smudge on my record."

"Like it or not, Carlyle, you're in this now. Do I need to remind you how much you've profited from this alliance? That makes you a criminal, as well. They need to be eliminated or we'll both end up in the clink." The bruise around his neck seemed to darken as John and Sarah stood in the snow, waiting for their fate to be decided.

"And do I need to remind you how we even found them here? You wouldn't be here without my deductive reasoning."

John turned to meet Sarah's gaze and nodded almost imperceptibly as he took a small step back. Could this be their getaway, with their captors arguing? Sarah also took a step back, worry creasing the delicate skin around her eyes, the dog stuck tight by her side.

"Who cares how we got here? We need to get rid of them, or that trial'll be a slam dunk."

"Fine." Carlyle took a step toward Jimmy. "But not this way. Your type may not care about leaving evidence, but I know a few things about crime-scene investigation, and I don't want a bullet left in them or questionable circumstances. Barns burn all the time in the Amish community, right? Wouldn't it be sad if someone got caught inside?" He affected a pouty expression, but it quickly morphed into a malicious smile.

If that was the plan, the sooner they could get away, the better. John took another small step backward, but before Sarah could follow—

"Hey! You're staying right here. Don't move." Carlyle's weapon rose a notch in their direction.

"Simon." An image flashed. John and Simon Carlyle

sitting in an unmarked car, talking and waiting. "Are you sure you want to do this?"

Silence reigned as a myriad of emotions seemed to tumble about the cop. Finally, he just shrugged, an air of resignation enveloping him. "So, you found me out."

John nodded. He remained silent, uncertain how much he should say. It wouldn't help their getaway to antagonize him.

"Yeah," Carlyle continued. "It's amazing what information people are willing to cough up for a police officer. Especially since you haven't told anyone of my involvement. I still have a spotless record."

The late winter afternoon was unusually dark, with heavy cloud cover and snow falling fast. But Jimmy jerked toward the road and studied the horizon and then turned back and motioned John and Sarah toward the barn. "There's no time to waste, not with this weather. Get in the barn."

Carlyle stepped close to John and nudged him with the barrel of his weapon. "And don't try any escape. We'll be right here." The odor of his breath, a smell of stale coffee, pushed John toward the barn door. "You're helpless though, anyway, aren't you? You couldn't have made it easier for us, hiding with the Amish. They don't have weapons. There's no fast car to get away in." He nodded toward Sarah. "She doesn't even have a phone to call for help with. Snow's falling. Everyone's staying at home, where the Amish belong. And barns burn all the time. Too bad that accident happened and took two lives." A snicker escaped through his nose.

He caught Sarah's gaze as he turned toward the barn. She stared at him, the wind whipping the tendrils that had escaped her prayer *kapp*, her beautiful brown eyes clouded by fear and worry, her full lower lip still trembling in the cold. He longed to gather her in his arms, warm her, comfort her, keep her safe. She didn't deserve this. She should be sitting by a fire, wrapped in a cozy quilt, sipping hot cider. Not at the mercy of two gunmen. He nodded, the only gesture that might convey to her that he would do his best. That all would be all right, whether they got away or whether they met their Maker.

Another nudge, harder this time, made him stumble a couple of steps. Jimmy the Bruise was beside Sarah, grasping her upper arm in his meaty hand.

"Let's get going. There's no time to waste." Carlyle pressed again. "We're going to wrap this up, once and for all."

Sobs, desperate to wrench free, filled Sarah's throat, but she choked them down. Slowly, she marched toward the barn.

She eyed the surrounding woods. Could they hide? Or would this snow and cold prevent any escape? The thought of being without her daughter caused more sobs to fill her, but it was better, at least, for Lyddie to have life than death.

Even a life without her mother.

But would an escape attempt mean an immediate end for them? Probably, except John's look had seemed hopeful. Perhaps he had a plan. For now, she would go along. Trusting *Gott* was not always easy, but it was always necessary. She would choose to trust John, as well.

John opened the large barn door and held it for her. As she passed him, she prayed that he would figure a way out, a way to help them, a way to get away. She couldn't help but glance at him, but he was kicking at the snow. She hesitated a fraction of a second, but it was enough to cause him to look at her. His eyes met hers, and she immediately warmed with the care and protection that issued from his expression. Stress projected from him, but she knew from his eyes, the light of the body, that he would even die to keep her safe.

Carlyle grabbed John by the arm and pulled him away from the door. "You come with me to get the buggy. We'll burn it up, too. Don't want to leave you any opportunity for getaway." He nodded to the man with the bruise-like birthmark. "Stay with her." Snowball ran after John.

Sarah trod into the barn, her muscles tense at the presence of the gun constantly pointed in her direction. A panic rose in her throat at the idea of Thunder and Lightning perishing in a fire. She turned toward her captor and faced his weapon. "Please, let the horses go! They have done nothing to you."

"Zip it, lady." The Bruise pushed her farther in with his weapon. "I don't care about no horses. Get in there."

John returned with the buggy and pulled it inside the barn. Sarah met his gaze as he settled the buggy to the side and swallowed down the lump that had taken up residence in her throat in her efforts to choke back the sobs. A few more minutes with him were minutes well spent.

The moment he finished, the one called Carlyle waved his gun again at her, stepping in too close for comfort. "Okay, in with the horses, you two." He ran his hand over the weapon and then pierced her with his hard stare. "See this? Don't even think about trying anything."

As Carlyle moved his hand toward her arm as if he was going to push her, Snowball rushed out from the other side of the horses. She barked and then bared her teeth to growl. The horses stamped their feet, shuffling nervously in the hay.

Carlyle pulled back from Sarah and stepped away from the horses, a look of vicious irritation clouding his face. "You better control that dog, woman. Or I will shoot it."

"Snowball, no!" Sarah put out her hand to stop the dog. The malamute slowed to a stop near Sarah, still rumbling from deep in her chest.

Before she could get a hold on Snowball's collar, the dog advanced toward Carlyle again.

In a blink, Carlyle swung out his leg and kicked the animal solidly in the ribs. Snowball's loud yelp of pain ripped through the silence of the winter afternoon. She dropped to her haunches but continued to growl.

"Snowball!" Sarah cried. She surged toward the dog, her throat tight, but John caught her and held her close.

"Take care of that mutt," Jimmy commanded.

Carlyle stuck out his foot toward the dog, and Snowball crouched again. Getting behind her, Carlyle chased the dog behind the barn. A moment later, he emerged alone.

Sarah swallowed hard. But other than soak up John's comfort, there was nothing she could do. To antagonize these men any further was a certain death sentence. With that thought, her strong facade crumbled. She could no longer hold her head up and face whatever may come. The best she could do was muffle the sound of her crying in her cape that she clutched to her face.

John pulled her as close as he could. His comforting touch dried up her tears, lending her his strength. She already dreaded the moment she would have to return that strength to him.

Chapter Sixteen

As Carlyle and Jimmy the Bruise conferred in the doorway, John massaged his temple, a vain attempt to assuage what he really ought to call a migraine. He kept one arm about her, but that would have to come to an end all too soon. She knew him, it seemed, better than he knew himself. Over the course of the past few days, she had proved to be an astute judge of character, and he would miss her insights when he left the Amish community and returned to his own home.

His home. Where was it, exactly? If they got out of this alive, he would have to go home, wherever it was. He might recall enough to testify, but he still couldn't remember where he lived. Could he go to his parents? He knew the names of his parents, but he would not know them if he ran into them on the street. Surely, hopefully, it would all return by the time he needed that information.

He hadn't taken his eyes off their two captors since he had pushed the buggy into the barn. They had promised to bolt John and Sarah in and burn the barn down, but so far, they just seemed to be arguing. All hope was gone for rescue. In good weather, an *Englisch* automobile at the schoolhouse would have raised suspicion. But no one was out in this snowstorm. There was no one to notice.

A sharp pain pierced his skull, and John resumed rubbing his temple with his free hand.

"Is your head hurting again?" Sarah seemed to have calmed after her cry, and now her soothing voice forced his attention.

"Yeah. It's worse this time."

Sarah nodded toward Carlyle and The Bruise. "Why do they wait?"

"I don't know." Angry heat rose within his chest, and the idea of rushing them flitted through the haze of his headache. "But we're stuck. We certainly can't look for a way out when they're still here."

If they survived, could he ever leave the world behind and be Amish? Or was too much of the world in him already? Could the Lord help him with his attitude and word choice? Of course He could. But would He if he asked? Sure, Sarah worried and got anxious, but through all their trouble and turmoil the past few days, she had seemed…unflappable. Composed and collected. At peace.

His chest ached with the desire to have that kind of calm peacefulness. God could do anything, couldn't He? Especially with a soul that was completely surrendered to Him.

The migraine radiated from his temples across the top of his head, and without knowing what else to do to ease the pain, he closed his eyes and continued to rub his forehead. It wasn't helping, but it wasn't hurting, either, and it gave him something to do with his free hand. There certainly wasn't any need for surveillance. They were in the clutches of the enemy.

"Are you remembering more? Is that bringing the ache?"

"I'm certainly trying, but so much remains fuzzy. I have a little bit that's clear, but then it blurs around the edges and disappears completely."

"Maybe if you talk about what you remember, that could help, both your memories and your headache. And that is information you will need if—when—we get through this."

He shrugged, wishing that roll of his shoulders could toss off his worries. But a glance at their captors in the doorway only tightened his muscles. "I suppose it won't hurt." He paused, trying to gather up the fraying edges. But it was useless. Everything was disjointed. There was no good place to start, to try to put it all together. "I remember a feeling of bitterness from when I was very young. I think my parents must have left their Amish faith with great resentment toward God. It's only bits and pieces, more so images, that have come back after what Mary told us. A little sister, a baby girl wrapped in a blanket, but there were problems. Mom cried. A lot. My grandfather—I guess that would be Mary's husband—had a long gray beard. It strikes me that he was very conservative, and my mom and dad seemed to be upset with him, although they did not talk much."

Sarah nodded her encouragement. "*Jah, Mammi* Mary said that her husband—your grandfather—would not let them go for medical help. Finally, your *daed* decided to go anyway, but it was too late."

John worried a fold of her cape between his thumb and first finger. "I remember a tiny casket. And there was so much crying. And anger. I remember lots of anger. At each other. At God."

Quiet engulfed them for a moment. John continued to stare at Carlyle and The Bruise. One was on the phone now. It was only a matter of time before they enacted their plan, and John's mind raced to figure out a way to escape.

"That was a long time ago. It will not help to hold on to resentment."

She was right, of course. But he could only stare through the open barn door at the snow swirling, trying to formulate an escape plan, as the sun set quickly behind the clouds. Were they waiting for the cover of darkness?

A new memory pinged, and he startled. "You know what? My dad told me his parents were dead. I remember now. That's what I grew up believing."

"I am sorry, John."

"Throughout my childhood, my parents rejected any kind of faith. I never went to church. And when I did have friends who tried to witness to me, I became too afraid to tell my parents because they ridiculed my friends who believed." He paused, letting his mind run to the edge of that memory, trying to absorb as much as he could before it disappeared into the amnesia. An image surfaced of him on his knees by his bed in a dorm room. "I became a believer in college, through a campus ministry. But because of my parents' bitterness, I've kept my faith a secret from them."

If Sarah was shocked by any of his memories, she didn't show it. There was that peaceful calm again, an aura that surrounded her and drew him in. "Pray for them, and let *Gott* work His will."

"Jah." This beautiful Amish woman had been a positive influence on him.

Carlyle and The Bruise moved to their vehicle but left the barn door open with a clear view of John and Sarah. This walk down memory lane was, most likely, not going to end with a happily-ever-after.

"They are still there?" She didn't have to specify who she was talking about.

"Of course. Their lives are at stake, and so that means ours are, as well." Another flash, like lightning, invaded his thoughts. Images of equipment, the odor of ink, the clanging of machinery. "Remember I said that Jimmy the Bruise is a counterfeiter? I need to testify at the trial because I was undercover. I infiltrated his crime ring. The case could falter if I can't testify. That's why he's so eager to eliminate me." An urgency like he had never felt before rose up within his chest. "What makes it all worse for him is that I can identify the other men involved and testify to their criminal activities as well as provide positive information on contacts for money laundering, not to mention equipment and materials used, as well as their locations." He ran through a mental list of names and information, details that Sarah didn't need to be bothered with.

"What about the man called Carlyle? He is a police officer?"

"Yeah, on the take. That means he's accepting cash payments from the criminals in exchange for keeping the police away from the investigation. If the ring goes down, they'll rat him out and he'll go down, as well." He had to get them free, and the sooner the better.

"How did you discover him?" Sarah glanced through

the door, an odd mix of curiosity and repugnance on her pretty face.

And the more he remembered, the greater the chasm between her Amish world and his *Englisch* one grew.

"A hunch. My captain suspected something odd, since we never seemed to get anywhere with an investigation. So, we kept it quiet, and I went in alone. It didn't take long to learn the identity of the dirty cop and just how deep his involvement was. The problem was, I had to withdraw too soon. I never got to report Carlyle to my captain. In the department, he still appears innocent with a clean record. I thought more cops were involved than just Carlyle, but I ran out of time. It had seemed at the time that the tentacles of the counterfeiting ring snaked further through the police department than just Carlyle, but I wasn't able to discover exactly who was involved. That means I'm not sure now who to trust, except for one officer. One friend. He's the one I'll call."

"But how did you end up out here in our Amish community?"

"I was stressed. Needed some time off before the trial." He pulled off his hat and ran his hand through his hair. "I think I thought that getting out of town would be a good idea. Apparently, I was right that I was in danger. But the danger followed me anyway."

John leaned forward, squinting toward the gathering dark outside. Carlyle and Jimmy the Bruise were returning from their vehicle, lighters in hand. The moment was at hand.

Snow flung into the barn and stuck to their captors. Sarah leaned against John and swiped a hand over her forehead. This was it.

She had had some good times in this widespread community, cultivated some lifelong relationships, made mountains of memories. But her time here was almost over. And if she did survive, she and Lyddie would move back to Lancaster County. Even now, her letter back to her mother rested in her apron pocket, jabbing her in the leg when she shifted her position, a persistent reminder that *Gott*'s will was best.

Her time with John was also almost over. She most likely wouldn't make it through the night, let alone make it back to Lancaster County. Her life was at an end. There was no way out, and it seemed for sure and for certain that the men quickly approaching them would achieve their goal.

Had *Gott* decided it was her time to go? Apparently so. Grief coursed through her. But a second emotion also ran through her veins. Gratitude.

She was grateful that *Gott*, in His wisdom and grace, had seen fit to give her two loves in one short lifetime.

Two loves?

Jah, she had loved her husband dearly and did not regret a minute spent with him.

But *Gott* had given her another love. Whether or not it could work was up to John. He probably was not willing to leave his *Englisch* life. So be it. But if neither survived what was coming, she at least wanted him to know how she felt. He had taken the huge risk back at the schoolhouse to reveal his heart's feelings to her. She should return the sentiment while she still had the breath to speak the words.

She would toss out her earlier logic that she saw no point in voicing emotions. She must have been *ferhoodled* by fright. The heart sometimes did not know logic.

Sarah loved him. John's desire to rejoin the Amish church was uncertain, even unlikely. But his care for her had helped her see that a loving *Gott* would not want her to be miserable. For that, she was grateful.

What she ought to do was clear. Tell him that she loved him. But her throat constricted as the men quickly approached.

John released her and took her hand in his as, together, they faced Carlyle and Jimmy the Bruise. She was grateful for the warmth of human touch in what would most likely be her final moments.

Chapter Seventeen

The snow beat furiously against the barn door as it swung on its hinges. How many days had it been since John had first arrived here in the Amish community? His mind couldn't quite figure it out, but it hadn't been that long ago. Lyddie had told about pulling him on the sled as he lay unconscious.

Now he was stuck, against his own volition. His arrival here had been the result of a lifesaving mission. His departure was to be the result of a life-ending mission.

Low muttering swirled about as Carlyle and Jimmy the Bruise pulled their collars up against the weather. "That storm will be helpful."

"Yeah, it'll cover our tracks, but the fire will still burn strong."

John couldn't tell which one said what, but did it matter? Neither could wait to light the match.

The barn added some relief against the storm as he followed Sarah deeper inside to join Thunder and Lightning in their stalls. He met Sarah's gaze as she stood near Thunder's muzzle, intending to say something encouraging to strengthen her. But instead, her eyes burned bright with determination.

"I will not remove their bridles." Her whisper was barely audible. "If we can find a way of escape, we will take the horses, as well."

John ran his hand down the length of Thunder as he exited the stall. The sooner he could identify potential exits, the better their chances of escape once these goons were gone.

"I'll check the perimeter," The Bruise was saying near the door. "Make sure there's no way out and all exits are blocked or locked."

Carlyle nodded. "I'll keep an eye on 'em here."

Jimmy jogged out into the snow, and Carlyle turned to see John. "So, you know our plan. It's a pretty good one, don't you think? I'm sure the Fort Wayne Police Department will give you a proper and honorable police funeral. I'll be your pallbearer. Maybe it'll be a memorial service, depending on how much of you is left. Either way, you'll be gone but not forgotten." A wicked grin slithered across his face.

Sarah had apparently finished whatever she was doing with the horses, and now she stood next to him. Her free hand slid into his, and he grasped her warmth. Whatever happened next, they were in this together, the two of them.

Carlyle stared for a moment at their intertwined hands. "Oh, now, Jed. Don't tell me you've gone and fallen for this pretty little Amish girl. Too bad that relationship won't go anywhere."

The Bruise reappeared in the doorway. "All's secure. And that troublemaking dog seems to be long gone after I chased him off."

With weapon in hand, the officer waved them back. "Back you go. Like I said, you won't be tied. But not to worry, there's no way out. One thing about the Amish, they know how to build a sturdy barn. But it's still wood. It'll burn fast enough."

The officer's gun trained on John and Sarah, Carlyle and Jimmy the Bruise stepped backward toward the door. Without another word, they both stepped outside. The door slammed shut. John raced forward in time to hear a scraping, as if they were securing it with a two-by-four or a strong limb. Either one would burn up in the fire, leaving no evidence of foul play.

John wasn't sure what they would do on the outside to get the fire going, but there were many ways to start a fire, even in a snowstorm. The danger was the same. Even as he stood there with those few thoughts, staring at the door, smoke began to filter in around the bottom edge. A moment later, a flicker of fire began to lick at the base of the door.

Adrenaline spiked in his arteries. His heart pumping and thumping, he rushed back to Sarah. "Whatever they're doing out there, it's fast. We have fire."

A mist formed around Sarah's eyes. "We're locked in. There's no way out. A barn can be completely engulfed, and horses can die from smoke inhalation within less than ten minutes."

"Then I'll hurry." He squeezed her upper arm. "Stay here. Now that Carlyle and Jimmy are gone, I'm going to search the perimeter for a way out." It may be a familiar barn to her, but that didn't mean that she knew every loose board, every knothole, every animal in-and-out.

He dashed around the inside edge of the structure, pushing on walls, trying doorknobs, searching for tools. As he worked his way through a tool room, he grabbed an ax.

Less than two minutes later, he returned to find Sarah swiping at her eyes with her apron, looking as if she fought desperately to stay strong and not let her mist turn into a waterfall of tears.

John hitched up his grip on the ax and then ran his free hand down the length of Sarah's arm, catching her hand. "Dry your tears. We're not going to die in this fire, and neither are Thunder and Lightning. I've found a way out."

Hope fluttered in Sarah's stomach as she looked up into John's shining green eyes. Could it really be? *Please, Gott!* Her death had been nigh, but now here stood a handsome and capable man telling her she was saved.

John dropped her hand to grip the ax, and a sudden chill shook her, despite the heat from the growing flames. She forced positive thoughts into her mind. Everything would be all right. She had to believe that.

"It never hurts to have an ax with you, for fighting fires or fighting the bad guys." Nervousness dimpled around his eyes, but he seemed to force a smile to reassure her. "The walls and doors are solid wood, so I can't chop through those in the few minutes we have before the smoke gets to be too much. But, Carlyle and his partner in crime forgot about the hayloft at the back of the barn."

"*Jah*, of course, the little door used to toss out the hay. It is to our advantage, then, that those men are not farmers." She followed John toward the ladder. Flames were inching farther up the door and the walls, and a small bunch of straw had caught. It would not be long before the entire barn was engulfed. Her breath caught in her throat at the acrid aroma of smoke.

John clambered up a few rungs, looking back to make sure she was coming behind. Smoke was beginning to billow upward. Sarah, despite shaking legs, stepped up to the first rung. Halfway up, he called down with a wobbly voice, "I'm not sure how we'll get to the ground, but at least we won't burn up."

"Oh!" A drum seemed to be beating in her chest. "The rope!" They could shimmy down the rope to the ground below. In the summertime, with the doors below open wide, children could swing on the rope in and out of the first level of the barn. Lyddie had begged time and time again to swing, but Sarah just never had the stomach for it. It seemed too dangerous. So many possible injuries just waiting to happen.

But now was not the time for caution. Even a broken leg after plummeting to the ground would be better than dying in the fire. A broken limb would heal. And surely the rope would provide some assistance in getting down to the ground.

With hay stacked neatly all around, John led them across the loft and to the door. It was secured with a chain and padlock, but a couple of blows from the ax broke through the wooden door handle. He slipped the chain off and swung the small door open, and a chill blew in for a moment. But then the fire, fed by the oxygen, roared up the ladder. Sarah inched toward the door, desperate for a gulp of the fresh air. Already she felt like she had smoke and soot all over her.

John scanned the yard and the nearby woods and, seeing no one, dropped the ax down to the ground.

"So no one gets hurt on the way down." He tugged on the rope and then hung on it, testing it for strength. Seemingly satisfied, he tossed the end out the door. It barely touched the ground. "I'll go first, to make sure it'll hold."

A moment later, John was on the ground. He held his arms up as if to catch Sarah, a signal that it was her turn and the rope would hold.

With one final look around the loft, Sarah grasped the rope, a fold of her skirt in each hand to protect against rope burns. With a gasp stuck in her throat, she stepped out of the loft and into the air. The gasp let loose as her hands slipped on the twine, her strength not adequate for the task. With barely both hands on the rope, she slid down to the bottom at a blurring speed. A moment later, strong arms held her. John had caught her in his embrace.

With her feet firmly on the ground again, snow swirling all around but doing nothing to stop the fire, Sarah glanced around the yard. Surely, Carlyle and Jimmy the Bruise had left.

"The horses." Sarah nodded as John breathed deeply of the fresh air and then stepped toward the back barn doors, leaving a void in his absence. Several strong ax blows to the solid crossbeams securing the barn door swung it open. The influx of fresh air fueled the fire, and flames leaped out the doors at the ceiling and around the doorway.

Pulling away from her surveillance, Sarah quickly untied her apron and jerked it off. "Here," she called to John before he could enter the barn. She folded it and knelt to wet the apron with some snow. "You must cover the horses' eyes, or they will not follow."

John rushed inside, leaping away from the flames that seemed to chase him. Too many heartbeats later, he reappeared, leading Lightning. The door swung shut just as he pulled away the blindfold and pushed the horse through. Sarah jumped forward to catch the door before it could hit the horse in the muzzle, and Lightning trotted free of the barn, circling around in the yard.

With one animal safe, John reentered the blazing barn. Sarah stood at the door, ready to hold it open, her eyes watering from the smoke and her throat aching for a long drink of fresh water. Just as the flames leaped larger inside, John appeared with Thunder. He pulled on the lead rope, digging his heels into the floor to lead the frightened animal out.

Heat closed in on Sarah as the horse finally rushed past her and out into the yard.

"Sarah!" John pointed at her skirt.

The hem of her dress was on fire. A ringing in her ears clanged loudly, and she saw John's lips moving, but she could not hear his voice. Flames licked up her skirt, but she stood immobile. Before she could form a coherent response, she was down on the ground. John shoved the damp, soiled apron at her and kneeled at her feet. As he scooped large handfuls of snow on her hem, she tamped at it with the piece of cloth.

The fire of her skirt was soon extinguished, and John pulled her to her feet. "Let's get the horses and get out of here."

She could only nod as she rubbed her hands together.

Lightning continued to prance around the yard back of the barn. But Thunder, with ears pinned back, tossed his head up and down. He stamped his feet in the snow, panic radiating from him. John spoke softly to him, but as Sarah crossed the yard in the deep snow to calm him, the horse stepped toward her. She held up both hands, her cry of "John!" trusting and desperate.

With a loud whinny, Thunder reared up, his hooves flailing over her head. Sarah froze. Even over the roar of the fire, she could hear her own scream.

Chapter Eighteen

Sarah's scream pulsed through her head, only extinguished when John pulled her to safety. Both fell in the snow as the horse trotted away from the barn.

With trembling hands, Sarah accepted John's help up, and they huddled together. "We must let the horses calm. They are panicked from the fire."

She nodded as she stroked her own arms, whispering a prayer and praying her own words would soothe her, as well. John's strong arms encompassed her, but Sarah also kept an eye on Thunder and Lightning. They were a crucial form of transportation and could not be lost, especially since they provided a speed that could not be achieved on foot. The barn was destroyed, or would be, by the time the fire was extinguished. But as she counted her blessings, she numbered quite a few. They had escaped, unharmed. John had saved both the horses. Lyddie was still safe. Between the intensity of the fire and the snowstorm, the bad guys should have been long gone. But the tension would not flow out of her. Her muscles bunched, and her hands shook as she thought of the long trek through the woods to get to the phone shanty.

The canter of the horses slowed, and Sarah broke free to approach the animals at a gentle pace. Grasping a lead rope in each hand, she led them farther away from the fire and behind some overgrown mulberry bushes where they would not be visible from the front of the schoolhouse or the road.

"I'm sorry there's no time to rest, but we need to move." John joined her behind the bush, his voice urgent. "We still need to get to the phone as quickly as possible. And I don't trust staying here, just in case they come back or are watching from afar."

"We will have to ride Thunder and Lightning then. The Amish do not often ride their horses. They are for pulling. So even without the fire, we would not have had saddles. Can you ride bareback?"

"I'll have to learn." His gaze swept down her long skirt. "What about you?"

"I learned when I was younger. My mother was not happy with me for riding, but I loved it. The freedom of it. The speed. The wind. It is true that it is not easy for an Amish woman to ride a horse, but my skirt is full enough for some give, and since it is winter, I have thick leggings on underneath." She looked from the ground to the height of the horse. "I could use a hand up, though, please."

He laced his fingers together as she hiked her skirt up and bunched it in one hand. It felt odd and uncomfortable, but what was that cliché? Desperate times called for desperate measures, and she certainly was desperate to get John to that telephone. With the other hand on his sturdy shoulder, she pulled herself up onto the horse. After she settled her full skirt about her, she looked around, but there was no sign of Carlyle and The Bruise. She tucked around herself a barn blanket John had managed to save from the fire.

John on Thunder, after receiving directions from Sarah, led them into the woods. Exhausted by the events of the day and warmed by the blanket, Sarah was desperate for sleep. Weariness enveloped her, but anxiety kept her eyes open.

The neighbor with the telephone was not far by *Englisch* standards, but the storm would slow the horses down. And though the wind had lessened within the trees, the snow lay deep. At least John knew who he could trust now. With the neighbor out of town visiting family in Ohio, John and Sarah would be alone at the neighbor's barn and not bring trouble on yet another family in the community. Besides, he would not mind if they sought shelter in his barn. The telephone was available for anyone to use as long as they paid their part of the bill.

The Amish took care of each other. That was what people did who loved each other.

Like John? Did she dare to hope that perhaps John loved her? For sure and for certain, he had done everything within his abilities to take care of her and assure her safety.

No. He was a police officer, most likely a good one. The doctor had said that despite the amnesia, John's instincts honed through training and his muscle memory would have remained intact. So, he was doing his job. Protecting people who needed him. That was all. He had said he cared, but wasn't that in his job description?

John turned and offered her a hopeful smile, and her heart flittered in her chest like the snowflakes in the storm. "The snow will muffle the sound of the horses. And although we'll leave tracks, I think they'll be covered up quickly because the snow is falling so thickly."

He pointed to the path behind Thunder, and she turned to see what sort of trail she was leaving on Lightning. But just as she verified that the snow was, indeed, filling in their steps, a tree just a couple of feet from her exploded. Bark flew in every direction. A piece smacked her in the cheek. Sarah spun back forward and hunched over, making herself as small as possible.

"They spotted us!" John's whisper seemed to echo through the woods. "They're shooting at us!"

A warm, sticky substance trickled down her cheek. Sarah leaned down to a corner of the blanket and pressed it to the spot. It came away with a circle of blood on it. The tree bark must have broken the skin, but it didn't seem serious.

John leaned forward on his mount. "Come on! Farther into the woods."

Those thugs must have seen them slip into the trees. And even though the men had to be on foot, John and Sarah couldn't outrun a bullet, not riding bareback and not with the fury of an increasing snowstorm beating at them.

Sarah huddled down farther, both for protection and for warmth. She urged Lightning ahead, and the horse picked up the pace. But with the snow flying even thicker and the temperature continuing to drop, time worked against them. They could last in the elements only so long, but they had no choice but to continue, no matter how long it took to reach shelter and safety.

Another bullet blasted into a nearby bush, the last few leaves from autumn flying off. Thunder sidestepped, and John stroked his neck as snow landed on his own head and eyelashes. His vision blurred as the snow melted on his face, and he swiped his hand across his eyes to clear away the wetness.

John peered behind him. Sarah was close behind on Lightning, leaning into the wind, her eyes squinting into the snowstorm. There was no sign of the shooter, although with the encroaching darkness and the thickness of the snowfall, he hadn't expected to see anyone.

At least there was no way those men could drive their car through the woods in the snow. And unless they had snowmobiles tucked away in the trunk, they would be on foot. They surely couldn't follow very far, not in that cold and the snow. He and Sarah would have the advantage with Thunder and Lightning to carry them and the horses' body heat to help keep them warm.

John held his mount back and turned to Sarah. "You go ahead. Lead the way and stay down as best you can."

Sarah inched ahead, but John rode close behind, pushing them deeper into the woods. Bare limbs scratched at them, and Sarah did her best to push them out of the way and hold them back, but a few snapped in his face. At the feel of warm stickiness, he feared he had a wound that matched Sarah's.

A crash came from behind them, followed by muffled voices. Carlyle and The Bruise hadn't given up yet, then. That meant that now John and Sarah were battling cold and snow as well as the two men who wanted them dead.

God, help! Did it take more than that? He suspected not, given their dire circumstances. But as he leaned over his horse and scanned the surrounding woods, he prayed for protection. Sarah would tell him that *Gott* would protect them if it was His will to do so, and she would be right. If they could just get to that telephone, he could summon law enforcement who would serve and protect.

But would they make it to the phone shanty alive?

A sliver of the setting sun filtered through the cloud cover, creating shifting shadows. John pointed to the closest shadow, and Sarah headed in that direction. The extra darkness might hide them temporarily, but what they really needed was shelter. Their speed had slowed, also, because they were riding bareback. John must have had some experience with horseback riding because he seemed to know what to do although he had no memory of it. Still, though, bareback was slippery enough without adding the moisture of snow. Some moments, it was all John could do to stay on. The thickness of the falling snow cut their visibility and further slowed them.

John drew close and pointed to a stand of evergreen trees. "Over there."

Sarah nodded and turned Lightning in that direction as the high-intensity beam of a flashlight swept across the snow just a few feet behind them.

"Go! Faster!" He kept his voice to a hoarse whisper.

John's heart thumped a wild beat inside his chest as the stream of light from the flashlight chased them to the cluster of trees. Craning his neck to watch behind, he thought a beam of light glanced briefly on his horse's foot. But the trees were straight ahead, and a moment later, Sarah and Lightning slipped behind the stand. He quickly followed on Thunder. Finally, he allowed himself to exhale a breath he felt like he had been holding since they left the barn.

He didn't have to motion to Sarah to stay quiet. She

hugged the blanket around herself and stared at him with eyes wide with fright. Through the branches, he could just make out the two men on foot. They swept their beams of light in a wide arc and stepped forward about twenty feet apart, communicating with hand motions. One beam swept across the evergreens, and he jerked back, holding his breath to keep from making a single sound. Thankfully, Thunder cooperated and remained still and silent, as well.

Eventually, after what seemed so long he half expected the sun to rise, the men began to move to the side and back in the general direction from which they had come.

Sarah's whisper sounded behind him, loud in the hush of the snow. "Are they gone?"

After one last visual sweep of the area in front of the trees, he turned Thunder to face her. "I think they've probably turned around. Despite the cold, we ought to stay here a bit longer, just to make sure that they are gone and we don't lead them to the neighbor's barn."

"*Jah*, I agree."

"Are you warm enough to wait it out awhile?" In the faint moonlight that snuck through the clouds, the pink of her cheeks accentuated her beauty.

"I am getting warmth from Lightning. I am fine."

Thunder stomped in the snow, perhaps because he was tired of standing still, perhaps to get the blood flowing again. Snow continued to swirl around them and add to the heaps of snow already on the tree branches and stuck against the tree trunks. John swept the snow from his shoulders and shook it out of his hair, water droplets clinging to his hands.

Thunder pawed at the ground and then turned in a circle. John clung to his mane so he wouldn't slip off.

"He is restless," Sarah whispered, her breath puffing a cloud. "He is tired of standing still and is ready to go."

"I'm ready to go, too, to get to that phone. But we're hidden here. I hesitate to take off and then be spotted. But Thunder is making it hard to stay upright." The horse swayed again, toward Sarah, causing John to grasp at Lightning's reins and neck.

Lightning also shifted, and the two horses bumped. John leaned to pat Lightning's neck and steady her. Sarah held out her hand, and John grabbed it for support. The softness of her hand startled him after the harshness of the chase, and her skin was surprisingly warm in the cold winter night. He shivered, but it wasn't from the cold.

As a few flurries continued to flutter down, the clouds parted. Moonlight flooded the clearing behind the trees, and he stared at her. Her skin was pinked from the cold, and her lips were parted slightly, her breath puffing out in small clouds.

With only the smallest flurry of thought, like the snowflakes that continued to drift about them, he leaned in closer, his lips almost touching hers. Without hesitation, she closed the space. Their lips met, and hers were as soft and warm as he had anticipated. The cold around him disappeared, and warmth flooded him.

I love her.

What? The startling realization forced him away from her. He pushed his foot against the horse and moved away, the winter chill seeping into the space between them. Before he turned, she touched her fingers to her lips, her expression a mixture of pleasure and confusion.

He urged Thunder a few steps away, his back to Sarah. He peered through the trees to make sure Carlyle and Jimmy had not returned, but he really needed the distance from her.

He loved her? It was true. Through the past few days, he had witnessed her compassion for others, her devotion to her daughter, her work ethic, her sweetness. What more could a man want?

But what could come of it? Since he had been able to infiltrate the counterfeiting ring and gather that information, he must, at the very least, be somewhat good at his job. But even with the return of his memory, there was still so much uncertainty in his skills after the period of not knowing himself. It felt wonderful to remember everything, but his confidence was unstable, both in himself and in his faith. If he had not even known himself, how could he know God and His will for his life? Maybe, with time, he could have more confidence in his abilities. He might have a job to go back to, but he'd feel like a rookie all over again.

He could not ask Sarah to leave her Amish faith to become a police officer's wife. Never. And if he left his job in law enforcement and joined the Amish community, how could he support a family?

Lord, You've brought me this far. If I'm to believe in Your sovereignty, then that means You've led me to Sarah. But what now? What do I do?

As he prayed, a fresh infusion of encouragement flittered down on him. A warm blanket of peace and joy filled him that could only have been from the Lord. With a *tch-tch* to the horse, he spun back to Sarah. She had her face to the sky, letting the last of the flurries alight on her face.

"I should have said it earlier," he whispered.

She fluttered open her eyes and looked at him. He shot up a prayer that that was hope he saw in her eyes, a hope that was probably mirrored in his own.

"I love you."

He leaned in close again and claimed her lips, the touch warming him in the bitter cold. Where this relationship might lead, he had no idea. But for the moment, being in the moonlight with her and her acceptance of his kiss were enough.

Chapter Nineteen

For sure and for certain, that kiss would warm her up.

But it couldn't last forever. When John pulled away, his mount shifting feet again and swaying him apart from Sarah, the cold invaded, even more bitter than before. The absence of his lips against hers chilled her to the bone.

The little warmth she received from the horse wasn't enough any longer to combat the snow and the wind. The shivering began in her arms but soon consumed her entire body.

John quickly pulled his blanket off and wrapped it around her.

"*Ach*, no, John. You will freeze." She began to remove the blanket, but he held out his hand in protest.

"I insist. We've been out here for quite a while with no sign of Carlyle or The Bruise, so let's hurry to that neighbor's barn. I'll warm up there."

She urged Lightning forward, John on Thunder following close behind. Only the moonlight and the peaceful silence accompanied them. Perhaps the threat really was gone, and their safety would be secured once they reached the telephone in the barn.

Shivers still consumed her now and then, but they soon rode out of the trees. The barn stood silhouetted against the night sky. Safety at last.

John dismounted and opened the barn doors. Warmth enveloped her as she entered, the wind and the snow and the chill left outside. John led Thunder to the nearest stall and quickly closed the doors.

As he helped Sarah dismount, she cherished the strength and sturdiness inherent in his hands as they encircled her waist. He had been a good protector and would be into the future...except, the telephone was in a shanty just adjacent to the barn and it would all be over soon.

Keeping the blanket wrapped around herself, Sarah showed John the door to the telephone. "It is just there. You can make your call and summon help."

"Right. Be right back." He ran his hand down her upper arm, then turned toward the door.

John returned a few minutes later and joined her near the horses.

"Did you reach who you wanted?" She kept her voice low, a practice she had adopted over the last few days of intense caution.

"Yes. Help is on the way." He scrubbed a hand over his chin. "What about weapons? For protection. Does the neighbor have a hunting rifle?"

"*Jah*. Most every Amish man has that." She moved to a nearby cabinet, her heart heavy. Inside sat a rifle with extra boxes of ammunition. All this time spent together, and John's first instinct was still to find a gun. He wasn't changed at all. Any hope she had had of a future with him in the Amish church was now shattered. "Please leave it there. It is for hunting only. I know you come from a profession that includes the use of weapons and violence. But *Gott* will protect us."

She clutched the bodice of her dress. Her heart felt like it would be torn into little pieces. John was so different, coming from the *Englisch* world. How could he ever choose to be a part of the *we* of the Amish community, let alone the *we* of—did she dare even to think it?—Jed and Sarah Miller? The *we* of a family with her and Lyddie?

No. She would not torture herself. She pushed it from her mind, although it took all her mental energy.

But the request was made. Now he stood staring at her. Love shone in his eyes, but it seemed there was also a sadness. Was he realizing just how different they were, how unequally yoked, and how impossible a permanent relationship would be?

He hesitated, seemingly torn between what was probably instinct and what, she prayed, was his faith working in him.

John knew what he needed to do, and Sarah was the encouragement to do it.

Amish vows would have to wait until the appropriate time, but he could, and he would, reassure her now. He would respect her and her faith, a faith that he wanted to be his again.

He stepped away from the cabinet where the rifle rested and closer to her, drawing her into his arms. "Sarah, I've already said I care about you. But I also want to say—"

The crash of the barn door interrupted him and sent

a pounding to his chest like he couldn't remember ever having experienced. Now, not only was his own life on the line, but also the life of the woman he loved.

He had taken too long. Too long to hide in the woods. Too long to finish their journey and reach the barn. Too long to make his telephone call.

And now the rifle still sat in the cabinet, too far away to reach.

The chilled wind and flurries of snow blew in with the two men, weapons pointed at John and Sarah. A sneer bedecked the angry face of Simon Carlyle, the dirty cop who had come to finish the job and eliminate the man who could testify against him. The black-and-blue birthmark of Jimmy the Bruise wrapped around his neck and down his arm, seeming to pulsate with Jimmy's rage.

As Jimmy pointed his weapon at Sarah, John grabbed her hand. Whatever happened, he wouldn't let her face it alone. A wicked smile snaked across Jimmy's fleshy lips. "So, she's your girl now? Love has blossomed under the pressure of the chase? Okay, then. You can watch her die first."

Carlyle tossed a glance at The Bruise. "Jimmy, you yap entirely too much. Get it done already. I'm sick of this problem."

"Fine. First, I'll have Jed here dig the hole for his girl. Then he can dig his own hole. All I have to do is fill the dirt in." His malicious smile grew.

John let Sarah's hand loose and raised both in surrender. "Now, guys, can't we work something out?" As far as he could tell, neither Carlyle nor Jimmy knew he had called the police. If he could just keep them talking, perhaps he could keep Sarah alive until reinforcements arrived.

"What do you mean, Jed? You're in? Ready to live a little beyond that miserable policeman's salary?"

John forced a casual shrug. "What did you have in mind?"

Jimmy growled at Carlyle, but Carlyle continued. "Well…"

A sudden movement flashed behind the two men, at the door. Something beige and brown and white. Something large. Law enforcement couldn't be there yet. John darted his gaze to see what it was. It was Snowball, teeth bared and eyes narrowed, ready for a fight.

Just as recognition flickered in Jimmy's eyes that John had seen something behind him, Jimmy turned. The dog attacked with a leap, flying right at his face.

Snowball's growl forced Carlyle to turn to see what was causing the commotion. As his attention refocused, John lunged for him. With a hand on Carlyle's wrist, John twisted the man's arm, but the weapon fired. A bullet shot up to the ceiling. Sarah screamed and covered her ears as she dropped to the ground. With one strong wrench, John took control of Carlyle's gun.

His hands covering his face, Jimmy tried to protect himself from the large and vicious dog. As The Bruise cowered on the floor, his knees pulled to his chest, John retrieved his weapon, now holding both guns on their two attackers.

"Sarah, the dog!"

Sarah sniffled and sat up. "Snowball! No!" She grabbed the dog's collar and pulled, stroking her back gently and speaking more softly to calm her.

Jimmy whimpered as he pulled his bloody hands away from his face.

"Rope, Sarah?"

She motioned to Snowball to stay. The dog seemed to have calmed, now that the two men weren't threatening her any longer. Sarah stepped away to riffle through a couple of cabinets, returning with a length of cord that was more than enough to tie up Carlyle and Jimmy the Bruise.

The faint scream of sirens sounded outside. A few moments later, the barn filled with several police officers, and Carlyle and Jimmy the Bruise were taken into custody. John handed over their weapons to the nearest uniformed officer and then sagged against the rail of the stall, his legs wilting underneath him.

With the quilt still draped over her shoulders, Sarah approached him. "May we step outside now? For some fresh air and a change of scenery?"

"Jah." A smile wobbled across his lips as he spoke the Pennsylvania German. "Sounds *gut.*"

Confusion flittered across her beautiful face, followed by a shy smile.

With fresh blankets thrown over their shoulders, John led her to the outdoor porch of the neighbor's house. Snowball followed and sat next to Sarah, reaching up to try to lick her hand. "The police will have some questions for you eventually. But you're safe now. It's all over. Life can go back to normal."

"Normal?" Sarah stared at the ground. "We are leaving Indiana. Normal for Lyddie and for me will be back in Pennsylvania." Something sparkled on her cheek. Was it a tear?

"No." His pulse raced within him as he pulled Sarah

into his embrace. "Let me finish what I was beginning to say before we were interrupted." Snowball barked, and John ran a hand over her head. He grabbed that moment to swallow over a sudden lump in his throat and toss up a quick prayer. "Sarah, I've said I care about you. I care about Lyddie, too. I also said that I love you. I love you both. Now that my memory has returned, I believe the Lord is leading me back to my Amish heritage. I want to speak to the bishop about joining the church."

A gasp escaped Sarah, and her arms found their way around his neck to pull him into a tight hug. "That is *wunderbar!*" She released him and pulled away, her beautiful face pink, probably with embarrassment.

Snow began to flit down again, but this time it was a gentle free fall of large flakes.

"I don't know yet what I'll do to earn my keep, but I'm grateful for how you've helped me find my way back, with a little encouragement. And—" he cleared his throat, fighting the lump that continued to grow "—I know where I'd like to settle."

This was it. This was the moment. What if she said *no?* What if he had misread her, and she was only helping him because it was her responsibility as an Amish woman who was true to her faith?

But as he looked down at her, it seemed that hopefulness shone from her soft brown eyes. As the snow flurried down around them, the chill of the winter air making him pull her even closer, he thought he could smell the aroma of cinnamon and home and hearth in her brown curls. God's peace settled on him like a warm quilt.

"I've already said it, but I'll say it again and again. I love you, Sarah. I need to wrap up a number of things, including testifying at the trial in a couple of weeks. And I need to figure out how I'm going to earn a living once I'm no longer a police officer. But if you agree, I'd like to write to you in the interim."

Silence seemed to settle around them, broken only by the pounding of his heart as he waited. Then, like the sun breaking free from the winter storm clouds, a smile lit her face. "*Jah*, I would like that. And John? I love you, too."

Epilogue

Two weeks later

Sarah plunged her hands back into the hot, soapy water and grasped another plate. A snowmobile hummed in the distance as she scrubbed, rinsed and placed the plate on the towel to dry. A letter sat propped up on the windowsill, but this one wasn't from her mother urging her to come back to Pennsylvania to marry again.

This letter was from her love, declaring that he was counting the days until he could return to the Amish community and to her. In fact, two other letters rested behind the first. The name John had served him well during his amnesia, but now he was Jed again, a good, strong name for a fine man.

She glanced at the calendar again, but it was still the same date as it had been five minutes ago when she had looked at it...the day of the trial of Simon Carlyle and the counterfeiter called Jimmy the Bruise. Today was the day for Jed's crucial testimony that would, he hoped, help return a guilty verdict for the men.

Snowball barked from outside, and the door opened

with a gust of cold winter wind, blowing in Lyddie in her black winter cape and bonnet. "*Mamm*, may I go to the sledding hill? I will take Snowball with me."

Sarah smiled at the plea of her daughter. Her daughter knew exactly how to ask for something by including her protective dog, for sure and for certain.

"*Jah*, but be back before sunset. That is not long from now."

"*Danki, Mamm.*" The child pulled the door shut behind her.

Sarah finished the dishes, straightened up the living room, and sat down at the kitchen table with paper and pen. She had written a brief letter to her mother to say that she would not be returning to Lancaster Country, but she had also promised a much longer letter with details about her adventure, the man with amnesia and his return to the Amish faith.

A late afternoon haze was bending low over the yard, signaling the coming sunset, when she tucked the folded letter into her apron pocket and stepped to the window to look for Lyddie to return. But instead, the Amish taxi pulled into her lane. With a lightness in her step, she retrieved her cape and pulled it on as she stepped outside to see who it could be.

Jed sat in the front seat. He stepped out of the vehicle, his large smile warming her from the winter cold. He retrieved a couple of bags from the back seat and moved quickly to her as the Amish taxi pulled away.

"You are done so soon? I thought it would be a few more days."

He grasped her hand in his, shaking his head *no*. "I testified at the trial, and guilty verdicts were returned for both early this afternoon. So, I rushed out of the courthouse, grabbed my few things, and the Amish taxi picked me up and drove me directly here. I didn't want to wait any longer."

"But you will have to return, *jah*?"

"Yes, but just to finish up a couple of things." He meandered toward the house, still holding her hand. "I just didn't want to wait any longer to leave that nine to five behind and slow down. Live simply."

"And eat pie?" She tossed a teasing smile at him, the pressure of her hand in his making her heart thump and bump.

"*Jah*, always pie." He returned the smile. "I know there will be hard work. But it'll be work with the satisfaction of a job well done, work with the strength of my hands as well as my mind."

"And your medical tests? You have results?"

"Yes. Everything came back clear. I won't have any lasting damage. I saw my parents, and, although they don't understand my return to the Amish, they don't disapprove either." The smile grew wider across his handsome face. "It feels good to remember again. To remember everything."

"That is *gut*. I saw your *grossmammi* yesterday, *Mammi* Mary. She has your room ready."

"Yes, she wrote to me that she was eager to make up for lost time. I think she's going to keep me up nights talking and reminiscing. And I meet with the bishop tomorrow about being baptized into the church. Then," he turned to her and drew her into his arms, gently touching his lips to hers, "we have something else to decide."

"*Jah*?"

The sun broke free of the clouds just as it hit the horizon. The rays of light shone in pink and purple across the snow and ice, and a thousand crystals sparkled in the sunset.

"A wedding date."

Sarah gasped as Jed put his fingers to her lips.

"I love you, Sarah Burkholder. It would be an honor if you would be my wife and if Lyddie would be my daughter. Will you marry me?"

Sarah's heart thumped a wild beat. Here was the moment she had been wondering over and praying about for the last two weeks. But before she could answer, Lyddie burst from the woods, pulling her sled, Snowball bounding beside her. She ran to Jed, and he picked her up, gathering Sarah back into his embrace, as well. "Jed, you are here to stay?"

"Well, that's up to your mother." He looked to her, pleading in his eyes, his eyebrows raised with the unanswered question.

A lump formed in her throat. How did she deserve all this happiness? All this answered prayer? She swallowed hard. "*Jah*, I will."

Jed squeezed them both tight and answered Lyddie's question without removing his gaze from Sarah. "*Jah*, little one, I'm here to stay."

"Will you become my *daed*?"

Sarah's heart danced within her. A tear squeezed out to expose her joy.

"As soon as the bishop will allow it, *liebchen*."

She leaned to give Lyddie a kiss on the cheek, followed by a kiss on Jed's cheek, and the letter to her mother that she had tucked into her pocket pressed against her. It wasn't the letter she had written a couple of weeks ago. That letter had burned in the barn fire, a fitting end to the intentions she had expressed in it.

Even then, she had known she didn't want to continue, especially not in Indiana, without Jed.

Now, she would write a new letter. A letter that explained it all. Jed was hers, and she was Jed's. Her home was here, with him, in Indiana. Sarah's lips found his as Lyddie hugged them both around the legs, completeness and wholeness settling over her like a warm Amish quilt.

* * * * *

WE HOPE YOU ENJOYED THIS BOOK!

Love Inspired®

New beginnings. Happy endings.
Discover uplifting inspirational
romance.

Look for six new Love Inspired
books available every month,
wherever books are sold!

Love Inspired®

Save $1.00

on the purchase of ANY
Love Inspired® or
Love Inspired® Suspense book.

Available wherever books are sold,
including most bookstores, supermarkets,
drugstores and discount stores.

- ✂

Save $1.00

on the purchase of ANY Love Inspired® or Love Inspired® Suspense book.

Coupon valid until December 31, 2019.
Redeemable at participating retail outlets in the U.S. and Canada only.
Limit one coupon per customer.

52616482

5 65373 00076 2 (8100)0 12431

"There won't be another bus going that way until the day after tomorrow."

"Are you sure?" Gemma Lapp stared at the agent behind the counter in stunned disbelief.

"Of course I'm sure. I work for the bus company."

She clasped her hands together tightly, praying the tears that pricked the backs of her eyes wouldn't start flowing. She couldn't afford a motel room for two nights.

She wheeled her suitcase over to the bench. Sitting down with a sigh, she moved her suitcase in front of her so she could prop up her swollen feet. After two solid days on a bus she was ready to lie down. Anywhere.

She bit her lower lip to stop it from quivering. She could place a call to the phone shack her parents shared with their Amish neighbors to let them know she was returning and ask her father to send a car for her, but she would have to leave a message.

Any message she left would be overheard. If she gave the real reason, even Jesse Crump would know before she reached home. She couldn't bear that, although she didn't understand why his opinion mattered so much. His stoic face wouldn't reveal his thoughts, but he was sure to gloat when he learned he'd been right about her reckless ways. He had said she was looking for trouble and that she would find it sooner or later. Well, she had found it all right.

No, she wouldn't call. What she had to say was better said face-to-face. She was cowardly enough to delay as long as possible.

She didn't know how she was going to find the courage to tell her mother and father that she was six months pregnant, and Robert Troyer, the man who'd promised to marry her, was long gone.

Don't miss
Shelter from the Storm *by* USA TODAY
bestselling author Patricia Davids,
available September 2019 wherever
Love Inspired® books and ebooks are sold.

www.LoveInspired.com

LIEXP0819

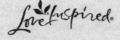

Nick took his seat next to her and picked up the reins, but before moving onward, he said, "I don't understand it, Lucy. Why is my caring about you such an awful thing?" His voice was quivering and Lucy felt a pang of guilt. She knew she was overreacting. Rather, she was reacting to a heartache that had plagued her for years, not one Nick had caused that evening.

"I don't expect you to understand," she said, wiping her rough woolen mitten across her cheeks.

"But I want to. Can't you explain it to me?"

Nick's voice was so forlorn Lucy let her defenses drop. "I've always been treated like this, my entire life. *Lucy's too weak, too fragile, too small, she can't go outside or run around or have any fun because she'll get sick. She'll stop breathing. She'll wind up in the hospital.* My whole life, Nick. And then the one little taste of utter abandon I ever experienced—charging through the dark with a frosty wind whisking against my face, feeling totally invigorated and alive… You want to take that away from me, too."

She was crying so hard her words were barely intelligible, but Nick didn't interrupt or attempt to quiet her. When she finally settled down and could speak normally again, she sniffed and asked, "May I use your handkerchief, please?"

"Sorry, I don't have one," Nick said. "But here, you can use my scarf. I don't mind."

The offer to use Nick's scarf to dry her eyes and blow her nose was so ridiculous and sweet all at once it caused Lucy to chuckle. "*Neh*, that's okay," she said, removing her mittens to dab her eyes with her bare fingers.

"I really am sorry," he repeated.

Lucy was embarrassed. "That's all right. I've stopped blubbering. I don't need a handkerchief after all."

"*Neh*, I mean I'm sorry I treated you in a way that made you feel…the way you feel. I didn't mean to. I was concerned. I care about you and I wouldn't want anything to happen to you. I especially wouldn't want to play a role in hurting you."

Lucy was overwhelmed by his words. No man had ever said anything like that to her before, even in friendship. "It's not your fault," she said. "And I do appreciate that you care. But I'm not as fragile as you think I am."

"Fragile? You? I don't think you're fragile at all, even if you are prone to pneumonia." Nick scoffed. "I think you're one of the most resilient women I've ever known."

Lucy was overwhelmed again. If this kept up, she was going to fall hard for Nick Burkholder. Maybe she already had.

Don't miss
Her Amish Holiday Suitor *by Carrie Lighte,*
available October 2019 wherever
Love Inspired® books and ebooks are sold.

www.LoveInspired.com

Love Inspired®

Discover wholesome and uplifting stories of faith, forgiveness and hope.

Join our social communities to connect with other readers who share your love!

Sign up for the Love Inspired newsletter at **LoveInspired.com** to be the first to find out about upcoming titles, special promotions and exclusive content.

CONNECT WITH US AT:

Facebook.com/groups/HarlequinConnection

 Facebook.com/LoveInspiredBooks

 Twitter.com/LoveInspiredBks

LISOCIAL2019